AF265138

Printed in the United States of America.

17   16   15   14   13   12   11   10   9   8   7   6   5   4   3   2   1

Werby, Olga

Mirror Shards : a novel / by Olga Werby

ISBN: 978-0-578-91558-6

San Francisco

www.Pipsqueak.com

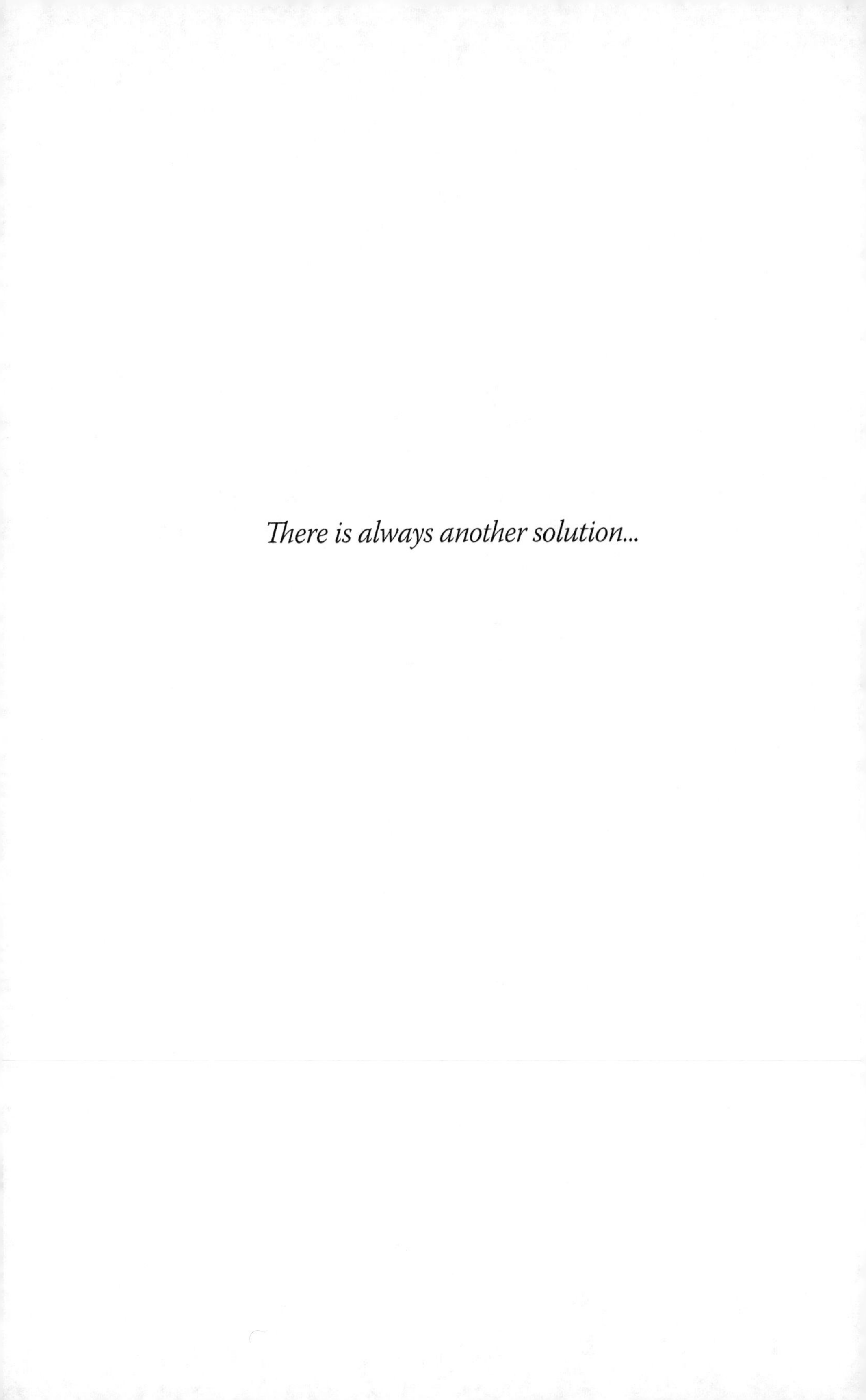

There is always another solution...

Table of Contents

Mirror Shards

Chapter One: The County Fair

I always loved my Uncle Charlie the best. He never looked down on me, even when I was still stuck in my wheelchair. He always listened carefully and never jumped to conclusions about what was "really good for me." And most importantly, Uncle Charlie loved me. He was everything an eight-year-old boy could ever want from an adult. Except that he lived very far away. But every fall, he would drive up to our house in his gleaming red convertible, with presents in the back for my baby sister and me and my mom, and stay for a few glorious days. Despite all that Christmas offered, the abundance of Thanksgiving, the nighttime fun of Halloween, and the rockets' red glare of the 4th of July, what I loved and looked forward to the most were those days when Uncle Charlie stayed with us. I waited for him to come all year.

I was a poor invalid boy all year except when Uncle Charlie looked at me. Then I was as healthy as any other kid my age. It didn't matter that I couldn't run, couldn't walk, really. Uncle Charlie saw me as an interesting and smart human on his way to adulthood. No one else saw me that way. What I loved most about him was how I saw myself when I looked in the mirror during those few days when he stayed with us. I learned to nourish that image for as long as possible, for I knew it would fade long before Uncle Charlie returned for his next visit.

The year I turned eight, Uncle Charlie came as usual, just days before my birthday. It so happened that year that the county fair coincided with his visit and my birthday. That had never happened before, and I think I went out of my mind with the anticipation of all the fun we would have when he arrived.

I remember that visit as if it was yesterday. Nearly a dozen years didn't erase a single detail, I believe. Uncle Charlie arrived later in the day than usual. Mom insisted that I go to bed. And as much as I protested, I ended up tucked under the covers, my crutches on the floor by my bed, staring out of the window, hoping not to accidentally drift off to sleep before I heard the telltale sound of wheels on our gravel driveway.

I lay in bed and listened through the floor as my parents argued in the kitchen. Back then, I didn't understand what they fought about. I bet most kids don't really understand their parents' arguments; they just feel the unhappiness in the air like a foul-smelling blanket. And since I didn't know any better, I just assumed all adults argued. All except Uncle Charlie. I'd never heard him say a cross word for as long as I could remember...back then.

*** ***

I never managed to stay up late enough to hear Uncle Charlie arrive, but he was there to greet me in the morning.

"Hey, Hig. Rise and shine!" He called me Hig for the atomic symbol for mercury: Hg. You might ask why? Well, my real name is Fred, like my father's and grandfather's, and everyone called me Freddie...except Uncle Charlie. He gave me a nickname taken from his favorite rock band of all time:

Queen. The lead singer was this dude named Freddie Mercury. So Hig, get it? It was our secret. Why I have that nickname is still our secret even now...mostly, although more people know me as Hig. The name Freddie got lost in histories.

"Uncle Charlie!" I threw my arms around his slender shoulders, and he lifted me gently out of bed. I was never embarrassed when he helped. He was so genuine and matter-of-fact about it all that it never felt wrong. When my dad tried to help, on the other hand, it always left both of us feeling awkward.

"We have to be quick," he said. "Your dad said that he would take the whole family to the county fair if we can get our act together fast. I volunteered you and me for breakfast duty!" That's how my uncle was; he didn't say he was here to help me get out of bed and wash up and get dressed. Instead, he talked about "us" cooking breakfast for the family! "Your mom is helping Nonaken," he added as he got me dressed. Nona was only a year and a few months old. Uncle Charlie added a diminutive to her name because he thought Nona was just too formal a name for a baby; Nona was named after Dad's grandmother. Nonaken stuck—even Dad called my sister that...perhaps because he used to call his grandmother Nona. Awkward.

I tried to be as helpful as my body would allow. My arms had grown stronger in the past year, so I was able to stand on crutches for a few minutes at time. The doctor said it was important for me to do so. But my legs were useless. They kept getting in the way of things. I once asked my mom to have them cut off, but she just cried. Well, they turned out to be useful in the end. Mom was right.

Uncle Charlie looked frail, but he was incredibly strong. He worked as a nurse in a children's hospital. I always thought those kids were lucky to have him. I wished I had him for more than just a few days a year. So he got me ready in no time and carried me down to the kitchen. Once I was settled into my wheelchair, he quickly organized eggs and bacon and toast. By the time my dad showed up, the whole kitchen smelled great.

"I can only go for a few hours," Dad said. "I have to return to the office."

"But it's the weekend!" I still remember how whiny my voice sounded. I immediately felt embarrassed in front of Uncle Charlie. "Sorry, Dad. A few hours would be amazing."

My dad grunted something in return and settled at the table to read the paper on his phone. Uncle Charlie winked at me and continued to juggle pots and pans to work a breakfast miracle. When Mom and Nonaken came down a few minutes later, all was ready. It was a great meal. I almost never got eggs with bacon and toast unless Uncle Charlie was in town.

"It looks amazing, Charlie," Mom said and got my sister strapped into a highchair.

"Freddie and I tried," he said, beaming back. All I did was set the table...badly. But I was happy to share in the praise. It was so rarely bestowed in my direction.

My mom was Uncle Charlie's older sister. I think there was just a two-year difference between them, but it felt much more to me. Uncle Charlie was fun and playful and silly, while my mom was the exact opposite. Dad just said that was because Uncle Charlie lacked seriousness of character. But I think it had more to do with the fact that he was still a child at heart. At least I felt that we were equal somehow.

When Dad finished with his coffee, the kitchen table was cleaned, the dishes washed and put away, and we were all dressed and ready to go. No one wanted to give Dad an excuse not to go to the fair.

My dad was dressed in a suit and tie; he planned to take

Uncle Charlie's car to the office directly from the fair. We were taking two cars so we could spend a bit more time exploring the animals, and food, and the crafts pavilions. In retrospect, my dad probably agreed to go to the fair so he could take that red convertible to the office. But I was none the wiser back then, and we needed the minivan for my wheelchair, Nonaken's stroller, and stuff. So, logistically, it probably did make sense. Still, I was just so happy to be going at all. If Uncle Charlie came a week later or a week earlier, we wouldn't have been going to the fair at all. Mom couldn't manage with Nonaken in a stroller and me in a wheelchair by herself. It was too much for her.

"Sissy." Uncle Charlie always called Mom "Sissy," short for sister, I guessed. "Why don't you put on that orange jacket I sent you? The one with all the wild flowers." The jacket was orange because it was covered with California puppies.

"It's not really practical, Charlie," she said, slipping into her frumpy gray sweatshirt. "What if I spill something on it? I can't even dump it into a washer. I'll save it for sometime special."

"So you will wear it sometime? You like it?" he asked, just like a kid.

"You know I do, Charlie," she said with a sad smile. My mom's smiles were always sad.

"Okay. But it better be soon. You look at least ten years older than you really are in that," Uncle Charlie said. He was wearing jeans and a colorful Hawaiian shirt that looked oddly feminine to my eye. "You know, I can babysit tonight, and you and Fred can go—"

"I've told that I have to work late tonight," my dad said. I didn't even realize he was paying attention. "I've agreed to this silly outing, it will have to be enough."

I was going to argue, but Mom gave me that look, and

I didn't say a word. We all piled into our minivan: Mom, Uncle Charlie, Nonaken, and I. Dad took Uncle Charlie's car. Thirty minutes later, we were pulling out the wheelchair and the stroller and a giant bag with extra diapers and food for Nonaken and other private things for me. Because of my disability, we could park right by the entrance to the fair, in the special blue zone. Dad waved us to go ahead as he looked for parking next to the exit. We already purchased the tickets and were getting ready to go in when Dad finally joined us. He missed all of the hassle and the ticket line and everything. Uncle Charlie just called him lucky. Mom already looked pooped. She got tired fast, I noticed.

✳✳✳

The fair was everything a kid dreamed it would be. There were farm animal competitions and even a small arena where kids could get a ride on a pony or in a goat cart. There was a humongous food court where restaurants and farms from all around our area set up booths and food trucks. Anything a kid would love: two-foot corn dogs, watermelon-sized spun sugar in rainbow color assortments, deep-fried Twinkies served in a tub of melted chocolate, any flavor of shaved ice by the bucket, fried chicken and BBQ ribs dripping with rich sweet sauce, roasted brown and crisp turkey legs, and a vast assortment of homemade stuff coming in a million combinations of sweet, sour, piquant, salty, pungent, and oleogustus. The last flavor was taught to me by Uncle Charlie. It meant the degree of fattiness. And boy oh boy was oleogustus well represented at the fair. There were also miles and miles of pies filled with so many combinations of fruits, berries, and even vegetables that there was no point in even trying to keep track. I really never understood how all those pie judges at the fair managed to do their job, but it was fun to imagine— *When I grow up, I will be a pie judge at a county fair.* It made me smile.

The fair also had a ton of amusement park rides, the kinds that spin and throw you around and even twist you upside-down. But I was never allowed to go on those, of course. And Nonaken was too young. She squealed with delight when Uncle Charlie simply rocked her stroller a bit too enthusiastically. She was easy to please. My dad was less so.

We tried to go see the chicken competition; the prettiest and smartest chickens were being shown off in one of the pavilions. But my dad said he couldn't go anywhere where there was hay or wood chips on the floor—it was bad for his shoes. So we went to one of the crafts pavilions. Some of my mom's friends had quilts in a competition, and she wanted to show her support. The place was huge, and we wandered around looking at cool things people made all year long to bring to the fair. There were cut crystals and homemade soaps in shape of crystals. Tons of honey in every shade of amber. Toys. More toys. Clothing and more clothing. One booth had nothing but hats. Uncle Charlie managed to surreptitiously buy a huge wide-brimmed hat with a whole bouquet of silk flowers pinned to the top for my mom. She refused to put it on, so Uncle Charlie wore it instead. It made Mom and me laugh. Frankly, I thought it looked good on him. Dad just frowned and walked ahead, pretending he didn't know us.

There is a smell and sound to the county fair. It's instantly recognizable to all those who've ever attended one, even once in their lives. We were soaking in the aromas and drowning in the sounds of the fair. It was more fun than anything I could remember since the last time Uncle Charlie came to visit and took me fishing. We didn't catch a thing, but it was still a load of fun. We even brought home some fish...that we bought off one of the fishermen. We tried to pass it off as our catch, but neither Dad nor Mom believed our fish story. It made for a good dinner either way.

"I bet even Nonaken will remember this," I said about the fair.

"She is too young, Freddie," Mom said, but she too looked a bit drunk on the fair's smorgasbord of sounds, colors, and smells.

"Oh, Nonaken will definitely remember," Uncle Charlie assured me. "She might not get all of the details—"

Mom laughed. My sister was snoring in her stroller, despite the din of laughter and the endless clamor of the place. "Nonaken is totally tuckered out, Charlie. We will be lucky if she doesn't throw a tantrum when we get home."

"Well, I did say all of this is just too much a little kid," my dad said. "You will just have to manage her overexcitement without me tonight."

"Don't worry, Fred," Uncle Charlie said. "We'll manage."

"You'll have to. I have to work hard to feed this family, Charles. You don't have the responsibilities of taking care of a wife and children. Life is simpler for you. I have to work all the time to help us manage."

I noticed the tension between Mom, Dad, and Uncle Charlie even back then. Dad always talked about the importance of being professionally successful. He said that he felt the pressure to get ahead more keenly because of me. He said that he would probably have to take care of me for the rest of his life. I hated that. I was sure that when I grew up, I would be able to manage on my own. Uncle Charlie told me lots of kids with spina bifida grew up to hold important jobs and live independently. He told me that Franklin D. Roosevelt, the president of the United States, was in a wheelchair when he did his job of running our nation. No one needed to support

President Roosevelt all his life. So, sure, I might need more help with day-to-day stuff than most people. But we all need help from time to time, Uncle Charlie said. I believed him.

As we started to make our way toward the crafts pavilion exit—Dad was trying to rush us out—we noticed a small booth run by a blind woman. You might ask how I knew she was blind. Well, her booth sign said she was, and she was wearing very dark sunglasses and used one of those long white canes with red stripes. Uncle Charlie stopped to see what she was selling. Since he was the one pushing my wheelchair, I stopped too. And my mom, with Nonaken sleeping in a stroller, paused to see what was going on. Dad almost walked out without us but turned back when Mom called him.

"Let's do it, Fred," she said. "Let's all go do it. It will be fun!"

"I second that," said Uncle Charlie.

"I third it!" I cried out. It was a Fun House Mirror Booth... with just one mirror! The sign above read, "Take The Test." Just that, no other instructions or explanations.

"It's just one mirror, Fred. It won't take long," Mom begged, and Dad grumped but agreed.

That's how we all ended up doing the "Mirror Test."

"You have to go one by one," the blind woman told us as she took off her glasses. Her eyes were a scary milky-white color all over, no iris, no pupils, nothing at all. "This young man," she pointed to me, "will need to use his crutches. Can you walk this far?" She spread her arms as wide as they could go to indicate the distance.

"Of course I can!" My crutches were strapped to the back of the wheelchair. It was easier to use crutches sometimes... like for the bathroom and stuff.

"Very good, young man," she said. "I would like the pretty

man with a hat to go first."

I laughed. Of course she meant Uncle Charlie. He and Dad were both wearing hats, but Uncle Charlie was the only "pretty" man in our group. Honestly, I'd always thought of him as pretty rather than handsome. He had big blue eyes and gently curling blond hair that framed his thin, delicately featured face. He looked a lot like my mother, except years younger. I overheard Dad say once that Uncle Charlie would have made a prettier woman than my mother. He was wrong, of course.

Uncle Charlie took off the giant hat and walked behind the curtain that contained the one mirror. We all waited outside. It seemed to take a very long time. Nonaken even woke up and was looking at all the colorful spinning and whirling wheels and thingies all round us—the garden sculptures that were designed to keep the birds off the fruiting trees sold in the booth next to the Fun House. The only bits of darkness among the exuberant explosion of colors were my dad's suit and the curtain that hid the blind woman's mirror.

When Uncle Charlie stepped out, we all turned on him.

"How was it?" Mom and I asked almost simultaneously. He just shook his head and lifted Nonaken from her seat. She wanted to touch a rainbow ribbon floating above our heads.

"Well," Dad said, looking at his watch. "I really need to go back to the office. So if you'd excuse—"

"It's your turn, Mr. Keen," the blind woman said. I don't know how she learned our last name, but it had an effect on Dad. He shrugged, went inside, and disappeared behind the curtain.

Dad took even longer than Uncle Charlie. At least it felt way longer. Nonaken was starting to get crotchety and was on the verge of tears. Mom took her in her arms from Uncle Charlie, who seemed unusually quiet for some reason.

Finally, the curtain pulled aside and Dad stepped out. He gave the blind woman a ten-dollar bill and, without saying so much as goodbye to us, left. I just watched him go. It was an unexpected departure, even for my dad. He always at least kissed my mom's hair before rushing out to go to work.

"Well, it's your turn, Mrs. Keen." The blind woman smiled at my mother. I noticed she had a bunch of gold teeth in the back of her mouth. I wondered if she knew about those, being blind and all. "Don't worry about the baby. She is too young to understand, and so it won't mean nothing to her," the woman added.

Mom nodded and walked in, carrying Nonaken. She came out almost immediately. I saw a tear running down her face. I wanted to ask if she was okay, but I was being hustled onto my crutches and into the booth. And then I was the one facing the mirror.

As soon as the black curtain fell closed behind me, all sounds and smells of the fair disappeared. That should have been my first clue that this was something out of the ordinary. But at the time, I was too overwhelmed to pay attention to those kinds of details. I was looking at a young man in the mirror. He was me and not me. I have to say that I generally didn't like to look at myself in the mirror. Who in my situation would? But the reflection looking back at me was more like the image of myself I had in my head: healthy, strong, able-bodied, not sickly at all. I was looking at an athlete, at someone who could jump over a fence or climb a tree without even thinking about it, at someone who could run to school every day and never ever get tired, at a boy who was confident and vigorous. The kid who smiled at me from the mirror would be chosen by other students to be on their teams first. So not like me. So me... I felt tears rolling down my face. I wanted more than anything to be that kid in the mirror. I almost hated the blind woman for showing this to me. I understood why my mom shed a tear—she probably saw something equally improbable when it was her turn.

I had to make myself look away. It was almost painful. I wanted that mirror to reflect reality so much. I closed my eyes and turned away. It was easier to turn once I couldn't see the evil reflection. I pushed the curtain and stepped back out into the pandemonium of the county fair.

That was thirteen years ago.

But to understand what's happening to me now, you need to know more about what happened after that day at the fair, all those years ago.

Chapter Two: After the Mirror Test

Once my dad left us alone at the fair, we wandered around, looking at the raucous chaos of food, toys, and entertainment still available for us to sample. We went to the chicken competition—Araucana won. Apparently that farm won every year, but it wasn't my choice. Yes, I focused on the feathers and size and demeanor of chickens on display to try to push aside what I saw in the mirror. I think Mom and Uncle Charlie did the same. Uncle Charlie even placed a bet on a Padovana chick, but he didn't even notice when the judging was over and he lost. Mom too seemed over excited about random stuff and at the same time almost catatonic for minutes at a stretch. It scared me. What did they see in that mirror? What did my dad see? He left us at the fair and didn't even say goodbye.

Finally stuffed with random food and totally exhausted from crisscrossing the fair dozens of times, we headed home, carefully avoiding coming anywhere near the blind woman's mirror booth. Dad wasn't home yet. In fact, he didn't return until we all went to bed. We didn't talk about it. And we didn't talk about the mirror or the blind woman at all. It was as if that never happened.

But in my bed, with the lights out, I could see the face of that boy so clearly. And I longed with all my heart to be him. I fell asleep crying.

In the morning, when I woke up, I lay there listening to the house. My parents were arguing again. I didn't want to know what it was about. Because regardless of what they said down there, it was about the mirror. Everything was about the mirror from that day forward.

Uncle Charlie left in the middle of the night, as soon as Dad returned with his car. I didn't realize that until I finally tried to crawl out of bed—no one was coming to help me. I managed to sit up by pushing off the mattress and was able to get the crutch off the floor. It was almost easy. One crutch, then another I accomplished getting to the bathroom and voiding my bladder all by myself. For the first time in many years, I didn't have an accident during the night. I should have been elated. You probably have no idea how it feels to be in a third grade and still needing a diaper. It's humiliating. But I was clean.

I brushed my teeth and got dressed by myself—another personal achievement. I was on a roll. I used my butt to slide down the stairs—a familiar maneuver that also seemed easier today—and hobbled over to the kitchen door.

"Did you say something to Charlie to make him go?" Mom was crying; her hands shook as she tried to pour coffee for my dad. Dad just ignored her. But he always did that, so it wasn't anything new. But Mom tended to do all her crying in the privacy of her bathroom, and Uncle Charlie never left without saying goodbye to me before.

"Uncle Charlie left?" I asked like an idiot. Of course, I figured that out already—his car was gone and the guest room door was ajar and bed stripped. What I really wanted to know was why he left.

"You made it down all by yourself?" Mom asked, ignoring my question. She rushed over to me with the wheelchair, and I collapsed into it. Getting down the stairs took everything out of me, but I forgot about it while grieving Uncle Charlie's departure. "You shouldn't have," Mom said. "You could have fallen down the stairs. You could have..." She let out a sob and stopped.

"I'm okay, Mom. See?" I smiled at her from my chair. I wished Uncle Charlie were here to cook breakfast for everyone again. We needed him.

"Leave him alone, Moira," Dad said. "A little independence is good for the kid." And without saying another word, he left. The front door slammed, and we listened as he drove away. He didn't kiss Mom's hair goodbye. That was twice in a row.

***

The following several months were crazy. Mom cried all the time. Dad was gone from early in the morning to late at night. He stopped coming home for dinner. All those missed meals turned into weight loss that Dad proudly mentioned any time we actually got to see him. He said that he had started going to gym regularly, thus all the absence. He dressed better. He looked great—even I noticed. Mom, on the other hand, didn't. She too lost weight, but on her it looked more like wasting than dieting. The word I learned from looking up Mom's symptoms online was cachexia—unexplained weakness and weight loss. She had in spades. I tried talking to Dad about it, but he refused to pay attention to me. He said it was his *me time* now, and I should let him enjoy life a little; he deserved it. I was at a loss. I was only eight.

Personally, I was actually feeling better than I could ever

remember. I was getting up, getting dressed, and getting my-self downstairs by myself on regular basis now. Sure, there was a fall here and there that set things back a bit, but I was obviously better. Even my teachers at school noticed. I tried to get in touch with Uncle Charlie to tell him my good news and to ask him for help with Mom, because she didn't want to listen to me either. She just nodded every time I brought up the fact that there might be something wrong with her and then just ignored me. I needed Uncle Charlie. He was the only one who could help—he was a nurse, after all—I was convinced. But I couldn't get hold of him.

First, I tried sending him a few texts to his phone and via social media and such, but he never responded. Three months after the fair, his number stopped working all to-gether. I knew the hospital he worked at in California, so I called their general number. Someone somewhere had to know what happened to my uncle. After multiple tries over several long weeks, I got hold of a night nurse on duty at the pediatric cancer ward, Nurse Megan.

"Is this Hig?" she asked after I introduced myself—ap-parently, she'd heard of me. Her voice was nice, clear as a bell. But I was surprised she knew my nickname, surprised Uncle Charlie would share something so intimate and private with a stranger. Of course, she was probably not a stranger to him. "Charlie told me that you might call, looking for him," she said. She sounded kind. I met lots of pediatric nurses over the years, and I could recognize a good one just by hearing the voice.

"I really need to get hold of him," I said. "It's a family emergency," I added, realizing that it was in fact that.

"He told me you would say that too," she said.

"He did?"

"But you see, Hig, Charlie had to take some time off...for

personal reasons. He told me to tell you that when the time was right, he would contact you himself. He asked you to be patient and not be too mad at him. Okay?"

"He said all that? But I really need him now. Really! I didn't lie about the family emergency. You see, I think there is something wrong with my mom," I told her. "I think it is serious."

"Huh."

"Uncle Charlie didn't tell you about my mom getting sick, did he?"

"No, he did not. What's wrong with your mom?"

"She lost a lot of weight. And before you say that's a good thing, it isn't. She was never fat. She was thin like Uncle Charlie. But now she's sort of skeletal. I can see her bones. She hides it by wearing bulky clothing, but she is so thin, it's scary."

"Did you try talking to her about it?"

"Sure. But she won't let me. She says everything is just fine. But it is not fine. She gets really tired too, now. I saw her needing to sit down on a couch. She looked like she was going to pass out. And she is having problems carrying Nonaken around."

"That's your baby sister?"

"Uncle Charlie told you about her, too?"

"I've seen photos. Nonaken, Little Nona."

"That's her! She's the only one who is still normal."

"What do you mean, Hig?"

"Well, Dad lost weight too, but he goes to the gym a lot and works out all the time. He got promoted at work and even bought a car like Uncle Charlie's."

"You mean that funny little red thing with no top?"

"Dad always thought it was cool. He used to borrow it from Uncle Charlie when he came to town. But that's not what's important. Something happened. Something happened at the fair." There, I said it. I didn't mean to. I wanted to discuss it all with Uncle Charlie, but he wasn't around.

"The fair..." she started to say, but stopped.

"Yes. Did Uncle Charlie tell you about the fair? About the Mirror Test?" It felt good to say those words out loud. I didn't dare before that day.

"He mentioned something about meeting an oracle at a county fair. He tried looking her up."

"Did he find her? Did he find the blind woman?" I was so excited, I practically yelled into the telephone. I never thought of trying to find the woman with the mirror. Of course, she was the person who could give me answers. *Of course!* "Did he?" I asked again.

"No, Hig. Charlie tried. He drove back to look for her—"

"He came back and didn't see us? Didn't stay with us?"

"Charlie had work, Hig. He couldn't—"

"But he didn't stay the full seven days with us like he usually does." I tried to argue, but it was silly. Uncle Charlie always stayed with us for as long as he could. But he frequently reminded me that there were dying kids waiting for him to return. He couldn't abandon them. I understood...sort of. "He didn't even call me..."

"I'm sorry, Hig. I'm sure he would have, if he could."

"Did he ever find out more about the blind woman?"

"No. He called the organizers of the fair and described her and her booth, but no one seemed to know what he was talking about."

"But that's crazy! We were all there. We saw her." Now I wished that we took some snapshots or something. But we were all so unsettled at the time, and Dad was...well, I wished I had some proof of that booth's existence.

"I don't doubt you...or Charlie," she said. But it sounded

like she did. "But Charlie never figured out how she got listed at the fair...or not listed. And the organizers said they've never heard of a one-mirror fun house booth. But he did look, Hig. Charlie was obsessed with trying to find this blind woman."

"Huh. But nothing?"

"Not as far as I know," Nurse Megan said. I could tell she would have told me if she knew anything else.

"Thanks anyway."

"Wait, Hig," she called into the phone. "Charlie promised to call me as soon as he could. We were best friends, you know."

For some reason that got me super angry—I was family. If Uncle Charlie called anyone, it should be me. "Where did he say he went?" I asked as soon as I could control myself, swallowing a painful lump in my throat.

"I really don't know, Hig. He didn't tell me, honest. But...I think he is still looking for this blind woman. I saw him get a list of all the county fairs for the upcoming year. I think he was going to go from one fair to another in person, trying to find her. I don't really understand what happened to you all," she added.

"I don't either," I said.

"But something did happen, right?"

"Yeah. Something." I thought of how handsome and successful my dad suddenly had become and how sick my mom looked...and how much better I was feeling. "Did you notice anything about Uncle Charlie before he left?" I asked. I never really considered it, but what did my uncle see in that mirror? Did he change somehow too? That blind woman said that Nonaken was too young, but the rest of us... "Did he change somehow?"

There was a long pause. I was even afraid that Nurse Megan hung up on me. But finally she said, "He got even prettier."

"Yes." I could see that.

"It was nice talking with you, Hig," she said. She sounded sad. "I really have to get back to my patients. But you be good and take care of your mom. Get her to see a doctor. Maybe you can ask for yourself and then explain at the office your concerns for your mom."

"It's a good idea. Thanks. Goodbye."

"Goodbye, Hig. And keep in touch. Just call this number from time to time." And with that the line went dead.

I held the phone for a long time afterward. Telling my own doctor about Mom was a really good idea. I should have thought of it. I dropped the phone of the floor and threw myself down. It hurt a lot, but I heard my mom rushing up the stairs to see if I was all right. I was, but I insisted we go to the doctor, faking pain in my leg.

Chapter Three: The Mirror Miracles and Mares

"It's been a while, Freddie." Dr. Ulf shook my hand. He was huge, a perfect Viking. When I was little, I wanted to grow up to be just like Dr. Ulf—a doctor who specialized in pediatric birth defects and someone who looked like he could take over Greenland barehanded. My hand disappeared into his, and I grinned the silly grin of a groupie. Dr. Ulf always managed to make me feel good, even when I felt awful. "You're looking great," he said. "I see you've been working out." He was feeling my upper arms, noticing improvements in my muscle mass. I was very proud of them.

"Freddie has been doing very well, Doctor," Mom said. "He managed to walk all the way here on his crutches from the parking lot. No wheelchair." That was the total of maybe one hundred steps, but still... Mom had Nonaken strapped into her stroller with multiple bags of supporting equipment for me and my sister. So it wasn't like there was a way for her to deal with my wheelchair too. I was happy I could make it to the office under my own power, even after I threw myself onto the floor. "But he did just have a nasty fall," Mom added.

Dr. Ulf was instantly on his knees, helping me with my sweatpants, looking at the damage. My leg did look bad. It was black and blue already. It would get worse before the day's end. I knew how these things went; I had plenty of experience. I now wished that I had been more cautious. There was no real need to hurt myself to see Dr. Ulf. Mom would have taken me as soon as I complained of pain somewhere. But I was a perfectionist. And I didn't want to lie...well, not more than I needed to.

"Looks like a bad fall," Dr. Ulf said. "Did you get a chance to ice it?"

"No, Doctor. Freddie insisted we go straight to your office. And I was afraid..."

"No worries, Mrs. Keen. We'll take care of your boy." He helped me up on the exam table and pulled some ice packs from a little freezer under the sink.

"Ah," I complained at the cold.

"Don't protest, dear," Mom was quick to intervene.

"I'm not. I'm just saying that it's cold." I rolled myself away a little. I did have far more upper body strength now. I'd bet I didn't even need help to get down.

"I'm very impressed, my boy. You are showing remarkable improvements, despite the fall," the doctor said.

"Freddie has been doing very well," Mom confirmed again. "There have been a few falls in the last few months, but nothing as bad as this. And he has been managing everything himself, even getting down from his bedroom to the first floor."

"Remarkable," Dr. Ulf commented again. He was gently lifting up my shirt and examining my spine. His fingers were probing but gentle. Very much like Uncle Charlie's.

"Dr. Ulf?"

"Yes, Freddie?"

"I have something private I would like to discuss with you." I gave a sideways look at my mom. Mom started to protest, but Dr. Ulf managed to quickly escort her out into the waiting room. He was very good at managing things and people.

"What do you want to talk with me about, Freddie?" he asked and settled on a tall spinning stool across from the exam table.

I was still lying down, cold packs pressed into my body. I considered sitting up—I wanted to be more eye-to-eye—but I didn't want to argue over my "treatment." I had more important things to talk about.

"Dr. Ulf," I said. "I didn't really come here because of the fall."

"No? It looks bad. It's okay to—"

"No, I get it. Really. I will always call you if it is really important. I promise."

"Good. So what's this all about then?" Dr. Ulf was always straightforward like that. It was one of the things I liked best about him. He wouldn't lie to me. If there was bad news, he would always tell me, not treat me like a stupid baby.

"I fell on purpose," I said quickly, before I lost my courage. Dr. Ulf started to speak, but I stopped him. "It was the only way I could think of to get my mom into a doctor's office. You see, my mom has been ill. Really ill. She lost a ton of weight, and she is tired all the time."

"Hmm, I did notice that she looked more worn-out than usual."

"She is. I saw her almost lose consciousness the other day."

"Did you talk with her about it?"

"She won't listen."

"And your dad?"

I was bad. I rolled my eyes, indicating how little my father really cared about what was happening to us at home. But when Dr. Ulf sat and waited for me to give a real answer,

I did. "I think my parents are having problems," I said. "My dad hasn't been around much. And he stopped kissing my mom goodbye."

"I see," Dr. Ulf said. "Do you think that your mom's condition has something to do with that?"

I hadn't considered that, but I was sure that was not it. "No. I think there's something medically wrong with Mom. I'm sure there is. And since I couldn't get her to see her own doctor..."

"You devised a way of getting her to see me."

"Yes. I know it is wrong. But I really didn't know what else to do. I'm very worried about her, Dr. Ulf."

"Well, young man. Do you think you can babysit that little sister of yours while your mom and I talk in my office?"

"Would you?" I felt so relieved, I almost cried. "It's no problem, Doctor. I babysit Nonaken all the time. It's easy."

A few minutes later, I was sitting on a floor of the exam room on a couch pillow from the waiting room with three cold packs strapped to my leg, while Nonaken sat in her stroller with a book she wanted me to read to her. Dr. Ulf and my mom were presumably discussing her health in his office.

A surprisingly short time later, Dr. Ulf and my mom returned. Mom looked like she planned on giving me a "talking to" when we got back home. But Dr. Ulf looked concerned.

"Well, I expect you back here in two weeks, Freddie," he said. I swear he gave me a wink. "I would like to see how your leg is healing. Would that be alright, Mrs. Keen?"

"Of course." But Mom didn't look happy about it. Perhaps she suspected that Dr. Ulf had ulterior motives.

"And please, Mrs. Keen, I think your son would feel so much better if you took some time to take care of yourself. As you've said, Freddie has been getting stronger and stronger. He and Nona can clearly take care of each other for short periods of time—"

"We'll see," Mom cut him off. She really didn't look pleased.

"Please, Mom?" I begged. "I told Dr. Ulf that I can't get better if I worry about you." Total lie, but I was sure Dr. Ulf would support me. "I can read to Nonaken in the waiting room while you see a doctor or something. It's no problem, see?" I showed the book Nonaken picked out for me to read. It really was easy. My sister was an easy kid—as long as everything went her way, she didn't protest at all. "You know I can take good care of Nonaken."

"I believe he can, Mrs. Keen." Dr. Ulf supported me.

We didn't discuss what happened on the way home, or that night, or even that whole following week. I went to school as usual, Mom took care of Nonaken, Dad was absent through most of it...all of it, really. I gave my mom inquiring looks; she avoided me. She didn't let me question her more. But she did seem grayer and grayer to me with each passing day. I couldn't understand why no one else saw what I saw.

✳✳✳

She collapsed while carrying Nonaken up the stairs. From my bedroom, I heard the banging as they both tumbled down and rushed out to help. It was just after dinner. We weren't expecting Dad home for many more hours still. So it was just me.

I saw Nonaken lying at the bottom of the stairs on top of Mom, not moving. It was probably the fastest I'd ever gotten down the stairs. I felt panic in my armpits. Cold sweat was running down my back. My brain was humming loudly, making it impossible to think. Then Nonaken looked up at me and screamed. It was a tentative scream. I think she hadn't figured out if she was hurt or not, but she was freaked. And so was I.

I dropped my crutches to the side and pulled Nonaken off my mom. My little sister's blue eyes were as huge as saucers.

"Are you good, Nonaken?" I asked. She wasn't *talking* talking yet, but Nonaken understood most things now. She nodded a bit and drooled on my lap. "Good girl," I approved. I carefully palpated her arms and legs and back—I've learned from the best—she didn't wince or anything, so nothing was obviously broken. "I'm going to put you down right here. And you be a very good girl, Nonaken, and don't move. Okay?" She just nodded again. "Good girl," I said and gently deposited her on the floor. She quickly turned over and sat up—she definitely seemed fine.

I turned to my mom. She was unconscious, not a good sign. I knew enough about not moving her—a spinal injury could get worse if the person was moved. I had plenty of ex-perience with that. So I crawled all around my mom's body, looking for signs of damage. I didn't see anything obvious like blood, and her body wasn't at any obviously bad angles. It didn't mean that nothing was broken, but it was a good sign.

"Mom? Mom? Can you hear me?" I called to her. I leaned over and gently pulled up one of her eyelids. Her eyeball was still there. I had no idea what I was expecting, but I saw people do that in some movie or something. "Mom?" I called to her again. I bent over and listened to make sure she was breath-ing. She was. I felt her pulse and couldn't find it. But she was breathing, so it was just my awkwardness. "Okay, Mom. I'm going to call an ambulance, all right? And I will call Dad too. I really don't know what else to do. But if you don't want me to do that, you have to tell me now. Like right now. Mom? 'kay, I'm calling..."

I crawled over to my mom's phone, which was lying a

few feet away. It must have fallen out of her pocket during the accident. The screen was locked. It was one of those that recognized the face of the user to unlock its function. I put the phone to Mom's face, but it didn't work. Did the phone know she was unconscious?

"Okay, okay, okay." I looked around. My phone was up in my bedroom. "Nonaken? Be a good girl and watch over Mom. I will be right back. I just have to go get my phone. Okay? Can you do that for me, Nonaken?"

My sister looked at me with those huge eyes of hers and nodded. She did understand. Good. I turned back toward the stairs and started to crawl up as fast as I could. I didn't bother with crutches—it was easier to just crawl, if not more dignified. But who cared? Still, it took me a while to get up there. My hands shook, and I could feel adrenaline flowing through me, making everything more hazardous. But I couldn't make a mistake and take a tumble. I had to be careful. My mom and Nonaken depended on me.

It felt like forever, but I was up in my room dialing 911.

"Operator? We need help. My mom fell down the stairs, and she is not moving." I knew I sounded like a very little kid. I was scared, and that always raised the pitch of my voice. But the emergency operator woman believed me, and I managed to answer all the rest of her questions just fine. I knew our address, and I had memorized my dad's phone number, so she called him for me, keeping me on the other line. I had to explain to her that Nonaken was just a baby and that I needed crutches to move around, so it would take me time to get back down to Mom. She waited patiently as I held the phone in my mouth and descended.

Mom was still nonresponsive. Nonaken was sitting next to her, holding her hand, and crying. I felt bad for her.

"It's going to be okay, Nonaken. Help is coming," I said as

soon as I got down and took the phone out of my mouth. It was covered in my spit. Still worked, though.

The nice emergency operator told me that a police car and an ambulance were on the way. I had to get to the door and open the locks, but if I couldn't do that, I shouldn't worry—they would just break the door down. I knew Dad would freak at that, so I left the emergency operator to talk to Nonaken and got up on my crutches and made it for the front door. I got there almost at the same time as the cops.

From then on, it was a blur. One cop was assigned to talk to me. He helped me to the couch and brought Nonaken for me to hold. She screamed if anyone else tried to do that. She clung to me for dear life, poor thing. The ambulance people were all over my mom, loading her onto a gurney and wheeling her out of the house. When I explained that Nonaken also took a fall, they came back for her too and took me along with them. We left together for the hospital. I hoped someone locked the front door.

***

Mom was admitted. Nonaken seemed okay besides a scare and a small bruise on her shoulder, but the hospital kept her "for observation" overnight anyway. My sister was too young to really say if something hurt, and frankly, they couldn't just release a baby into the custody of an eight-year-old, could they? So I was in the room with Nonaken, who finally fell asleep around midnight. I had no idea about Mom—I asked, but the nurses told me that they would get back to me later and that I should take a nap on a cot they wheeled into Nonaken's room. I haven't heard from Dad. But I also managed to lose my phone in all of the hassle and shuffle. I hoped it was just back home somewhere; Dad would go ballistic if I *lost it* lost it. It was very expensive, and I only got it because I was a crippopotamus—not being able to walk did sometimes get one a cool phone, but I wouldn't recommend it. There really were very few benefits to having a congenital birth defect. I should know.

I woke up because Nonaken was crying. Light was already streaming through the window, so it was morning... but very early. I got out from under the blanket that someone must have put on me in the middle of the night and hobbled over to my sister. Out of consideration, someone had moved my crutches over to the corner of the room, neatly out of the way. I wished people were a bit less considerate and left them where I could reach them. Surprisingly, I hardly needed to grab at things on the way to the crib. I usually made fun of myself for "brachiating" across rooms and such, but my legs supported me just fine the four feet of open space I needed to cross over to get to my sister.

"What's up, Nonaken?" I asked and sat on a stool next to her hospital crib. "Hungry? Wet?" I realized that we didn't bring a diaper bag with us. So not only I had nothing for Nonaken, but I didn't use anything myself overnight. Yet I knew I didn't have an accident. I was so relieved and surprised that I almost cried, too.

"How are you guys doing?" A nurse walked in on us at that moment. Somehow, all nurses everywhere have developed a supernatural ability to sense pain and discomfort. I guess it's their superpower.

"Fine?" I answered. My voice squeaked, and it came out as a question. I cleared my throat and wiped a stray tear. "I think my sister needs her diaper changed, but I forgot to bring her stuff with us. And I have no baby bottle or anything." I felt guilty for letting my mom down like that. I was old enough to know better. "And my mom—what's happening to my mom?"

I knew I should have asked right away, but there were too many things happening at once. I never had to be responsible for my sister for so long by myself, and at a hospital, no less.

"I have everything our little girl needs right here," the nurse sing-sung her way over to Nonaken. "Come here, sweetheart. There you go." And just like that, she lifted Nonaken and checked her diaper and cleaned her up. She was like a miracle worker. One, two, all done.

"Thank you," I said. "She probably needs some food too."

"I have it right outside the door," the nurse said and brought in a large tray with bacon and eggs and orange juice and a big bottle with formula. My mouth watered. "A bottle for our girl, and some eggs for you, young man. Also, here's a hygiene kit—a toothbrush, some toothpaste, and a comb. The bathroom is through that door." She pointed to a door just inside our hospital room.

I took the little plastic bag with goodies, grabbed my crutches from the corner next to the crib, and made my way to the bathroom. There was no point in showing off my prowess to the nurse. She had no idea how remarkably well I was moving. She had no baseline. And I could easily have tripped and fallen and ruined everything. Crutches were easy, familiar, reliable.

When I came out, the nurse just finished feeding Nonaken, who looked happy now and was playing with some toy the nurse brought for her. The woman thought of everything! I dug into my food, which was still warm. I didn't realize I was ravenous. The eggs were good, but not as good as Uncle Charlie's, obviously. I so wished he was there.

"The doctor will come soon and talk with you, Freddie," the nurse said. "He will come with a social worker—"

"What?" The idea of a social worker got me spooked. "Why? We don't need a social worker." The nurse looked at me kindly and smiled. But instead of making me feel better, it just made me even more scared. "You didn't tell me about Mom. How's Mom?" I asked again.

"You know how hospitals work, Freddie. We are not allowed to discuss patients—"

"But I'm family!" I knew exactly how hospitals worked; I'd been here too many times.

"Why don't you finish your breakfast, dear?" She changed the subject. And I could tell that she wouldn't tell me anything. I just had to wait.

I finished up the food—*who knows when I will eat next?*—and took Nonaken on my lap while the nurse straightened up our room. We sat in a "family" chair, and I played with my sister's fingers and toes—this little piggy... She always loved that.

We didn't have to wait long. Several doctors, nurses, and social workers crowded into the room. If I were a normal kid without the extended experience with hospitals and their staff, I would not have freaked. But I knew. They all had that look—kind, grieved, sympathetic, serious, and "we know what's best for you, child." I knew that look oh so well. It always came with the worst news.

"Fred Keen?" the doctor asked and walked over to shake my hand. Nonaken started to cry again. She didn't like being around so many strangers. A nurse that fed and changed her tried to take her off my lap, but Nonaken screamed even louder. It confused all those people. They looked around at each other, trying to figure out what to do about us.

"Doctor? Can you tell me what's happening to our mom?" I asked, putting Nonaken over my shoulder and gently petting her back. She hiccupped and stopped wailing, keeping to just a few tears and lots of snot and drool. A nurse kindly supplied a towel to protect my already soaked shoulder. I guessed Nonaken was teething, on top of everything else. As she settled into chewing the towel over my shoulder, I asked again, "Mom? I need to know about Mom."

"Your mom was very ill," the doctor started.

"I know. I told her she needed to see a doctor," I said.

"Do you know what was wrong with her?" someone asked.

"No. But she lost a lot of weight and was tired all the time," I said. There were many more symptoms, but this was a hospital, and they were all professionals; it was their job to figure out what was wrong with Mom and fix it. I was happy that she was finally getting help. I told them as much. That seemed to confuse them even more.

"We are getting hold of your father," the doctor said. I swear they teach verbal jiu-jitsu in medical school—all the doctors and nurses I've ever met were very practiced in question avoidance. All but Dr. Ulf.

"My doctor, Dr. Ulf, knows about my mom," I volunteered. "He spoke to her just a week ago."

"Dr. Ulf?" I saw a woman scribbling notes and then stepping out of the room. I figured she would look up Dr. Ulf and call him. I felt a little better. There were too many strangers who knew nothing about our family or our problems. I knew they were all trying to help, but they didn't feel helpful...yet.

"Thank you, Freddie. It's okay to call you Freddie?" the doctor asked.

"Sure. Everyone does. Fred Keen is my dad. I'm Freddie," I told them. "You've said you couldn't get hold of him yet?" I could swerve and dodge conversationally as well as they could. At school, it was my best defense—confuse them silly with words and they leave you alone...mostly.

"We are working on that, Freddie," a woman not dressed in a hospital uniform said. I figured she was the social worker. For some reason, I hated her. It wasn't rational. She didn't do anything to me...so far. "You don't happen to know if your dad is out of town? On a business trip, perhaps?" she asked.

"I don't think so," I said. But I really didn't know—Dad was absent so much lately. And he stopped telling us when he traveled. Sometimes, when we crossed paths in the morning, I'd noticed a rolling bag, and then I knew he would be gone for a few days. But I didn't notice anything yesterday. "I haven't seen my dad since last morning," I said. "It's possible that he might be out of town."

"I thought so," the woman said and exchanged glances with the doctor. "Do you have other family in town, Freddie? Grandparents? Aunts?"

"I have an uncle in California. Uncle Charlie."

The woman wrote something in her pad. "Would that be Charles Keen?"

"No. Uncle Charlie is my mother's young brother. Charles Labelle," I said. I was proud of myself for knowing. Somehow, I'd only learned Mom's maiden name just a few weeks ago, accidentally, when I overheard her arguing with Dad through the floor of my room. It paid to eavesdrop, occasionally. "He used to work at Oakland Children's Hospital. Uncle Charlie is a nurse. He helps kids with cancer." I was very proud of him. "But he isn't there right now."

"Do you by chance know where he is?" the social worker asked.

"No." I didn't want to tell them about the conversation I had with Uncle Charlie's friend. That was private. "But can you please tell me about Mom? How is she feeling?" I didn't like how they were all avoiding telling me about her. "Can I go see her? I know it would make her happy to see her kids," I added. And it was true.

You might have guessed by now that Mom died that night, and the doctors, nurses, and the social worker were just stalling until they found my dad. No one wanted to tell an eight-year-old and baby that their mom was dead. I couldn't blame them.

We stayed in the hospital through that day until they finally managed to locate Dad. He came to pick us up in his new red convertible. It didn't have a car seat for Nonaken or a booster for me. I held my sister tight on my lap until we got home, hoping that there wouldn't be an accident on the way. I'm not sure what was more terrifying—my dad's total lack of appropriate emotions or the ride home with the top down. Nonaken seemed to like it, though.

Chapter Four: New Life, Old Fair

Things happened fast from then on. We moved into an apartment Dad bought downtown. It was on the sixty-seventh floor, and I spent hours watching the city from above, patrolling it for fires and other emergencies. Dad got us a housekeeper slash babysitter, Ms. Marta, a plump woman of indeterminate age who became the grandmother Nonaken and I never had. We both loved her fiercely. When she first arrived, Ms. Marta spoke little English, and Nonaken and I learned her Spanish. Ms. Marta was worth it. She had a strange accent, and we both picked it up. Nonaken became completely fluent in no time; she had the Spanish language skills of a native...of some country or other. I was not as good as my sister, but I got by. And it gave my sister and me a language in common that Dad...well, most everyone couldn't understand. That was very useful.

Time flew... After the move, we went to new schools, private ones. I can't say they were better than the public elementary school I attended when Mom was alive. But it wasn't worse. Nonaken—slender, blue-eyed, with waist-long blond hair—looked a lot like Mom and Uncle Charlie. Her looks made her one of the popular girls. I looked more like Dad, even as I desperately wished to look like Mom, just to spite him. I even dyed my hair blond once. I was punished—Dad made me shave it all off. I stopped acting a fool after that. That was back in seventh grade, way before my prefrontal cortex came online—that's my excuse, and I'm sticking with it.

The most amazing thing was that by about a year after Mom's death, I stopped needing crutches. And by about the tenth grade, I was participating in sports like any other kid my age. I played soccer. Can you believe it? Soccer! All that running and twisting. I could do it all! Dr. Ulf kept asking Dad to bring me by so they could study my amazing progress, but Dad told him to bugger off. Dr. Ulf and his medical team eventually stopped trying. I missed him. Despite trying to pry into my medical history, I sort of remembered Dr. Ulf as a good man. He wasn't able to save Mom, but I think he tried. I found it hard to remember, it was so long ago now.

In all those years, Uncle Charlie never called. I used to hate him for it. Hated him so much it hurt. Why would he abandon us like that? Did he ever love us? Ms. Marta would rock me to sleep on days it got real bad. I was her "gran chico," yet she still tucked me in and sang to me and stroked my dark brown hair until I got too tired of crying and feeling sorry for myself and fell asleep. Nonaken, of course, never experienced any of this. She was too young to remember Mom or Uncle Charlie. She grew up with Ms. Marta satisfying all of her parental needs.

Dad wasn't around much. He became a very successful businessman. He traveled all around the world. Sometimes, we didn't see him for months at a time...which was fine by me. It made Nonaken angry, but he always managed to buy her good graces with expensive exotic gifts. He hardly talked to me at all, although I think he was glad that I wasn't a cripple anymore. It made it so much easier to show us off to his important friends at dinner parties he threw in his pent-house. Yes, Nonaken, Ms. Marta, and I lived in the original apartment he bought right after Mom died. Dad lived by himself in an upgrade in the same building. He said once that it was too awkward to bring home dates when we were around. It made me hate him, but Mom was dead, and so there really was no reason Dad shouldn't have been dating. And it was considerate to us...to me that we didn't have to meet his endless parade of "step-sins," as Ms. Marta called them. She called them worse in Spanish, but there was no point in repeating it.

I graduated from my elite high school with honors and went off to an elite college on a soccer scholarship. Can you just imagine? The little crippopotamus was the captain of the team now. Amazing.

That was when everything changed yet again.

✳✳✳

I was an English Lit major; she was studying economics. Her name was Klaire. We met in freshman English. She was wonderful! But it took me a few years to figure that out. We didn't go on our first date until my junior year. That was mostly my fault. I went home for as long and as often as I could get away from my school, my team, and my studies—Nonaken was home alone, and she needed me.

But somehow, in the first semester of my junior year, a bunch of my friends and I ended up going to a county fair one Friday afternoon. It was a long weekend, early fall, harvest time. Klaire went as my date with an invitation to spend the rest of the weekend at my home with Ms. Marta and Nonaken. She'd already met my sister during one of the on-campus family weekends, and I was sure Nonaken would like the company. Ms. Marta wouldn't have minded either—she always told me to find someone to be happy with—and she was a great cook. Best tamales this side of the border—she told me so herself. It was going to be fun, eating homemade food and watching stupid movies late into the night, huddling under a blanket on a sofa.

You might think that given my history with the county fair all those years ago, I would have been wary of going again. But I had successfully repressed all those memories. I pushed aside all the years in the wheelchair, all the endless times in the hospital, my mom... And I pushed out the mirror test and its old blind minder, burying it all deep inside, so deep that it was only once we were walking the fair that a strange sensation started to come over me. As we walked the temporary dusty "avenues" of the fair, I remembered my past more and more. Random visual memory vignettes overlapped reality, making me stumble like a drunk.

"Freddie? Are you okay?" Klaire asked. She was wearing a white summer dress, which was a nice contrast with her dark golden skin and long black hair cascading down her back in loose curls. She was holding my hand. It felt super nice. I kicked myself mentally for not asking her out before this.

"Yeah. It's just..." I mumbled, considering what I could tell Klaire without freaking her out. "Did you ever have a feeling of déjà vu?" I finally asked—a mysterious and yet safe topic of conversation. It was not what I was feeling. Mostly I felt dread: dark, thick dread. But I couldn't tell this happy beautiful woman at my side that I was scared of the county fair, now could I?

She thought about it for a moment and said, "Not personally, no. But I read about people who have, and of course I've seen movies that used déjà vu as a plot device. Why? Are you feeling it now?"

"Kinda." And I stumbled again, reaching out to grab hold of something, searching for my long-discarded crutches. I almost fell then, but Klaire caught me.

"Are you okay, Freddie? Do you want to sit down or something?" she asked, concerned.

"Yeah, do you mind?"

She waved off the rest of our gang, who went on to stand in line for some spinny ride. I was definitely not going on any of those. That old feeling of crippopotamus washed over me, even as I was in perfect health and very physically fit.

"Perhaps it's the sun," Klaire said. "You are so fair. People with these many freckles don't tan—they stroke. Why don't we go inside one of the crafts pavilions? I've always loved those. And perhaps we can find you a great big sun hat. Might be a good look!" She smiled brightly at me and pulled us forward.

What could I say? Should I have told her that I was scared to go inside? Nope. So I let Klaire lead me into the giant fairground building divided up into thousands of colorful booths, selling everything under the sun...well, under the roof away from the sun. I just hoped the blind woman was not there...or perhaps I was secretly hoping she was? I was so confused...and clumsy, all of a sudden.

Klaire decided that I needed to get something to drink, and we walked toward the back of the building where the food courts were. I insisted on walking through the middle of the building. Somehow, I just assumed that the one-mirror booth would be off to the side somewhere. That was its location thirteen years ago. And no, I wasn't superstitious...not really. We walked. I scanned the crowd. Klaire talked about going to the county fair every year as she was growing up. She grew up on a family farm just outside of a small town, and the county fair was a big deal there. She and her family—she lived with her two aunts—went to the fair multiple days in row.

"Did you ever go to the fair as kid?" she asked. She always assumed me to be a city kid. I guess I was. We moved from the 'burbs when I was just eight. I'd spent most of my life living in a giant metropolitan area.

"We went a few times, when I was little." I gave her vague answer.

"I knew it!"

"Why?"

"The way you move around here. It's like you know where you are going, like a regular."

"Huh."

"It's okay. I won't think badly of you for liking the simple pleasures of a county fair," she said and gave me one of the most dazzling smiles I'd ever seen. The only one who could ever match it was Uncle Charlie. He was such a beautiful man...wasn't that what his friend from the hospital told me all those years ago? "You seem unusually quiet, Freddie. Are you still feeling ill?"

"Sorry. I was just thinking about something that happened the last time I was at a county fair." I just blurted that out without thinking.

"What?" She smiled again and pulled on my t-shirt. "What, Freddie? Did you get kicked by a mule? Did you fell off the wagon? Did you step into—"

"No!" I jokingly pushed her away. She made me laugh. "Nothing like that. We had a fun day with my whole family. My mom was still alive. Nonaken, my little sister, was just a drooling baby."

"Don't talk about Nona like that. I'll tell." Klaire was teasing me, trying to make me feel better, to lift the darkness that was trying to strangle my body and soul. I tripped again; she caught me. "Are you sure are okay? Perhaps we should just sit down somewhere." She put her arm through mine supportively. We must have looked silly—she was at least a foot shorter than me, and I was probably twice her weight. But I needed the support. I felt dizzy, lightheaded.

"Yes," I said. "Let's go sit down somewhere. Maybe it was just too much sun." But at that point we both knew it wasn't that. Klaire was looking at me with those huge chocolate eyes of hers. She was really worried about me. It made me feel happy and scared all at the same time.

She guided us toward the exit. There were some benches set up in the shade. We walked fast past all of the Technicolor booths selling all kinds of wonderful wares. I wanted to look, I wanted to get something wonderful for Klaire—a handmade hair clip for those long locks of hers, or a tie-die scarf—but my feet felt like they were getting tangled. My back was starting to hurt. If I didn't sit down soon, I was going to collapse.

"Should I call for help?" Klaire asked, her voice full of worry. I was putting more and more of my weight onto her. "Tell me what to do, Freddie. Please." She whispered "Please," and I could tell she was starting to get scared. There was something obviously not right with me.

"I think I will be fine once I get some fresh air," I lied.

And then there it was. Same sign, same woman. She hadn't changed one bit. I practically crawled over to the entrance of her booth.

"Well, hello, young man," she said. "Hig, wasn't it?" She remembered!

"Who is Hig? Freddie? Do you know this woman? Excuse me, ma'am, my boyfriend is not feeling too well. Too much sun. Do you mind if he just rests here a bit?" Klaire was wonderful, and she called me her boyfriend! I should have been over the moon, but instead I wanted to vomit.

"Of course, dear," the blind woman said. "Here, take my

chair. I have some water in the back. I'll get it."

"Thank you!"

I plumped down into the little collapsible chair. It groaned under my body...oh, it could have been me making all those strange sounds. "Whatever you do, Klaire, don't look into her mirror," I managed.

"What mirror, Freddie? And why did she call you Hig?"

"Hig is an old nickname my Uncle Charlie gave me when I was just a kid. And the mirror..." I motioned my head to the sign above: *Fun House Mirror, Take Your Mirror Test Today!* "Promise me that whatever you do, you won't go inside, okay? Promise me, Klaire. It's important." I squeezed her hand hard. I didn't want to let go.

"I promise." Her eyes were huge; she was taken aback by my intensity. But I couldn't put Klaire in jeopardy. We were already too close, and it was my fault. I made us come there.

"Here's some water." The blind woman handed me the bottle right into my hands. "Drink it. You'll feel better. It's a hot day."

"Hot day," repeated Klaire. She was watching both of us, moving her head from me to the old woman in rapid succession.

I drank the whole bottle in one go and sat for a bit with my eyes closed. I did finally start to feel better. As soon as I was able, I was going to take Klaire out of there.

"I told you," the blind woman said. I'd swear she hadn't changed one bit. I would even swear she wore the same skirt and blouse as last time, when I was eight.

"Thank you," I said. "We'd better be going now." I wanted desperately to get Klaire as far away as possible from that mirror behind the flimsy black curtain.

"Are you sure, Freddie? Perhaps a few more minutes? I'm worried about you." Klaire was wonderful; did I mention that already? I saw her looking at the blind woman for help in trying to convince me to sit a bit longer. That felt dangerous to me.

"I'm fine now, Klaire. Thank you very much for the chair and water, Ms. ... Ms. ..."

"According to the sign, I am the Mistress of the Looking Glass of Fate, but please call me Mistress Kismet, Hig." The woman smiled. I could have sworn she looked me up and down. But her eyes were empty—there was just a dull white where her eyeballs should have been and nothing else. I wasn't sure that was how her eyes were back then, when I was eight and went to look into her mirror. But how else would we have all known she was blind?

"Thank you, Ms. Kismet," Klaire said and helped me up.

We rushed away with Klaire continuously looking over her shoulder.

"What was that?" she asked when we were back outside in the bright sunlight.

She probably meant all of it—the Mistress of the Looking Glass, Hig, me feeling sick... I decided to answer the easy one. "My Uncle Charlie liked Freddie Mercury. You know the rock group Queen?"

"What? Oh. Of course!"

"Well. Mercury's sign is Hg in the Periodic Table. So, Hig, get it?"

She smiled. "Yes. I like Hig. Do you mind if I call you that?"

"I'd like it," I said. For some reason it made me really happy, too. It was a silly nickname, but I missed using it. No one used that name for thirteen years. It was special...but so was Klaire. "But it'd be for just between us, okay? Back when I was a kid, only Uncle Charlie called me that."

"You must have loved him very much," Klaire said. "Did

he die a long time ago?"

"He..." I felt flushed. I didn't really know how to answer that. How would I explain it all to Klaire? Would she want to have anything to do with me after that?

"Oh, Hig! It's okay." She threw her arms around me. "It's okay to miss your family. It makes me like you even better." I felt horrible...but I didn't correct her.

Chapter Five: Awkward Introductions

Nothing much else happened on the way home, except that I was still too much of a coward to correct Klaire's impression that Uncle Charlie was dead...well, he might have been. Over a decade had passed. He hadn't contacted me even once. He was dead to me, for all intents and purposes.

We got to the apartment later that night. Ms. Marta had left us some dinner in the fridge and gone to bed early. Nonaken was on the phone with a friend of hers—that was easily two, three hours for us to be alone. I turned off all the lights in the living room and we sat on the windowsill among the many orchids that Ms. Marta was so fond of growing—she had an obvious green thumb—eating leftovers directly from their containers and watching the lights of the city at night. The evening was unusually clear, and we could see for miles and miles from our high perch. All of my aches and pains were long forgotten.

"When I was a kid," I said, "I would watch for fires all across downtown. I felt like it was my duty to call the fire emergency as soon as I spotted smoke."

"Did you?"

"What?"

"Did you ever call the fire department?"

"Three times...until they told me to cut it out. It turned out I was lousy at discerning smoke from steam. Some owner of a laundromat got pissed when the firemen broke through his door. I was given a talking to."

Klaire quietly laughed. It wasn't a mean laugh; it was a kind of a gentle chuckle that told me she was in on the joke with me rather than laughing at me. I put my arm around her. We watched the city. It was perfect.

We heard the keys in the lock, and the apartment's front door opened. A click, and the overhead lights blinded us.

"Here's where my kids live," my dad was saying. "They are mostly grown up now. Fred Keen the Third is almost done with college. He is the captain of the soccer team, you know. Nona is still in high school." We couldn't hear the response from my dad's guest, but it was a woman. Dad obviously didn't know Klaire and I were there.

"Shh." I pressed my fingers against Klaire's lips. It felt nice.

"You don't need to see the view from here," my dad went on. "It's much, much nicer from my penthouse. Come on, dear. Let's go up."

But for some reason they stayed, and moments later Dad and his guest stepped into the living room and saw us.

"Fred? I didn't know you were home this weekend," Dad said. He sounded perturbed. We hadn't spoken for at least a month.

"I'm home almost every weekend," I said. "Dad, this is Klaire. She is a friend from college."

"Nice to meet you, Mr. Keen," Klaire said.

"Huh." Dad was obviously confused. He clearly didn't want to have a family reunion tonight...with his date there and all.

"I'm Cherie." A beautiful woman came forward. Her voice was deep and velvety. She was wearing a jacket decorated with hundreds of little buttons that made slight click-click sounds as she walked. She was tall and thin, with beautiful long, slightly curly blond hair, which looked like it would tangle with all those buttons in a painful way. "Cherie Hydrargyros," she introduced herself with a little half-smile.

"Cherie is Greek," Dad explained. She didn't look Greek.

"Nice to meet you," I said and shook her long, thin fingers. She was breathtaking...and so familiar. I just couldn't place her.

"The pleasure is all mine, Fred," the woman said. She looked at me like she was trying to dissect me with her blue-as-a-summer-sky eyes, but not in a bad way. Just strange. Intense. "Well, we better go, dear. We don't want to disturb these young people." And with that, she turned and led my dad out of the apartment, turning off the lights on the way.

"That was..." Klaire started.

"Strange," I finished for her. "Dad rarely brings anyone down here."

"He never introduces you to his girlfriends?"

"Never."

"Is he embarrassed by you?"

"I have no idea," I said. "But I don't think so. Dad just prefers to have as little to do with Nonaken and me as possible. But don't feel bad," I added as Klaire's eyes expanded into huge saucers of sympathy. "It's really better this way. We have Ms. Marta. And we have each other. And after Mom died, it would have been too weird to have him bring other women to meet us. I'm glad he never did."

"I see," Klaire said and squeezed my hand. She didn't really understand our family dynamic. How could she? But for me, I'd rather there was as little contact between Klaire and

Dad as possible. I didn't want anything to ruin my budding relationship with this amazing woman.

"And that woman? Cherie?" Klaire asked after an awkward pause. "Are you sure you've never met her before? The way she looked you over...it was very disconcerting."

"Yeah, that was very strange," I agreed. I didn't think Klaire was really questioning me or feeling jealous, even if Cherie was undeniably a very beautiful woman. It was just... "She did feel very familiar, but honestly, I don't think we've ever met. I would have remembered that name: Hydrargyros. It's Greek for water-silver."

"Mercury? Hg."

"Yeah. So I'd remember, right?" I smiled at her. Sometimes being an English major had some advantages—I was good on my roots.

"Huh. Strange." Klaire didn't smile back but did take my hand in hers. I liked it. Her fingers were long and smooth and cool.

We didn't talk much after that and went to sleep soon after. We both started that day with super early classes and were pooped. Klaire got my bed; I slept out on the couch in the living room. It was still very early in our relationship, and I didn't want to jinx anything by rushing things. Before retiring, Klaire gave me a quick kiss on the lips and left me in a daze. I ended up lying awake for hours, staring out of the window at the lights from the distant rivers of traffic—red blood cells floating along the city's arteries...

✻✻✻

The next morning, we had a family brunch. Ms. Marta treated us to pancakes and bacon. She always believed in feeding me when I came home from school. I couldn't understand how Nonaken stayed so skinny—she ate at home all the time. But my sister took after my mom's side of the family, obviously. I, on the other hand, always had to be careful and watch what I ate, although soccer practice burned off most of the extra calories I consumed at home.

"Tell me about Freddie as a big brother, Nona," Klaire asked. She insisted on calling my sister Nona, and Nonaken just ate that up. It made her feel grown-up, I concluded. I could see that she would soon insist I did the same. Well, she couldn't make Ms. Marta do that. Ms. Marta operated by her own rules...which were mostly focused on loving us. So all's good.

"Freddie has been a good brother...mostly," Nonaken said and gave me a furtive look. Klaire was the first girl I'd ever brought home like this. Nonaken and I hadn't yet worked out how we were going to handle interactions with our significant others. We both felt awkward. "I think he is worth the effort," she added diplomatically. I was grateful; it could have been so much more embarrassing.

"Of course Freddie is worth it!" Ms. Marta said and slid another pancake onto Klaire's plate. "Eat. Eat!" No one ever left Ms. Marta's table hungry. "My Freddie is best of boys." Ms. Marta's English language skills had improved a lot over the years she had been caring for us. She learned it by reading the obituaries in the paper every day—it was one of her most morbid fascinations. Nonaken and I teased her behind her back by calling her Ms. Morta, not something I am very proud of. But don't we all have something we do that we might not be too proud of, but we do it anyways? We had Ms. Morta. Ms. Morta had her obituaries. In any case, if Ms. Marta spoke ungrammatically now, it was always for effect. Her English was pretty perfect structurally, even if her accent was still pronounced at times. "He is a good brother, too," Ms.

Marta added. "You are very lucky to date him."

"Ms. Marta!" I was instantly embarrassed, but Klaire squeezed my hand under the table and smiled.

"I couldn't agree with you more, Ms. Marta," she said. "Freddie is a very nice young man."

"Nice" wasn't what I was hoping for from my new girl-friend, but one didn't get to argue compliments. And Nonaken was making faces at me—so immature.

"Freddie has always taken care of our little Nonaken," Ms. Marta continued. My sister just rolled her eyes. I swear if she was any more expressive, her eyes would have fallen out of her head and rolled around in the maple syrup on her plate. She was such a drama queen. "Mr. Keen is not around much, so Freddie is our man of the house," Ms. Marta said proudly. Nonaken stuck her tongue out at me. I gave back as good as she gave and felt like a little kid. Fortunately, Klaire laughed.

"I met Mr. Keen last night," she volunteered unexpectedly.

I watched as Nonaken's face fell. My sister always looked to our dad for approval. She desperately wanted him to pay attention to her. He never did, and yet she kept trying. I felt sorry for her. I'd mostly stopped caring after Mom died.

"I'm sure your dad was just busy..." Ms. Marta said, trying to soothe Nonaken's hurt feelings. But Klaire was unaware of the dynamic. How could she know?

"Oh, Mr. Keen just stopped by with his date to show off the apartment," Klaire clarified. I thought Nonaken would burst into tears right there and then, but she managed to collect herself. She didn't want to lose face in front of my girl-friend, I guessed. "He seemed nice," Klaire continued, oblivi-ous. "And his date was gorgeous, like a Greek statue, but with arms. She's Greek, apparently. Cherie...Cherie... What was her name again, Freddie? Something quick-silver in Greek."

"Cherie Hydrargyros," I said. "Water-silver."

"That's it. She seemed very nice," Klaire added in a small voice, finally noticing that we all got quiet. "I guess I put my foot in it, didn't I?" she said. "I'm sorry. I really should have known better than to say anything. I'm very sorry if I upset anyone. Really." Klaire's eyes got huge, and she really did look sorry.

"It's okay," Nonaken said. I made a vow to call her Nona from then on—that was very big of my sister. I knew how upset she really was, and yet she managed to be kind and make Klaire feel welcome. "We don't get to see Dad much. He's always very busy or traveling."

"More pancakes?" Ms. Marta asked. Her solution to most emotional upsets was more food. "They won't be good reheated." I grabbed one more just to make Ms. Marta feel better. Klaire and Nonaken...Nona refused seconds. Or was that thirds?

Ms. Marta busied herself cleaning up the kitchen. Klaire wanted to help, but Ms. Marta gently pushed my girl back down into her chair. Ms. Marta didn't want strangers meddling in her kitchen realm. I noticed that every time she passed Nona, Ms. Marta gave her a gentle squeeze on the shoulder or adjusted her hair or gave her a little kiss on the head. It pained Ms. Marta when she saw us kids suffer. She was a real mother bear. I loved her.

"I saw a wheelchair in your room, Freddie," Klaire said, trying to change the subject. "When did you get hurt?"

I saw both Ms. Marta and Nona give me frightened looks. My birth defect was not something we ever discussed. Especially not with people who didn't already know about it... of which there were none, really...other than Dad.

I took a deep breath and said, "I was born with a spinal condition." If we were going to be together, Klaire should know, right? "But I've been much, much better for a very long time now."

"You were in a wheelchair as a kid?"

"Until about eight or nine years old," I confessed. "Then it was mostly crutches. And then nothing."

"Did they do surgery on you or something?"

"No...well, yes. I had many surgeries when I was a kid." Klaire had never seen me without a shirt. She didn't see the scars that travelled like zippers up and down my back. Might as well prepare her for that. She would see those eventually...I hoped.

"What was it? Scoliosis?"

"Spina bifida." There, I said it and it didn't kill me. No one back at school had any clue, not even our coach. I never changed out in the open in our team's locker room.

"I didn't know that was curable," she said.

I didn't like the way Klaire was looking at me. Her eyes were full of pity. That was not right. Pity is a bad emotion in a romantic relationship. "I'm totally cured now," I said. "A walking, running, soccer-playing miracle, you might say."

"I'm sorry...I mean...that's great! That's amazing, Freddie. I really had no idea. Aside from that time at the county fair, I've never known you to be sick at all, much less have a serious birth defect."

"My boy has no birth defects," Ms. Marta barked out. She didn't like when anyone mentioned my "problem." "Freddie is as strong and beautiful as an oak."

"Of course he is!" Klaire was waving her hands trying to erase whatever wrongs she just conjured up by her careless words. "I didn't mean anything by it. I'm sorry, Freddie. I—"

"It's fine, Klaire." I took her hands in mine, stopping the panicked windmilling. "I want you to know everything about me. No secrets," I lied. I didn't want Klaire to know about the mirror test...although that was going to come out, wasn't it? It was just a matter of time. But I could push it further into the future, giving us a bit more time to bond and all.

"You went to a fair without me?" Nona finally spoke up. "Freddie has been promising to take me to the county fair for years! I've never been."

"That's not true," I said. "You've been that time when..." I felt the blood drain out of my face.

"Freddie? Are you okay?" Klaire was all concern. And Ms. Marta rushed over and grabbed my face in her hands to do a quick "medical" diagnostic. Ms. Marta knew how bad I used to be. I think she secretly dreaded that something was going to happen me and I would wind up back in that chair.

"I'm fine, Ms. Marta. Really."

"He just feels bad for not taking me to the fair," Nona said. She didn't really remember anything from back then. I didn't think she even really remembered when I was in that chair all the time. She was too young when I stopped needing it.

"The fair is still happening this weekend," Klaire said. "We can take you today."

"Would you? I would love to go! Please, Freddie. I really want to go. And Ms. Marta, I have finished all of my homework. I didn't really have plans at all for today. And we ate a big breakfast, so we don't even really need to spend a lot of money at the fair on food..." Nona seemed so excited at the prospect of going; she was talking nonstop, trying not to allow any room for a "no."

"Sure," I finally said. "We can go for a few hours. But Klaire and I have to get back to school tomorrow. So—"

"A few hours is great! Ms. Marta? It's okay, right? You don't mind if we go for just a few hours?"

"I..."

"I just want to go on a few rides, that's all," my sister

pressed. "Just a few rides and then we'll go home. There and back again in no time. Just a few rides…"

"Are you really feeling okay, Freddie?" Ms. Marta pulled down one of my lower lids to check for…what? She was no medical doctor. She just wanted to reassure herself. "You look a bit better," she decided. "Why don't you sit quietly for another half hour or so. And then we'll see."

Ms. Marta had no real say over my actions anymore, but I agreed anyway. Not only would I have done anything to keep her happy and worry-free, but I also wanted to figure out how I would deal with the Mistress of the Looking Glass…Ms. Kiss-something. I'd already decided that neither Nonaken nor Klaire would come anywhere near that woman if I could help it.

Chapter Six: Cherie

We got to the fair by one that afternoon. Nona promised to let us go home by five, no delays, no whining to stay longer. Not that Nonaken ever whined. She was never that kind of kid.

I noticed that Klaire was watching me like a hawk. She had her arm through mine, and it felt more like a medical thing rather than an "I want to be closer to you" thing. That was really not good. I didn't want Klaire to mother me. I had Ms. Marta for that.

"Should we go directly to the rides?" I asked. Those were located safely on the other side of the fair from the crafts pavilion...and the mirror booth.

"I'd rather walk around a bit," Klaire said. She sounded worried. "And I would love to show Nona around. A real county fair is not so much about the rides, although those are good too. It's more about the other stuff. You know, when I was in elementary school, I belonged to the 4-H club."

"Really?" Nona sounded so excited. "I always wanted to do that. But it's not a thing if you live downtown. It's not like they would have let me raise chickens on our balcony or anything."

"Funny you say that," Klaire said. "That's exactly what I raised. I had four. A white Silkie, a big Rhode Island Red, and two Plymouth Rocks. Of course, I raised them in a barn."

"I didn't know you lived on a farm," Nona said. "I wished we did."

"And I always wanted to live in a big city," Klaire said. "It's always like that—the city kids want to live on the farm, and the farm kids want to run away to the city." She chuckled. "But I did love raising my chickens. They are very intelligent birds, and each had a unique personality."

"I thought part of the 4-H program is that you have to eat the chickens," I said...like a dumbass. Both girls gave me "are you crazy" looks, and I shut up.

"Why don't we go to a chicken-judging competition?" Klaire said and led me in the direction of the barns. As long as we were not going to the crafts pavilion, I was good. "And for your information, I raised the chickens for their eggs," Klaire added.

Of course she did. I was so stupid. "I like chickens," I said lamely.

Klaire didn't stoop to a response. Nona just huffed at me. I deserved it.

We walked the dusty lane between food trucks, getting a giant blue Slurpee of undefined flavor for all three of us, toward where the animal competitions were going to be held. Each 4-H contestant, Klaire explained, got some space in the barn, where their animals could rest up from the trip to the fair. It was not good for animals to be stressed. And when the time came, they were taken over to the little arena where the judges and the audience sat on bleachers made out of hay bundles. Not all competitions were like that. Sometimes the judges simply walked around the different animal stalls and gave out awards. But the chickens were exhibited in front of an audience. I guessed they didn't mind too much. It would have been harder with a goat, right? What did I know? I liked chickens. I liked Klaire. She didn't seem to be angry with me any more while she talked chickens with Nona. My sister was happy. And we were nowhere near the mirror booth.

We got there in time for the chicken beauty pageant. Who knew? Girls—it was mostly girls—brought our their birds and placed them on a raised table in the middle of the arena. You might think all chickens were simply chickens, sort of like pigeons. But chickens came in all kinds of colors, and sizes, and shapes, and plumage.

"That one," Klaire pointed, "is a Padovana. See the punk feathers on its head? That's a tell."

"They're awesome!" Nona exhaled. "I always wanted a chicken for a pet. Dad always said no."

"You've asked?" I couldn't believe Nona even tried. Of course she couldn't have a chicken in a high-rise. It was probably bad for the chicken, too—if it jumped the coop, so to speak, would it fall dozens of stories to the pavement below or suddenly learn to fly? I was contended to leave it as a hypothetical question. But I got another dirty look from the girls and shut up. Why antagonize the fans? I made a decision to sit quietly on the hay and watch and let the girls have their fun. And I liked chickens, I really did, although perhaps not in the "this is the most beautiful bird in the world" kind of way.

There were dozens of crazy-looking chickens shown, all exotic breeds. I'd heard of none of them before. Klaire seemed to be able to identify all of them on sight. She gave continuous commentary on each bird contestant—rarity, disposition, breed, color, and even historical tidbits. I had no idea she was so into chickens. Not that it changed how I felt about her one bit. Klaire was still the most wonderful girl I'd ever met, *and* she was also the world's preeminent expert on chickens. A person could be both.

I have to say that my appreciation for chicken beauty was not as well-developed as it was for Klaire and Nona. My eyes started drift around to the audience. Who were the other chicken fans in the crowd? Mostly, it seemed to be the parents and friends of the 4-H presenters and other contestants. It was a very supportive group—lots of cheers and clapping. It felt more like a party than a competition. I liked that. I scanned the judges—all very serious dudes. And suddenly, my eyes caught a pair of blue eyes staring at me from behind a hand fan, one of those old-fashioned affairs that little old ladies in the South used; I'd seen the pictures; I was an English Lit major. It was like electricity passing through me. Uncle Charlie!

I wanted to cry out to him, to run there, to hug him, to hit him for leaving me like that. I jumped out off my bail, but the fan motioned for me to go outside and the eyes disappeared into the crowd.

"Freddie? Are you okay?" Klaire was instantly on her feet as well. "Are you feeling badly again?"

"What?" Nona didn't know about my problems the last time I went to the fair. Why tell her? "Is there something wrong with you? Klaire? Is he okay?" It was amazing how fast women were able to bond. None of my male friends would have questioned me in a situation like this. If a dude had to go, he had to go.

"No, no." I waved both of them down. "Just need to go find a restroom. I'll be right back." I could see that Klaire was scanning my face for paleness or some other sign of sickness. Thank goodness for the dark shadows of the barn where the competition was held—all the spotlights were on the beautiful chickens. "Be right back," I said again and jumped down from the back, eager to show off my good health. It worked; the girls turned back to the competition, and I ran out of there.

The sunlight hit me hard, and I could hardly see after the dimness of the barn arena. Everything felt fuzzy. Where was Uncle Charlie? What was he doing here? Those eyes...he didn't seem surprised at seeing Nona and me here. I didn't even question how he managed to recognize us after so many years. I looked nothing like the eight-year-old cripple he knew. But that thought never even entered my mind.

I walked all the way around the barn but didn't see him. Then someone tapped me on the shoulder. I turned and...it was Cherie, Dad's newest squeeze, the step-sin.

"Excuse me," I said. I really didn't have time for this, for her. "I've got to get to the bathroom." I rubbed my belly demonstrably and was about to rush off, and then...

"Hig? It's me. It's Charlie," the woman said and raised her fan to cover most of her face. Only the eyes remained. They were Uncle Charlie's eyes.

"Uncle Charlie?" I felt faint. Like there was not enough air or something.

"Let's go sit down somewhere for a moment. I won't keep you long," he...she said. I was taken by the elbow and led to the side to a bench in the shade of a large tree. The bench looked familiar. "Thank you for coming out to see me, Hig. I can't tell you how much it means to me," Uncle Charlie... Cherie said.

"So do I call you Uncle Charlie?" It was a stupid question, but I was stunned. I didn't in my wildest dreams ever expect anything like this. Who would have?

"It would be simpler if you called me Cherie," Uncle Charlie said and smiled. He still had that smile... He had lipstick on. It looked good.

"Okay." There were so many things I wanted to talk to him about, and now nothing. I had nothing to say. Except perhaps, "Why?" That seemed to cover all of it, really.

"You always asked the right questions, Hig," Cherie said.

"Thank you, I guess."

"Do you remember that day at the fair?"

I nodded. My throat was suddenly dry. I looked left, beyond the tree. There was the entrance to the crafts pavilion. And just behind that door...

"Do you remember the Mirror Test?" he...she asked. "Of course you do. Do you remember what you saw, Hig?"

"I do." I could still see the face of the young man in that mirror—my face. I saw that face everyday in my bathroom mirror for the last decade.

Uncle Charlie smiled. She looked sad and nodded knowingly.

"Oh." And everything clicked. In a flash of an eye, I saw how life must have unfolded for Uncle Charlie after the mirror. He must have seen this woman in its reflection. He went back to California but things...he started to change. Fast. He left his job. He had to. If his change from Uncle Charlie to Cherie was as fast as mine, he would have been halfway there within a year or so. I had a hard time explaining to everyone around me what was happening to me. I stopped seeing Dr. Ulf. It must have been impossible for Uncle Charlie. We moved. He ran. He couldn't really come and see me like this, could he? Would I have understood? Would Dad? Definitely not Dad... *Dad!* "Does he know?" I asked, my voice sounded strangled.

"No."

We looked at each other for a long time. What did I really care if my dad was dating my dead mother's younger brother? What did it mean to me? I couldn't really answer that question.

"Why?" I asked again.

"Why I saw what I saw in that mirror? Why I didn't reach out to you earlier? Why I agreed to go out with Fred?"

"That's a good start," I said. "I'd add, why didn't you go to your sister's funeral? Why didn't you try to talk to us right away, before all this?" I waved my arms at her face and rather large breasts. "Why did you leave us alone?"

"I'm sorry, Hig. It wasn't my intention. I was scared. My body was changing. I couldn't stop it. I didn't want to stop it."

"You didn't?"

"Your mom probably never told you, but I always wanted to be a girl. I used to dress in your mom's sundresses as a little kid. It was funny at first. But then I started to get punished for it. So I hid but did it anyway. Your mom, Sissy, was supportive. Well, she was until she met Fred. Then she told me not to ever do that again. She didn't want him to catch me at it."

"Huh. I didn't know."

"Of course not. You were too young back then."

"Are you happy now?" I asked. Cherie didn't look happy.

"When your mom died, I lost my best friend."

"You mean that woman at your hospital? Nurse Megan?"

"Wow, you still remember her name."

"I've tried to find you for years. I needed you. Mom died, and I needed you. *We* needed you. And you weren't there. You ran away." I felt hot tears in my eyes and turned away, using my shoulder to wipe my nose.

"I'm so sorry, Hig. I know I shouldn't have abandoned you like that. I know."

"You knew and yet you did. It was horrible when Mom died. Horrible." And then it struck me—I saw a healthy kid in the mirror, Uncle Charlie saw a woman he became. "What did my mom see? What did she see in that mirror that made her die?"

"I gave that a lot of thought over the years. I was obsessed."

"And?"

"When you were born, Hig, Moira was diagnosed with postpartum depression. It's very common, you know. Something like eighty percent of all women experience the 'baby blues' after giving birth. And some, like Moira, struggle with a clinical depression. As much as twenty percent."

"Twenty percent..."

"She got better, obviously...and then had Nona. I saw the darkness return. Your dad knew about it, too, of course."

"But you didn't save her," I said.

"She was getting better, Hig. I was sure of it. But then the Mirror Test. I think that's why she died. I think that's what Sissy saw in that mirror—death," she said almost in a whisper.

"But she didn't commit suicide, right?" I was trying hard to put my world in a whole new order. Mom was suffering, and I didn't even know it. I didn't help.

"No. But given our outcomes, she didn't have to. She only had to look into that mirror to get her wish."

"And she wished for death."

"Or for an end to suffering, which might have amounted to the same thing in her head."

"And Dad? What did he see?"

"What do you think?"

I thought about it, and it was obvious: "He wished for success."

"I believe you are right."

We sat in silence for a moment, trying to digest what was just said.

"Are you going to run away again?" I asked finally.

"I was hoping to stay," she said.

"With Dad?"

"For now. This way I can be close to you and Nonaken

again—"

"It's Nona now," I corrected her.

"Nona." She laughed a sweet sad laugh. It almost brought me to tears again.

"She doesn't remember you, you know," I said, probably to hurt her. "Nona doesn't remember Uncle Charlie. She was too young."

"But you do."

"I do. I'm not sure I'm good with you dating Dad. It's wrong. It feels wrong."

"We'll see."

"Hmm." I felt angry and happy, relieved and confused all at the same time. I wanted to hug Uncle Charlie and didn't really want to touch Cherie. "Nurse Megan said that you went to look for the blind woman. Traveled the country looking for her."

"For years," she said. "I've looked for her for years. I thought that maybe I could do something to make it right."

"But you like being a woman?" I said. "And I definitely like not being a wheelchair."

"I do. And I'm very happy for you too, Hig. But Moira..."

"You mean we can get Mom back?" The idea was so incredible, it felt akin to being struck by lightning. "To get Mom back..."

"I never found the blind woman, Hig. I looked and looked. Traveled all over U.S. and Canada and even Mexico, hoping to see her again. But I never did."

"She is right here." I nodded. "Just behind that door. She calls herself the Mistress of the Mirror or some such pretentious crap."

Cherie jumped up. There was a crazed look in her eyes. "I..."

"There you are!" Klaire and Nona walked over to us. "We

were looking all over for you. You can't just disappear like that." She finally saw Cherie next to me. "You!"

"Cherie Hydrargyros." Cherie extended her hand to Nona, her expression still wild. "I was a friend of your Uncle Charlie."

"So that's how you knew Freddie," Klaire said. "It makes sense now. Nice to see you again. Glad we were able to run into you." She smiled, but it was an uncertain smile. There was tension in the air. Uncle Charlie was ready to bolt. I felt sick. I didn't know how to process any of what just happened.

"Nice to meet you, Ms. Hydro... I'm sorry, I didn't catch that," said Nona.

"Please call me Cherie."

"Okay. Nice to meet you, Cherie. You've met Klaire already?"

"We met last night." She didn't elaborate.

Klaire looked at me, and I just shook my head. It was not the time to get into it. My Uncle Charlie was dating our dad! Too much. I could hear blood rushing through my body.

"Well, I was just saying goodbye—" Cherie started.

"No," I said. It came out more forceful than I intended, and I got questioning looks from both my sister and Klaire. So be it. "I would like a way of getting in touch with you. A real way," I said. I wasn't letting him...her go this time. Not again. Not when there was so much to figure out.

"I'll be in touch, I promise," she said. She smiled and turned to go.

"No!" I practically screamed. And I reached for her, but Klaire stopped me.

"Let her go, Hig," she said softly in my ear. "Let her go." And I watched Cherie disappear through the door of the crafts pavilion.

"What was that?" Nona asked confused.

"Let's go home," I told her. "I need to get back right now. I'll explain later." Surprisingly, neither Nona nor Klaire protested.

***

I refused to discuss anything on the way home. We rode the train practically in silence. I dropped my sister at our apartment, grabbed my and Klaire's overnight bags, and left. I knew Nona was very worried about me. I promised that I would talk to her soon. Just not right then.

"What was that about?" Klaire asked when got back to our dorms at school. I was grateful that she waited until we were alone. "Were you feeling sick again?"

"No." She just looked at me like I was lying to her. And in a way, I was. It just wasn't in a way she thought.

"You know, Hig, I want us to be a real thing," she said.

"I do too."

"Well, we can't be for real if you lie or hide things from me. It's not how real, grown-up relationships work."

"I'm not lying to you," I insisted stubbornly.

"Okay then, you are not telling me the whole story, Hig. Who was that woman, really? What's her connection to your dead uncle? Did you know that she knew him?"

"Huh." I took a deep breath, looked out in the hallway, got up, and closed the door of my dorm room. I lived in a single, so the only intrusions would have been from my floor-mates. I didn't want them to interrupt. I didn't know how much I was even planning on telling Klaire, and I didn't want others at school to know...anything.

Klaire sat on my bed, patiently waiting for me to get it together. "So about my Uncle Charlie..." I started.

"Yes?"

"He is not dead."

"No?"

"I didn't lie to you the other night, Klaire. I really had no contact from him at all since I was eight. He could have been dead...or alive. I just had no idea."

"Okay."

"Today I learned that he is in fact alive."

"From this woman, Cherie the Greek?"

"Cherie Hydrargyros. Yes."

"No wonder you were so flipped out back at the fair, Hig." Her face was full of sympathy and compassion. I felt guilty. "I'm so sorry," she said. I loved the sound of her voice. "Do you trust that woman? Do you think she told you the truth about your uncle? People can be—"

"Klaire," I stopped her. "She told the truth." Now that I knew, I saw Uncle Charlie's face in Cherie's. I had no doubts about his...her identity.

"Are you sure?"

"Very."

"People lie all the time, Hig. Some are into manipulating. Finding ways...finding vulnerabilities..." She stopped and studied my face. "Okay, so that's not it. You trust her." I nodded. "And she just happens to date your dad? Don't you think that's—"

"That's bad, Klaire. I told her so. I think I told her to cut it out."

"You think?"

"It's hard to remember now. It was so...so unexpected."

"I'm sorry, Hig." She leaned over and gave me a hug. And I swear I just wanted to cry into her hair. My mom chose death... She chose death over being with us, with Nonaken and me. "Are you okay?" Klaire asked.

"No. But I'm working on it." My voice sounded terrible. I

felt very vulnerable indeed.

"So do you want to go see him?"

"Huh?"

"Your Uncle Charlie. Do you want to go see him? We can go together, if it's easier."

I thought about it. I didn't just want to see my uncle, I *needed* to see him. I needed to understand what happened to all of us. "I will go see him. I have to."

"I'll go with you. I can wait in a car or in another room. But I think you need someone with you when you go. You said Nona has no memory of your uncle, right? And I figure your dad is not very interested—"

"Klaire, stop. It's more complicated. It's more...more weird than you can ever imagine."

"Tell me, Hig, I'll understand. That's what happens in real relationships. People trust each other even with the weird, complicated stuff. Trust me, Hig. Please." And she just looked at me with those chocolate eyes of hers. What could I do?

"Okay. I'll tell you everything. But please, please don't judge me...just don't. Promise?"

"Promise," she said. And for the next hour I told her all about the spina bifida, my life in the wheelchair, Mom, Uncle Charlie, and finally the Mirror Test. She made little sounds. Nothing like "I don't believe you" sounds or anything. Just high-pitched little oh's and ahh's.

The story came out like a rambling river of strangeness. I would not have believed half of what I told Klaire myself. But she saw the wheelchair and crutches in my room. She saw how Ms. Marta reacted. She believed at least that part of the story. And then Cherie. Klaire picked up on how strange she was, how intensely "off" our first interaction was, and how disturbing the second.

When I was finally done, Klaire sat and looked at me for

a long time and then said, "I believe that you believe it, Hig. But—"

"You're about to tell that it's all paranormal nonsense, right? Nothing like this happens to normal people, is that it?"

"Yeah. That mostly covers it," she agreed but didn't let go of my hand. I didn't remember her holding it. "But something happened to you all," she said. "Your family is damaged. This Uncle Charlie is somehow mixed up in it all. Well, it's Cherie now. But have you considered that your uncle could have just undergone a sex change operation? People do that, you know. It didn't have to happen by magic. It could have been a simple surgery...well, not simple, but—"

"I get it, Klaire. Yes, you're right. Yet, I feel like it's more than that. You were with me when we saw the Mistress of the Mirror. She knew who I was. She was blind, and yet she knew right away. I was in the wheelchair back then, all those years ago. I was a sickly little kid. And yet she recognized me."

"There could be a perfectly reasonable explanation for that. It doesn't have to be a magic wish-granting mirror, Hig."

"I guess so."

"And I think she called herself Mistress of the Looking Glass of Fate. Kismet, for short."

"Kiss?"

"Kismet. I looked it up. It means fate, destiny, or some such. A bit pretentious even for a stage name."

I agreed. The blind hag chose that name to intimidate, intrigue, and lure innocent visitors into her evil booth.

"So we go and confront your Uncle Charlie..." Klaire stumbled over the name. "Your Aunt Cherie," she corrected herself, "and try to get her to confess. And we can also go back and visit that old Kismet woman. She's clearly a charlatan and preys on the sick and the vulnerable. You were sick. Your mom was depressed. Your dad had issues. And your uncle was...he had a lot of issues, obviously. People like that old blind woman have to be stopped before they hurt more people. And it sounds like she might have been the cause of your mom's death. Indirectly... Your mom might have had suicidal ideation due to postpartum depression, and the woman said something to her to push her over the edge. That's a crime, Hig."

When she put it like that, it all made a lot of sense. More than...what did Klaire call it? The magic wish-granting mirror.

"We'll take a few days off from school, starting tomorrow," she said, "and go and see this woman first. We need to report her to the authorities. Then we will find your Aunt Cherie. Okay?"

"Okay." I was so drained and emotionally exhausted that I couldn't say no. Not then. You see, I still believed that the mirror was magic and that Klaire might be hurt by that blind Kismet or whatever she truly was. I agreed, but secretly I made decision to go back to the fair that night, as soon as Klaire left for her own dorm. Without her.

I smiled. We kissed. It felt good. We made plans to leave first thing in the morning. She went away. I crept into the dark and took a midnight train to the fairgrounds. I hoped Klaire would forgive me—real relationships were about forgiveness, too, right?

Chapter Seven: Back to the Fair

The train was empty but for me and some man in the far corner, reading a newspaper. I couldn't read. I couldn't really focus. I stared out of the window. Neighborhoods were rushing by, the metropolis abruptly transformed into suburbia and then changed into stretches of farms interspersed with small town centers—the train stops. It was amazing, really, how fast the human population density dropped off. It seemed like people either wanted to live right on top of each other or be as far away from their neighbors as possible. I still remembered when we lived just a few miles away from the fairgrounds—practically walking distance for every kid but me. Wide streets, tons of big climbing trees, freedom to run… nothing I could really enjoy back then. I was actually happy to get away into the big city center. When you are stuck in a wheelchair, it helped to be close to everything. Distance was the enemy back then; it kept me confined to my home, inside my room…without friends.

But what if we never went to the fair on that day? With Uncle Charlie's work schedule, we could easily have missed the fair altogether that year. Dad would never have agreed to take us. Mom wouldn't have done it on her own. If we didn't go, would life have stayed as it was? Would I still be stuck in that chair? Would I have even gone to college? Dad's success had direct advantages for me and my sister. We lived very well. We didn't want for anything...other than Mom and Dad...the kind of dad that had dinner with us every night and talked with us over food, discussing politics and science and the latest movie plots. Nona and I didn't get that. But we had Ms. Marta. We loved her and she us. We weren't deprived kids. No, we weren't. Sure, it would have been nice to have a real mom...and Uncle Charlie. Nice but clearly not necessary, not for survival, anyway. We got along.

Was he happy as Cherie? It must have been a shock to wake with breasts and...well, the other thing was probably missing now, right? I felt embarrassed even to think about it. It was none of my business what body parts Uncle Charlie gained or lost in the process of becoming Cherie Hydrargyros. He must also have lost his profession, right? Uncle Charlie loved being a nurse. He loved helping kids through the darkest days of their lives. Sometimes all the way to "the other side." He never really talked to me about that, but Mom said once that the dying kids always requested Uncle Charlie for their last nurse. It must have been something to be wanted... needed like that. That must have been more of a loss than the other thing. Did Uncle Charlie...Cherie manage to work in her chosen profession after the change? Did he want to? Nurse Megan told me that he left to chase the blind woman from the fair; at least that's how I remembered it. It was so long ago. What if Uncle Charlie wanted to change back? Could he? Would he see something different in that mirror if he looked today?

Lots of random ideas swirled around my head to the monotonous beat of the train speeding on its rails. But there was one train of thought that I tried to avoid at all costs.

The important one. The one that really mattered. Mom... I couldn't go there—there was too much at stake.

I got off the train way after midnight and walked several miles along the dark, empty roads to the fairgrounds. It was strange to walk these streets as an able-bodied man. I mostly remembered it as a bumpy ride. A very different perspective now.

The fair was locked up for the night, of course. But the people who traveled with the fair—the artisans and the cooks, the clowns and the ride operators, and all the others who lived from fair to fair—were still in there somewhere. I remembered Uncle Charlie telling me all those years ago about the trailer park out in the back, where the visitors didn't go. He said that some people traveled with their motorhomes and lived and worked at the fair. It was like a small town, a neighborhood of people who all moved together and lived together and worked together. The location changed, but the town stayed together. Spring in Alabama, summer in Maine, fall in Pennsylvania, winter in Florida. Modern nomads. There was an appeal to that. I felt it when I was a kid; I still felt it creeping along the fence of the fairgrounds that night.

I saw some lights flickering in the distance—campfires. The fence was a simple twisted wire, temporarily installed to keep unauthorized people like me out. It was eight feet high at that point, but I was very athletic. It took less than ten seconds and I was on the other side. Easy.

It was hard to get my bearings in the dark, but I noted where the fires burned and walked the other way. I wanted to get inside the crafts building, where the one-mirror fun house booth was. I decided that I needed to see if my reflection showed something different now. I also had a feeling I might find Cherie there. Where else would she be? Uncle Charlie had been chasing that mirror for over a decade, and he finally caught up with it.

I walked by the animal barn, where the chicken competitions were held. I could find that place by smell alone. It wasn't unpleasant, per se, just barnyard-y. Then I rushed by the big trees, with the now very familiar bench at the base, and made it to the double glass doors of the crafts building. Inside it wasn't completely dark. There were some emergency lights and other illumination that I couldn't exactly place by pressing my face into the glass. The doors were locked, obviously. For some stupid reason, I thought they'd be open—the whole fair's perimeter was locked, so why bother with the door? But there were wares and cash registers and other valuables inside. It made sense that the crafts building was secured tight for the night. It was probably set on the alarm, too, now that I thought of it. I would make a terrible criminal.

I slid over to the glass door, peering into the gloom. The point of that? I had no idea. I was making it up as I was going along. Just as I had planned on doing with Klaire—I knew she would be mad at me for going without her. But I was protecting her; she couldn't hate me too much for that, could she? I remembered the mirror booth being very close to these doors. It should have been visible from my vantage point. Sure enough, I could see its black curtain through the door. My mind jumped to thoughts of Klaire again. I knew she would be pissed, and yet I couldn't come up with a way of making things better with my new girlfriend. I just hoped she was still willing to be mine after all of this was over. My mind bounced all over the place, fueled by adrenaline.

With doors locked, I decided to walk around the whole building—perhaps there were windows left open or some side utility door or something. Things slip, people forget... The crafts pavilion was huge. Twenty thousand square feet, easy. Maybe more. I walked with my fingers trailing the side of the building, scanning for anything accessible above and below. I found a small metal door on the backside of the building and pressed it gently, testing how far it would give. No go. I kept going. I came onto the side of the building housing a big industrial kitchen. Sometimes there were bakeoffs and cooking classes held there during the holidays, when the fair moved on for the year and the building was available for rent to other events. I remembered Mom talking about those and how she learned to cook a turkey at one of the Butterball demonstrations. During the fair, though, it was rented out to a local restaurant and used to cook food for the visitors who preferred to eat something familiar in the cafeteria, which was in addition to all of the food trucks stationed around the picnic table area in the central quad of the fairgrounds.

Bathrooms were also located on that side of the building, the good kinds—those that had hot and cold running water and special stalls for wheelchair people. I remembered just how important such facilities used to be to me. Abled-bodied people just don't get what a crippopotamus like me had to put up with...or just parents with little kids in strollers and such. I looked up, searching out the bathroom windows. Those were usually left open during the day for ventilation, and with luck, they still might have been. But nothing obvious was. So I jumped and pushed on each window in turn until one swung about its base. Bingo!

I looked around. It would have been stupid to be caught by a night guard...or a security camera. But the coast was clear. I pulled myself up and snaked through a narrow opening. A few more acrobatic maneuvers got me inside the utility closet for the bathrooms. There were stacks of toilet paper and cleaning supplies from floor to ceiling. I was in! And I was so glad that I didn't knock anything down.

The door to the supply closet was locked from the outside,

but those kinds of locks were made to keep people out, not in. A twist, a turn, and I was out, carefully leaving the door slightly propped open with a toilet paper roll. It was dark in the main hall of the crafts pavilion, but not pitch black. I took a few seconds to adjust my eyes and started to carefully make my way back toward the other side of the building, where the mirror was located.

Have you ever been to a toy store after hours? Or a children's museum after dark? Going through the rows and rows of booths at the crafts pavilion was something like that. The displays that looked happy and fun during the daylight hours looked creepy and grotesque under the emergency lights. Not that I was scared or anything...well, only of being discovered by a security guard. But I didn't think those patrolled inside the fair buildings at night.

The twists and turns of the rows of booths were disorienting in the dark. Uncle Charlie once told me that they designed the booths layout to make it harder for people to simply leave. The fair people wanted visitors to become shoppers, so they made leaving as difficult as possible. It was like the mall elevators—they were placed purposely to make people walk all the way around to get from one floor to the other. I figured it was to give people enough time to develop impulse-buying desires. I just found it confusing, and when I still used crutches, practically unmanageable. I ended up having to double back several times when the aisle I was walking down turned back away from where I needed to go.

It felt like it took forever, but I finally made it to the double glass doors again. The mirror booth was there. And now that I was right there, I did feel real fear. What if I saw myself in the wheelchair again? It was not what I wanted. But could the mirror really work to change me back into crippopotamus? And could Klaire have been right about all this magic crap? Perhaps I simply got better? Dad could have advanced in his company based on his own hard work. He did work very hard all the time. That was more plausible than magic, wasn't it? Same for Uncle Charlie. It was amazing what was possible with modern medicine nowadays. Yet I knew that wasn't true. It was the mirror. And now it was just feet away from me, paralyzing me with fear.

I heard voices. I almost cried out but managed to get hold of myself and dove under the black velvet curtain of the one-mirror booth. I crouched next to the chair that I sat on just a few hours ago, amid the endless boxes of stuff, and practically stopped breathing. The voices were getting closer. Given what the mirror did, of course I wouldn't be the only one who'd be interested in visiting it after hours.

It was a man and a woman. They were whispering but didn't seem overly concerned about stealth—I could hear their echoing footsteps from way away.

"It this it?" the man asked. He was clearing talking about the mirror booth.

"Yes," the woman said, still in a hushed whisper. "Are you sure the old woman is not in there? I wouldn't put it past her to sleep with it." Cold sweat irrupted out of my every pore—I didn't even consider that. The Kismet hag could be right here...with me!

"She has a traveling wagon that expands into a sleeping tent. Roger said that he saw her go in. He'd text me if he noted something different."

"Good."

"Roger is solid," the man said. "We've been doing these fairs for years." The woman mumbled something in response that I couldn't understand. "Don't worry, Cherie," the man told her. "He'd let us know if the old crone so much as goes out for a pee." So it was her. I knew it! At least the blind old witch wasn't lurking somewhere behind me.

"She took her sweet time about going to sleep, though," Cherie said. She sounded uncertain. Scared. Well, so was I. But it was good to know that Roger was keeping a look out... whoever he was.

I considered—*should I be scared of Cherie and her friend finding me here? Should I just come out—Hi, what a surprise to find you here too?* It wasn't like they'd do anything to me... But I decided there was no rush. If they found me or if the situation warranted it, I'd crawl out and let them know I was there. If not, I could learn a lot just by listening. Yes, I was a coward. I didn't really want to look into that mirror again; I just knew that I must. I pulled a large dark scarf, which was left hanging over the back of the chair, over myself and stilled.

"Do you want me to look first?" the man asked. "I don't mind. Not only do I not really believe in all that crazy magic shit, but my life has been sucky lately, and a bit of change might be nice." If only he knew...

"No, Vic. You've helped enough as it is," Cherie said. "And just having you here—"

"We've known each other for a long time, Cherie. And have been friends for nearly as long. You know I'd do anything for you," Vic interrupted her. "I guess I'm just saying you're not alone. Whatever happens."

"Thanks, Vic." I heard what must have been a kiss on a cheek...well, I hoped it was a cheek—Cherie was dating my dad...*Yak! All-around yak!* And then the curtain moved and Cherie stepped inside.

It was darker inside the booth than out there in between the fair stalls. Cherie pulled out a flashlight, and a narrow beam of stochastic light bounced about the tiny space. I stopped breathing. Cherie didn't see me. She stumbled over the box and cried out, dropping her flashlight. Vic rushed inside, knocking the chair into my side, hard. I let out a sharp groan. Vic grabbed me by the back of my sweatshirt and then punched me with enough force for the world to go dark.

***

"Hey, buddy. Wake up."

The first thing that came fully into focus was my throbbing jaw. I'd never been hit hard enough to lose consciousness before. Soccer led to bruises and an occasional bloody nose, but no one tried to hit you in a face...on purpose!

"There you go." I was finally able to understand words. *Vic, was it?* "Sorry about that, buddy. I didn't know you were Cherie's nephew. Figures. But just finding you hiding under the chair like that? Well, I just didn't expect it, that's all. I hope I didn't break anything important." He gave me a twisted grin. It wasn't funny. "Move your jaw back and forth," he instructed. I did. It hurt. But it moved. "That's a boy. Looks good to me. Girls will be all over you, trust me. Scars are very attractive—"

"Stop bugging him." I heard Cherie's voice, and something very cold touched my face. Ice. "How are you doing, Hig? Sorry about that. Vic was just trying to protect me, I guess." I felt my uncle's expert fingers palpate my jaw. He hadn't lost his touch—he was gentle, yet thorough. If something was broken, he would know. He would take care of me. She. "Feel your teeth. Anything loose?" My tongue moved around. Cherie watched me. Nothing was obviously wiggling in a wrong way. "Now, say something," she ordered.

"Why?" I mean I knew why, but the question was still on my mind.

"Well, buddy, you don't look a thing like your aunt here. How was I supposed to know you were related?" Vic said. "I didn't mean to hit so hard. Just the surprise of it all." *He* was surprised.

"He took after his father's side of the family," Cherie said. "You should have seen his mom—Moira, my sister." Now that I really looked, Cherie did look a lot like my mom, a spitting image, really. And like my sister, too. For some reason, I hadn't noticed before. "What are you doing here, Hig?" she asked.

"What are you doing here?" I answered. It sounded garbled. And, boy, did it hurt.

"See?" Vic said with forced cheerfulness. "He's just fine. Won't even be able to see a mark on him by morning."

I didn't agree. I felt like I wouldn't be opening my mouth fully for at least a month. *No chewing. And no more kissing Klaire...not like she would let me after I ran out on her like this. Damn.*

"Hig? Did you look into the mirror?"

I shook my heard. That hurt too.

"Don't move," Cherie said. "I want that ice pack to stay on your face. Just move your lips...a little."

"Okay," I mouthed.

"Good. So did you look?" she asked.

"No." There was no time.

"Good." Cherie sounded relieved. Vic stepped back and was just observing us. I was stretched out on a bit of carpeted floor in front of the mirror booth. The black scarf I was using as cover was now rolled up under my head as a pillow—I could see the splayed ruffles out of the side of my eyes as a halo around my head. For some reason I worried that the water from the melting ice pack would damage the silky material.

"Did you look?" I asked.

"No. I'm scared to."

"Are you going to?"

"Or for god's sake, you two," said Vic, and I watched him pull back the curtain and march inside.

"Victor, no!" Cherie called after him but didn't try to really stop him.

There was rustling of cloth. A curse, as Vic apparently also hit something hard in the dark. A flash of light from a flashlight or perhaps his cell phone, and Vic called back to us, "No mirror."

Cherie jumped up and rushed inside the booth. I waited for what felt like forever as there were more frantic noises back there, but then Cherie came and shook her head.

"It's not here?" I asked like a dumbass. *I mean, obviously.* "Perhaps she takes it back with her for the night?" I suggested, but that couldn't have been true. The mirror was at least six feet tall and four wide. It looked heavy, too—big ornate gilded frame. It would have been crazy to move it back and forth every day.

"It could be on wheels," Cherie said as if reading my mind. "No, I agree. It doesn't make any sense. Vic? Did Roger notice the old woman rolling back a big mirror? Or anything large like that?"

"Not as far as I know," he said. "Roger would have mentioned it. Perhaps we should look some more?"

"No, it is really not back there, Vic. We've both searched already," she said. "So, Hig, are you ready to move yet? How do you feel?"

I felt like shit. My jaw felt like a giant cast iron pan that had been welded to bowling ball—not too well at that—and every movement hurt and pulled in all the wrong ways. But I turned over and got up anyway. I felt woozy.

"Easy there, buddy."

I wished Vic stopped calling me "buddy." We were not

friends. And I hadn't even planned on forgiving him yet for knocking my lights out, much less had done so.

"Hig?" Cherie's voice was full of concern. She came closer and put one of her arms around my waist, and I put one of mine over her shoulder. I was much taller than her. Was Uncle Charlie always this short? Height, at least, couldn't really be affected by surgery. Did the mirror make Uncle Charlie shrink in size too? Made him more demure? More petite? Like Mom...

"Hig? I would like us to walk back to camp. Vic has a nice motorhome in the back of the fair. I don't think it's a good idea for us to hang around here, okay? Do you think you can walk yet?"

Could I? I took a few tentative steps. I felt strangely embarrassed by not being able to manage by myself. It was like I was eight and a cripple all over again. But my head was spinning too much. And I wanted to vomit. I was just not ready to walk that far yet. I gagged. Vic saw and rushed to grab something. It wouldn't have been good to leave a mess in front of the mirror booth. But I'd bet that the blind woman would notice regardless that someone was there; I'd bet she would even know who. For a blind person, she noticed a lot.

"Okay," Cherie said and guided me back into the infamous chair. "Sit here for a bit." She lifted one of my eyelids with her finger and than turned back to Vic. I could see she was furious with him.

"Concussion?" I managed.

"Perhaps," she said, facing me again. "We can sit here for a few minutes. It's okay. It's still very early." It was about three in the morning, I guessed.

We sat, and I finally got to look around the front section of the mirror booth, the one in front of the curtain behind which the magic mirror was hidden...was supposed to be hidden, but wasn't now. There were boxes everywhere, the type of boxes that held paper files, the type no one got anymore. Some looked very old and beat-up.

"Should we snoop?" asked Vic. We were all looking at the boxes, trying to figure out what they were all about. "It's not like they are locked or anything," he added. They were not, but they were taped. Only some had the tape so old that it stopped being functional and just draped loosely over the edges of the cardboard like a sad ribbon. But we were trespassing. These were not public papers; these were witch's private property.

Cherie leaned over and lifted the lid on one of those. They were full of files, like I guessed. Each file was labeled with a date and a name of a newspaper. Cherie pulled out one at random and opened it. All three of us looked.

"The *Plain Dealer*, Cleveland. November 23rd, 1978," Cherie read out loud. The clipping was old, yellow, seemed fragile. "Pete Johnson, the distant uncle of Mayor Dennis Kucinich, won the Bobcat Trail Marathon at fifty-three. Mr. Johnson had never ran a marathon before and only took up running a few months prior after being diagnosed with diabetes. We are happy to report that today, the mayor's uncle is free of the disease, as well as super fit and enjoying the fame that comes with winning our city's proud race."

"Lucky dude," Vic said. "My grandpa died of diabetes. Never ran a marathon in his life, though."

"Here's another one." Cherie pulled out another clipping folder from the middle of the filing box. This one had a blurry black-and-white image of a smiling woman. *"Dayton Daily News*, June 3rd, 1967," Cherie read.

"Wow, 1967?" Vic whistled.

"Mrs. Helga Haggins celebrates her one hundredth birthday..."

"Let me see." Vic took the clipping from Cherie's hand. "Nope. This gal can't be a hundred. Seventy, maybe, and even then... Nope. Just nope."

Cherie gave me a look and then pulled out another one. "*Laramie Daily Boomerang*, Wyoming. May 17th, 1963." She took a deep breath and continued reading. "A miraculous recovery for Mr. and Mrs. Willington's baby girl. Their daughter, born in January 1958 with limb deformities, suddenly grew out healthy arms and legs. Little Suzie's congenital condition involved malformations of both arms and legs, which resembled flippers. Miraculously, just a few months after her fifth birthday, the child's limbs had a remarkable growth spurt. Little Suzie is now running around like any other little girl..."

"Is there a photo?" Vic asked.

"No," Cherie said, her voice flat. She dropped the clipping, and Vic picked it up and reread it.

"Huh."

"We now know," Cherie said, "that this type of birth defect is caused by thalidomide, a drug commonly given to mothers in the late fifties and early sixties to treat morning sickness. It caused horrific limb malformations in a generation of kids."

"Did those kids ever grew their limbs out?" Vic asked.

"No. It's not possible," Cherie said. "It was a very horrible thing. There is no cure, no treatment. No one grew new arms or legs. We gave this drug to mothers, and we just didn't know back then that this was going to happen."

"But this baby girl Suzie grew hers back," Vic said, still holding the newspaper clipping.

"January 1958. May 1963," I said, stating Suzie's date of birth and the year given by the paper when her limbs grew back. It hurt to talk, but who cared? "That's just over five years old. Old enough."

"Old enough for what?" Vic asked.

"Old enough to pass the mirror test," Cherie said. I saw her hands shaking. We both looked at the piles of boxes, each clearly stuffed to capacity with news clippings. There must have been records of thousands and thousands of minor (and major) miracles in those.

I saw both Vic and Cherie take a few of the newspaper clippings from Mistress Kismet or whatever. There were dozens of boxes full of such clippings, and I saw how careful Cherie was about arranging them to look like nothing was disturbed. But I was sure that somehow the old woman would know anyway. But who cared? What could she do about it? And, more importantly, what did it all mean?

Chapter Eight: History

Vic and Cherie walked me back to his motorhome just as it started to get light. I was still a bit nauseous but good enough to walk half a mile or so back to camp. And by the time we situated ourselves in Vic's "living room," I was really much better.

"Lie down and keep that ice pack on your face." Cherie ordered me to Vic's bed. I didn't protest too much. I was dead tired...and wired all at the same time. It was a surreal sensation that strangely fit the mood. Vic and Cherie crowded to his laptop and pulled out the clippings.

"Read aloud, please," I asked. From the bed, even if it was just a few feet away from the fold-up table, I couldn't see anything. And I wanted to understand the magic mirror's influence on the world almost as much as I wanted to reduce the swelling around my chin.

"*Ashland Daily Tidings,*" Cherie started.

"Is that in Oregon?" Vic asked. He was typing in the information into a search engine.

"Yes," Cherie said and continued reading, "September 8th, 1979—"

"Do you have anything past the nineties?" Vic asked. "It would make the Internet search easier."

Cherie shuffled through the stolen clipping, looking for

another one. I vowed to read all of them later, even the ones not backed up by online sources. All of the clippings looked genuine to me—they were obviously cut out from real newspapers and magazines.

"Okay," she said. "October 31st, 1998."

"Halloween," Vic murmured, but I saw him enter the date into a search field.

"*Grants Pass Daily Courier.* Also in Oregon."

"Thank you."

"Eleanor and Davy Wood of Grants Pass invite family and friends to celebrate the life of their daughter, Jenny. After four years of battling breast cancer, Jenny will pass away peacefully among her loved ones—"

"Assisted suicide?" I asked from the back. I remembered reading about those. I was obsessed at one point, after Mom died and when I was still in need of the chair...and adult-sized dippers on occasion. Suicide seemed like an easy way out. But there was Nona. An easy way out was never an option for me, not after Mom died, anyway. Someone had to stay behind and care for my baby sister.

Vic typed furiously and then said, "Oregon's Death with Dignity Act was passed on October 27th, 1997. That's almost exactly a year before this announcement."

"So it would have been legal," Cherie said. "But still not very common back then. But this clipping is obviously about a death party."

"But what does this have to do with the mirror?" I asked.

"Not sure."

"Perhaps the old hag met those people," Vic said. "I see here that there was a county fair not too far from Grants Pass in September of that year. They could have went to the fair and saw her there."

"Hmm. Let's read another one," Cherie said and shuffled

the clippings, looking for the more recent ones. "Here's one from 1997. I know that was still the early days of the Internet, but..."

"Let's see if it comes up," Vic said. "Read me some of the details."

"May 13th, 1995. *Great Falls Tribune*, Montana," she read aloud and stopped and scanned the rest. "The article talks about a motorcycle accident. A bunch of 'road warriors' from Great Falls were racing through National Bison Range and smashed into some bison."

"Predictable," Vic murmured as he typed. "Must have come up winner in the Darwin Awards..."

"Vic! They all died! Well, all but one. One woman made a remarkable recovery. She was paralyzed from the waist down and lost one of her arms in the accident. She also suffered some brain damage...ooh, it was bad." I could see Cherie's hands shaking from my vantage point. And she was a nurse!

"There is a picture?" Vic leaned over. "Not good," he said after glancing at the clipping in Cherie's hands. I didn't ask to see; I didn't need to.

"So this woman had a complete recovery?" I asked instead. "Another medical miracle?" I was very familiar with those. "Did she grow back her arm too?" I knew I was being too flippant, but...

"Doesn't say," Cherie said.

"I can't find this story," Vic said. "Before the 2000s, lots of information simply disappeared. It's not like today, when data storage is cheap and everyone has a long history of every little thing they've ever done documented online. Don't ever Google me, buddy." He shook his head.

"I won't," I promised. I didn't even know his last name, although his motorhome was packed with knives and swords of every kind, in addition to metalworking tools. I figured he made those and sold them at fairs. Probably why he almost broke my jaw "without meaning to"—Vic was a blacksmith, for goodness sake. He was probably totally ripped. And he was at least a head taller than me. I had no interest in messing around with him. None. If he wanted to keep calling me "buddy"... But Vic would be easy enough to find online, I'd bet.

"So," I said, "do we believe that this crash survivor went to the fair, visited the magic mirror, and then got better?"

"Perhaps," Cherie said and started to read another one. "November 13th, 2012."

"Now we're getting somewhere!" Vic looked ready for the search.

"*Montana and Bitterroot Valley Church Bulletin*," Cherie went on. "A fight broke out at a holiday crafts fair."

"Got that," Vic said. "Ooh, nasty enough to get into the papers. People went to a hospital. Damn! It was about Christmas presents, of all things. People, you should be nicer to each other."

"Is there any mention of the mirror online?" I asked.

"Nope, not a thing."

"It says here that the fight started at the fortune teller booth." Cherie gave us both a look. "A man accused his wife of cheating on him. One of his kids wasn't even his, according to this."

"I wonder what he saw in that mirror," I said. But I could see it in my mind's eye—man and wife went in together and saw the reflection. The reflection showed the wife with another man, probably smiling, holding hands with a kid. Perhaps there was more, but it was enough. The man flipped out and...

"She cheated on her husband with his best friend," Cherie added.

"I'm surprised the mirror wasn't broken right there and

then," Vic said. "But nothing like that is in the police report I'm reading. And there's nothing about the mirror in the local papers. There's lots about the fight that wiped out a whole bunch of holiday crafts booths. People lost all their wares. Thank goodness it wasn't one of mine. My knives are sharp." Vic confirmed my guess of his profession—he was a cutler.

There was a knock on the door of the motorhome, and a smallish man with glasses and an impish grin walked in.

"Hey!" he greeted Vic and Cherie. He didn't see me lying in the back. "So, your blind gal just left her trailer."

Vic and Cherie jumped up. "Was she carrying a large mirror?" Vic asked.

"No, just her white cane. You know, for visually disabled people?"

"Okay. I'll go and see what she's up to," Vic said. "Thanks for keeping an eye out, Roger."

"Sure thing, Vic. A pleasure to see you, Ms. Cherie. Always a pleasure." He smiled widely at her and followed Vic out. Cherie blew him a kiss.

She explained that Roger was a traveling accountant. He lived in a giant, two-bedroom motorhome and provided financial services to the little one-person corporations—the fair artisans. It was a very useful service, and the people held Roger in high regard. Cherie knew him personally. She seemed to know a lot of the fair people personally. But I guessed that after years of chasing the blind old woman and her one-mirror fair booth, one got to know the regulars.

"What do we do now?" I asked when Cherie and I were alone.

***

Now that I had some time to get used to her, I could see that Cherie was beautiful...in an ethereal sort of way. She was very slender and had long blond hair and piercing blue eyes. Her skin was translucent; one could almost study the anatomy of circulatory system by just looking at her. But she also looked kind and caring—those main traits of Uncle Charlie's were still there in Cherie. Everything, including the extreme vulnerability and extra human strength, all rolled into one decent person. She looked very much like my mom did in the photographs from her college days. Looking at Cherie made me miss Mom terribly.

"How are you feeling, Hig? On the scale of zero to ten, how's the pain?" she asked.

By then, I really resigned to calling her a "she," even in my head. It wasn't a smooth transition, though. "About a five," I lied. It hurt more, but why go there?

"Not a fracture then," she said, and I instantly regretted my lie. *Should I be getting an X-ray or something? What happens when you break your jaw? Could I...should I talk? Eat? Can I damage my face more through movement? It's going to be so damn inconvenient.*

"Ah," I started to ask, but Cherie cut me off.

"Roger knew me as Charlie," she said. *Well, that was unexpected.* "I helped his little boy die. Lucca had glioblastoma, a brain cancer. He was only three when he died. Roger held his little boy in his arms when Lucca took his last breath. I held Roger afterward." I saw tears in her eyes. "Roger quit his job and joined the fair caravan. He used to work with stocks or something. Something very high-paying and demanding. But none of his life advantages saved his son. So he just packed up, sold everything he owned, and bought that motorhome."

"Huh. And what about Lucca's mom?"

"I don't know. I never met her."

"She wasn't there for her son in the hospital?"

"No. And as far as I know, Roger is not married. Perhaps he never was."

"I'm sorry." I didn't know why I said that. I didn't even know what I was really sorry about.

"Thanks," Cherie said.

"How was Roger when...you know?" I motioned at Cherie's breasts as a shortcut for the transformation she went through.

"Very caring. I stayed with him for several years until things stabilized and I was comfortable to face the world as a new me. As Cherie. And like Roger, I rejected my old life, never going back."

"I see." Not really. But I too went through a transformation, and I too was glad to lose the past that remembered me as a little crippled boy. So there were some parallels.

"Did you know when Mom died?" I asked.

"Not right away, no. I would have come. Even with these." Her face was graced with a sad smile as she pointed out the same body augmentations. She looked like a Madonna in a painting or something. "I would have come for you, Hig, and for Nonaken."

"Nona doesn't remember you," I reminded her again and knew it was cruel. But I hadn't forgiven Uncle Charlie for abandoning us, even as I was beginning to forgive Cherie. "She doesn't remember Mom either, though." That was a little amends. I could see how much I hurt her just then. "When did you find out about Mom?" I asked again.

"A few years after. When things stabilized somewhat. When these stopped growing." She flashed a sad, twisted smile. "I wanted to reach out to you guys. I thought you'd forgive me for being Cherie. I really had no way to reverse it at that point."

"Several years...things changed a lot by then."

"I read. I mean I looked you guys up. Saw that you moved downtown. Watched you walk around, no wheelchair, no crutches, no nothing. I knew what you saw it that mirror."

"You spied on us?"

"You guys are my only family. I've missed you. But I didn't know how to approach you. I wanted to reach out to Sissy but couldn't find a way. Then I learned... I'm so sorry, Hig. It must have been devastating." Tears were running down her perfectly formed cheekbones.

I didn't know how it happened, but we ended up crying on each other's shoulders. I sobbed so hard, my jaw was aflame. Cherie cried just as hard. I guess some losses never stop hurting.

***

We decided to go see Roger. He was good with statistics. Perhaps he could see something—a pattern or some recurring variable—in the newspaper clippings we stole. We wanted to make sense of what we were dealing with. Vic wasn't back yet, but he texted that he was "on the case." He was as silly as a little boy playing at being a spy. He did mention that the hag didn't come dragging a mirror. So it seemed safe enough to wait on going to see her. Somehow, without her mirror, she seemed disarmed. And it made more sense for us to arm ourselves with some information first.

We laid out all of the clippings on Roger's dinning room table, surprisingly large for a motorhome.

"What do you want me to focus on?" he asked.

"I don't know, Roger. Anything," Cherie said. "I have no

idea of what's important. Dates? Locations? Outcomes?"

"Some of the stories talk of happy endings," I said. "But some describe deaths and... And you know about my mom, right?"

"Cherie told me," Roger said. "I'm very sorry. I know how hard it is to lose a loved one." Of course he knew—he watched his son die of cancer. From my expression, he must have guessed that Cherie told me about that. "Don't say anything," he cautioned. "It was a long time ago. And, yes, it still hurts."

I just nodded. A day didn't really go by that I didn't think of Mom one way or another. I was no longer continuously sad like when it just happened, but still, it was hard. Some days, very hard.

"Why don't we start with your family as the first set of data points," he said. Cherie and I sat across the table from him. I nodded. His suggestion made sense to me. I guessed since Cherie didn't say anything, she agreed too. "Good, good." Roger pulled out his computer and started typing. He seemed to have a spreadsheet already made for the task. "So everyone in your family looked into the mirror: Cherie, you, your mom, your dad, and your sister."

"Nona was too young," I said. "Nothing happened to her."

"Yes, if I remember correctly, the old woman who owned the mirror said that Nonaken was too young at the time," Cherie clarified. Roger just nodded and took some notes. "You know my story, but perhaps I should fill it out a little bit for Hig's benefit? We didn't really have a chance to talk things out yet."

Roger sat back, and I settled in to listen. Cherie had this way about her; you just couldn't help but be mesmerized by her voice. I didn't know if that was always true. Personally, I loved talking with Uncle Charlie even back when he was my uncle. So perhaps that didn't change.

"I started to feel it almost as soon as we left the booth," she said, her expression distant, as if she was reliving that day all over again. "There was a dizzy sensation, and my nipples hurt. These didn't pop out right away, obviously." She pointed to a rather well developed pair of breasts. I looked away, embarrassed. "But I felt pain in my chest," she continued, "almost right away. Here, under the nipples. Well, maybe not right away, but by the time we got home that afternoon for sure. And by that night, I could feel something hard about the size of a frozen pea under my skin. It hurt. I was scared that I had a sudden onset of breast cancer. It happens to men too, you know. Except it felt too symmetrical. One painful pea under each nipple." She laughed. "I'm a nurse. I knew the symptoms of breast development in girls, but it still took me a few hours to put it together. And by then, I was totally flipped out. I wanted...needed to leave in the worst possible way. And your dad," she turned to me, "didn't come home until late." I remembered that. We were all waiting for him... "As soon as Fred got there, I jumped into my car and raced out of there. I was scared, confused. I'm sorry I left you guys like that."

I just nodded. It wasn't forgiveness, but I understood. Cherie gave me a weak smile. She knew it would take a while for us to be whole again...if ever.

"Ms. Cherie, please just stick to the story," Roger said. "You can do that emotional stuff when I'm not around." I wondered why he called her Ms.? It was a strange affectation.

"Sorry, Roger," she said and continued. "I obviously never learned what Fred or Hig saw in the mirror that day. And by the time I was trying to reach out to Moira, she was already dead."

"Hmm. So you don't really know what your sister saw?" Roger asked. It was a question that I'd spent many years thinking about.

"Moira was clinically depressed—"

"You knew and didn't get Mom into treatment?" My voice sounded angry. Uncle Charlie was a professional; he should have helped...especially if he knew my mom wasn't all right.

"Take it easy, Hig," Roger said. I wasn't sure how I felt about him calling me by my nickname. Ticked, most likely. "Ms. Cherie was going through some serious shit at the time." I was about to say that we had it worse, but he shushed me. I was too upset to really argue, so I let it go.

"Moira suffered from depression for a long time," Cherie said. It sounded like she was trying for another apology. "And back then, I didn't realize that the mirror showed us our most fervent desires." She took a deep breath. "Many who suffer from depression just want their suffering to end. I've seen that many times."

I caught her give a quick glace toward Roger. *I guess it wasn't a surprise that he was depressed after his kid died.* He made it, though. Mom didn't. I didn't know how much "Ms. Cherie" helped to get Roger through to the other side, but I sure knew that she didn't help Mom. My mother needed her brother, and he wasn't there for her. Nona and I were just too young back then. *And Dad?* Somehow I was angry with Dad in a whole different way.

"I was so wrapped up in my own...transformation," Cherie continued, "that I didn't realize we all must have seen something in that mirror. Once it hit me, I tried to find out surreptitiously."

"You did?" I asked. I'd searched for Uncle Charlie for years, without success. But she made it her business to disappear. We didn't go far...just downtown.

"I read Moira's obit in the paper after I learned about..." Cherie took a deep breath, paused, and tried again. "The local library helped me find it. I also read about Fred's promotions.

But it was all later, much later. I also have a whole book of clippings of your accomplishments." She smiled at me again. And again it felt like an apology. "Every time you've made it into a local paper as a boy who succeeded. All your soccer wins—"

"You saved those?" I did too, but not anywhere anyone would ever find them. It was my little stash of proof in case one morning I woke up a cripple again. Who knew how long this magic shit was going to last?

Cherie nodded as if reading my mind. "I searched my bathroom mirror every morning for signs that it was fading somehow. Still do."

There was an awkward pose. Cherie and I understood each other. We both experienced this fear of reversal. "It's like I cheated," we said at the same time.

"Hmm. So I'm going to guess that everyone who looks in that mirror has similar feelings of being a fraud and a fear of reversal," Roger said. That made sense. "I've known Ms. Cherie for a very long time. I saw her being scared of buying a bra for the fear of not really needing it. And yet she still looked for this old hag and her damn magic mirror."

"Why did you look for her?" I asked. I knew why, but I asked anyway.

Cherie didn't answer right away. A tear, which spilled out of her left eye, had time to roll down her cheek and reach all the way down to her perfectly formed chin. We both knew what she was about to say. "Moira," she finally whispered. "If I revert to how it was, would she revert as well? I don't know if it even makes sense—"

"If we change back, she might live," I finished for her. *If we sacrifice out hearts' desires, can we bring back my mom? Perhaps...*

Chapter Nine: The Mirror

Vic rushed through the door of Roger's trailer. "She is seeing customers!" He sounded out of breath. He obviously ran all the way there from the crafts building.

"Why didn't you just send a text?" Cherie asked.

He showed his phone, clutched his side, and slid into the chair. "Dead," he exhaled.

"We should go!" I jumped up and tried for the door. Three pairs of arms grabbed me.

"And what would you do?" Vic asked. He sounded so winded, yet his grip on my shoulder was like a vise. In our short time knowing each other, Vic managed to never let me forget he was a blacksmith.

"It's stupid to go without a plan," Roger said, grabbing my coat. Unlike Vic's hold on me, Roger's wouldn't have taken much to break. He might sport a superior intellect, but he had the muscle strength of an undernourished chicken.

"We haven't decided," said Cherie. She held my hand in both of hers. Her fingers were cool and somehow tender...and desperate all at the same time. She couldn't have stopped me if I wanted to go, but she made me feel like I shouldn't.

All three spoke at once, but the obvious consensus was that I wasn't going to be allowed to run back there and confront the old crow at that moment. And frankly, I didn't even really want to. I just needed to... I went limp. I wasn't going to fight them. I sat down and put the icepack back on my face. My jaw...my face hurt a ridiculous amount. I couldn't imagine it hurting more if it was really broken. The pain was actually good. It was a valid reason to stay. It was a punishment for not going. And it kept me in the moment—hard to make long-term plans when one's brain felt so sluggish.

After they figured out that I wasn't going to run out on them, Roger turned to Vic and asked him to describe what he saw. Cherie handed him a bottle of water, which Vic drank before answering. The quiet moment gave us time to cool down a bit. We were all at a flashpoint with our emotions, and any little spark could have made any of us go off. In such a state, it was easy to make a stupid decision. Even I realized it.

Vic placed the empty water bottle on the table and began. "She just flipped the 'open' sign pinned to her curtain, and people started to line up." He was talking better after drinking the water. "She didn't let everyone in, though. She interviewed people. I couldn't really overhear what she was telling them from my position—I didn't want to be too obvious."

"You were with Missy?" Roger asked. I looked at him, confused. "Missy sells apple-faced kuklas—Russian for pretty doll—from the stall across the booth with the Mistress of the Looking Glass of Fate," he explained. I saw Vic nod.

"Missy and I are old friends," Vic said. "So it wasn't suspicious or anything if I hang out with her. And the old hag is blind anyway, right?"

The three of us looked at Vic as if he was crazy. For a blind person, the Mistress had a particularly astute sense of her surroundings. She didn't miss a thing. We all obviously believed that. Vic would have been better off borrowing Missy's phone... Well, no one accused the man of being the sharpest tool in the shed—not yet, anyway—despite making such tools.

"Let me get this straight," I said, trying not to show exasperation...not that emotions were easy to read on something as puffed up as my mug was at that moment. "You've all been going to these fairs for years, right?" I asked all of them. They agreed. "You know most other artisans and vendors who travel the country from fair to fair." They nodded, almost in unison. "But you've never, in all this time, run into the blind lady and her magic mirror before yesterday?"

"Nope. And I've looked for years," Cherie said. And despite how unlikely this seemed, I believed her. Cherie, like Uncle Charlie, had this way about her—people couldn't help but trust her. There was something magnetic about her personality—it was easy to see its effects on Roger and Vic...and me, if I were honest with myself. Cherie was like the center of gravity, and we all orbited around her.

"I think I might have seen her a few decades ago," Vic said. "Some time when I first started my knife-making business. But once I learned that Roger and Cherie were looking for her, I began to make inquiries. But I've never even heard of the old hag being mentioned by other people I know who do this sort of thing for a living."

"And that's strange, right?" I asked.

"Very," Roger agreed. "I've asked around a lot. I wanted to help Ms. Cherie. But as hard as we've searched, we've never came up with anything until this fair. And I've only arrived here early this morning, after Ms. Cherie notified me that the Mirror Booth was here. I drove seven hours straight. I didn't want her to have to face this alone."

That made sense with what I knew so far. I'd looked online for some news of the mirror from time to time. Not too hard...not really to find it or anything. Mostly I did it out of guilt and fear that all of its effects might suddenly dissipate. In all that time, I'd never come across any reference to it. Now that I knew I was searching for all the wrong things, it made sense. The clippings we found were like brilliant beacons in the night... I just didn't know how to look before. Roger and Cherie were also probably searching for all the wrong clues, focusing on finding the woman and not on seeking the evidence of the mirror's effects on its visitors—the ripple effects of the changed lives. But the mirror was here now...or at least its blind minder was. And since the old woman had just arrived, Cherie couldn't have been waiting on me to start her investigations. Our unexpected night encounter was just a coincidence...an unfortunate bit of luck. I rubbed my jaw; it felt huge. Yet something about the way Roger said what he said sounded off to me. I didn't know what it was, but something rang false. Perhaps it was the whole "Ms. Cherie" thing. It was very annoying. But Cherie didn't complain, and what right did I have to get unhappy at a silly nickname? *Once a cripple, one never forgot...*

"So did you see anyone go in and confront the mirror?" Cherie asked Vic. *Yes, that!*

"I didn't wait that long," he said. "When I realized my phone was dead—"

"Yes, yes. You ran all the way here." Roger dismissed him. Vic's face fell and turned red again. I felt bad for the guy—Vic was only trying to help. "So what do we do? What do we want to do?" Roger asked. "What do *you* want, Ms. Cherie?"

It was as if my wishes didn't count. I almost moved for the door again, but Vic's iron arm pressed me down into the chair. I wasn't allowed to rush out there on a whim. And I knew I was grateful for that...pissed, but grateful.

"I think we should all go and watch what she does and then confront her," Cherie said. "There really is no point in doing it surreptitiously."

"I agree," said Roger. "I bet she knows anyway."

"Right."

"That still leaves us with 'what do we want to accomplish' decision,'" Roger reminded us.

Frankly, I had no idea anymore. I hoped Cherie did. The guilt of not going and asking about Mom was overwhelming, but so was the fear of what that might lead to. I didn't want to go back into the chair. I'd rather die. So it really was my life for my mom's. I was such a baby.

***

We watched an endless procession of fairgoers walk up and down the aisle between Missy's stall and the booth with the mirror. Missy allowed Cherie and me to sit on the two extra folding chairs at the entrance to her stall. I guess I looked pathetic enough to let me sit. Vic and Roger hovered about. We made Missy's stall look more crowded, which she apparently thought was good for business. Personally, I always purposely avoided crowded spaces, but what did I know about retail?

Vic observed correctly—Mistress Kismet turned down most people. She asked a few questions and sent most on their way. But somehow that just made her even more popular. The line to look into her mirror was snaking out of sight. Why? What did she tell them? What did she tell Mom and Dad...and Cherie when it was our turn so many years ago? I didn't really remember a conversation prior to our looking. But then I was just a kid...a kid in a wheelchair. I was used to waiting to get things I wanted and needed. It's just how it is for people with restricted mobility, relying on others to help them function in this world. Still, I didn't remember a line that long back then.

For every five people who wanted to look into the mirror, four walked away without getting access to it. But would the lives of those who got to go inside change as much as mine? My breath caught every time the curtain was pulled aside to let the unwitting in. Was it evil not to stop those people? Did they understand the bargain they were making? I didn't. I was now sure that Uncle Charlie didn't either. These people's lives were about to transform. I tried to find changes in the faces of people exiting the booth. Did their demeanor shift as they left? Honestly, I didn't notice much difference.

I guess I zoned out watching the queue move. The sound of Klaire and Nona's voices felt like a bucket of cold water dropped on my head. *What are they doing here?* Sitting as we were, I couldn't really see the girls. I jumped up, and Vic did his Vulcan move, pinching my shoulder and pushing me back down into submission. I was ready to kill the oaf! My sister and girlfriend—I hoped Klaire was still my girlfriend—sounded like they were about to walk into the dreaded booth.

"Stop!" I screamed. And the world obeyed. All eyes turned on me.

One heartbeat. Two. On the third, the human anthill burst into action. Someone screamed, presumably jostled aside as people starting to run in all direction, trampling over each other. If I yelled "fire," the reaction wouldn't have been much different. I felt a strong hand clump hard over my mouth and blacked out from pain.

***

"—everything with you has to be brute force," Cherie was saying as the world came back into focus.

"He needs to go to the hospital! Now. Right Now!" That

was my sister. She sounded freaked.

"I called an ambulance." I heard Ms. Marta. Her voice was like a tonic—she'd spent half my life caring for me through my colds and flus and taking me to endless doctors' appointments...until I didn't need those anymore. "They should be here any minute. Now, step away from my boy!"

I recognized the feel of Ms. Marta's rough warm hand on my forehead and opened my eyes. She was leaning over my face and exhaled as our eyes met. Her expression was love contorted by worry. I knew that expression well and came to rely on it over the years after Mom died. Ms. Marta was the woman who would give up her soul for me, I was sure. For me and my sister. She loved us as if we were her own flesh and blood.

"It's not broken, Ms. Marta," Cherie said. "I'm pretty sure." I would have been happier if she was really sure about that. Cherie was somewhere behind my head as I was lying back on the ground in the now familiar position of repose. I saw Ms. Marta give Cherie a dirty look. I'd never seen Ms. Marta so mad. She probably only thought of Cherie as my dad's girlfriend—not something that would have predisposed our beloved nanny to like her. *Step-sin indeed.*

A soft hand squeezed my fingers. *Klaire! She still cared;* I exhaled. "I think I'm okay," I managed to mumble out, hoping that I wasn't drooling too much.

"And we will keep it that way," Ms. Marta said. "You're going on a little trip to the emergency room." Her tone brokered no objections. None were raised.

Chapter Ten: The Fracture and Other Maladies

Many hours and multiple exams by dozens of specialists later, I found myself alone with Klaire in a small space carved out by a privacy curtain around my hospital bed. I was lying with an IV line full of painkillers, and Klaire was sitting on a little rolling stool next to me, still holding my hand. I was waiting for her to really let me have it for running out on her like that, but instead she simply broke down, silently sobbing right there next to me. I felt horrible. I didn't deserve this beautiful woman.

"Klaire," I started. Her name came out jumbled. I tried again, "Klaire—"

"Please, don't," she told me. "The doctor told you not to talk." She squeezed my hand when I opened my mouth again; it wasn't very gentle. I shut up. "You really freaked me out, you know? With everything you've told me...all that stupid magic and mirrors and your mom dying...I thought...I thought...I really worried that you might do something stupid."

"Even more stupid?" I tried for levity. She smacked my arm. I deserved it.

"Shut up or I'll call that crotchety nurse back," she said. My emergency room nurse was very nice, but I got her point.

I kept quiet. "I spoke with your sister and Ms. Marta as we drove to the fair," she continued. "Nona doesn't know anything, but Ms. Marta was really scared. She didn't want us to call your dad. I thought that weird, but she was adamant we leave him out of it. She said that you were over eighteen, and so parental consent for whatever we were going to do to you wasn't necessary."

She gave me a questioning look but squeezed my fingers painfully when I tried to speak. *What did Ms. Marta want to do to me?* "I don't know if your dad even knows now, Hig. As your parent, shouldn't he be notified that you are in a hospital? Don't answer that!" Klaire inhaled deeply. "Good," she said when I didn't say anything. "Then I had a chance to speak with Roger." *She did?* "He is a super nice guy. He said that he knew your dad's girlfriend, 'Ms. Cherie,' for many years. And that, by the way, is too strange, too. Did he know she was your Uncle Charlie? I'm sure I'll get to the bottom of it all, but honestly..."

I realized that I would have a lot more explaining to do when Klaire and the doctors allowed me to talk again. But how did one explain it all? *Damn.*

"Knock, knock. May I come in?" a male voice spoke outside of privacy curtain—Dr. Ulf, my pediatric orthopedist. *How did he find me?* I felt bile rise up in my throat. There was something, I didn't know what. It felt like a slimy memory trying to come to the surface, but even thinking about it was making me feel nauseous. It happened in mere moments, and then the curtain pulled aside and Dr. Ulf walked in. "Freddie! Long time no see, my boy. Glad you are doing so well...well, perhaps not as well as you were before your unfortunate encounter with a concrete floor."

So that was the story Cherie had told the doctors and Ms. Marta? I wondered if Klaire knew the truth. But I didn't really want Vic in trouble. So floor it was. Dr. Ulf could certainly confirm my prior clumsiness.

"I presume you are Klaire?" Dr. Ulf turned and shook Klaire's hand and smiled at her. He looked happy for me. "Pleasure to meet you, young lady. I've been Freddie's doctor since he was just a kid." That wasn't really true—I hadn't seen Dr. Ulf for years...but it was sort of true. In any case, what was the point of arguing? And how could I?

"Nice to meet you," Klaire said, and I could tell she was uncomfortable. Our relationship was just at the budding stage, and here we were in a hospital, in middle of strange magic, all and everything up in the air. I'd never even gotten a chance to tell her just how much I liked her. Now, she would probably kick me if I even tried to open my mouth. How long would Klaire stick around with all this weirdness? I squeezed her hand. She squeezed back, and I felt higher by her touch than from all the drugs in my IV...not that I wasn't grateful for a bit of pain control. There was no way my jaw wasn't broken.

"It seems like you've managed to fracture your jaw," Dr. Ulf said. *I knew it!* "It's what is called a condylar fracture, not a bad break. Lucky for you, the fracture is quite small," he continued, "but there won't be any chewing or talking for at least ten days." He turned to Klaire. "I know you will take good care of our boy here, Klaire. He is known for remarkable, I might even say miraculous, recoveries." I wished he wouldn't. "So just use your phone to text each other or whatever else you young people do nowadays. I mean, you of course can talk, Klaire, but Freddie has to communicate with his fingers only. And, unfortunately, only liquid foods for a while. No chewing, no grinding, no talking, and no kissing." He flashed a self-satisfied smile. Clearly, he enjoyed making us uncomfortable. "But seriously, if Freddie could keep his jaw immobile for a week, the restrictions might ease up faster and he might avoid screws." *Screws?!* "Didn't the doctors tell you? No? Well, they must have spoken to Ms. Marta while you were resting."

"Dr. Ulf? Are you saying they might have to screw Hig's... Fred's jaw shut?" Klaire asked; her voice was shaking. *Hell of a way to start a relationship.*

Dr. Ulf looked over my chart again and said, "Doesn't seem so." *Thank goodness!* "You are one lucky young man. But you know that already, don't you, Freddie?" *There we go...* "You know, I've tried multiple times to reach out to your father over the years. In all of my years of practice, I've never seen such a complete recovery. In fact, before you, I would have said that such progress, while hoped for, was simply not possible."

"Really?" Klaire asked and then looked me. Something in her look changed; she might finally believe me. I squeezed her fingers again—*we'll talk about this later*, I implored her with my eyes. She gave me the slightest nod. *Later.*

"Before Freddie here, I would have said that spina bifida wasn't a curable birth defect but rather a manageable condition," he said. *I'd disagree—"manageable" was not how I would have described trying to navigate public school bathrooms in a wheelchair.* "So I'm so glad to run into you, Freddie, because my team and I would like to do some studies. We would like to be able to chart your progression—"

"No," I managed and shook my head for emphasis. That hurt.

"But—" Dr. Ulf tried again.

"That part of my life is over, Doctor. I don't want to be studied." That was what I meant to say. What actually came out was all garbled, but we all understood the gist of it—I didn't want to be part of any study. Period.

"Dr. Ulf?" Klaire spoke up. "Perhaps now is not the best

time to ask or make plans—"

"Yes, yes." Dr. Ulf was visibly shaken by my outburst. Then he took hold of himself again, and a pleasant, neutral expression slid back onto his face. "We will speak again later, Freddie. Get well. Don't talk. And I'm sure I'll see you again very soon." He smiled at me and Klaire and walked away.

When Klaire was sure he was too far to overhear, she leaned in and said, "So it's all true?" I just nodded. Life would be so much easier if Klaire believed me.

***

I was released from the hospital in the middle of the night, having spent over eight hours in the emergency room doing god knew what...but no surgery, no wires. By the end, I felt giddy to be let go. Ms. Marta drove Nona, Klaire, and me back to our apartment. I didn't get a chance to talk with Cherie or the rest of the fair gang. I just hoped they didn't do anything rash without me. *Well, not with me either.*

When we got home, Ms. Marta fussed over me. I was made to lie in bed with dozens of pillows supporting me on all sides, as if she was afraid I'd accidentally roll out and hurt myself again. I was pretty sure that Ms. Marta didn't believe the whole story about falling down and hitting the pavement with my chin. And I now had a growing suspicion that she knew more about the mirror than she let on. In all our years growing up under her care, Nona and I never went back to the fair. Ms. Marta always found an excuse for not going...not that Dad didn't support her. I bet he didn't want to go back either—*no take-backsies, please.* I felt the same.

When Klaire and I were finally alone, while Ms. Marta made me some chicken soup mush and Nona went to buy thick milkshake straws at a convenience store across the street from our apartment building, we had a chance to finally talk about what really happened. Well, talk wasn't really right. I got my phone out and typed all I knew about Cherie, Roger, and Vic...and Mistress Kismet. I never pressed *send*. In fact, I erased everything as soon as Klaire finished reading it, which she did as I typed. I didn't want to leave any evidence. She didn't interrupt, just read. I didn't know what or how much she believed. When I finished, she stood up and walked over to my bookshelf, which had some of our old family photographs arranged between the books and plastic superhero models and picked up a holiday card with Mom, Nona, my dad, me, and Uncle Charlie. She looked at it for a very long time, then put it back down and came back to sit on the side of my bed.

"Well?" I asked.

She hit me again. "Stop talking."

My bad, I typed. *So what do you think?*

"I don't know," she said after a long hesitation. "It's a lot to process."

And Uncle Charlie? Cherie?

"We'll see," she said.

I had no idea what that meant, but at that moment, Ms. Marta came in with a tray of great smelling mush. And I realized I was starved!

＊＊＊

I slept until the following evening and woke up feeling much better. The swelling was way down, and the pain was back to tolerable. Dr. Ulf sent me an email with my X-ray scans. The fracture was tiny. In fact, if they didn't point it out—it was highlighted in red on the digital image—I wouldn't even have noticed it. Granted, I'm no doctor. When I was around eight or so, I was shown my spine X-rays that clearly displayed the full extent of my spina bifida. I felt nauseous; I couldn't even hear the doctor's voice for the hum in my ears. But these images looked fine. The X-rays of my jaw, more than anything, I believed, were responsible for the marked improvements in my symptoms. *I know, I'm just very susceptible that way.*

So, feeling much better, I got up, got dressed, and went to look for the rest of my family and Klaire. Was she still in our apartment?

I found Nona sitting on the windowsill, watching the car lights of the city streaming like some modern art exhibit.

"Cool, huh?" I said.

She immediately hit me on the leg. "Stop that! No talking."

What's it with women? Why are they all hitting me?

Sorry, I dutifully typed on my phone and showed her.

"Better," she said, still sounding annoyed. "Ms. Marta told me to tell her if you tried talking."

I shot my eyebrows up—*really?*

Nona just shrugged. "You have no idea just how much you freaked us all out," she said. "Klaire got hold of Ms. Marta first, you know. I'm not sure what she had told her, exactly, but the next thing I knew, Ms. Marta pulled me out of my ballet class and the three of us were driving to the fair."

"Hmm." My lips were tightly shut, yet I still got that "I'm warning you" look from my baby sister.

"Klaire tried to tell me about some magic mirror, but Ms. Marta shut her down so fast. She is always so nice; I never even imagined she could get so angry. Ms. Marta said you were a fool that would screw everything for everybody. I still don't understand what she went on about. Klaire just sat in the car with those huge chocolate eyes of hers opened up to saucer size. She was trembling. Trembling!" Nona turned away from me, back toward the city lights. "I'm not sure what to believe," she added quietly.

I sat next to her and typed, *Did Ms. Marta say anything else?* For all of its advantages, texting wasn't an efficient method of communication for important stuff. I pushed my phone in front of my sister's face. She didn't bother to read. I started to say something but got hit again.

"Stop it, Freddie. Just stop it." Nona sat for a while, staring out the window, pointedly ignoring me. And then, "I felt it. When we were getting close to that mirror booth...and then standing in line... I felt it, Freddie."

"It?" I asked. She didn't hit me this time.

"It was like being high, I guess. Like having millions of lucid dreams all at the same time." *Getting high?* Nona was just a tenth-grader! "It was dizzying. I felt like I was drowning. I couldn't breathe. I couldn't wait to leave, and yet since we left, all I want is to go back."

"No—"

"It's more than just a desire, Hig." Nona had never called me Hig before. That was a name left behind when Uncle Charlie left us. But she must have overheard Klaire call me that...*or Cherie?* "I feel like I'm drawn back there by some force. It's physical, like a rope that starts at my belly button and ends at the mirror...or at least at that booth. It's so taut that it hurts." She hugged herself across the middle.

"Did you actually look into the mirror?" I asked, dread spreading though me like poison.

"No. Never got a chance. Ms. Marta was like a banshee. She didn't let us talk. She held our hands, Klaire's and mine, like we were little kids, practically dragging us there and out. The only time she let go of us was when she saw you lying on the ground. I thought she would have a heart attack right there. She turned gray. It was terrifying."

Tears were rolling down my sister's face, and I reached out and pulled her in for a hug, like when she was a baby... when Mom just died. I used to have a permanent little wet spot from Nonaken sucking on my shirt, just over my heart. When she was upset, I'd hold her, and she would suck my shirt like a pacifier. I didn't really remember that until just then, as her tears were soaking though my t-shirt. It was breaking my heart. But as upset as I was by her crying, I was freaked out of my mind by what Nonaken just told me. She couldn't be allowed to go back there again. She shouldn't be anywhere near that mirror and its blind minder. Not ever!

I held her and rocked her for a long time. Then she pulled away from me and turned back to watch the traffic lights. Her arms were back encircling her body like she was trying to hold herself together. She looked in pain. And I had no doubt that she was. What was I to do?

Chapter Eleven: Revelations

Nona didn't go to school the next day, or the day after that. Obviously, I was staying home, too. Ms. Marta wouldn't even hear of me leaving the apartment. She called my sister's high school and told them Nona got food poisoning and would be staying home for a few days. Then she went and gathered my sister's assignments directly from school. She didn't have to do that—everything was posted online—but I think Ms. Marta thought that if she showed up in person, her lie about my sister's condition would be more real somehow. Old people always struck me as having a strange version of morality...not that Nona wasn't really feeling ill. She was in a lot of pain. I could hear her moan through the door of her bedroom. Ms. Marta shooed me out of her room on the grounds that both of us needed rest. That was certainly true, but I had a feeling Ms. Marta didn't want us to talk to each other. That was concerning.

Klaire, in the meantime, was back at school. She sent me a ton of schoolwork, too. In our third year, we couldn't simply take off too many days without making it too difficult to catch up. So I worked—there wasn't much else I could do—and she worked. And occasionally, we texted. The whole magic mirror thing was never mentioned by some undeclared mutual consent. I decided to give Klaire time to sort things out; she obviously hadn't yet.

And, obviously, we had no word from Cherie and her friends from the fair. There was nothing I could do about that—I had no contact information for her. I considered asking my dad for Cherie's number but decided against it—too weird, too hard to explain. I just hoped she was okay.

We were in this holding pattern for almost an entire school week. And then Nona screamed. I rushed to her before Ms. Marta could stop me...as if she could at that point. Nona was sitting on her bed, pale green in complexion, her golden hair matted to her head, unwashed and unbrushed, eyes wild. I'd never seen her like that.

"Nona?" I sat gently on the side of her bed. "What's wrong?" She was still clutching her stomach; it looked like newly acquired habit. "Does it still hurt?" I asked, idiotically—of course it did. Why else would she have screamed?

"Stop talking," Ms. Marta barked at me and handed Nona a glass of water. "Here, honey, drink it. It will make you feel better," she said in a silky smooth voice. I was immediately suspicious of the contents of that glass. But Nona took it and drank it in one go. "Good girl," Ms. Marta cooed over her and pressed my sister's frail body back into the pillows. "Rest now, dear. Rest."

She was about to push me back out of the room when we heard the lock turn on the front door of our apartment. Ms. Marta gave me a dark look and left to deal with it. I stayed behind in Nona's room.

"What happened, Nona? Why did you scream?" I asked quietly. I took her thin, almost transparent hand into mine. Her fingers were cold and clammy. My sister was very unwell.

"It snapped," she said quietly.

"What snapped?"

"That rope thing that was linking me to your magic

mirror. It snapped. And it feels like it ripped something from me."

I just stared at her like she was insane. *This can't be happening, this can't be happening.* The thought turned round and round inside my head.

"We need to talk with Cherie," she finally said after what felt like eternity. "Something happened. Something... I think the mirror is gone."

"What do you mean gone?" I whispered. "Like the fair is over?" Today, Friday, was in fact the last day of the fair. I kept close track of that via the county's website.

"I don't know," Nona said, still clutching her stomach. "There was a night-day variation in the power of the pull, in addition to occasional spikes in intensity." She winced just thinking about it. "But this feels different."

I thought about it. "You mean like it was out during a day and closed for the night?" She didn't answer. "But Cherie and her friends never saw the mirror inside the booth," I pushed. "And Vic never saw the blind woman dragging the mirror to or from her booth."

"I don't know, Hig. I only know what it felt like," she said. Her voice was so hollow, it was frightening to listen to her. "Perhaps when I felt the pain spike was when the mirror was actually being used? I don't know..."

"Like when people looked into it?"

"Maybe? I don't know. I don't know," she kept repeating. "I just don't know, Hig. But we need to find someone to ask, right? And the only one I can think of is Cherie."

"What about Cherie?" Dad spoke from just inside the door to Nona's bedroom. I was so focused on my sister that I didn't hear him walk in. I felt my leg muscles turn to jelly. Thank goodness I was sitting down.

"The kids ran into your girlfriend at the fair." Ms. Marta

spoke from behind Dad's back.

He turned so fast, he almost knocked her down. "You went to the fair?" he barked practically into her face. Ms. Marta didn't even flinch. I was very impressed.

"I left you a message about it, Mr. Keen. I informed you that your son had a fall when he visited the fair with his college friends. Klaire was with Freddie, too. I went down there with Nona to get him into emergency care. And we happened to run into Cherie. She recognized Freddie as your son and stopped to help. It was very fortunate."

That was not at all how any of it happened. But Ms. Marta was so calm and collected that Dad believed her. I believed her! How could one not believe Ms. Marta? Except it wasn't true.

"I see," Dad said and looked me over. "Well, you seem to be doing better, Fred." I did look better. The facial swelling was practically gone now, and the color of the bruise was a dull yellow green, hardly noticeable given my freckly complexion.

"I'm better, Dad," I said and hoped I sounded as convincing as Ms. Marta. Technically, I was still under doctor's orders not to talk.

"Glad to hear it," he said. "And Nonaken? How are you feeling, sweetheart? Did you eat something at the fair? Those food stalls could take down a bull..." He was evaluating Nona very closely.

I didn't really know all that Ms. Marta told Dad about our illnesses, obviously, and so I decided to keep quiet. Nona clearly made a similar calculation. She leaned back against her pillows and closed her eyes. Ms. Marta rushed to her side and placed her hand against Nona's forehead, as if feeling for temperature.

"Okay, it's time we let our little girl rest," she said

possessively. "We can go and continue our conversation in the living room." She turned pointedly at my dad.

Dad immediately left. I stood up and started to walk out but saw that Nona's eyes were pleading with me. I guessed she wasn't too thrilled at the idea of being left out of the "conversation." But Ms. Marta gave no ground. She pulled me outside and shut Nona's bedroom door.

I leaned in close to Ms. Marta's ear and asked, "What are we going to—"

"We won't be talking," she said, emphasizing the "we" part. "You are still forbidden from moving your jaw, young man. So no talking for you. Only listening." I felt instant relief.

Ms. Marta and I walked into the living room together. Dad was standing by the window, looking at the city below; he wore the expression I recognized as one of Nona's. Genetics were funny like that. I tried to remember him from when I was just a kid in a wheelchair. Was he always this tall? Always this good-looking? This distinguished? How much power over our lives did that mirror have?

"How's Nonaken?" he asked without turning to face us.

"She had a very bad case of food poising," Ms. Marta told him. "But she is finally on the mend."

"That's good. And Fred?"

"Small fracture on the very top of the little jaw bone that goes into the cheek bone." Ms. Marta touched her face and moved her jaw up and down. Dad did the same, mirroring her movements, touching the area where she was showing him. "Freddie should be as good as new in a few weeks." I distinctly remembered the doctor telling me that it would take at least six months for my jawbone to fully fuse, but I wasn't about to argue.

"I see." Dad finally turned to face us; his whole body and face were dark against the brightness of the window.

We were just standing at attention across the room. I didn't even consider sitting down; I guessed Ms. Marta didn't either. It felt like we stood ready for action across a battlefield. I never felt as much resentment for my father as I did then, not even when Mom died. He never even tried to get her back. He never looked back; just got the life prize the mirror awarded him and ran as far and as fast as he could...into the future.

"Sit," he ordered and indicated the sofa across from the two armchairs next to the window. He sat in one of those. We obediently did as he told us. I slouched. Ms. Marta sat as straight-backed as if she had a sword tied to her spine. I loved her for that. She was getting ready to fight for us, for Nona and me.

"What do you want to talk to us about, Mr. Keen?" she asked without a hint of worry in her voice. Her English was perfect now. Dad never bothered to learn Spanish. Why should he? He was never around long enough to need it.

He looked from her to me and then started talking, addressing me only, as if Ms. Marta didn't even exist. "When Moira died, I didn't think I would make it. I didn't think I could go on after that." He called Mom Moira as if he was talking to some adult, someone other than her son. It was strange. I didn't know how to feel about it. "With Nonaken just a baby," he continued, "and you with all those medical problems, the world felt overwhelming."

Yes, I remembered that well. I remembered feeling dark hopelessness then. But Nonaken needed someone to love her, so I did. Where was he? Gallivanting around the globe on business trips; moving us away from the only home we'd ever known until then, the home that smelled like Mom; giving us a replacement parent while he dated anything on two legs freed from any family obligations. I didn't say any of this, of course. I just stared at his half-lit face, hoping that my emotions wouldn't betray me by spilling tears down my cheeks.

"I knew it was hard for you too, Fred."

"Are you trying to make some point, Mr. Keen?" Ms. Marta interrupted him.

He turned on her then. "I'm allowing you to stay, Marta. Don't make me regret that decision." Ms. Marta flinched as if he had slapped her. I thought I saw guilt flicker across Dad's face, but he soon gathered himself again, dismissed her, and continued. "You might not believe me, Fred, but I loved your mother very much. Moira and I were very close." I didn't believe that for a second. "But with you being born the way you were and then another baby...we had a very hard time of it. I had to work all the time to make sure you got the medical attention and surgeries you needed. Moira was left struggling to take care of you and the baby. It was grueling."

I wanted to yell at him that it was not how it was. He was gone because he made a choice not to be around for the difficult stuff. He left us long ago, way before Mom died. But I sat completely silently, trying not to move at all, focusing exclusively on his face, trying to catch any false emotion or untruth. I was no longer a child. I thought it would be much harder for him to lie to me now.

"Your Uncle Charlie's visits were like sunshine piercing the darkness of our lives." There was a hint of wistfulness in Dad's voice. "Charlie had a talent for coming and lifting everyone's mood. Life was simply more bearable when he was there. I understood why he made such a great nurse. People like Charlie are rare in this world."

I didn't know why he was telling me this, and I was hating him for doing it. He didn't even like Uncle Charlie. I sat motionless, hardly breathing, listening to Dad's voice.

"I'd known Charlie long before I've met your mother, did

you know that? No?" *Why is he telling me this?* "I was traveling through California and managed to get pretty banged up surfing. Beginner's folly...and luck." *Dad surfed?* "Charlie worked at SF General as an emergency night nurse back then. He made everything and everyone okay...effortlessly. I've never encountered anyone so full of life and charm, warmth, and empathy. I was completely taken with him." He hesitated and then took a deep breath and continued. "We went on a few dates. It was San Francisco, after all. But...it just wasn't for me. I loved Charlie, but I just couldn't..."

I felt like the world was spinning out of control all around me, and I might fall in. *Charlie? Dad? What?*

"He introduced me to Moira. She had a lot of Charlie in her. She was like a pale shadow of him. But I fell for her so hard...almost in relief. All of the feelings I had for Charlie were gathered up and remolded into love for his sister. Charlie was happy for us. He told me so." Dad got up, poured himself a drink, and returned to his armchair to face us...me.

I wondered what Ms. Marta thought of all of this. Could Nona overhear any of Dad's revelations from her bedroom? Did I have an obligation to tell her, if she didn't? I watched Dad take two big gulps of cognac, and his face scrunched as the liquor burned the insides of his mouth. I knew the sensation—I had helped myself to his cognac several times. He sat quietly for a few moments. No one said a word. It was his confession.

"Moira told me she wanted to just walk away from it all," he said after finishing his drink.

Lie! I almost screamed out, but Ms. Marta squeezed my arm firmly, and I managed to collect myself. Dad noticed, and one of his eyebrows shut up, twisting his face into a scary grin.

"Believe what you will, Fred. But don't think it was easy

for either of us. Dr. Ulf was very good at describing for us what it would be like as you grew older. It was ugly." I shivered. "Moira cried for months after that *consultation*." He infused the word "consultation" with so much venom that I almost believed him. "By the way, dear old Dr. Ulf contacted me the other day, asking if I would agree to let him study you."

"You didn't—" It just slipped out of me.

"Of course not. That self-righteous prig. I told him to never contact me or anyone in my family ever again. He called you a throwaway baby."

"My goodness." Ms. Marta caught her breath. "He seemed like such a nice man..." He never did to me; in that I was in agreement with Dad.

"Moira didn't take that well. Charlie came out and spent a few months with us after that to help out. Without him, I don't think we would have made it." Dad poured himself another drink and took another deep sip, swirling it in his mouth. "In so many ways Moira was just the opposite of Charlie. She couldn't deal with sickness and death. She couldn't stomach it."

"And you?" I asked.

"I don't think I was much better. If not for Charlie... I guess what I'm saying is that it is very hard to have a child who is sick and has no chance at getting better."

"Do you think it was easy on me?"

"Oh no, Fred. I didn't think it was easy. I looked at you getting ready for school every day in that wheelchair of yours, and it blew my mind. I couldn't have done it. I couldn't even visualize it. When I tried...well, I just couldn't. I couldn't imagine living like that. Charlie told me that I needed to try, you know? That I needed to try to understand how it was to be you, to be her. It was important for empathy or something... I cared. I really did, but I couldn't..."

"So you ran away?" Ms. Marta asked.

"No. I never ran. I worked as hard as I could. I looked for any possible new therapy or drug trial that was coming up. Anything. I was willing to pay or do anything to help Fred get out of that chair. Moira knew what I was doing. She wanted to ensure we had enough money to take care of our son...for the rest of his life, if necessary. That was going to be longer than our lives, we hoped. We dreamed. Those were bad dreams. We shouldn't have fantasized like that. The letdown..."

I didn't notice when I started crying, but by then I didn't really care. I knew how he felt. I didn't want to live in that chair either. I didn't want to be in that chair so bad that I would let Mom stay dead. If my dad was a monster, then so was I. *Who am I to judge?*

"The mirror..." The word just fell out of my mouth in defiance of my terror, I think. "We have to go back. We have to get her back..."

"What mirror?" Dad asked. And by the look on his face, I realized he had no idea what I was talking about. It shocked me.

"The blind woman? The fun house mirror that granted us wishes all those years ago?" I said like a dumbass.

"Did Fred get a concussion?" Dad turned on Ms. Marta. His expression was grim. Angry.

Ms. Marta shook her head, but there was horror written on her face. Was it because of what Dad just revealed? Or was she thinking I had brain damage? Or was it the mirror? I didn't know what to think. A loud hum filled my ears.

"I think I need to go lie down," I said and stood up. My legs still felt noodly, and Dad rushed in to support me. "I'm okay," I lied. Dad escorted me back to my room and helped me into bed.

"Get some rest, son. I'll call the doctor to find out about

your injury. Not Dr. Ulf, don't worry. I should have been involved from the beginning. Marta gave me an impression that you weren't very hurt, mostly embarrassed. I let it go. I shouldn't have." He turned to go and then added, "I'll call Cherie, too. You said she was there? She saw you fall? Hmm."

He closed the door, and I was left alone in my room to cogitate on all that I'd just learned. I didn't really know what I believed. Everything I assumed all my life seemed to be wrong.

Chapter Twelve: Research

A week later, both Nona and I were back to our respective school schedules. I moved back into my dorm room with strict instructions to be a "good boy" and not use my jaw too much. Ms. Marta gave me a blender so I could purée all of my solid foods into mush before consumption—*liquid pizza, yum-yum.* I told her would absolutely do just as she had instructed. But in reality, I planned to stuff the blender under my bed and never touch it again. I just had too much on my mind to worry about food consistency...or my jaw.

I didn't know what Klaire told everyone about what happened to me, but people at my dorm went out of their way to be nice. Even the professors tried to be accommodating—miracle of miracles. Actually, they were always nice to me; I had nothing to complain about. My coach, on the other hand, had a conniption. I was banned from playing with the team for at least the next two semesters by my team's doctor. I was in the middle of my junior year, so that meant no games until almost the end of my college career. I felt horrible, but there it was—don't break your jaw if you want to play sports in college. I was welcome to come to team practices, but what was the point? So all of a sudden I had a ton of extra time on my hands.

After a few days of getting my academic life back in order,

I decided it was time to do some serious research. If there was a magic, life-altering mirror in our world, then someone, somewhere must have seen something and then written about it. I was in college; I had access to the best research papers in the world for free. And now I had the time. I called Klaire and asked if she wanted to help out on my extracurricular project. We didn't really have time to fully discuss all that happened, so I wasn't sure how she would feel about me chasing that mirror again. But she agreed right away, and we met in the library on the third evening after I moved back into my dorm room.

We hugged, and I awkwardly tried to kiss her on the lips—I didn't really know where we stood, and frankly it hurt. She smiled kindly and pointed to an empty, out-of-the-way corner of the reading hall with a small table tucked away between weekly periodicals and the window.

"So you haven't told Nona?" she asked almost immediately.

I was taken aback—how could Klaire know about Dad and Uncle Charlie? I hadn't spoken to anyone about what he said...*oh, right.* Klaire meant the mirror, of course. "Well, not exactly tell her—" I started, but she interrupted me.

"I called your apartment—"

"You did?"

"—and Ms. Marta answered. She said that Nona had been sick. Something about stomach flu."

"It wasn't a flu," I said.

"I didn't think so."

"Why?"

"I asked to speak with your sister, and Ms. Marta wouldn't let me."

"I see." It was a bit strange. But then Nona was ill...

"I'm not sure you do," Klaire said. "I heard your sister talking in the background. She sounded fine."

"She really was sick, Klaire. Ms. Marta didn't lie about that."

"I'm not saying she did, Hig. It's just that I got a strong feeling she didn't want your sister to speak with me." She waved her hands. "Don't interrupt, please. You don't need to defend Ms. Marta. I think she is a wonderful woman. I really do."

"She is," I said stubbornly.

"Right. But she didn't want us to speak. I believe she didn't want me to mention the mirror to Nona. I don't know exactly why I think so. Ms. Marta didn't come right out and say so, but I just can't help but think that she knows something about it, Hig. You should have seen how she reacted at the fair when she saw you lying there next to that stupid Looking Glass of Fate booth. She was horrified. Really scared. And it wasn't just of you being hurt. I know you might not believe me, but I just..."

I took her hands in my mine across the narrow wooden library table. "I believe you, Klaire."

"Thank you." She looked visibly relieved. "So, what have you managed to tell Nona about the mirror?"

"Well...actually not much. She was sick." I started spinning excuses. "And I wasn't allowed to speak. And she kept hitting me every time I opened my mouth." Klaire smiled at that and squeezed my fingers. "But now that I think of it, Ms. Marta was a bit keen on us not spending time alone together, wasn't she?"

She nodded. "I thought so."

"The strange thing was that my dad really didn't know about the mirror."

"Really? How do you know?"

"He came over to talk." She looked at me skeptically—by then, she knew how strained my relationship with Dad was.

"Yes, I know. It was strange." I was trying to decide whether I should tell Klaire about Uncle Charlie and Dad. There was nothing intrinsically wrong with Dad dating Uncle Charlie before he met Mom. But...it felt wrong. "When I brought up the mirror, Dad had no idea what I was talking about," I said instead.

"Was he lying, you think?"

"No. I believed him. Dad spoke about how difficult it was for him and Mom to have a crippled child and a baby."

"You weren't—"

"But I was, Klaire, I really was. Dr. Ulf apparently didn't think I was viable."

"You are very viable!" she practically yelled. And everyone in the library turned to see what was going on. Klaire turned bright red and waved everyone away. "Sorry, Hig. It's just that you are the captain of our school's soccer team, how can you not be—"

"I was. I'm not any more. And I resigned from the team this morning. It was the right thing to do. I was banned from playing until the second semester of my senior year. It just wasn't right."

"I'm sorry, Hig." She squeezed my fingers again, trying to show her support. "I know how important that was to you."

Actually, I didn't think she really did. After years of being confined to a wheelchair and then years more making my clumsy way through the world on crutches, to arrive at a place where people had enough confidence in my physical prowess to gift me the leadership role on a team... Being the captain of my team was more than just important to me. It meant...it meant...

"Hig?" She sought out my eyes. "You were a great captain. It wasn't just that you were an amazing player—while I'm no expert, I was told you had moves." I was glad it wasn't my physical abilities that had won over Klaire. Those seemed to be particularly transient at that moment. "You were kind," she continued. "You helped others on the team to become their best. I bet your teammates didn't want to release you from that responsibility." That was true, but... "But I think you did the right thing. You stepped aside and allowed someone else to shine and lead. That was very generous of you." She held my gaze for a few moments and then switched the topic completely. "So what do we do about this mirror? Have you learned anything I don't already know?" She was awesome.

"I'm sorry I didn't take you with me to the fair, Klaire." There, I finally said it. Meant it too...sort off. She didn't respond. She just watched my face expectantly. Klaire didn't accept my apology...not yet. I still had work to do. "So, right. The mirror. Cherie's friends at the fair, Roger and Vic—"

"The idiot who broke your face?"

"Vic? Yes. Well, he was trying to protect Cherie—"

"Please don't ever protect me by breaking people's faces." It made me smile, and I yelped in pain. "Right. And don't go breaking bones for me either. Got it, Hig?" I nodded. "Good. So what did you learn before having your jaw broken?"

"It was really after..." Klaire's eyebrows went way up, and I stopped myself from saying more stupid shit. "Yeah, right. So Vic and Cherie stole some papers from the...what's her name?"

"You stole from Mistress Kismet? You guys are just..." She stopped herself from yelling at me. "Right. So what did you learn?"

"She had boxes and boxes of old newspaper clippings full of stories of miracles that resulted from people looking into her mirror. Well, at least this is what Roger and Cherie believe."

"Do you believe?"

"Yeah. Yeah, I do. Not all stories were good. Some

described assisted suicides; people who were in too much pain to live. But others were of a more miraculous variety. There was one story of kid who was born with flippers for arms and legs. But then she grew them back."

"Arms and legs?"

"Yeah. Cherie said it was an impossible thing."

"Obviously. But you all believed it?"

"Yeah?"

"Well, that would have made all the papers, right?"

"Well, it did…"

"You saw one mention, Hig. There would have been hundreds."

"Maybe. This was a while ago, if I remember correctly. And there could have been more, but we only took a few clippings from the boxes. And as Roger and Cherie were reading them, Vic was doing Internet research to see if things matched up. He found police reports and other things that correlated with some of the stories we read."

"So you stole only a few of these clippings?"

"Maybe a dozen? I'm not really sure. I wasn't feeling well—"

"So did you find a pattern or anything? Did you find enough information to do a library search, for example?"

I shrugged—I simply didn't know. "There must have been at least two dozen boxes stored in that booth. Some looked very old. And even from a few stories that we managed to pull up, it felt like they all described life-changing events. Not all positive, but definitely life-changing."

"Like with your family."

"Like with my family."

"So what would you look for if you were to search for a story that might be the outcome of looking into the mirror? I mean, we don't really need the clippings from those boxes. Because, ultimately, we don't really know if they are connected or not. Mistress Kismet might just be into collecting crazy stories. The stories in themselves are not proof of anything. You get that, Hig, right?"

"Well..." I hadn't considered it that way. "You mean she could just be a crazy old lady with a stupid mirror and a weird hobby of collecting tabloid miracle stories?"

"Aside from your personal miraculous recovery, nothing that happened to your family is all that unusual. Tragic about your mom, but... You still don't really know if your uncle simply had a sex-change operation. Right? It's not like you have a DNA proof that he is a woman now—"

"Huh?" *Would Cherie have two X chromosomes now?* I hadn't even considered that. "That is great idea, Klaire. If we had Cherie's DNA sample, we would know for sure, right? I mean, if he became a woman on a molecular level—"

"So, how do we get that sample?" Klaire was obviously more the practical of the two of us.

∗∗∗

We didn't get a sample of Uncle Charlie's...Cherie's DNA—I still didn't even have her contact information. But we did stumble on something almost as good. A librarian pointed us toward stacks of old medical case studies. You see, in the world that shared all information, true or not, indiscriminately online all the time, it was very difficult to sift through strange articles documenting miracles. There was just so much crap out there. Klaire and I started to look up a few things and gave up after a few minutes. And almost immediately, the librarian showed up and asked what we were trying to research because of our public RUBY search history. *Damn!* Our school had its own private version of Reference and Universal Bibliography Yields function built into its library computer terminals, RUBY. Let's just say I was glad we didn't do our research at home on our personal computers. There was just no way to explain it.

When librarian questioned us, I was too tongue-tied to come up with some plausible explanation for our RUBY searches, but Klaire had no trouble at all. I would never be sure from now on if she was told me the whole truth or concocted pure fantasy out of bits of truth. She was that good.

"We are writing a paper on medical facts and fictions as told via old print media," she said in a bright, studious voice. "Something very fantastical that can't possibly be true but which was reported that way in some local newspapers, or almanacs, or such. People growing out new limbs; sudden onset of bilingualism; virgin conception... Just strange things people believed to be true. What would you recommend, ma'am?"

The librarian, who obviously didn't get a lot of student attention, perked up and walked us over to the back, where old medical case histories were compiled into giant folders.

"Now, some of these stories have appeared in the local papers," she said. "Some didn't. But each has a bibliography and references, so you might be able to track things down that way. Just let me know if you have any problems. I'm here to help." She smiled directly at me. "Glad you are feeling well enough to return to your studies, Mr. Keen. I've heard of your unfortunate accident. I'm sure the whole school feels your loss on our team."

I didn't even say thank you. I just stared at her as she turned and left us to our research. How did she know? Did the whole school know?

"Klaire? Was there a school newspaper story about me?" I asked with dawning realization of gaining a very unwanted notoriety. A librarian knew who I was by sight, for goodness sake! As if I needed more complications in my life. But Klaire just ignored me—I bet she knew and just wasn't telling me—and pulled me deep into the medical mysteries files.

It was like we were doing research for some *House* episode—*and now, Dr. House will meet a patient who falls into a deep depression, sleeps for fourteen hours, and wakes up fifty pounds heavier. Strange? Yes. True? Maybe? It was hard to tell.* But we were obviously on the right track. Apparently, medical mysteries and miracles were a thing and people loved to read them. There were *New York Times* articles that regularly covered this topic. There even existed an online database of medical cases that were being solved by the readers, *CrowdMed*—the wisdom of crowds and all that.

"Let's focus on the very old cases," Klaire said. "Something that only has one or two references to it, so it would be easier to track down. Okay?"

I was game. It was as good a place as any to start. And I got to spend my newly found free time with the girl I really liked. *Bonus!* We pulled a bunch of giant folders from about a hundred years ago and set ourselves up on a large wooden table. Why a hundred years? Well, we figured if the mirror was magic, then it wasn't really a new phenomenon. And if it was, we could simply go forward in time and see when the "mirror miracles" first started to pop up. And we had to start somewhere, right?

We didn't bother to whisper and commented back and forth in normal, non-library voices—we were the only ones in this section, deep in the bowels of the building. I'd have bet that we were the first to visit this part of the library in years. There was dust everywhere, despite the air-purifying, particle-sucking machines working hard in every corner.

It was probably the hum of those machines—or perhaps

the overhead old-time florescent lights in dire need of an up-grade—that prevented us from hearing her footsteps. I was completely oblivious until Klaire stifled a scream by literally shoving her own fist into her mouth.

"Hi," Cherie said from behind my back. "Not really a surprise finding you here, I suppose." I practically saw her reflection in Klaire's eyes, which dilated to the size of saucers. "Klaire, right? A pleasure to see you again. How are you feeling, Hig?" Cherie asked in her velvety-smooth voice. If Uncle Charlie had a sex-change operation, if was very successful.

"Hello, Cherie," I said as soon as I was able. "Glad you found us. You never gave me your contact information. So..."

"Sorry about that."

"Hello, Ms. Hydrargyros," Klaire finally managed.

"Please, just Cherie."

"Cherie," Klaire said, her voice returning to normal. My heart, on the other hand, was still pumping at twice the normal speed—I could feel each beat painfully in my jaw—but my facial swelling and bruising hid my unease well, I hoped. "We decided to do a bit of research on the effects of the mirror," Klaire said. "We are starting with old medical miracles. Would you like to join us and help?"

"I would," she said. "But let me make a recommendation on how to narrow the search space." Cherie pulled out a portable computer from her purse and placed it on our table. "There are lots of medical miracles in the world—I too have been doing a bit of research on this subject. But we are only interested in those that happen to be located around some large social events that would allow for the mirror to be shown to the public."

"Like the county fairs," Klaire said.

"Precisely. And World Exhibitions. Any big attraction that would hide a few miracles among the noise of other activity."

That was brilliant—*cross reference the "mirror miracle" candidates with World Fairs! Add geospatial component to the search.* We would have come to that eventually on our own, I was sure, but Cherie just saved us a ton of time. I saw Klaire's eyes sparkle—she agreed.

"Do you have a fair in mind?" she asked.

"The 1901 Pan-American Exposition in Buffalo, New York," Cherie said without hesitation. "It wasn't too far from here. It's an old event but not too old to be covered well by journalists in a more or less modern way. It was of a short duration—easier to narrow things down in time. And it was the first fair to introduce an X-ray machine. So there was a strong scientific component overlaid on the basic lack of scientific knowledge of the general public."

"Perfect," I said.

"I had time to think about it," Cherie said. "A World Fair is a perfect place to set up the Looking Glass of Fate. People expect strange futuristic exhibits. It wouldn't draw too much suspicion—"

"But why hide?" Klaire asked. "What does Kismet get out of all this?"

"Mistress Kismet," Cherie corrected her. "That too should be something we are giving deep thought."

So she had no idea either. In some way, it was comforting. Cherie—Uncle Charlie—didn't know how to think about this "mirror miracle" phenomenon either. Not even if it was good or evil.

***

Time flies when you're having fun...not. We must have spent five hours sitting, reading through newspapers and medical cases documented just after the fair—it took some time for the changes to take effect, for the miracles to manifest, as we already learned.

We were just about to call it a night when Klaire stood up and said, "Nina Morgana!"

"Morgana as in the *League of Legends*?" I asked stupidly. I used to play lots of games when computer games were the only thing I could really be good at. "Or as in King Arthur's half-sister?" I asked when Klaire looked at me like I'd lost my marbles. I used to read a lot of fantasy books, too—people had a tendency to get magically healed in those. "Sorry, you were saying?" I said in a small voice.

"Nina Morgana was a little kid, daughter of Italian immigrants, who sang at 'Venice in America' exhibit at the 1901 Pan-American Exposition."

"Oh."

"Was there something particularly extraordinary about that girl?" Cherie asked.

"Well, it says that she later performed just after 1906 San Francisco earthquake for the benefit of the survivors. That's way on the other side of the continent."

"Hmm. That would have been a big trip back in 1906. Anything else?"

"Well, the girl became famous. Her siblings were exceptional too. Her brother Dante Morgana—"

"Dante? Really? Sorry, I'll just shut up," I said. *But Dante? Really? Did I mention what I majored in at school?*

"Dante Morgana was a famous eye surgeon—"

"What? In 1900s? What was he good at? Taking eyes out?"

I just couldn't help it. But after Cherie and Klaire stared me down, I vowed to just shut up and listen. With a broken jaw, it actually hurt to be snarky.

"Sounds like he had vision issues as a boy," Klaire said, completely ignoring my outburst.

"A blind eye surgeon? Is that our medical miracle?" I asked.

"Oh, no, sorry," she said, even blushing a bit. It looked good on her. "I got tired of reading the med files, and I'm just surfing the net now, looking for interesting characters that attended the 1901 fair, per Cherie's recommendation. I'll go back to the files." She sighed and reached to our seemingly undiminishing stack. "But...well, David Morgana, Nina's other brother, became a Trappist monk." She looked at Cherie for support. I did, too.

"That's interesting," Cherie agreed. She quickly typed on her computer and then read out loud, "Trappist monks take three vows: stability, fidelity to monastic life, and obedience."

"What does that even mean?" I asked. What I didn't know about monastic orders...

"I think these guys make cheese and beer," Cherie said after scanning her computer screen.

That I understood. "So these were the good monks," I said. Again, the women ignored me. But it was late, and I was clearly getting punchy.

"They also raise sheep," Cherie added. "Anything else, Klaire?"

"There is another brother—Charles." Klaire and I both looked at Cherie for a reaction.

Cherie noticed, smiled, and said, "So Hig told you?" Klaire nodded. It was awkward, but it could have been so much more if Cherie wanted to make it so. She didn't. "Good," was all she said. Suddenly, things were a bit simpler between us—fewer secrets. I didn't even notice that I was keeping tense around Klaire and Cherie, and now that Cherie knew that Klaire knew, something let go, and I could breathe a bit easier.

"Hmm. So, Charles," Klaire said. "Charles Morgana was personally selected by Henry Ford to be an executive at his motor company."

"Strange little family. Did Nina, the little girl singer, become big?" Cherie asked.

"Sang soprano at Metropolitan Opera, married the general manager of the New York Philharmonic, who just happened to have died suddenly just weeks after their wedding. But she lived to be almost a hundred. Even had a son from that marriage who became a TV producer. So I'd say a very successful family, except for a few minor details."

Yes, a few minor details like the death of a loved one. "So a little nobody kid goes to a fair, sings at some attraction, and becomes a famous opera star," I summed up.

"She was ten when she performed at the World's Fair in Buffalo," Klaire said.

"I was only eight," I said. "So definitely old enough to pass a mirror test."

"So our little Nina goes to the fair with her brothers, comes across the Looking Glass of Fate booth, and they all look into the mirror?"

"But how can we prove that?" Klaire asked. *Good question.*

"We look at the registry of all the exhibits at that World's Fair," Cherie said. "It costs money to have a booth at the fair. There would be financial records."

It took just under half an hour to locate the list of fair exhibitors. Our school library happened to have it on a microfiche, and the good librarian helped us scan it. One, two, three, and there it was: Mme. K., the owner of the Booth of

Future Fates in the New York State pavilion that later became the home of Buffalo History Museum.

"Do you think this is our Mistress Kismet?"

"Could be. The pavilion was designed to look like the Parthenon in Athens," Klaire added. "I bet she dressed as a Greek goddess or something, in a toga."

"During a Buffalo winter?"

"Well, perhaps not then. But if this is one and the same, it would make our mystery lady way over a hundred," Cherie said. "Given what we suspect, that's probably okay, right?"

"There is only one way to find out," I said. "We need to find a photograph. If my memory doesn't deceive me, Mistress Kismet looked the same thirteen years ago as she did thirteen days ago."

"I took a photo of her on my phone," Cherie said. "It's not very good—there was a lot going on—but it's something. If we find other visual records, we can compare." Klaire and I both nodded. Somehow it didn't cross my mind to take pictures.

"It says that even as the fair was only opened for a year, lots of families and school children went," Klaire said. "They estimate almost a million visitors. That's a nice-sized crowd to hide many miracles."

"But why?" I said. "Why hide? Why do it at all? What does Mistress Kismet get out of it all?"

"Something we have to find out, don't we?" Cherie said. "And also, is our Mistress Kismet the same woman as that Mme. K. from the 1901 World's Fair?"

✳✳✳

A little trip to Buffalo History Museum in Cherie's little red convertible—not a good car for a winter outing in Upstate New York, but that's all we had available—got us into state historical archives the next day. Newspaper articles, photos, cards, and even artifacts from the 1901 fair were stored in the basement of the museum. Klaire's "we are just students doing a school research project" got us access. Incredible, but I truly believe a beautiful woman could get access to Fort Knox if she wanted to.

A nice man ushered us into the archives section in the basement of the museum. We were made to put on special gloves. And with his permission and under his watchful eyes, Cherie was allowed to carefully look through the photographic archive. If it were me, I would have had all of this stuff digitized and available to the public online, for free. Oh, and I would have made it searchable, too.

As it was, we spent hours in that basement. But it was worth it—we got a blurry image of the Future Fates booth as part of a background of some family outing shot. Four kids dressed up in old-fashioned clothing—the girl in a sailor dress outfit and the boys in short pants and caps—stood and smiled. One boy had thick glasses. The Morgana family children. What was the chance of that? Zero...but here we were.

"Oh, I see you found it," said the nice man, who was also the museum's conservator. We all turned and looked at him. He smiled and added, "For some reason people find this image particularly fascinating. We even had it blown up and installed upstairs as part of the exhibit on the 1901 fair. Charming family."

"Yes, charming," Cherie said. Klaire and I were too stunned to comment. "So do you mean to say that other people were looking for this image?" she asked in a sweet voice.

"It's surprisingly popular," the man confirmed. "As is the one group photo we have with all of the fair's exhibitors—"

"Can we see that one?" Klaire and I spoke at the same time. What was the chance of that?

The man just smiled a knowing smile and pulled out a folder with a photograph in a special plastic sleeve. "Just like every other visit," he murmured.

We bent over to study the photograph with the big magnifying lens he gave us. It was badly damaged. Water stains had turned some parts of the photograph completely indiscernible. But perhaps...way in the back...in the back row, dressed in black.

"Do you think it's her?" I asked.

"Could be," Cherie said.

Yeah, but it wasn't definitive. "Is there another photo, perhaps, that shows the exhibitor for the Future Fates booth more clearly?" I asked.

The man nodded knowingly, like he was expecting this question. "Not here. But from what I've learned from other visitors doing this research—a popular topic, apparently—there is a photograph of a similar booth from the 1964 New York World Fair. Fortune tellers have always had an unhealthy attraction among the unscientific audience," he added.

We briefly exchanged glances, and Cherie thanked the museum conservator profusely for his time and tip. She was so charming that he walked away from us beaming with pride. Klaire and I hardly uttered another word. We didn't really have to.

On the drive home, Klaire and I did research on the 1964 New York World Fair. We found the Mistress of the Looking Glass of Fate in the records of the exhibitors. No photographs. Not online, anyway. But perhaps our school librarian could help us with that.

Chapter Thirteen: Loss and Revelations

About an hour out from the school, I got a phone call from my dad—he never called me. Ever. We both tried hard to avoid talking with each other...especially after our last conversation. And yet here he was...

"Dad?" I said, and Cherie instantly turned off the music in the car. I heard Klaire take in a deep breath.

"Have you heard from your sister?" He didn't even bother to say hello, and his voice was shaking.

"No? What's going on with Nona, Dad?" In the quiet of the car, Klaire and Cherie could hear my dad's voice through the phone.

"The school called and told me she didn't show up for school today or yesterday. I tried getting hold of Marta and couldn't locate her either. Do you know where she is?"

"I saw Nona just a few days ago, but we haven't spoken since then. I saw Ms. Marta then too. Just before I left for school, late on Sunday night."

"So you didn't get an email or a text or a phone call from your sister? You have no idea where she is?"

"None." I felt my phone slip—all of a sudden the palms of my hands were sweaty. "Sorry," I said after I recovered the phone from the floor of the car. "Did Nona go to school at the start of this week? We were both going—"

"She was present on Monday," Dad said, but he seemed distracted. "I have to go, Fred. If you hear anything or re-member something, please get hold of me right away. I'm at the police station now. We are going back to the apartment to scan for fingerprints."

"Fingerprints? Dad? Did someone break into our home? Dad? Dad? Dad!" But the line was dead. "She is missing," I said in a flat voice. "Nona's gone missing, and Ms. Marta can't be found."

I felt the car accelerate. We were flying on the dark high-way. Cherie didn't say a word. Klaire just put her hand on my knee as I furiously typed messages and tried to call my sister and Ms. Marta. Neither answered. I felt sick.

＊＊＊

We parked a few blocks away from the apartment in a small garage. Cherie's car was too noticeable—she didn't want my dad to know she'd spent the day with us. We walked out together. Cherie wrapped a big black scarf around her neck and lower part of her head. It wasn't much of a disguise, but at a distance? She gave Klaire and me her number so we could contact her if we had to separate. Cherie didn't want anything to do with police. I understood. But my mind wasn't processing information well. How could my sister be miss-ing? How could Ms. Marta be gone? Nothing made sense.

We approached my building from the other side of the street. Three police cruisers were parked at the front doors of our lobby. Klaire pointed out two more around the corner. Police was taking my sister's disappearance seriously. I was at once relieved and freaked out. Seeing police cars made everything more real.

There was a small convenience store directly across the street from our apartment building, Abba's Snacks, Gifts, and Coffee. We ducked inside. I knew the guy who ran it, Abbas. He was the son of a man who ran the store when we moved into the building when I was eight. Abba used to give me sweets for free, and, most important, he allowed me to use the large handicap-accessible private bathroom in the back of the store, which saved me time when I was still using crutches and a wheelchair on regular basis. Such kindness allowed me more time on the playground with Nona and Ms. Marta. Abba was a super nice guy, knew our family well...well, Nona, Ms. Marta, and me. I don't think he ever met my dad. His son took over running the store a few years back. Abbas was also friendly, but it was never like it was with his father. Yet I still felt a sense of "home" when I stepped into Abba's store.

"Mr. Keen," Abbas called from behind the counter. I was always "Mr. Keen" to his dad, even when I was just a little kid, and Abbas kept up the formal address. He called Nona Ms. Keen, too; she loved it. At the sound of his voice, we all turned in unison from watching the flashing blue and red lights. "Come with me, please," he said with a smile and beckoned us to follow him into the storeroom, out in the back next to the bathroom.

"I—" I protested.

"Please," he said again and motioned for me to get inside. "Ladies, too, please," he said in a pleasant voice.

I was too stressed to argue and walked into the storeroom with Klaire and Cherie right behind me. After we were inside, Abbas closed the door with a click. He stayed outside. Klaire let out a cry. I spun around...and saw Ms. Marta. She was huddled by the wall next to the door and stacks of toilet paper. Her eyes were swollen and red. She had obviously been crying. She pulled me into a hug and sobbed into my shoulder; she was easily a foot shorter than I was.

It was such a strange reversal of roles that I didn't really know how to respond. I stroked Ms. Marta's back and looked at Cherie and Klaire for help.

"Ms. Marta?" Cherie said. "Would you like some water?" She pulled a water bottle from a case and grabbed some tissues as well. "Here, drink a little. And please sit down." She flipped over a water bucket used for cleaning the floors and placed her big scarf as a cushion on top. I gently lowered Ms. Marta down.

We crouched around her and watched as she downed the water bottle. Ms. Marta looked so fragile to me then that I was worried something bad was going to happen to her. She was no longer a young woman. Frankly, I had no idea how old Ms. Marta was. It never came up.

"Ms. Marta?" Cherie crouched in front of her, peering up into her face. "What happened? Where's Nona?"

"You look just like her," Ms. Marta said. "I knew from the first moment I saw you."

"What did you know?"

"You are just like me. Just like them. Just like my *gran chicos.*"

We exchanged glances, and I got down on my knees and asked, "Ms. Marta? Are you talking about the mirror?"

She took my face into her hands and gently moved her thumb over the bruised area on my jaw. "What did they do to you?"

"I'm fine, Ms. Marta. It's just a stupid—"

"There are always accidents around Madam Karma. There is never a clean getaway. She always takes her price in blood. Always."

"Madam Karma?"

"I lost my children in a horrible accident," Ms. Marta said. Her expression was beyond grief. "The details are too horrible to tell, too horrible to relive through retelling. At the time, I just wanted to die. And for many months I think I was just like the living dead. I went to bed, I slept, I woke up, I ate, I went to work. The work saved me. Gave me purpose, I suppose." She stopped and stared into space, her eyes unfocused and unseeing.

"What did you do?" Klaire asked when the pause became unbearably long. It was almost like Ms. Marta forgot that she was talking to us.

"I worked as a forest hostess."

"What's that? I've never heard of such a profession."

"You wouldn't." And the way Ms. Marta said it made me shiver. "My job was to introduce an urban forest to its visitors. It was a very small forest, and it had very few visitors, so my job was really just walking about and talking to the trees, seeing to their needs. I was good that. Every tree knew me..."

I was beginning to worry that Ms. Marta had suffered a full breakdown. She had stopped making sense. I was about to say something, but Cherie placed a hand on my shoulder, stopping me.

"What happened next, Ms. Marta?" she asked.

"The government consul for recreational activities—"

"The what?" Klaire asked. Cherie glared at her, and she cowered back, mouthing "sorry."

"—they wanted to organize a big forest reception as part of an agricultural celebration of some sort. It was long ago, I don't really remember what they were celebrating...and the details tend to slip in time. It's the way of it. My job then was to prepare the forest for the onslaught of all those visitors. My forest was shy. Inexperienced. I did my best, but when the day came, the trees started dying anyway. Too much stress…"

"I'm sorry. It wasn't your fault," Cherie said. Her voice was like a balm; it always helped, no matter how bad the pain.

"There were many exhibits set up in the glens of my little forest. People came, explored, had fun. They didn't really know they were killing my trees. How could they? The life of the forest happens on a different timescale from that of people." She took a deep breath, and I could swear Ms. Marta saw her forest in her mind's eye. It almost made me see it too, if my mind didn't rebel as hard as it did at her narrative. "On the last day," she continued, "I was assessing the damage and looking for ways to help my forest recover. I ran into this woman. She said that she could show a life one hadn't lived. I wanted to see my life as it would have been if my babies never died. She said that she could do that. All I had to do was look into her mirror. She said that what I saw in the mirror was the real truth, I had to believe. I looked. A few months later, I met your mother." She looked right into my eyes. "She gifted me you and Nona."

Ms. Marta took another water bottle from Cherie and drank the whole thing again. She looked exhausted.

"How could Hig's mom give him and Nona away?" asked Klaire.

"The mirror told her that her babies would be safe with me. You see, Moira needed to rest but couldn't because she couldn't stop caring for you. And I needed children to care for. Trees weren't enough."

"Huh."

"When you were studying Social Studies at school, Freddie…" Ms. Marta stared at me with such intensity that I backed away a bit. She smiled and continued, "I noticed that here, President Kennedy died and his wife lived. For me, it was Mrs. Kennedy who was shot. The president lived for a year longer. He died of complications from a back surgery. I remembered that clearly. I knew then...well, I've known earlier. But somehow the story of President Kennedy's death was a shock. I was very careful never to talk history to anyone after that. Never did another Internet search."

There was a knock on the door. Abbas looked in and said, "The cops are gone."

"Thank you." Cherie smiled at him. "We will go too. We used some supplies..." She handed Abbas a twenty, but he refused to take it. He helped Ms. Marta to her feet, and Klaire and I walked her back to Cherie's car, supporting her on both sides.

***

Cherie decided it was too late to wander the streets of the city looking for Nona. And the cops would probably do a better job of it anyway. Ms. Marta agreed, and Klaire and I just followed their lead. The older women seemed to know better. I had no idea what to do...what we should...could do. We needed a safe place to regroup, to tell each other what we knew, to air some secrets, to do some research. Cherie took us to her place.

She lived in one of those hip industrial spaces converted into an apartment. Hers used to be a button factory. One of the exposed brick walls was covered with thousands of buttons carefully arranged to make a mosaic of fantastical flowers. It was stunning.

"I had a lot of time on my hands," Cherie said when she noticed us looking at the button patterns on her wall.

"You did this?" Klaire asked. She was obviously impressed as well. Cherie acknowledged with a little bow. I knew Uncle Charlie was artistic, but Cherie was on a whole other level.

"Roger bought this place for me a few years back when I got tired of traveling from fair to fair—"

"You were living in the same city as us? All this time?" I practically shouted out.

She shrugged. "Where else would I want to be?"

I didn't know how to answer that. She never even tried to reach out to us...

"Your friend bought you this place?" Klaire asked. I guess that was strange, too.

"He had the money." Cherie said it as if that happened all the time...as if it was normal. "And he likes staying here when he's in town," she added.

I was oscillating between feeling betrayed and being furious and...I wasn't clear on what I was feeling. Nona was missing!

"I see. Are you and Roger—" Klaire started to ask.

"No. Nothing like that. Roger is the oldest friend I have... as Cherie. And as Charlie too, I suppose. We go way back."

"It was nice of him," Klaire said about the apartment.

Cherie's place was large and open, with brick arches dividing the space into charming nooks for resting, working, and cooking. There was a huge stove against one wall and a giant wooden table with mismatched chairs. On another wall there was a fireplace with a big, ornately framed mirror above and some wooden logs stacked on the floor beside it. And next to the fireplace there were overstuffed leather couches and chairs with thick blankets hanging off the arms. Even I saw that it was cozy.

Cherie indicated for us to sit and went to fuss over the fire, getting it lit almost instantly.

"Gas assist," she said, blushing. "Roger insisted. He said I was never a boy scout." She got us comfortable and asked if we wanted some tea and cookies. We all declined. It had been a horrible day. Nona was god knew where. And...and I suddenly I wasn't really sure what we were all doing here... other than hiding from Dad and the police. But what could we really tell them? That Ms. Marta came here from another universe? A parallel history? I could see all of us locked up in some cell for mentally unstable. That wouldn't help locating Nona.

"So," Klaire said when Cherie finally came to join us, sitting down in an armchair closest to the fire, wrapped up in a fluffy blue blanket. The blue matched her eyes. I didn't know why I noticed that, but I did.

"Back in my world," Ms. Marta said, "I was a scientist. A forester, to be sure, but still a scientist. I tried hard to understand what happened to me. I refuse to think this is all some sort of magic. It's not how the universe works."

I heard Klaire exhale. "Good," she said. "I'm very uncomfortable with magic, too. So what else is it?"

"In my world," Ms. Marta began, "our scientists had a theory of many parallel, coexisting universes. Something along the line of every possible history that can exist exists. Some histories are more probable than others, to be sure. So the universes that contain those are more certain somehow. In the beginning, I tried to look for something similar among the theories of this world, but I was, frankly, too afraid to look too hard. I stopped looking altogether after the Kennedy incident. I got what I wanted." She looked directly at me. "I got you and Nona. What if by examining this gift too closely, I might accidentally revert back to the world where all I had was a patch of dead trees? Or worse... I was too scared to take that chance."

I understood. Cherie and I spoke of similar fears, just not in the same terms. "I think we have similar theories in our world," I said. "We studied those ideas in an introductory science class, Physics for Poets. Not the most scientifically rigorous course, I grant you, but what you are saying sounds an awful lot like a multiverse supposition our professor talked about."

"I haven't heard of that," Ms. Marta said. "Or perhaps we are just calling the same thing by different names? Do you remember how your theory goes?"

"Klaire? You were a better student..." It hurt to admit it, but I wasn't very scientifically minded. Klaire, on the other hand, had a mind of a mathematician...an applied mathematician.

"I think what we are trying to talk about is something called Alternate Timelines," she said. "I'm no expert, obviously, but it fits what you've just said about every possible history coexisting together in some quantum probability matrix." She looked at our awed faces and shyly added, "That's about all I remember. Sorry."

"This gives us enough to start looking things up," said Cherie and pulled out a small portable computer from the side pocket of her armchair. Clever. "RUBY, link display." A mirror above the fireplace turned into a screen that mirrored Cherie's laptop. "This way, we can all see what I'm looking at," she said with a small shrug.

"You got RUBY?" Klaire asked.

"Yeah, Roger is into all of the latest gadgets. He set up RUBY—a home operating system version, of course—to control all of my tech. I could have lit the fireplace by just asking RUBY to do it, but I kinda like doing it myself."

"Nifty," Klaire said. It was. "My aunts didn't want to get a RUBY. Said it was like having a spy at home."

"Roger assured me that he turned all that stuff off." I watched as Cherie typed *alternate history, timelines, multiverse* into a RUBY search box. "Anything else?" she asked.

Klaire stared at the big screen and then shook her head.

I couldn't remember much from that class and so I wasn't much help. Seemed like a good start, though, so I just nodded and felt useless.

"Before you do that, Cherie," Ms. Marta said. "I need to explain what I saw in that mirror all those years ago." Klaire, Cherie, and I collectively inhaled. "I didn't look in that mirror and see Baby Nonaken and Freddie. I knew that I could never have kids due to the nature of my accident, and so that never even occurred to me."

"Sorry," Cherie said quietly. And Klaire reached out and touched Ms. Marta's arm in support. The women were showing empathy. I was just freaked out. I had no space in my soul for any other emotion at that moment. I pulled my knees up to my chest and tried to hold myself together.

"What did you see, Ms. Marta?" asked Klaire.

"I saw an old woman surrounded by dozens of family members of all ages. My grandchildren and great-grandchildren. I was in heaven. More than anything, I didn't want to die alone. And there the mirror showed me my heart's desire."

"Oh." Klaire watched her with her giant chocolate eyes. "That's beautiful."

"Seductive," Ms. Marta corrected. "I believe the mirror, or whatever that device is, allows the lookers to make a choice to walk away from the vision they saw or to embrace it, to turn it into their reality. I didn't have to choose the future I saw in the mirror, but I did because I wanted it so badly."

"Device," Cherie echoed. "That makes more sense than a simple mirror."

"Yes. I believe it is a machine of some kind," Ms. Marta said. "Some kind of time-link, a bridge between alternate possibilities, different histories. But I do think that I could have rejected the choice it offered me. I don't know how I know this, but I'm sure. Just as I'm sure that emotionally, I couldn't do so."

"Did you see just the one image? One choice?" Klaire asked.

I haven't even considered the possibility, but of course! The mirror-device wouldn't have just linked two possible histories; it would have been a junction, an intersection of many histories, of many future potentials.

"Wouldn't it be like a crossroads for many possible alternate timelines?" Klaire expanded on her idea, echoing my thoughts. *Exactly!* I was glad Klaire was there with us...with me. In more ways than one...

"It was long ago, and emotionally a very difficult experience for me," said Ms. Marta. "What I remember is just that one image—a reflection of a happy possibility. I accepted it right away."

"And what about you, Cherie? What did you see?" asked Klaire.

Cherie turned beet-red, and she moved to hide herself under the blanket. "I saw Fred," she said in a small voice. "I've always loved him. When I looked in the mirror, he was smiling back at me, extending his hand to take mine."

"You didn't see yourself as Cherie?" I asked like a dumbass. It was what I always assumed Uncle Charlie saw...well, I assumed so, since I recognized him in Cherie just a few short days ago. "You didn't see yourself as a woman?"

"I was happy being who I was," she finally managed. "Cross-dressing is not such a bad thing. No one really cared what I did as a private citizen. Well, your mom did, but that was after...after she met my Fred. I didn't need to be a woman to be who I was. I just needed to be a woman to be with Fred."

"You and Hig's dad?" Klaire asked, looking back and forth between me and Cherie. I realized that I'd never told her about the conversation with Dad. There really was no right time.

"It's complicated," I said.

"You knew?" She looked at me with astonishment mixed with betrayal. "Is there anything else I'm missing here?"

"Sorry," I said. "There was no time." There was all the time on the ride in the car to and from Buffalo. But it was a wrong time, so... "Dad confessed to dating Uncle Charlie before he met my mom."

"I see. Does Nona know?" Klaire asked. I shook my head ambivalently—Ms. Marta could have told her. But I knew she didn't; she wouldn't have. "No? Are you sure? Do you think this is what might have made her run away?"

"Nona wouldn't have run away..." I started saying and then stopped. *Would she?* I didn't take the news well, so why would Nona be any different?

"I don't believe my Nona would run away, regardless of what she learned about her dad," Ms. Marta said. "I raised her to be a very tolerant and open-minded young woman. She doesn't remember her mom or Uncle Charlie. She has a complicated relationship with her dad." That was an understatement...at least for me. "But she wouldn't just leave. Not without leaving a word."

"Are you sure, Ms. Marta?"

"Yes. Without a doubt. But Nona did look into the mirror-device once, even if she was a baby at the time. And she came into close proximity to the device again just a few days ago, at the fair. Freddie had a strong reaction, I recon, to being close to the mirror-device, even without looking into it again. Right?"

I thought about it. My jaw had nothing—

"He was stumbling," Klaire answered for me. "At the fair, when we were there together, even before we walked into that building where the booth was. He was stumbling, and I had to support him."

"That's true." I almost forgot about that. "Did you feel anything?"

"Panic," said Ms. Marta. "Sheer panic. But I'm not sure if it was from seeing you on the ground, looking dead...or recognizing the booth and its blind master. It was too confused. I just wanted to get you guys out of there as fast as possible. How about you, Cherie?"

"Splitting headache. Nausea. Perhaps hallucinations. I'm not exactly sure either. I do suffer from migraines...they started right after the transformation began. And I always get these visual hallucinations just prior. But..."

"Yes?" we asked almost in unison, leaning in toward Cherie's diminutive frame huddled under a thick blanket.

"I saw visions," she finally said. "Nothing clear. Just greens and blues and some flowers. Windoms mostly."

"Windoms?"

"The flowers on that wall? You know, windoms? The ones pollinated by these little nocturnal insects that glide instead of fly? They glide on the wind from flower to flower. Windoms?"

I looked from Klaire to Ms. Marta. It was obvious that none of us ever heard of such plants or insects before.

"Here, I'll look them up," Cherie said and started typing into her computer. And a moment later, her fingers contorted, her face spasmed, and the computer slid onto the floor. The screen above flickered something resembling the flowers in the button mosaic across the room and reverted back into a mirror.

Immediately, I was on my knees in front of Cherie, trying to keep her from falling out of the armchair. Klaire was helping. But Ms. Marta just sat there, eyes opened almost as wide as her mouth.

It took a few minutes, and slowly Cherie started to breathe regularly. I got her bundled into her blanket, and she lay there with her eyes closed, clearly suffering. I moved to sit back on the sofa. But Klaire picked up Cherie's computer and was about to finish the search for windoms.

"Stop!" Ms. Marta cried out. "Don't look. Don't search." We both turned to look at her. "You won't find those, and you better not look."

It took a few seconds for me to realize what she was trying to say. Klaire understood right away and dropped the computer back on the carpet like it was burning hot. I tried to remember what I saw on the big screen but couldn't. The memory was too slippery. But there was still the mosaic. I refused to turn around and look. Somehow, this world seemed less solid than it was just seconds ago.

"But how do we figure things out if we can't even look them up?" Klaire asked. "How do find out what happened to Nona?"

Chapter Fourteen: Histories

I slept. In my dreams, I kept running from someone. Every time I was about to get away, I fell through a mirror into another universe, where a whole other set of evil was chasing me. It didn't make much sense, and I was completely exhausted when I woke up.

It was still dark. Ms. Marta slept sitting up in the corner of the couch. Klaire was curled up with her head on Ms. Marta's lap, and the old woman—an alien being from another history—had her arm around my girlfriend's shoulder. Cherie was gone. Her fuzzy blue blanket was on the floor next to the armchair. The fire was out. I got up quietly, not wanting to wake Ms. Marta and Klaire, and went to look for Cherie.

I found her sitting at a small desk in front of her laptop in a room that was obviously her bedroom. Pictures of me and Nona and my mom and dad were all over the room—on the walls, on the dresser, on a bedside table, on her desk, even stuck into the frame of a mirror. It was like my whole life was on display for Cherie's private viewing. It felt wrong somehow.

"Come in, Hig," she said and pointed to her bed, the only other place to sit in the whole room beside the chair she was using.

I perched on the very edge, trying to see the screen over her shoulder. "What are you doing?"

"Looking for limits of things that are safe to search for," she said.

"And?"

"I think one gets used to it," she said. I noticed a large water bottle on the desk, now almost empty, and a wastebasket full of tissues at her feet. There was a vague smell of sick in the air. "I've been sucking on mints." She pointed to a small, nearly empty can of candy next to her computer. "It helps...a little."

"Did you find anything useful?"

"I think there are lots of intersections. Always have been, probably. Humans have always talked about miracles and other strangeness that didn't have rational explanations."

"It doesn't mean that all those are people traveling between alternative histories."

"No, Hig. I don't think so either. But some are. Must be, right?"

"Are you saying that there is more than one mirror-device?" I'd already considered that. That was what my dream was about, I decided—endless doorways into other possible histories. "Or is it more like a persistent crossroad over a long period of our history?" That was my other theory—the mirror-device had always existed, for as long as humans were around.

"If it is a device," Cherie said, "then someone had to make it. And as with anything man-made, it would break periodically. Someone has to repair it, or another device has to be made. Perhaps someone can even improve on its design. Progress and all that."

"I guess that makes sense...if it's a device," I said. "But if it is some kind of natural anomaly, like a black hole or something, then it might be the only one, right?"

"A discovery that's been harvested and locked up into the

mirror?" Cherie said softly.

"Something like that. We just need to understand it enough to get Nona back. Enough to stay away from it."

"Or to try to get Sissy back."

That. Yes, I didn't want to think about *that.* I didn't want to go into a timeline where I lived my whole life in that chair as a cripple. But perhaps I didn't have to? Couldn't I find an alternative history where Mom lived and I wasn't born broken? Was that possible? Was that too much to ask for? I would even take a timeline where I wasn't born at all...

"Your mom made a choice, Hig," Cherie said as if reading my mind. "She wouldn't choose her own happiness over yours. No mother would."

"But—"

"A mother is only as happy as her unhappiest child. That is very old saying, but it is true...always been true. Your mom is not looking for you to sacrifice your life for hers." She turned and took my hands in hers. "I'm sure, Hig. I knew Sissy far longer than you. She would choose your happiness over hers every time. Every time, Hig."

And just like that, I was crying again. "And Nona?"

"She would want Nona to be happy, too. All these years, I've been looking for that damned mirror, feeling guilty, hoping to fix everything. But I think I finally realized that was impossible, right?"

"Huh?"

"Well, if there are thousands, millions, billions...I don't know, an infinite number of histories, then it would be impossible fix all of them, right, Hig? There will always be timelines—that's multiple, more than one—where Moira dies. There are not enough of me...of us to fix all of them. We all made a choice of a future that would be best for us and our loved ones. Perhaps I was selfish. I wished to be with your dad, with a man I always loved. You wished to be healthy. How is either of those desires wrong? Ms. Marta wanted to be a mother. Was that wrong? Was that evil of her?"

"And Dad? He doesn't even believe in the mirror, Cherie. When I asked him, he was stunned. He had no idea what I was talking about."

"I don't believe everyone understands that they are making a choice when they look into that mirror...into that device. Fred might not have. Perhaps Moira didn't."

"Dad said Mom just wanted out. That she was tired... tired of taking care of us."

"Oh, Hig. Even if she was tired, she still loved you. She still looked for an alternate life that granted you and Nona happiness. Don't fault her for that. She wasn't selfish when she gave you Ms. Marta and your health."

"Mom also gave you Dad," I added quietly. And that was true. I was sure of it. Mom must have known how Dad and Uncle Charlie felt about each other. And she made a choice to let them have it. Cherie was crying too now.

We sat for a while, wallowing in our...relief? Cherie just gave us a permission to be happy by finding an interpretation for a multiverse existence that would make that possible. Did I want to throw that out? No. I wanted to grab on to it for dear life. I wanted to be happy. I wanted to be healthy. I wanted to have a normal life...with Klaire, if possible. I wanted to have a family, kids...kids who didn't have genetic defects. So, yeah, we were pathetic in our mutual permission granting to allow ourselves, each other, to be happy...while Mom stayed dead... in this timeline.

"But Nona?" I finally said. Yes, there was a matter of my missing sister. She was missing in our timeline. And I wanted...needed her back. I might have been able to let go of resurrecting Mom, but Nona was a deal-breaker.

***

Cherie made us all breakfast. She wasn't as good a cook as Ms. Marta, but her eggs were excellent. We all sat at her slick granite counter and ate without talking. I noted that Klaire kept looking from Cherie to Ms. Marta and me over the rim of her coffee cup. She tried to be discreet, but I was sure we all noticed her doing it.

"What is it, Klaire?" Cherie finally asked. And we all knew what she meant.

Klaire turned bright red, easily noticeable even underneath her dark-golden skin. "S-sorry," she managed to stutter out.

I reached out under the counter and squeezed her knee. I was grateful she was there, that she stayed despite being the only one... *Oh!* Cherie, Ms. Marta, and I, we all managed to change the direction of our lives by switching our time streams. That made us all aliens in this timeline, right? Only Klaire was a true native of this world history. Was that the right way to think of it?

I felt Klaire squeezing my thigh for support. I didn't notice when I dropped my hand from her knee and just sat there, staring at her. "I'm sorry." It was my turn to be sorry.

"How do we even know who belongs and who doesn't?" she asked. "I mean, how do we know which one is the one true history?" And from the look on Cherie and Ms. Marta's faces, I could tell we were all thinking the same thing.

"I don't know of any telltale historical or botanical anomalies," I said. "To me, this world, this history has always been the one I've lived in. I've changed. I know this. I have proof—the photographs, the crutches, the wheelchair, Dr. Ulf's medical records. But I don't perceive the world as different. It was a smooth transition for me from cripple to normal."

I looked at Ms. Marta. For some reason, I thought she knew more.

She shrugged. "I always knew," she said. "Even the language...even my Spanish was off. Aside from a few words that were clearly not in the dictionaries of this world, I had people asking where I was born all the time because they couldn't place my accent."

"How did it work with the authorities?" Cherie asked. It made sense that she thought of it—I bet she had a hard time explaining her "differences" too.

Ms. Marta laughed. "Bureaucracies! Every history has them." That made sense. But...

"Was there another Marta whose place you took?" I asked. "I mean, Cherie was Uncle Charlie. And I was me, but a poorer version of me. And Dad...well, Dad just became more successful, I guess. But we all lived here already. But you?"

"I woke up in hospital several weeks after my mirror-device experience," she said. "And that was the transition for me into this history."

"Were you sick before?" Klaire asked. "I mean in your other history?" It felt awkward speaking about alternate timelines, but here we were.

"After my forest started to die off, I got very depressed... well, and before, obviously," Ms. Marta said. "I was in various medical facilities on and off. They...well, there are medications, but I didn't want to take them..." I could see that she didn't want to talk about it. I was just about to say something empathetic and then...

"You tried to commit suicide," Cherie said. She was looking at Ms. Marta with those eyes, the eyes of a nurse who'd seen it all before, seen the pain that wouldn't go away unless one took the ultimate step to try to stop it. I overheard Mom and Dad talking about it in the kitchen one night, through the floor of my childhood bedroom. Mom understood, Dad thought it crazy—one had to fight to the end, he said. "You woke up here, in our world, after that," Cherie finished.

Ms. Marta nodded. "I just didn't see the point. When I woke up, a woman was in the same room with me. She was young, beautiful...well, she was beautiful once and her few years lay heavy on her, smothering her fragile body."

"Mom?" I asked. I didn't remember Mom being in a hospital. Well, we were there all the time, but it was mostly about me. I didn't remember her staying in the hospital because of how sick she was. She simply refused. Refused until it was too late. At least that's how I remembered it.

"Moira talked about her life. How sometimes it was just too much. She talked about having the baby blues." I glanced at Cherie; she knew and didn't help Mom. "I told her about my babies," Ms. Marta continued. "She was kind. She understood. She cried with me. She told me about you and Nona. I told her that I could help. I had no family of my own, and I was retired, available. She was so desperate for someone, anyone, to help her."

I glared at Cherie. She should have been there for her sister. But she ignored me; she just stared at Ms. Marta with those huge blue eyes of hers.

"When did you know?" Klaire asked. "When did you know you switched timelines?"

"I spoke of forest bathing—it's something that was commonly prescribed to depressed patients in my history. One could walk through the forest and commune with the trees. Our trees were high on emotional intelligence. It was common for individuals to maintain their moods just by taking daily walks through nature."

"It didn't work for you, though," Cherie said.

"No. My trees were dying. So the combination of losing

my children and losing my forest were more than I could bear. But Moira didn't understand. I explained about special baths placed deep in the forest glens, usually kept hot by some local thermal springs. A patient would walk into a forest barefoot and find one these places to cleanse their souls."

"Hydrotherapy and naked commune with nature. We called it Kneippism," Cherie said. "It was a nineteenth-century treatment for mood disorders. Sounds similar."

Klaire and I exchanged glances. I'd never heard of this Kneippism and clearly neither had she. But that didn't mean it wasn't a thing in this timeline. It could have been our own ignorance, nothing more. *In fact*, I realized, *many people who switched timelines accidentally probably never learned of the change. The world is large; we are familiar with just a tiny bit of it. Easy to get lost, especially if changes were small.*

"Kneippism? It does sound similar," Ms. Marta agreed. "But as far as I can tell, the botanicals here are not very highly evolved on the cognitive scale. Not like in my timeline, anyway. Trees are just trees here. So that's how I truly knew I was someplace else." She took a deep gulp of her coffee. *Sentient trees?* Hers seemed a far jump between histories. "Moira and I became close," she continued. "It was nice because I didn't really have any English skills. And Moira's Spanish was good enough to have a conversation but not so good as to have her notice my particular linguistic eccentricities. I needed her help with the doctors and nurses. She was kind. She introduced me to Fred, your dad. He seemed nice too. Harried. Stressed. Tired. But nice. He hated hospitals and all things medical. It always felt like he couldn't wait to get out of the hospital as soon as he arrived. I was released before Moira. I offered my help with their kids. He took it."

"That's not how I remember it," I said.

"Your perception of events leading up to your mom's

death might have been different," Ms. Marta agreed. "But that's how it was for me. The only regret I have was telling Moira that I had everything under control. She looked so relieved then. She died the next day. It was almost like I gave her permission to let go. To leave."

Cherie and I exchanged glances. I felt sick. My spine felt off, twisted, bloated somehow. I wanted to vomit. I got off the stool and stumbled into the bathroom. After emptying my stomach into the toilet, I sat there on the cool, white tile floor, head full of bees. No thoughts, just endless buzzing.

✲✲✲

There was a knock on the bathroom door, and Klaire poked her head inside.

"Hig? Is it okay if I come in?" she asked. I nodded, and she stepped inside and closed the door. "Nice ceiling."

I looked up. Galaxy-like spiral patterns made out of different shades of blue and gold buttons spread above my head—another one of Cherie's works, obviously. "Nice," I said. I hadn't even noticed it before Klaire pointed it out. She nodded.

"Cherie and Ms. Marta are discussing how even talking about alternate history splicing might cause nausea." She looked me over. "Are you okay? Are you in pain?" She crouched next to me and took my temperature by touching my forehead. I guessed that was a universal female gesture of medical concern.

"I'm not feverish," I assured her. "But I agree with Cherie and Ms. Marta about the sick feeling. Do you feel it too?" I inhaled deeply to balance my stomach. "Perhaps it only happens to outsiders."

"You mean like people who got here from another

timeline?"

"If true, it would be a useful tell."

"Yeah. If true. Ms. Marta said that Nona had it in spades."

I sat up. It was true. Nona got it bad. Worse than me, worse than Cherie, from what I'd seen. Nona was sick for days. "Did Ms. Marta say she had it too?"

"I didn't hear," Klaire said and sat on a little blue, fluffy rug. "But Hig?"

"Yeah?"

"I think I felt it too. Not as bad or anything. But some. Lightheadedness. A strange feeling like my stomach was doing the flips outside of my body. Or something."

"Sounds like you had the splicing history illness thing."

"The SHITs?"

We both dissolved into laughter.

The door opened, and Cherie stepped inside. "Sorry to disturb you," she said, "but I just got a text from Roger. He found Nona." I looked at her like she was crazy—Roger had never even met my sister. *How would he even know?*

And then it hit me—all those photos in Cherie's bedroom. *But of course!*

I jumped up and pulled Klaire up to her feet. "Let's go!"

Chapter Fifteen: The Dream Land Music Festival

Klaire's phone rang just as we all were trying to squeeze into Cherie's car. Ms. Marta sat in the passenger seat next to Cherie. Klaire and I sat in the back.

"Hello?" It took her five rings to get the phone out of her pocket—we were sitting comfortably close...just not for complicated maneuvers like phone extraction. Klaire pressed the phone tightly to her ear. I couldn't hear who was on the other side, but I saw her eyes get bigger and bigger.

"What?" I mouthed. "Who is it?"

"Okay," she spoke into the phone. Her voice shook a little. "I'll make sure he gets the message." Klaire hung up and turned to face me as she spoke in a loud voice for everyone in the car to hear. "That was the nice man from the Buffalo History Museum."

"Really?"

"He said Cherie's friend left his scarf there."

"What?" Cherie and I said at the same time.

"A man visited the museum right after we left, apparently," Klaire said. "He said he was Cherie's friend. Described you and Hig enough that the curator knew who he was talking about. Said he was late to meet us there. Asked if we were done with our research and if he could briefly see what we saw so that we could all be 'on the same page.'"

"No."

"Yes. The curator showed him the photographs of the Morgana Family and the group shot of 1901 World's Fair exhibitors."

"And?"

"He thanked him and left. And apparently left his scarf behind. I gave my name and number as part of the form we filled out to get access, remember?"

"You said we were working on a school project," I said, still stunned.

"So the man called and asked if we could tell Mr. Hill that he left his scarf behind. It's cashmere." She shrugged, as if that explained it.

"Roger followed us to the museum?" Cherie asked, and the car swerved a little.

"Roger Hill? That's his name?" I asked. "Why would he follow us?"

"How did he know to follow us there?" Klaire asked. That was a better question.

"I don't know?" Cherie said. It came out as a question.

"Just drive. We'll know in a few hours," Ms. Marta said. We were travelling south on a highway out of the city toward the Dream Land Music Festival that Roger told Cherie about. He and Nona were there now, according to him.

***

How many miles did we do in just over twenty-four hours? Whatever we did, we did in near silence. I didn't know what everyone else was cogitating about; I was focusing on trying to remember when exactly I slid into a different timeline, all those years ago, as a kid. And the more I tried to reconstruct the flow of events in my memory after looking into the mirror-device, the more I became certain that there wasn't a one moment—I wasn't in one history and then instantly in the next. I came to believe that the movement between alternate histories had to be a gradual process. More like switching lanes than jumping from one stream into another. One had to get close to the lane of choice, line up to it, match speeds, and then carefully merge. And perhaps during this process there was a way of merging out—a certain time period when one didn't commit to driving in that particular timeline and there was still a way of getting off. But at some time later, the lanes had to diverge. As we lived our lives, we did things, events happened, history unfolded, and the time streams no longer flowed side by side. The more life happened to us, the farther apart the alternate histories grew. There was never going to be a way for me to jump back in time to the moment when I chose this new life. Too much had happened, not only to me, but also to everyone around me. My life made ripples that affected others, however tangentially—if nothing else, I was the captain of my college soccer team, for goodness sake—and there was no taking it all back. By living my life here, I made this timeline different. And that had to be true for Uncle Charlie, Ms. Marta, Mom, and even my dad, even if he didn't believe in this whole thing. He lived a life and made choices, and those choices changed other people's lives, and so on. Which meant that if I ever faced the mirror-device again—and I never wanted to—I would never be presented with a choice of reentering my old timeline. That history was too far diverged from this one by now. In a way, that was a relief. If true.

After hundreds of miles, I managed to convince myself that I shouldn't carry the guilt of choosing a happy life. I wasn't even an adult back then, for goodness sake. What did I know? I just wanted to be free of that chair, to be like every other kid on my block—happy to run around the county fair, to go on stomach-churning rides, to eat corn dogs, and to vote on which chicken was best. To do all of the simple things that young boys wanted. Cherie and Ms. Marta might have a heavier load of guilt to ditch—they were adults, and they knew what they were choosing. Except not really. The only person who really knew what was going on was Madam Destiny or whatever she was calling herself these days, in this timeline. She knew.

She knew and yet allowed all those people to look into her mirror-device and make life-altering choices. There was something evil in that. The people who looked didn't know the implications of the reflection of possibilities they were seeing. They just hoped and dreamed. Some of those dreams were dark and ugly. Those led to timelines full of misery and pain. Or death. But those people didn't know they were making a real choice. They couldn't be held responsible for bad thoughts. Everyone was allowed to have ugly thoughts; it was the acting out of those bad ideas that was criminal. Thinking was not illegal. Or shouldn't be. But if thoughts could actually hurt people... The Mistress of the Mirror was responsible for all the pain the slips in the timelines caused. She had to be evil. And we were chasing her. Because why would Roger have gone to this Dream Land Music Festival if not to find the Looking Glass of Fate booth? Why else would Nona have tried to go? She had talked about being pulled...

I wished Cherie would drive faster. I was all philosophy'd out. I needed action.

***

The Dream Land Music Festival was one of those affairs I could never have gone to if I was still tied into my wheelchair. It was massive—several acres of rolling grass and mud, four separate music stages, several streets of novelty gift vendor booths, a massive food court made of circled food trucks, and rows and rows of porta-potties. In other words, a total nightmare for mobility-challenged...or just parents with small kids.

It was a three-day event; Friday at noon was the official start. But people who worked it got there almost a week before, of course. It took time to set things up. We arrived at the back door, vendors' entrance, before the festival opened to the public.

"We are with the IATSE," Cherie said as we rolled up to the security gate. She opened her glove box and pulled out some credentials. The guard checked Cherie's papers, smiled, and waved us through. It was as simple as that.

"What's *eaties*?" asked Ms. Marta.

"International Alliance of Theatrical Stage Employees, Moving Picture Technicians, Artists and Allied Crafts of the United States, Its Territories and Canada," Cherie said without skipping a beat. "Vic and Roger are members. They made me join a few years back."

"Oh," said Klaire. "What do you do? As a member, I mean."

"I have my EMR certification—emergency medical responder. It's not as good as my certified ICU registered nurse designation, but..." She shrugged. "It was the best I could do. And I am handy in a medical emergency." That was true. Uncle Charlie was the best. Assuming Cherie didn't lose anything in a slide between timelines, she would keep all his old skills, medical knowledge, and years' worth of experience.

"And Vic and Roger?"

"I guess you haven't seen Vic's knives and swards, Klaire. He makes stage-fighting gear of all kinds and teaches how to use them properly, too. As for Roger, he provides his financial services, as usual. Everyone needs a good accountant. Artists most of all."

"I see."

"Look around for Roger's double-wide," Cherie said, scanning the rows and rows of trailers, tents, and other temporary dwellings set up at the back of the fair to house the men and women who worked it—a little temporary city for the folks who made the fair possible. I'd bet some of the musical acts were housed here as well. People were out and going around saying hello to each other and grabbing supper and locally brewed craft beer from roaming kitchens and open-air bars—just folks relaxing after a hard day's work. It looked very much like the "back stage" of the county fair and had the same feel.

I didn't remember what Roger's trailer looked like, other than it was huge...for a portable house on wheels. But Cherie managed to spot it almost immediately. It looked like it was one of the last ones to pull up into the available camping spaces. It didn't really fit, splaying out half on the grass and half on a concrete surface of a parking lot converted into the designated staff living area. There were no lights on—Roger probably didn't have much time to plug his home into the "grid" here. He must have done quite a bit of driving himself in the last twenty-four hours. I wondered how he managed to find Nona...or was it Nona who found him?

"Do you feel the SHITs?" Klaire asked.

"What?" Ms. Marta and Cherie asked together.

"Sorry. It was what Hig called the shitty feeling that rolled over him in proximity to the mirror-device or just, you know, talking about it too much." Of course, it was Klaire who came with that name...

"Huh, I don't feel it," said Cherie.

"Me neither," said Ms. Marta.

They all looked at me. I just shrugged. Frankly, I didn't know what I felt. I was tired and stressed and worried and overthinking everything. And Nona... How could I even tell if I got the SHITs with everything else I was feeling?

"Well, we better find them before this place explodes with overexcited visitors," said Cherie and got out of her car. Klaire and I climbed out after Ms. Marta stepped out. We stood and watched Roger's trailer like it was some kind of trap. Then Ms. Marta exhaled and went to knock on the door.

"Mr. Hill?" she called.

"Roger?" Cherie tried to look through the window. "I don't think they are in there."

I didn't know why she assumed Nona would be with Roger. I was just beginning to suspect that Roger might have lied about finding my sister just to get us here for some reason. Yes, I was feeling very SHITy.

"Can you call him?" I asked.

Cherie took out her phone and started texting. Well, at least if his home was here, the man would surely be around, right? Ms. Marta sat down on the front door stoop. She looked old to me. Tired. What did switching timelines do to a person's longevity? How old was our beloved Ms. Marta? She was always just old to me before. I'd never thought of her as a person of a certain age. But I didn't think of my mom or dad as having an age either. They were just adults...and I was their kid. Except now I was an adult, too...sort of. A little bit.

Roger didn't respond to Cherie's texts or her attempts to call him. But just before we decided to split up and go look for him and Nona, we saw him running up the road toward us. He was holding his side and looked pale and out of breath by the time he got to us. Roger was not an athletic man, obviously.

He held up a hand when we jumped on him with questions. "Sorry," he managed. "Give me a moment..."

We took a step back and watched him try to pull himself together. Finally, Ms. Marta mattered something, went to Cherie's car, grabbed a water bottle, and gave it to Roger. He looked at her with a mixture of gratitude and apology. We just watched. This man spied on us. Followed us. Found Nona... I didn't think we should trust him and knew that Cherie did. I glanced at Klaire. She just shook her slightly, her puffy hair catching the evening light like a golden halo. She didn't think highly of Roger either, apparently. At least Klaire and I were on the same page. I couldn't read Ms. Marta.

"So, Mr. Hill," she said. "You said you found my Nonaken?"

Roger looked at her with a start. "Nice to see you again, Ms. Marta was it? And Klaire? Glad you all came. Thank you, Ms. Cherie, for getting everyone here." He stopped to take a few breaths; he was still holding his side. "Why don't we go inside?" He fiddled with key.

"How do you know Klaire and Ms. Marta, Roger?" I asked. I just didn't understand, but everyone clearly had met before.

"Oh, you were unconscious when we met," Klaire said. And suddenly it made more sense—Roger met Nona, too. He wasn't just spying...although following us to the museum was very odd behavior.

We all stepped inside, and Roger got the lights on—he apparently did have time to plug into the temporary grid. I wondered how long he was here...not too long if he left his scarf in Buffalo less than twenty-four hours ago.

"Mr. Hill," Ms. Marta said as he gestured for her to sit down, "we don't have time for pleasantries. You know the whereabouts of my little girl. I need to know where she is right now. I need to know she is okay." Yet she sat down. She looked so worn out. I placed my hand on Ms. Marta's shoulder. I didn't know how else to support her. I just needed her to feel that I would.

Roger wiped his face with a paper towel and sat down at the table, the same table we were doing research on Mistress Kismet's news clippings. I looked around for those files. As far as I knew, they were still here in his trailer. What I saw instead was a big stack of newspapers, obituaries page up. Some of those were circled with yellow highlighter.

Roger followed my gaze. "Obituaries were the natural place to look, don't you think?"

And another thing clicked into place—Ms. Marta had been looking for Mistress Kismet and her mirror, too...for years. Just like Cherie... I picked up one newspaper from the top and scanned. A woman was declared missing after a year's absence. Her obituary focused on her love of travel and adventure. Could be... I dropped it.

"So, Nona?" I said.

"She contacted me few days back. Said she remembered my name and I was easy to track down," he explained before I was able to ask him why. "Everyone knows how to contact their accountant, apparently." He gave us a small smile. None of us returned it. "Nona asked if I knew about the Mirror of Fate. I told her I did. She said she could feel it. She wasn't good at explaining what she was feeling, just that she needed to find that mirror. It was very important, she said. I told her I was sympathetic, but I had no way of tracking Madam Kismet or her mirror. I've tried for over a decade, and this month was the first time I came across it...by accident."

"That's true, Ms. Marta," Cherie said. "We've searched for years. Nothing..."

Ms. Marta nodded. I had a feeling it was her experience,

too.

"Nona asked a bunch of questions," Roger continued. "Nothing very revealing. How did I look? Where did I look in the past? Did I feel anything weird when I was close to it?"

"Did you?" Klaire asked.

"As I've said, my first real contact with the mirror was just this month. Before, it was all theoretical." He glanced at Cherie and went on. "And when everything was happening. Freddie...sorry, Hig, and his broken jaw and Ms. Cherie...I was so pumped up on adrenaline, it's hard to attribute how I was feeling. Sorry I can't be of more help there."

"Nona?" I asked again. Even I heard the edge in my voice. Roger had to stop talking nonsense. His eyes shifted back and force between us, my hands curled in stress. I felt Klaire's hand on my shoulder. But underneath my fingers, I felt Ms. Marta's body tense up.

"Right, Nona," Roger said. "She said she knew the location of the mirror."

"She felt it again?" I asked.

"Again?" Everyone turned on me now.

"She said that she felt it like a rope tugging at her gut," I explained. "But not all the time. Just sometimes. She thought perhaps it was only when it was working or something. So Nona said she felt it again?"

"She felt something. She wasn't specific. Just said that she knew where it was. Not the address or anything. Just that if we drove, she could keep pointing toward its location," Roger said. He looked guilt-ridden. I felt my teeth grind. "We drove through the night. We had to stop a bunch when she wasn't sure. But then she would know, and it was like she was pulled here, like a physical thing. We got here early this morning. By then, the pull was gone, but the fair made sense. We both agreed that the mirror would be set up at music festival somewhere. So we were going to wait until your sister felt it again."

"And did she?"

"I guess."

"What do you mean?"

"I fell asleep, Ms. Cherie. I'm sorry. I've been up for hours, driving. And...I just closed my eyes for a second. When I opened them, she was gone and it was dark already. I rushed out. I called for her. I asked everyone if they saw her. I ran around the fair..."

"But you didn't find her," Ms. Marta finished for him.

"No. I'm sorry."

"Well, we just have to look for her now," Ms. Marta said and stood up.

"Wait," Cherie said. "Mistress Kismet. She would be a registered vendor here. We can look her up. Find out where she's set up. Roger?"

The man jumped up and grabbed his computer. His fingers flew on the keys. It was stupid that he didn't look before. We all leaned over his shoulder as he scrolled through the names of various booths. "Looking Glass of Fate" wasn't listed. Neither was the "Mirror of Fate" or "Kismet" anything.

"Try Madam K," I said. But Roger was already searching by the names. The blind hag wasn't here, not officially...or not yet.

"She might have other names," Ms. Marta said. "We can assume that throughout history, here and in other timelines, there would be many different variations for a name of a woman offering to change one's fate. Kismet is just a nineteenth century Arabic variation on a theme."

"There could be thousands," Cherie agreed.

"But this is a country music event. We should be able to look through the list of vendors and performers and find something that stands out, right? Something that doesn't belong?" Klaire said. I think I was in love with her by that point. She wasn't a woman easily deterred. "And if not, then we split up and search on foot. It's only a few acres."

"Right, let's go," I said and pulled Klaire toward the door. "You guys search from here. Text us if you find something. We'll go out and look for Nona."

I was happy to get out of Roger's trailer. I needed to actually do something. I needed to run...while I still had the ability.

Unfortunately, because it was late, we were barred from going practically everywhere. Security was present at every gate, and there were patrols driving around on little golf carts. I'd never been to a music festival; I had no idea if this was normal. There were guards at a county fair too, but those seemed more concerned with lost kids and giving people directions to toilets than enforcing peace. But perhaps it was different at night; I'd never been to a fair after dark. *Well...* I started to yell something about my sister at the guard who was screaming at me. I was not in a good way. Finally, Klaire grabbed hold of me and pulled me away, apologizing to the woman officer working the late shift.

Once we were out of earshot, she turned on me. "Hig, what do you think you were doing?"

"Nona—" I tried, but she just talked over me.

"Your sister didn't inform you of her whereabouts, did she? She didn't tell Ms. Marta where she was going. She kept your dad in the dark—"

"So?"

"So perhaps she had a good reason."

"But—"

"I don't know why she kept it secret that she was going here or looking for the mirror. But Hig, if you yell and make a big fuss and alert the whole camp that we are here looking for her, do you think she will just come and find us? Or do you think she will hide harder, deeper?"

I hadn't considered that; I hadn't considered much of anything, obviously. "So what do you propose we do?"

"We go back to Roger's trailer and lie low. If Nona returns there for the night, great. If not—" I was about to argue how we would have to go looking for her, but Klaire stopped me. "If not, we will find her in the morning, when the show opens. We won't get ourselves arrested and booted out of here by sneaking around after hours."

"We won't?"

"No, Hig. We won't. Come on, let's get some food and sleep. If not you, Ms. Marta needs it." That was very true. I was really worried about her.

We spent the night sleeping on the floor of Roger's trailer. Well, some slept. I was mostly up thinking. What made Nona leave? What did this Fate woman want of her? Of me? Of us? If I switched my history lane, did Nona move over too? Did it work like that? Or was I living with an *alternate* sister all this time? Or perhaps it was her that lived with an alternate me. I desperately needed to understand the rules of this game, and without additional data, all my ideas were just desperate guesses. What if I guessed wrong and lost Nona? Or Ms. Marta? Or even Cherie? Or, god forbid, Klaire? Did Klaire even exist in another timeline? Did she like me there? I did not want to lose this woman. I listened to Klaire breathing next to me. She too took a long time to fall asleep, but we didn't speak.

Nona never returned that night.

Chapter Sixteen: Director of Destinies

By morning, the only clue we had was that no one who matched Nona's description left the festival grounds in the meantime. Given the tight security, Roger assured us that we would know if Nona was no longer on the fairgrounds. So my sister was still here, either with some backstage crew or out on the public grounds somewhere. There were only a few more hours before the official opening of the festival, and people were rushing around like worker ants at a disturbed anthill—easy to hide among all the hullabaloo if one wanted to. We had a lot of ground to cover.

Roger gave Klaire and me a couple of Dream Land Music Festival "runner" t-shirts—red with the official festival logo featuring a guitar twisted into a spiral with musical notes spraying out from its center. A bit on a psychedelic side, but it looked good on Klaire. Everything looked good on Klaire. Roger explained that "runners" were people who filled in the gaps in work that needed doing, like doing errands or standing in for people who got sick or got pulled to do something more important. He said that runners, or floaters as they were sometimes called, were indispensable to running any music festival. There were endless tasks and never enough people to get it all done. He directed us to pick up official staff badges from the festival administration office—no badge, no entrance. Klaire grabbed her oversized purse with long fringes, and I grabbed Klaire's hand—my basic long-term plan was never to let go—and we took off.

The staff area was enclosed by a ten-foot chain-link fence inside another ten-foot barrier surrounding the entire festival grounds. There were at least a hundred portable structures set up in there: trailers, campers, tents, busses, vans, and even a few teepees. In the central area, there was a food court and a large temporary medical facility with several ambulances parked next to it. There was also something that looked like administrative office on wheels. There we were issued staff badges, and Klaire and I become official runners for the Dream Land Music Festival...except all the running we were planning on doing was to look for Nona.

With our badges and runner t-shirts, we were able to get onto the actual festival grounds with all of its music venues, crafts booths, and endless food trucks—we got discounts on the food, too. We could even go backstage and all the other places that had "restricted, staff-only" signs posted at the entrances. We were staff!

Roger, Cherie, and Ms. Marta decided to walk about and ask the regulars. Someone might have heard about a one-mirror fun house booth or a girl with long golden hair. Klaire and I went straight to the public section of fairgrounds to look for Nona there among the exhibits, booths, and musical stages.

Aside for the lack of animal barns, it all looked awfully familiar. The visitors, who started to stream in from the main entry gates even before noon, were a bit different. While the county fair that I'd been to had always been a family affair—tons of noisy kids, parents with strollers, even hordes of middle schoolers out on school trips—the music festival had a different vibe to it. For one thing, people seemed to be over twenty-one or older—drinking age. Most were college kids there to blow some steam. It even smelled a bit like Spring Break...and it was still very early in the day.

Everyone tried to stand out in some way. There was a lot of clothing that looked like it had an unfortunate encounter with wild animals or abusive driers prior to being worn at the fair—not good at protecting its wearers from the elements or even at maintaining modesty. But that was clearly not the point...or the point. I was taken aback at first—I've been going to private schools with strict dress code most of my life—but then saw that it was a thing after the umpteenth girl sported the look. I noticed that most didn't have much on underneath the shredded fabric. I loved Klaire, but I was male.

"Their hotness will keep them warm," Klaire remarked as we wound our way among thicker and thicker crowds, encountering young women with less and less on. "Or they'll die from a sunstroke...or a cold. Or both." Klaire obviously did not approve...or perhaps didn't approve of my staring. I wasn't, though...not really.

The visitor numbers grew exponentially, and I was beginning to feel desperate. There were just too many here already. What looked like a large, open, grassy park in the early morning was turning into a dense self-activated, artificially rowdy crowd...fast. We gave up running. Klaire waved her badge over her head, and between that and our official Dream Land Music Festival t-shirts, people did part to let us by. But I still felt trapped.

"With so many people, how are we going to find Nona?"

"I think Nona will stand out," Klaire said as a group of girls walked past us, looking like a postapocalyptic gaggle of clowns. Their heavy makeup shimmered and changed colors in the sun. "Why don't we start with a systematic search of the booths? Madam K might have registered under some more exotic name this time, but I'm sure we would still be able to spot her. And if nothing else, we might feel the—"

"Don't say it, please," I begged. Klaire broke into a huge grin. I knew she was just trying to keep my freakout to a minimum, but I just couldn't... Laughing felt wrong while my sister was missing.

"Look, Hig, Nona is here, all right? So we will find her. She is no longer *missing* missing. She is a very sensible girl. Nothing bad has happened to her—"

"Yet."

"We won't let anything happen, Hig. We are here now. It will be okay." She squeezed my hand, and I did feel a bit better. "Let's go look for that mirror-device," she said and pulled me toward the festival's creative court—a collection of booths selling random stuff that the Dream Land Music Festival visitors felt compelled to buy.

We walked past booth after booth of artisans selling festival attire. In addition to expensive rags, we could purchase see-though clothing, scarves in any shade of neon, giant hats, and tiny fascinators that blinked-out messages of hope and love via embedded microchips and LEDs, programmable jewelry that morphed based on the wearer's mood, and augmented reality glasses that promised enhanced viewing experience for all of the musical acts at the festival. Quite a few people were already wearing those.

A woman walked past us holding a chicken—one of those exotic breeds that Klaire pointed out at the county fair just a few weeks back. The chicken was wearing "therapy animal" designation on its leash harness. It blinked, *We can talk about the elephant in the room, or you can leave the elephant at home.*

"That's just animal abuse," Klaire hissed. The woman pretended not to hear us and kept walking toward a vegan seed bar. I vaguely wondered if she was looking for a healthy morning snack for herself or for her therapy chicken.

"People spend an insane amount of money here," Klaire said, pointing to a price board at a place selling florescent-colored beer. It looked like poison. Some bottles even smoked.

There was a feeling that people came to this festival to escape reality. Three days of something completely different. Total sensory emersion into the weird and strange. No wonder the medical facilities out back were so expansive. I hoped they had a vet on standby, too.

We turned the corner and almost collided with a group all dressed in billowing, hooded capes with spiral galaxies printed all over them. The galaxy decal on our "runners" t-shirts was clearly a homage to these robes. In addition to the galaxy-wear, some of these people were holding up signs over their heads decorated with even more spirals of all sorts. The spirals looked like they were moving.

"Optical illusions?" Klaire asked.

"Got to be. They look like ordinary prints." But I was getting dizzy looking at them.

There was a crowd gathering around. Some were chanting something that sounded like a Gregorian chant. There was drumming, the kind one could feel in one's chest and made one's heart fibrillate.

"What are you guys advertising?" Klaire asked one of the girls standing off to the side.

"Siming is performing tonight after sundown," the girl said. She had so much makeup on her face that it was difficult to describe her features. She would be impossible to identify, I thought, and felt a touch of morbidity. For all of the strangeness and color and over-the-top face paint, these were just folks out to have some fun. They didn't look evil or anything. Just a bit on a crazy side...or drunk.

"Siming?" Klaire prompted. She wasn't deterred by strange facial-ID-defying paint.

"The Director of Destinies. They are going to lead the audience into a transformational experience at sundown."

"I bet they will." Klaire and I exchanged looks. "This evening? Which stage?"

"Oh, it will be held at the prayer circle." The girl motioned over her shoulder toward the center of the festival grounds, its highest elevation point. There were large speakers set up in a semicircle like some new age Stonehenge. "Like it always is," the girl added.

"It happens every time?" I asked.

"Sure. That's why most people come to this festival. It's not for the music, you know."

"Of course not. Thank you for clarification, dear. Stay safe tonight. Stay hydrated. Drink plenty of water—"

I pulled Klaire out of the tightening circle of chanters. "What was that?"

"Just good advice. Didn't you see the helpful safety hints back on the office wall?"

"No. I must have missed that," I said. "So, this Siming?"

"Yeah. The Director of Destinies. Must be our girl, don't you think?"

"So no booth this time? No mirror-device?"

"Oh, I think we should still look for the booth. And maybe we should get a pair of those capes, too. Blending into the crowd and all that."

"Right." I looked around for the booth that sold those. It couldn't be that everyone just happened to have one of the exact same galaxy-patterned hooded capes on hand prior to coming to the festival.

"Pick me up," Klaire said. She motioned to my shoulders. "I might be able to spot it that way."

We fumbled a bit trying to figure out a way for me to lift Klaire up, and then I crouched down and she just climbed on. I stood up, and Klaire zoomed above the mob.

"There!" She pointed somewhere.

It was amazing having her pressed against me this way. I felt giddy, almost light-headed. She tried to slide down, but I held her and moved through the sea of visitors in the direction I thought she indicated. I felt weightless; Klaire felt weightless. It was crazy how good it felt.

We threaded our way among the growing number of galaxy robes until we almost collided with yet another row of vendor booths. I could swear they were breeding—I didn't think there were so many crafts people here when we first arrived at this section of the festival grounds.

"The last one," Klaire said into my hair. Her hot breath made my scalp buzz...in a nice way. "It's covered in the same material and galaxy pattern as the robes." That made sense— a booth that's its own ad. *Very practical.*

We watched a couple go by, pulling on their newly purchased galaxy-wear. Their robes still had tags on them. Klaire grabbed on one and pulled. The robe almost slid off the man's shoulders, but then the thin thread attaching the tag gave and we were able to pass each other without the man knowing what Klaire did. I stepped into a narrow space between two adjacent booths and lowered Klaire down...reluctantly.

On one side, the tag simply read "Siming Enterprises. Made in China." The backside was covered in the same galaxy swirls as the robes.

***

The crafts booths at the festival were arranged on a grid pattern in rows of twos with narrow alleyways in between, at the back. While the "streets" were packed with visitors, the alleys were for staff only, and we were the only ones there after squeezing between two adjacent vendors.

"I'll look up Siming Enterprises," Klaire said. "You text Cherie and the rest. Let them know what we've learned so far."

"We didn't learn anything useful yet," I protested. What was I supposed to say? *We noticed some people wearing galaxy robes?* So what? People were wearing all sorts of crazy shit around here.

"Look." Klaire ignored my tantrum and pulled me closer to show a webpage she loaded on her phone.

I leaned in. Klaire had Wikipedia up: *Siming is the Chinese deity who holds the title of Director of Destinies...*

"Siming Enterprises was some car company in China," she said. "So that didn't work. But this? Perfect, isn't it? Most definitely linked to the performance tonight, don't you think?"

"Yeah." Klaire was so fast. I barely managed a few words of complaints while she identified the right reference among thousands. *Brilliant...brilliant and beautiful.*

"Stop looking at me that way." She punched me.

"Ouch." I robbed my arm in fake pain.

"Let's go get us some fancy robes. The right costume is apparently everything around here." And she waved her badge again. True enough.

We jogged over all the way to the end of the back alley. The galaxy booth was massive—it took up a double-wide space as a cap edge of a crafts "street." The dark material printed with colorful spirals, stars, and nebulas made for interesting shadows on the ground, shimmering in the slight breeze of the afternoon. I noticed that in addition to the sun, there were several well-positioned spotlights that added to the effect. I guessed the weather didn't always cooperate, and the owner of the booth wanted to maintain the mysterious aura, even on cloudy days.

"Nifty," Klaire said. "Hey! Nin hao!" She waved at the people manning the booth.

"Nin hao?" I was taken aback by her use of Mandarin. I didn't even know Klaire knew any Chinese.

"It's a Chinese deity," she hissed at me. "Yes, you!" She motioned to a girl in a galaxy robe working the back of the sales counter. "So are there any staff discounts on these things?"

"Good thinking," I whispered into her ear. And then looked at the prices. Damn. "Klaire? Do you have any cash on you? I don't think I have enough to buy half a hotdog here, much less one of those robes."

"Not enough," Klaire said. "But I'm sure they take e-credit; everyone does."

"That's a lot of money, Klaire. Are you sure we need those? We could just go as staff, you know."

"Perhaps Roger can loan us some cash? We can return the robes tomorrow and give it back."

"You want me to ask Roger for money?" I wasn't comfortable with that.

"He bought your uncle a whole button factory. But I guess not." She looked around. There were boxes and boxes stacked in the back alley, probably full of those robes.

"We can't," I said, following her gaze. "It's just wrong. And we don't even know... Well, we don't know a lot."

"I was just looking, I wasn't really going to take any." She sounded defensive.

"I know, just..."

"Why don't we ask them for a brochure or something? We really just need more information, right?"

"Right." I exhaled, feeling better. I didn't want to commit a crime or have Klaire do it.

"So, do you want to buy some robes?" the sales girl finally came over to us and asked. "We do staff discounts," she added, looking us over. "Especially for runners. They don't pay you guys much, do they?"

"Nope. In fact, we are volunteers—no money for our work at all," Klaire said. She used one of those friendly, conspiratorial voices: *We are all in this together.*

"I'll see what I can do," the sales girl said. "Just wait here." She pointed to a stack of boxes and went to look for someone with authority, probably.

Klaire and I sat down. It didn't feel like folded cloth. Klaire fingered the edge of one of the boxes—stacks of paper. She looked at me as one of her eyebrows inched up. I shrugged. Getting some marketing crap wasn't like stealing. She carefully pulled a colorful folder from the box we were sitting on. The design on the cover matched the galaxy pattern of the robes, of course.

"Oh, I see you are getting familiar with our activities," said a man, dressed incongruously in a closely tailored black three-piece business suit and the shimmering galaxy cape. His smile felt artificial. I glanced over at Klaire; she looked like she was caught with her fingers in the chocolate box. She was. "We do need an extra volunteer for tonight," the man added. "I'm afraid only one." He spread his arms as if he was sorry about that. He wasn't. "Would the young lady be interested? You already have our brochure..."

"Yes, she would," I replied for her. Klaire just stared at the man like she had lost her ability to speak. "Klaire?"

"Yes?" she managed.

"Excellent. I'm sure we'll have something in your size." It didn't make any sense—Klaire was a normal-sized girl, not unusually short or tall or wide or skinny. Just normal. The man smiled again and added, "We start promptly after sunset. That's 6:47 at this time of year at this latitude." And with that he turned and left, leaving the sales girl to handle the details.

"That was oddly specific," Klaire said after letting out a lungful of air.

The sales girl came over with a packaged robe. It had a big M for medium, sticker stuck on top.

"There you go. The tag is your ticket into the show. Please don't lose it, and don't be late. In fact, we ask all of our volunteers to arrive at least fifteen minutes early. Crowd control and all that. Is that okay with you?"

"That would be fine," said Klaire and took her robe and stowed it into her bottomless bag. "I'll be here."

I fingered the tag in my pocket. *So will I.* I didn't even feel guilty.

***

We squeezed back outside and wandered the festival. It felt like we were breathing fresh air after the suffocating gloom of the back alley behind the galaxy booth. The sun was making Klaire sneeze. It was strangely endearing.

There were even more people now, hordes and hordes of revelers ready for a good time. A good percentage were wearing the galaxy robes. What were those people hoping for from this experience? What was the Director of Destinies offering that they all wanted? Did they even know?

I tripped and broke into a cold sweat. The paranoia over losing my physical abilities was now an almost constant companion.

"Are you all right, Hig?"

"Yeah. Just thinking about life changes and alternate histories and all."

"I see." She looked at me suspiciously. "If you start to feel... well, you'd tell me right away, right?"

"Of course. Do you feel it?"

"No." She put her arm through mine. It felt more like a medical rather than an emotional support. I almost pushed her away...but didn't. I liked her body next to mine.

"Klaire?" I was about to say something stupid; I couldn't help it. "Would you even have given me a second look if I were still in my wheelchair?" It was a stupid thing to ask her. How could she know? We would probably never even have met if not for my transformation...change in destiny...slip into another time stream. Stupid. But I practically stopped breathing waiting for Klaire to respond.

We walked on, and she didn't answer. I thought she would just ignore me—I deserved that—but then she stopped, turned, and said, "No. I don't think so, Hig."

"What?" I was hoping she was answering a different hypothetical question.

"I don't think I would have been with you if you were still disabled. I don't think we would even be friends. Sorry, Hig. But it's the truth." I must have looked totally stricken, for she took both of my hands in hers and looked up straight into my eyes. "Hig, people need an initial push or a starting place that they can share. If you were in that chair, we never would have found an opportunity to interact, to talk even. And I never would have learned how amazing you are. You would still be you." I didn't think so. "But without some reason for us to come together, how would we ever have found each other?"

"You mean if there was some reason for us to meet but I

was still a cripple, you would have still wanted to be with me?"

She didn't answer, just squeezed my hands, let go, and started to walk away. I almost let her, but then I ran up to catch up with her. I wasn't that stupid, I decided.

We circled all four musical stages and even looked at the backstage preparations. Neither of us had ever heard of any of the bands listed to perform. A few people stopped asked us for directions to food courts and bathrooms and even where the vendor booths were set up—we were literally a few yards from the crafts city, but whatever. Klaire actually had a map; she'd grabbed one from the office while they were printing our badges. I was impressed all over again.

I was even more impressed when she started to inquire of the visitors who were asking us for directions why they came to the festival. That never even crossed my mind. Almost everyone we spoke to said something about the Director of Destinies. It almost felt like we had stumbled into a cult gathering. These people had all met each other online at special social group chats maintained by the Siming Corporation. And now they were seeing the real people behind the avatar masks and they were giddy with expectations.

"I think most of them are going to be disappointed," Klaire murmured into my ear after a particularly exuberant encounter with group of girls, all wearing the galaxy robes over some ripped t-shirts and slashed jeans, all sporting that color-changing metallic makeup.

"Why?"

"They've built up all these fantasies about this gathering and about each other. It's hard to live up to one's imagination." That made sense...sort of. "And," Klaire continued, "not one of them explained exactly what is going to happen tonight or even talked about it using the same words. It might turn really ugly."

"Huh. I hope we find Nona before sundown."

"She might be hard to identify underneath the robe and all that iridescent beetle face paint."

"My sister doesn't wear—"

"She will if she is trying to blend in. Haven't you noticed that all of these people are trying hard to blend in? To make sure everyone recognizes that they are part of *it*?" She put a heavy emphasis on "it."

I haven't considered that but peered even closer into every hooded face that passed us...except, of course, Nona would recognize us. We stood out. And if for some reason she didn't want us to find her, these Director of Destinies groupies were making it very easy to do.

Why did Nona come here? Was she being "pulled" by the mirror string again into all of this? *All of what?* My mind was just going around and around in circles. We had to find Nona.

Chapter Seventeen: Fates

It was dusk, and we were still circling the hill where the Director of Destinies was going to perform. We hadn't gotten any farther in our search for Nona or in figuring what was actually going to happen...in just under a half an hour from now.

"Cherie and Ms. Marta said they would meet us here," Klaire said, looking around. With so many people, it was hard to see more than a few feet away. And neither Cherie nor Ms. Marta was a tall woman. "Roger is already supposed to be here."

"It's time," I said. "You've got to pull on that robe thing." I helped Klaire rip the plastic bag open—which was surprisingly difficult—and shook out the dark, galaxy-covered material, careful not to lose the tag. The inside was lined with one of those space blanket materials—metallized polyethylene terephthalate—gold-colored, of course. It was rather beautiful and felt well made. It would keep all those girls in hole-y clothing warm during the evening chill.

"Quality," Klaire said as she slipped it over her shoulders. She looked good. *Great.* "So you've said Cherie, Ms. Marta, and Roger, all have these?"

"That's what Cherie said." I bit the tag off Klaire's robe and gave her the ticket to go inside the fenced-off area.

"Thanks." She looked around at the sea of galaxy robes. "It will be impossible to spot them." I totally agreed. "Okay, Hig, I've got to go and volunteer. Stay out of trouble, okay? Text me if you find anyone or spot something of note. Don't be brave and stupid, okay?" She leaned in and gave me a light kiss on the lips, and before I could even kiss her back, she was gone into the crowd.

"Klaire?" I said softly into the ever-growing mass of galaxy-clad fanatics. "Don't let anything happen to you," I whispered. And with that I turned and walked purposely toward the back entrance of the galaxy-covered Director of Destines stage, erected over the last few hours on highest point of the festival grounds. I was staff, and I had a ticket. *What are they going to do? Deny me entrance?*

After anticipating all this drama, getting inside the backstage of Director of Destines was as easy as flashing a smile...and the robe tag. People were busy and just waved me in. I tried to look purposeful—people who looked lost or idle were quickly assigned tasks, as Klaire and I had just discovered. In the few hours of running around the fair looking for Nona, we had managed to get roped into selling mineral water, manning a ticket booth for some show coming up in a few months in Iceland, and even helping rig the sound system on one of the smallish stages. *With any luck, those musicians would be able to fix whatever we managed to miswire on the spot. Fingers crossed...or wires...whatever.*

I walked fast, keeping my eyes straight ahead—a man on a mission. I used my peripheral vision to scan for Nona and now Klaire. Cherie, Roger, and Ms. Marta would be somewhere in the audience already; they'd texted earlier. Hopefully, they got a spot close to the front of the stage—people had a hard time saying no to Cherie, so I wasn't very worried about them.

"You there!" someone yelled behind me. I ignored it and kept walking toward the little changing booth labeled "talent." "Hey! Didn't you hear me?" A hand grabbed my shoulder and spun me around. "What's the matter with you? Deaf?" a bespectacled man barked at me, and then his eyes widened underneath his thick lenses. "Oh, if you are, I'm so sorry." I found his reaction almost comical.

"I was told to check the sound system?" I put it as a question, trying to make my voice sound gruff and full of electrical experience. Having spent almost an hour wiring the other stage, I was almost a sound engineer...or at least I could sound like one—I had picked up some vocab. "Some idiot used the wrong wire gauge earlier," I said. "And as you know, the fatter the cable, the less resistance between the amp and the speaker." That was the full extent of my knowledge, but by the look on the guy's face, I was as far above him in my expertise as a slug was above the amoeba in evolutionary development...neither of us capable of doing any sound equipment wiring. "So what do you want?" I tried to come across as busy, important—I had all those wires to check.

"Sorry, sir!" I was promoted to a sir. "I just need a hand moving that stand over there. But really, I'm sorry. I'll find someone else. Just make sure Mr. Valdytojos has sound wired right. This is his first time in South Carolina. He usually sticks to Eastern European DD events. Siming had a time of it... We are lucky to have him, of course. But... Sorry for running my mouth. Just nervous. It's almost time. Go. Go. Go." And the guy practically pushed me toward their sound system...and away from the curtained-off "talent" section.

I gave the guy a thumbs up, which he didn't see since he was screaming for someone else to help him with his stand or something. He did look very stressed. I rushed behind the speakers, crouched next to the thick wires, and pulled out my phone.

Valdytojos from Eastern Europe is performing at the DD tonight. Does this ring a bell, anyone? I typed into a group chat for Klaire, Ms. Marta, Roger, and Cherie. I fiddled with the cords with a stern expression. *I'm very busy, and this is careful work*, I tried to project to people rushing around me.

Roger answered first. *Deivės Valdytojos refers to seven goddesses from the Baltic pagan tradition.* This explained why this guy performed mostly in Eastern Europe, I guessed. *They weave the garments made from human life strands*, Roger added.

Huh. Like the Greek fates? I asked.

Don't know.

Well, that was something. Not much, but something. The lights started to flash around me—a backstage warning that the show was about to begin. I stood up and rushed off the stage to hide behind one of the giant speaker monoliths. It was a good position—I could see practically the whole performance and the first few semicircular rows of the audience from there. I branded myself as a sound guy, so people wouldn't just push me out, hopefully. If only I had earplugs—the speaker was massive, and there were seven of them...like the number of Deivės Valdytojos. *Coincidence?*

It was very faint at first, almost subliminal, but it built and built. Finally, I recognized it as the music from Khachaturian's Masquerade Ballet—not what I was expecting. I knew the music well; my sister took ballet classes. I went to all of her performances and many rehearsals. But while I recognized Khachaturian's score, it took me by surprise. Why Masquerade? What was the connection? Personally, I'd always found this score to be hypnotic, almost trance-inducing. I secretly played it when I had trouble sleeping, just in my earphones, so no one knew. Somehow, the frantic melody reminded me of my mother...at the end, when it felt like she was dying, abandoning us. There was falseness about it, a fake exuberance. And something otherworldly in the way it made my spine prickle and my scalp tingle. I loved this music and never told anyone about how it made me feel. Why was it playing here? Now? Another coincidence?

I looked through the purple darkness of the evening at the audience. Some were swaying with the music, some even hummed along—they seemed to know what to expect. There was a strong beat component, which had a hysterical vibe to it. The swaying of the audience slowly coalesced, undulating like deep ocean waves. Colored lights ran the perimeter of the round stage. The lights were synchronized with the music, which was synchronized with the audience and the strange deep drum beat—some complicated variation on the one-two-three waltz tempo. I wondered if all of it was preprogrammed or was there someone actually working some percussion instrument somewhere, carefully taking a measure of the audience and leading it into a kind of induced frenzy? The effect, however it was achieved, was very strong. I felt as if my heart was beating with the rhythm: thump thump-p-p, thump thump-p-p, thump thump-p-p. One two three, one two three, one two three. My chest muscles felt like they were fibrillating. It almost hurt...but in a nice way?

We were at the *Galop* section of the Khachaturian's Masquerade—the too-fast headlong rushing into the melody, the place that always made Nona stumble. The music crescendoed and dropped...and the audience exploded in cheers. A man with long dark hair, dressed in the galaxy cape and holding a cane with a large crystal on top, walked to the middle of the stage, the silky dark material billowing behind him. It was a cool effect, but there were no fans, as far as I could see...which was disconcerting. Where was the "wind" coming from?

The music swelled again and dropped to near silence. The audience stopped their cheering as if on cue as the man, presumably Mr. Valdytojos, raised his hands, cane held high above his head. The crystal was shinning brightly, pulsating with the same strange beat as the lights and the background percussion.

"Greeting, Fate Seekers," he said. His voice sounded off, like it was heavily processed or something. It made me shiver—there was something very wrong with the sound. Perhaps it was because I was experiencing it from the back of the speaker? I twisted my fingers into fists, trying to control the strange tremor that spread to my extremities.

"You're gathered here because something is missing, something is not right. Your life is not as it should be. You know it. You feel it." As he said it, the crowd groaned, sounding truly in pain. He was like some kind of bedazzled mountebank, a snake oil salesman...but the crowd was buying it.

My body shook as if I were in a particularly uncomfortable position. I wasn't. I tried to shift my legs underneath me so that I could put of the weight on my butt. I was an athlete; this should have been easy for me. We—my team and I—practiced meditating and remaining still in one position for a quarter-hour at a time. I was good at it, and yet no position was comfortable. I felt like I was contorting my body into more and more outrageous poses in an effort to still myself. Yet each muscle seemed to vibrate at some variation of the rhythm...some subfrequency of the beat of the drums that kept going despite the muting of the Khachaturian's score.

I looked into the crowd. No one seemed as uncomfortable as I felt. They stood—more than I could—and cheered the generic nonsense that the Director of Destinies speaker was laying on them. It was the worst pep talk ever. I felt cranky, nauseous. I was tired of this...

"—other people's fates." Mr. Valdytojos spoke in a deep voice of a practiced orator. "But we are here to try. To try to grab our destiny from thousands...no, millions of better fates that could be our own. How do you find the life that's right for you? The perfect fit... Sure, everyone tells you to work hard and study hard and practice hard. But no matter how hard you try, you won't bring your loved ones back to life. Right?" The audience wailed and cried and agreed. "You won't find love by trying hard, will you?" More screams. In anger or agreement, I couldn't tell. I could barely tell what I was feeling. "They say find your hidden talent. Explore what you're good at. But how can you do this when you are trapped in someone else's life? When you are a prisoner of a wrong destiny? You are spinning some other hamster's wheel. Running all out to nowhere." Surprisingly, I found myself nodding. Agreeing? "Could you be a pilot if your vision was bad? There are no blind fighter pilots, are there?"

People screamed "no" and yelled obscenities. Some even threw their glasses up in the air. And even as I thought it stupid—those people might truly be blind now and could have problems getting home without their glasses—I was screaming something too. The sound just ripped itself out of my mouth like I had no control over what I was saying... screaming. I looked around backstage. Other people who worked there were also screaming. The man who had asked for my help earlier was stomping his glasses into the deck of the stage, grinding them to bits. He looked half-crazed. What was happening?

"What do you see when you look at yourself in the mirror each morning?" the man asked, his hair and robe flying behind him like wings. He looked like an oversized crow...or some demon angel; the thought flashed in my mind unbidden.

He was making strange waving moves with his cane. I found myself staring at the glowing crystal at the hilt, unable to look away.

The crystal spun and pulsated. And then it split. And split again. My eyes were crossing as I was trying to follow the multiplying lights. There were so many. Someone in the audience screeched, and I lost my balance, sprawling on the stage floor, tangling myself in cables. I lost contact with the lights. When I looked up, I saw that there was not one but seven of Valdytojoses standing on the stage now, each holding a glowing crystal-tipped cane. Their undulating capes merged into something resembling the waves breaking on the rocks of the ocean shore.

I looked out into the audience. It too had split. It was almost like looking into a mirrored hallway—endless self-reflections out to infinity. Except it wasn't perfect. I noticed a woman with red hair that used to be in the front row was now farther away. It was still the same woman, I was sure. I tried to spot Cherie, Ms. Marta, and Roger. They should be close. I should be able to see them.

There was another scream. I snapped to the sound. It was Roger. He was pointing at a reflection of himself and screaming. It was a primal, guttural sound. I followed his gaze. There was another Roger; he was holding a hand of a little boy. The boy was smiling. I knew that Roger must have thought it was Lucca, his son who died of a brain tumor. But that couldn't be—parallel histories didn't result in backward time travel. At least that was my impression—one could slide sideways, but not back. Lucca would be an adult now, not a little kid. But Roger—our Roger—pushed his way toward his other self with the little boy. I saw four arms trying to stop him—Cherie and Ms. Marta. Yet Roger wouldn't be denied. He half flew, half fell into the other image. And then he was gone.

Other people in the audience started screaming and pointing at other versions of themselves. Some rushed toward the reflections they liked, falling into the, merging, disappearing. The music sped up. The lights were spinning at an insane rate. It was pandemonium. I tried to call to Cherie and Ms. Marta. I was worried that they too would find a destiny they liked better.

I managed to stand up, and from my new perspective I saw Nona. She was dressed in a flowing, loose dress of the same make as the robes, hanging off her small shoulders by thin, dark straps. Her white skin and golden hair was even whiter and more glowing against the darkness of the material.

"Nona!" I screamed.

She turned. He eyes were milky white...like the Mistress of the Mirror.

I gasped. She turned back to face Valdytojos and wrapped her fingers around his cane. The crystal glowed even brighter. I looked for Ms. Marta and Cherie. Did they see Nona? We had to stop her. Stop this...

I stumbled toward the front of the stage. The robes parted in front of me like water. Still, I felt almost a physical resistance as I tried to get to my sister. I was almost there. I looked out and saw myself...thousands of me. Some looked happy, some were recoiling in horror; some were on crutches, some strapped into electric wheelchairs, their bodies twisted by the disease. I wanted to run. I wanted to get to my sister... to get away.

There were more screams in the audience. People seemed to be leaping and falling and melting into some other realities. One scream was closer, one more insistent. I couldn't focus on it; I didn't have enough attention bandwidth to be able to. I stretched my arms.

"Nona," I gasped, trying to reach her.

The light from the crystal expanded and engulfed me. I felt hands grabbing for me, holding me tight. And then I fell. The light went out. It was dark. Nighttime. Cold. I felt snow on the ground.

Chapter Eighteen: Time Streams

"Hig?"

"Klaire?"

She had her arms wrapped tightly about me. I was just able to feel the pressure from her arms, feel her breath on my neck. The galaxy material was covering us like a blanket.

"Oh!" she cried out. I turned and saw a body wrapped in the matching galaxy robe lying in the snow on the ground next to us, one hand stretched out, fingers curling around my ankle. The fingers were twisted, bloodless.

We bent down and turned the body over. Ms. Marta's dead eyes were staring at us.

"No, no, no." I leaned close and tried to find her pulse. "You can't die, Ms. Marta. You can't leave me."

Klaire got close too, but she didn't let go of me. One arm held on so tightly, like her life depended on it. She brushed Ms. Marta's hair from her face with her other hand, stroking her gently, muttering something I couldn't hear...understand.

"CPR," I cried. "We need to do CPR." I knew how. My soccer team got formal training. I moved to straighten Ms. Marta's body, but my own didn't respond. It hit me like lightning—I couldn't feel my legs. I couldn't feel Ms. Marta's fingers clutching at my uncle. "No, no, no."

"Do it, Hig. Don't worry," Klaire said. "Just do it."

I pulled myself over. Klaire obviously hadn't figured out yet that I was a cripple again. I pushed on Ms. Marta's chest in rhythm to "Staying Alive." "Ooh ooh ooh, staying alive..." Press, press, press, wait. Press, press, press, wait. Press, press, press, wait.

I don't know how long, but at some point, Ms. Marta's eyes focused on mine. She was alive. And we were in an alternate time stream.

***

The sky was beginning to gently glow with an early dawn. Ms. Marta was feeling better. She sat up and drank from a water bottle Klaire produced from her bag. That girl... The chalky whiteness was gone from her face, and Ms. Marta's skin tone had almost returned to her normal delicate brown hue. From what I could observe, Klaire and Ms. Marta weren't markedly different from who they were in our timeline. Shaken, but still the same. I, on the other hand, couldn't walk. That was going to be a problem. A big problem.

We were sitting in a middle of an empty field, perhaps the same one we were on before, but all the people and structures were gone. No Nona, no Valdytojos, no one at all, just a few streams of smoke over the horizon beyond a distant row of naked trees. Klaire and Ms. Marta still had their galaxy robes over their warm weather clothing—a good thing, too, with the snow on the ground. We left all of our winter stuff at Roger's; I was only wearing the Dream Land Music Festival runner t-shirt and jeans. It was a warm day back in our history; it was cold, below freezing now. We couldn't stay there.

"I think it's the same geography," Klaire said. Her breath

made a visible puff in front of her.

She draped half her robe over my shoulder, holding me close by the waist. I'd managed to sit up, but my legs were a no-go. I worked hard to beat panic and bile every time I looked down at those useless appendages. Surprisingly, not only the robes, but all of our stuff was the same as before the transit to here, wherever "here" was. But my legs looked deflated underneath my jeans. I was too scared to touch and find out what was under the flattened cloth. Klaire politely tried not to notice. But I saw her look, saw her turn white, saw her pretend like she hadn't.

"Look over there." She pointed. "That's where the Director of Destinies stage used to be. It's the highest point. So we are like dozens of feet away from our starting position. And that tree? That's where the office trailer was. Remember they hung all those lights all over the brunches?"

"The tree is different," Ms. Marta said. We didn't argue— she would know. "The one in our time stream was an old laurel oak. This one is something else. And it has no leaves." I noticed that too.

"Do trees lose their leaves in the winter in South Carolina?" Klaire asked.

"I don't think so," I said. "It too far south, right?" Actually, I had no idea. I was talking just to keep talking, to keep from freaking out.

"These are not my trees," Ms. Marta said. "So not my timeline."

"And not ours...well, not mine." Klaire gave a quick glance in my direction. "We need to find out where we are."

"Where is a difficult concept," Ms. Marta said. "But, yes. We can't stay here. We need shelter. We need food."

"We need information," I said.

"And we need help. I will go get some." My brave Klaire

disengaged her arm from my body and stood up. I immediately shivered. She started to undo the clasp of her robe, but Ms. Marta stopped her. She moved over to sit right next to me and took me under the wing of her robe. These women were not giving up on me.

"Thank you," I whispered, trying not to shed a tear. "I'm sorry I'm so useless."

"You are not useless," they said at the same time.

"Hig." Klaire bent down and faced me. "You know what you asked me before?" I knew exactly what she was talking about. I nodded. "I don't care about it. It's inconvenient right now." *The understatement of the year...of a lifetime.* "But we will deal with it. I'll walk toward that village there and get some help. It'll be fine. You just wait for me here. Don't move, okay?" She smiled at me. Ms. Marta took Klaire's hand and squeezed gently. "I'll be back quick. That chimney smoke can't be too far away. Five miles tops. Easy!"

She stood up again and refastened her robe. Thank goodness for that emergency material lining. The galaxy robes looked strange, but they would keep us warm. Klaire passed her water bottle to Ms. Marta. She also gave us a small bag of roasted nuts we had purchased some time during the festival. I ate all of mine. Klaire squirreled hers away for later. I was just crazy about this girl. I needed to slip back into a time stream where I was a fully able person. *It isn't just for me, it's for her,* I told myself. Klaire didn't need a crippopotamus in her life. The old nickname I gave myself popped unbidden into my psyche.

I didn't say anything as Klaire walked away; I didn't trust myself. I huddled with Ms. Marta under her robe and tried to think us out of this situation. How could we get back home, into our own timeline?

"You know, it didn't happen all at once," Ms. Marta said

after Klaire disappeared behind the hill.

"What?"

"It took time for the switch to become final. For days... weeks, I encountered people, objects, and places that were from my time stream. At first, it was very confusing. One moment I was walking down the street in your history, the next I was seeing my trees lining the street. It was unnerving. But over time, it settled down. And eventually, I stopped seeing any phantoms of my worldline."

I thought about it. It was like that for me too, sort of. My ability to walk developed slowly. It took years, actually. But I didn't remember seeing anything that "didn't belong," and I told Ms. Marta so. Our experiences of transition seemed different.

"I wish we had more time to talk all of this over," she said. "Cherie had a lot of interesting data to add, I'm sure. It would have been helpful."

"Yeah."

"Gran chico?" She hadn't called me that in forever...days, at least. And somehow Ms. Marta saying her baby name for me made me at least ten degrees warmer. I stopped shivering; I didn't even realize I was doing it before. "It will be all right," she said. "We'll find a way of getting us home. I believe it takes time to switch timelines, and we haven't committed to this one yet."

God, I wished with all my heart that it were true. I leaned on Ms. Marta's shoulder and watched the direction Klaire ran—yes, she actually ran toward an unknown civilization to get us help. The sky was steadily getting lighter and lighter. Little white clouds started to pop up—evaporating condensation. It was even getting a bit warmer, although without the space-age lining of the galaxy robe I was sure we would have been suffering from hypothermia. Birds began to sing. It was not anything familiar, but what did I know about birds? Birds of South Carolina? I'd never been to this state before yesterday. Was it even South Carolina in this timeline?

"Ms. Marta?"

"What is it?" I felt her body startle awake. She must have fallen asleep. I was such an idiot for not checking first. She was practically dead just a few hours ago. She needed the rest.

"Sorry. I didn't mean to wake—"

"What is it, Hig?" I really liked that she had started calling me Hig, recognizing my preference.

"Thank you," I said. And she tilted her head in acknowledgment. "I just wanted to know if there were states, like in the United States, in your timeline...from before?"

"Yes," she said. "But it wasn't exactly the same."

"Was there a South Carolina?"

"There was just one Carolina."

"I see." Damn. We really should have discussed this more, but I felt that telltale nausea that came when the differences between alternative histories were plainly identified. I tried to control my breathing and focused on watching the sky. Calm, collected...

"Damn!" I shouted and practically fell over. Ms. Marta had to grab me to help me remain in a sitting position. Those damn useless legs... It would take time to get used to having a body that didn't work again.

"What is it, Hig?" I felt her arms wound tightly around me, supporting me.

"There are no contrails," I said, pointing to clear violet skies above. She looked at me like I was crazy. "Nothing. Not a one. Not anywhere in the sky." She still looked at me blankly. "No contrails means no planes, right?"

Understanding slowly flooded her face. She pulled down the hood and swerved around, looking up. The sky was indeed empty, blank, no white streaks caused by planes. We sat and searched the sky some more in silence. We saw no planes. Aside from birds, there was nothing above us. In our timeline, back home, we would have seen a dozen planes overhead, if not more. I'd never seen skies so devoid of traffic.

"Could we have moved into a timeline without technology?" I asked. I felt around the front pocket of my mostly empty jeans. My cell phone was still there. Ms. Marta saw what I was doing and grabbed for her own purse. She pulled out her phone before I got mine.

"Mine still works," she said.

I typed my password, unlocked my phone, did a few operations. Everything looked normal except for the lack of a cellular signal. Ms. Marta checked hers out, too. She shook her head.

"We would still be able to share data just between our own phones via connector cables," I said.

"Why would that be helpful?"

"I don't know. It's just that we can. Or I can set up a local hot spot, and we can do Wi-Fi..." I was stopped by the look on Ms. Marta's face.

"We might have problems getting these charged up," she pointed out. "I don't even have my charger with me. I left it at the Cherie's button factory apartment. In the rush to leave, I just forgot."

"I don't have mine, either. But Klaire might." I bet she did—that girl was so prepared. She probably had a spare cable or two in that bottomless bag of hers. "But if these people don't have electricity..." I looked in the direction of the rising chimney smoke. These people might not have advanced technology. *These* people...

"Put that away, Hig. Hide it," Ms. Marta said urgently. "Our IDs won't be any good here either. We should have made a plan before Klaire left." She shook her head. "Well, that's water under the roots." I never heard her use that expression before. "Give me your wallet and phone. I will hide them in my skirt. I have a secret compartment sawn in." *She did?* "Perhaps searching little old ladies is not a thing in this timeline."

I handed her my personal items and hoped she was right. I was even more nervous for Klaire now. Was searching beautiful young women a thing here? Would Klaire know not to reveal her identity? She was very smart, but how often did one had to deal with—

There was a low whooshing sound coming to us from behind the Director of Destinies hill. Ms. Marta and I both turned to watch. The winter grass—what was left of it—was moving strangely. The noise was getting louder. And then something resembling a very large drone—six big motors attached to a chassis in a hexagon pattern with a cabin suspended between them on the bottom—rose up into view and moved toward us at about five feet above ground and the speed of a good sprint. Perhaps ten miles per hour? Maybe a bit faster. Klaire was one of the passengers. There were two more people with her...wearing uniforms.

Another drone rose up.

***

Two of the largest drones I'd ever seen settled down on the frozen grass next to us. One drone looked like a medical vehicle by its markings—*a sky ambulance?* The other was clearly a police drone with two officers and Klaire, sitting inside a wide circular cabin.

Once on the ground, a policeman helped Klaire out of the drone. It was easy, though—the doors opened, and everyone simply strode outside. There was a small step, but one even I could manage...*probably.*

"Mama!" Klaire cried out and ran toward us. "Hig! How are you guys doing? I'm sorry it took so long."

"Mama?" I mouthed, but Ms. Marta elbowed me underneath the cape. I shut up.

"Hello, officers," she said in a voice that was both somehow pathetic and very officious. "Thank you for coming. I'm afraid we had quite an adventure. Klaire told you about it? Did she per chance mention Hig's disability?" Ms. Marta was obviously a master at saying nothing and asking leading questions while appearing not to do so to get the information she needed. I had to learn that skill in a hurry.

"Mama, I told them that we had Hig's med-assisted drone stolen, with all of our papers and credits and such," Klaire said as one of the men who was obviously a medic from the other drone bent down to examine me. The officers stood back a few feet. One was taking notes on a simple paper pad with what looked like an ordinary yellow pencil with a pink eraser on top, while the other was observing all of us carefully.

The medic, a tall man in a light gray jumpsuit and with an easy smile, palpitated my legs. I didn't feel his touch. I guessed that the expression on my face conveyed the horror I felt at the lack of sensation, because the man patted my shoulder and said, "It will be all right, young man. Hig, was it? We'll take good care of you. You'll be just fine." He turned to the other medic—his partner or assistant, perhaps—and the man rushed back into their ambulance drone to get something that looked like a carry sling. I was all too familiar with those; I could recognize one from this or any other timeline in a heartbeat.

"Ms. Marta?" The police officer who was not taking notes finally spoke. "Your daughter tried to explain what happened to you all last night. She was too distraught to give us the full story—"

"It was awful, just awful, Officer," Ms. Marta lamented.

"I'm sure. Did you by chance see the person who could have done such a thing?" he asked.

"We went for an evening dinner picnic," Klaire jumped in. "It was a full moon." *Was it?* She tugged on her robe. "My mom and I try to go once every few months. You know, for religious..." She just sort of tapered out there, but she managed to convey a lot of information—she'd been telling wild tales, it seemed. We had to be careful not to make too many contradictions. I decided just to keep my mouth shut. The women obviously had this under control.

"We are familiar with followers of the Kismet rituals." The officer helpfully stepped in. "But we try to encourage people to stay with their groups and to avoid desolate areas. There is no need to flout fate." He chuckled at his own witticism, and I saw Ms. Marta smiling at him. "Nice robes, by the way. I haven't seen any of such high quality for a long time. The gold lining is a nice touch."

"Thank you, Officer," said Ms. Marta. "My sister sent these to us from up north. Apparently they work well in warm and cold weather."

He just nodded and walked around us, looking at the ground. "So what happened to yours, young man?"

"What?" I said like a dumbass. I wasn't quick enough for this. And the medics were lifting me off the ground and helping me get into a sling to be carried into their drone. It was awkward. I was awkward. But it covered up my inability to answer the officers.

"Your robe? Was it taken too, son?"

"Mine?"

"Yes, Officer," Klaire jumped in again. "It was left in his..."

She pointed vaguely behind her back.

"Aah," he said. "I'm sorry. There are people who don't play by social norms. Someone probably noticed these robes and saw that it would be easy to take." He motioned his head toward me as I was being carried away. "Some people... Well, these robes would be easy to track! I'm sure we will be able to get it back for you."

I saw the officer and Klaire help Ms. Marta to her feet. She seemed a bit unsteady. Klaire hugged her and even theatrically wiped a tear from the corner of her eye. But the officer was concerned. He looked at the ambulance drone and at me. And then back at Ms. Marta.

"I think we should take your mother to be checked out at the clinic as well," he said. "We can fill out all of the paperwork after that. No point in taking a chance. Right? It was a cold night... Mevrouw, you are not a young woman anymore." He smiled patronizingly at Ms. Marta, using the Dutch honorific.

How she managed not to yell at him, I'd never know. If I had to bet on who was tougher, I wouldn't lose by placing all my bets on Ms. Marta. But she just took the officer's arm and leaned heavily on it. She made a big show of needing support to get into the police drone. Klaire followed behind, looking very concerned. Well, at least we were all going to the same location, albeit in different drones.

Once we were settled inside—me in the reclining chair at the back of the ambulance drone and Klaire and Ms. Marta in the back seats of the police one—the officers did another walkabout the place we "picnicked," probably looking for clues. There wouldn't be much.

I noted that the other officer, the one who didn't talk, never stopped taking notes.

Chapter Nineteen: New World

The village we landed in was quaint; there was just no other word for it. It was a mix of two-story square Dutch houses—exposed black beams, white stucco, pointy roofs—and houses built on a circular footprint. The round houses were modern-looking—they were made mostly out of glass, steel, and concrete—and more numerous. There was something vaguely familiar about their architecture, but I couldn't really place it. The people, including the two policemen and the medics who came to our recue, were also not typical in their build or features. At least they didn't really look like people who lived in South Carolina of my timeline. Most everyone we met—at the drone parking lot and at the lobby of the modern hospital, built like a set of overlapping circles—were obvious descendants of Native Americans, tall, lean, with thick black hair, straight-as-a-cleaved-rock noses, dark brown eyes, and light brown skin. If their features reminded me of anyone, it was Ms. Marta. Except she was not a tall woman and rather on a plump side. I, with my super-white skin and light brownish hair, and Klaire, with her obvious Caribbean genetic ancestry, were distinctly different. We stood out.

After being carried into the hospital in a sling, I was swarmed with attention. I was placed in some kind of levitating drone of a chair and had an IV stuck in me even before I had a chance to protest. From the corner of my eye I saw that Ms. Marta got a chair of her own, and the doctors in gray jumpsuits were working on her IV. Klaire just stood to the side and gawked. Things were very different indeed in this timeline.

They must have given me a sedative, for I started to feel woozy. I closed my eyes, and that's when I noticed it. The random noise that was always present behind my eyelids, the one that looked like gently floating dust on sunny days and swirling stars at nights, was moving decidedly from the top right to bottom left corner. That had never happened before. It wasn't bad, per se, just different, perhaps a bit nauseating. I wondered if the nausea we felt early was related to this strange drift. But I fell asleep before I came to any conclusion about it.

***

I woke up in a bed in a sunlit room. It took me a few moments to figure out where I was. The room didn't feel like a hospital, at least not like a modern hospital. I could recognize those without opening my eyes by smell alone. All hospitals made the same olfactory assault on one's senses—a mixture of sick, desperation, and strong cleaners. This room smelled... nice. There was some floor-cleaner odor but it was distant, not overwhelming.

I looked around. I was alone in a partition of what felt like a much larger room. The IV was out, and a glass of water was standing on a nightstand next to my single-width bed. A big window, letting in all that sunshine, had lacy geometric curtains—very inappropriate material for hospitals, I was taught. The curtains looked very bright, happy. The bed had blindingly white sheets underneath a soft woolen blanket with alternating chevrons of ochre, gray, and beige. The floors were dark brown oak—another inappropriate material...at least not what I was expecting from a hospital. The bed was wrought iron, painted white. There were two rolling partitions on either side of me that blocked the view of my neighbors, so I couldn't really tell how big the room was or how many beds it had. But from the echoing footfalls in the distance, I guessed it was at least thirty feet long. I could see the wall in front of me, opposite the window at my back, which made the room about ten feet wide. I also noticed the slight curvature of the walls—I was in one of those modern round buildings. The partitions didn't go all the way to the wall in front of me, creating a kind of informal corridor that allowed medical staff and visitors to move from patient to patient across the length of the room. It was a good design. Light, not oppressive like the hospitals back home that I was used to.

There were soft footsteps, and Klaire's head peeked from behind the partition on my left.

"Hig? Are you awake yet?" she asked, coming over and sitting at the edge on my bed. She smiled, and the room seemed to get even brighter. I vaguely wondered whether the carefree lightness of being I was experiencing was my own feelings or the drugs they gave me. "Hig?" Klaire called again.

"I am awake," I finally answered. "And Ms. Marta?" *Did they give her happy drugs, too?* I shook my head to dispel evil thoughts. So far, everyone has been super nice to us in this timeline.

"Mama?" And there was a twinkle in Klaire's eyes. Her eyes were no longer chocolate. There were gold and green stars sparkling in the sea of brown. That was new...shockingly new. Her eyes were more like Ms. Marta's now. Did Klaire know?

"They are working on requisitioning a new personal drone for you," she said, oblivious to my staring, "to replace the one you lost. The police is also creating us temporary IDs so we can go back to New Amsterdam." She squeezed my fingers to keep me from expressing my surprise too loudly. As if I could. I was too "surprised" out. "I had a few hours to decompress and read the papers in the family waiting room," she continued, "while the doctors looked over you and Mama. She is doing well, just a bit of a chill from spending the night outside. And her blood pressure seems elevated. But the doctors are not worried. They say it is to be expected after the ordeal we've been through. They gave her a sedative, and she slept for a few hours. She needed it. After she eats some lunch, we will walk over to the police station and work on the paperwork."

"I see," I managed. "Should I go with you?"

"No. Sorry, Hig." She squeezed my fingers again. "The doctors are planning on taking a few more images of your spine. Apparently it is necessary to make sure the drone fits properly."

"But spina—"

Klaire stopped me with another squeeze. I shut up.

"You have a fractured spine that severed your spinal cord." She repeated "fractured" and "severed" to make that sink in.

My eyes felt like they were bugging out of my skull. "W-when?" I stuttered out.

"I think the doctors will be done with you by late this afternoon, just in time to catch the evening train up north." Klaire knew it was not what I was asking, even if the information she was feeding me was valuable and necessary. She leaned in to give me a kiss on the cheek, and as she did, she whispered in my ear, "Childhood accident, most likely. You don't remember how it happened." I nodded slightly to show her I understood. "Well," she said as she got up. "I have to go and help Mama. You be good, like a good godson." *Godson?* "We should be back in a few hours. I explained to the staff that you are not much of a talker. They'll be nice to you, I promise."

With that she blew me a kiss and left. I wished we had more time to coordinate our stories. "Don't talk much?" "Ms. Marta's godson?" What did she mean by that? Was I supposed to act like I had brain damage? Not that it would be a stretch, the way I felt. I wished that I could "decompress" with some newspapers right now. Where were we? What was this timeline?

✳✳✳

It was surprisingly...shockingly easy. It felt like the bureaucratic red tape that was always present in everything we did in our timeline was virtually absent in this one. We were issued new temporary passports based on the information Ms. Marta and Klaire provided without a shred of proof. And just like that, she became Klaire Marta. I was Hig Keen. Our one-page, laminated IDs stated our names, dates of birth—the time flow was identical between histories, even if events weren't—and our home state...New Amsterdam in this timeline.

The train tickets were free. All public transportation was free. The reason there were tickets at all was to ensure that the railroad could keep track of the flow of passengers and make reasonable accommodations for the number of trains needed to service them. With free public transit, most people didn't even own private vehicles...which would have been drones in this timeline. There were no internal combustion engines and nothing on wheels. The word "cars" referred to train compartments on levitated mag rails. Everything seemed to fly or hover or levitate in this timeline; it was as if these people invented airplanes before the wheel. Well, not airplanes...

We would have to be very careful how we spoke and even thought before we learned the differences between our timeline and this one. A tell-tell sign when we approached a "wrong" subject was a slight wave of nausea that hit just before the words tumbled out. It was a handy clue, even if it wasn't immediately apparent what was making us feel that way. For example, when I told Klaire about her eye color change, we both vomited. It almost sent us back into the hospital. Ms. Marta managed to do some fast-talking to get us on that train for New Amsterdam, the last one for the day. But when I asked for something to treat my headache, resulting in another wave of nausea, we didn't know if it was appropriate to ask for medicine, or if headaches themselves were not a thing, or there was some other reason for the sickness that came when histories collided. *Still useful.* I just had to suffer the headache.

My mobility drone was amazing, better than any wheelchair back home. For one thing, it could hover high enough to have eye-to-eye conversations with people, and stairs were just not a problem. I could zip up and down faster than Klaire. All doors in this timeline were made wide enough to allow for such "personal assistant" drones to float through. Even bathrooms were easy to manage. *If we ever got back home, I will "invent" mobility drones for all those people whose life is limited because they don't have one,* I thought. But for all that, I was the only person I saw who was disabled enough to use a personal medi-drone. Were their medical techniques more advanced or...? I leaned over to side to heave dry again.

"Hig?" Ms. Marta was instantly by my side. "What is it?"

We all now recognized the symptom, and apparently merely contemplating "wrong ideas" could be bad enough to cause the timeline collision sickness.

"It's nothing," I said, dizziness making it difficult to concentrate, pushing all thoughts to the side.

"Think about the weather, the sun on your skin, the wind in your hair," she said. We discovered that the best way to manage the sickness was to anchor ourselves in the here and now. Often focusing on our direct senses—touch, smell, sound—was the easiest. I inhaled a few times, breathing in the soft, lavender-like smell of the train car, and after a few moments, I did indeed feel better; the nausea had passed.

"Sorry," I mumbled after regaining my composure. I didn't like to feel so weak, so out of control, especially in front of Klaire.

"That's fine." Klaire tried to reassure me, and that made it worse. "It will be quite an adjustment for all of us. This thought control..." She made a face. "So how's the weather?" she said, working to overcoming her bout of sickness. She closed her eyes and turned her face toward the window. I did the same...as a preventive measure.

"It gets better," Ms. Marta said, shaking her head. Of the three of us, she was the most experienced at making this kind of transition. Translation? Side-slide? But I had a feeling it might be difficult for us to talk about it, to share information. Well, perhaps when we got someplace private, when we had the freedom to puke at will.

"I was given a recommendation for a place to stay in New Amsterdam. A halfway house for the medically challenged," Ms. Marta said and pulled out a piece of paper with some writing on it. "Morgana House for Challenged Children, Youth, and Adults."

"You mean for crippopotamuses like me?" I said, feeling

bitter and sorry for myself. Klaire gave me another one of her hand squeezes. I liked it and hated it at the same time. Pity was not what I wanted from her.

"Morgana? Why does sound so familiar?" Ms. Marta said, robbing her forehead.

Klaire sat up and her eye lit up like jewels. "Nina Morgana? The soprano from the World Fair?"

"Oh yes," Ms. Marta said, "that family."

"Do you think it's just a strange coincidence?" Klaire asked.

"When histories collide, there are no coincidences," Ms. Marta said, and all of us had to close our eyes for a while, riding in the quiet of a train that never touched the ground.

I worked to relax and let go. The sun, slanting into the train window, reddish in the sunset glow, felt warm on my skin, even through the thick sweatshirt I was given by a social worker at the hospital. She was one of the few people with light skin, blond hair, and blue eyes I'd seen in this timeline. That woman slipped me a small metal pin with a colorful cloisonné of a spiral galaxy and the word "Kismet" spelled out in stars on its surface. She did it furtively, while no one was looking. She put the pin into my hand and curled my fingers closed over it before I gave it barely more than a casual glance. "May the eye of fate look favorably on you," she whispered into my ear and rushed off. It was strange, but there was no time to dwell on it or the interaction. The pin was still in my pocket.

Chapter Twenty: Morgana House

Morgana House for Challenged Children, Youth, and Adults was located in an old button factory, *the* button factory—Cherie's apartment. We stood—well, I floated, surprisingly quietly—in front of the door to the three-story building.

"I think it was only one sto..." Klaire managed before gagging.

I agreed with her and experienced a touch of dizziness. I wondered if there was some medication for seasickness we could buy, something that wouldn't result in our getting ill just from asking for it.

"Should we?" I asked and flew toward a large iron zipper-shaped doorknocker. It was literally shaped like a large zipper slider, hanging over the teeth chain, each the size of my hand. It was a very contrarian decoration for an old button factory. I used the pull-tab suspended from zipper's bridge to knock against the base to announce our presence to the inhabitants of Morgana House. The sound was nice and solid.

I knocked and pulled back from the door. We waited outside for a few minutes, and then the door opened, and Uncle Charlie stepped outside. My heart almost exploded out of my chest.

"Hello," he said, looking each of us over. "Welcome to Morgana House," he said with a sad smile. "Carolina Medical said to expect you. Please come inside, I'm sure we can find some accommodations for you folks."

I felt like I'd lost all my ability to think and function. Ms. Marta and Klaire stepped to either side of me and helped to gently glide my drone through the entrance. Both women had seen photos of Uncle Charlie from our family album, but they didn't have to have seen those—Uncle Charlie looked just like Cherie...just male. He was instantly recognizable.

He led us into a small room off the great hall, the one that had flowers mosaicked out of buttons by Cherie in our time-line...but not in this one. The small side room had a stove and what looked like a refrigerator; so it must have been the same space as Cherie's kitchen but enclosed. My eyesight doubled as I thought about the architectural and design changes, so I made myself stop thinking about that. But then there was still Uncle Charlie. Was he my uncle in this timeline? Was there another me here too? I felt very sick.

"They sent us your X-rays, Hig," Uncle Charlie was saying casually.

He obviously didn't recognize me. Did I look different now? The way Klaire changed her eye color? I wasn't sure and tried to maneuver my drone toward the darkest corner of the kitchen, as if that would help.

"Broken spine," Ms. Marta said, sounding helpful and yet not really.

"Yes," Uncle Charlie said. "It is unfortunate you were not able to get your godson into medical care fast enough to get it fixed at the time of the accident. But I guess it was over two decades ago?" He looked to Ms. Marta for confirmation. She moved her head noncommittally. "I'm so sorry. But I'm sure we can help you, and we can definitely find ways of keeping Hig comfortable." He looked at Ms. Marta and Klaire's galaxy robes and nodded. "It might be a good idea for you two to put away your robes. Down south, I hear, it's no big deal to expose yourself so openly, but in New Amsterdam..." He spread his arms and gave a sad smile. "We, Morgana's staff, of course don't care either way. We have several stays who practice openly. It probably helps to believe in fate when..." He glanced at me but didn't say it. "But...let's just say around here it's a good idea to keep these beliefs to yourself, that's all."

"All of our cold-weather clothing was stolen," Klaire said. "We don't have anything else that could keep us warm." It was even colder up here than back in Carolina.

"Yes, I've heard about that, too. Just shows that even down south... Yes, we'll of course find something appropriate for all of you. Still, perhaps you would like to take them off while inside? Is that a problem?" He was clearly uncomfortable with whatever religious expression he thought we were exhibiting. Klaire and Ms. Marta quickly took of their robes and folded them up. They were surprisingly compressible, and Klaire managed to stuff both of them into her bag. "Thank you," said Uncle Charlie, and I practically saw the tension drain out of him. I wondered what was going on. What about this Kismet religion that was putting people on edge? We needed to find out right away, obviously.

"Thank you for taking us in," Ms. Marta said. "Allow me to introduce us. I'm Rose Marta." After all those years of her taking care of us, I had no idea Ms. Marta's fist name was Rose. I was such a baby. Uncaring baby... "And this is my daughter, Klaire Marta," Ms. Marta continued. "And this is my godson, Hig Keen. You've obviously been informed about him. And what is your name, sir?"

He shook our hands in turn. I could recognize those

fingers anywhere...in any history or any other.

"I'm so sorry." He flashed a broad smile, the smile that always made the clouds go away when I was a kid. That same smile... "I'm Charlie Labelle. My sister, Moira..."

He said something after that, but all I could hear was that my mother was alive. *Alive!* In this history, my mother didn't die. I was hyperventilating. I felt a pressure on my shoulder. Ms. Marta came over and held me, and I realized that she had been my mother longer than my real mother was my mother. I felt ill. I had to force myself to focus, to pay attention.

"...we have been running this place. We are both medical technicians, but of course we work with doctors and family members, too. It takes a village..." Another brilliant smile lit up the room, and we were all grinning back at him. It was just like being around Uncle Charlie.

"Pleasure to meet you, Charlie," Klaire said. "It's okay to call you Charlie, right?"

"Of course!" He flashed another smile and turned to the stove. "We had some pasta for dinner earlier. I saved you some, knowing you had a long journey and all. Is that okay?"

"We would love to!" I finally found my voice. Uncle Charlie made the best pasta. *...and I might see my mom...*

⁂

We were given two rooms, one for me and one for Ms. Marta and Klaire to share. Uncle Charlie managed to gather some basic hygiene supplies and even a change of clothing. And he got me the medical supplies I needed...diapers. I was back in diapers for the night. We...I couldn't stay in this history. Well, a few weeks with my mom and then... Mom was worth a few nights in diapers.

Ms. Marta came to help me get ready for bed. It was a long time since she had needed to do that. It should have been awkward, but somehow she managed to make me comfortable about the whole thing. After all, she said, it wouldn't be like this forever. *We are just undercover agents here, really.* It worked...but I didn't want Klaire to be anywhere near me. We couldn't even talk about it beyond just the two of us in the room...well, perhaps Uncle Charlie could help, too. He did for eight years of my life.

"Hig?" Ms. Marta said after getting me situated in the bed. The drone did most of the lifting. It was like a Hoyer lift in addition to being my personal transport. "I don't want to scare you, but I want you to be fully aware of the extent of your disability in this timeline." I caught a slight heave of her chest as she said it. I too felt a bit nauseous, but we had to discuss this. I steeled myself; I could do it. She nodded at me, gave each of us a bottle of water, sat on a chair across from my bed, and continued. "You have a very slim neurological connection to your legs and your lower body. The break happened at the fourth lumbar vertebra."

"What does it mean?" I asked.

"As you can tell, there is very little feeling in your legs. You do have some bladder control, but it will probably be good idea to use these all the time as we slip further and further into this timeline." She motioned toward a large stack of adult diapers. "I'm sorry, Hig. We'll get you out of this. I promise."

I didn't say anything. Couldn't. I felt on the verge of tears. I remembered promising myself that I would rather die than grow up needing those.

"On the positive side," she continued, "there was never a break in your jaw."

I felt the side of my face where Vic's fist connected with

it. I didn't feel any pain at all. With everything that happened, I missed that the low-grade ache was gone. "So that never happened?"

"It did, but not here."

"I don't understand."

"It takes time for things to balance out, to reach equilibrium, an accommodation between our previous timeline and this one." We both took a deep gulp of water to suppress the bile that was trying to rise to the surface. "Your hair is blonder. Klaire's eyes are hazel now, more like mine. Other things, probably."

"I knew about Klaire, but..." I pulled out a strand of hair from my head. Sure enough, it was more like Uncle Charlie's and Mom's. It was longer, too. "Huh. Do you think he is my uncle still?"

"I don't know. We will try to find out tomorrow. We also need to find a way of locating and getting to the next Kismet meeting." *Yeah, we do.* "So get some sleep. Just tap on the wall if you need me. I'll be right on the other side. And don't worry about Klaire. She is a good girl. She cares for you. She knows that none of this is permanent." Ms. Marta leaned in and hugged me. "It will be all right, gran chico. It will be all right," she said softly into my hair. And I cried. I just couldn't help it. I cried like a baby.

***

Uncle Charlie came to help me get dressed in the morning. For all my terror, it was fine. He was my Uncle Charlie; he helped me get ready in the morning thousands of times. Somehow it didn't feel wrong when he helped. He pulled up my socks and tied my shoelaces. I could have done it myself, but it was so much easier... It could be so easy to fall back into dependency. I had to force myself not to, I decided. But Uncle Charlie smiled at me, and my resolve simply dissolved.

"How long have you worked here?" I asked as he helped me into my new drone.

"Almost two decades. Ever since my sister lost her family..." I saw his expression change; it was like storms clouds passing in front of a sun—dark, brilliant, mesmerizing.

"How did it happen?" I asked, not really sure I wanted to go there and knowing I had to find out.

"We were at a county fair," he began. My breath caught in my throat, and I had to will my heart to keep on beating. "We went to one of those Kismet booths, you know, just for fun. Neither Moira nor I believed in that stuff, of course. It's just a bunch of nonsense superstitions. But we were out to have a good time. Moira just went through a difficult pregnancy and childbirth, and we were celebrating life and fun and... Well, just as it was our turn to go in, the roof of the county fair building collapsed. They pulled Moira and me out of the rubble. My sister's baby and her husband didn't make it. There you go." He stood back after tightening the belt that helped keep me upright in the drone chair and looked me over. I must have looked bad, for he leaned in and put his hand on my forehead, face a mask of concern. "Hig? Are you okay? Do you need—"

"I'm so sorry for your loss," I said, almost without any sound. I had no air in my lungs.

"Thank you, Hig." His smile was sad. "It is very kind of you. But it happened a very long time ago. And time heals, it really does. My sister and I are doing fine. We dedicated our lives to people who have suffered tragedy. It made a huge difference to us. And we hope it makes a difference to people like you and your family."

I just stared at him. In this timeline, my sister wasn't

even born. I died as a baby. My dad died. It was a lot to take in. A slight wave of nausea washed over me, but I pushed it down. Not now.

"Hey," Uncle Charlie said. "Cheer up. We are fine, really. I'm more worried about you and your family."

"I'm sorry. It's just... I can't even imagine what it must have been like for you."

"It was a long time ago, Hig. Let's go get you some breakfast, shall we? I bet your godmom and sister are already there."

He helped move my drone out of my room, and we maneuvered into the great hall. I wasn't good at driving the thing yet; I didn't even know what all of the controls were for. Everyone just assumed I knew how to operate one of these, and I didn't think asking for instructions was a good idea. I figured I'd get used to it eventually.

Now, in the daylight, I got to see the great hall of the old factory in all its glory. There was open brickwork and giant metal beams crisscrossing the walls, just like back in New York. But in New Amsterdam, the converted building was bigger. The great hall was obviously the heart of the place, just like back home. The ceiling here was double the height, and there was a balcony running all the way around the perimeter, with many doors leading to what must have been private rooms or offices. Our assigned rooms, of course, were on the ground floor, just around the corner from the kitchen. We'd already noticed from outside that this building was three stories high, so there must have been one more floor above what I could see. Cherie's place was just a single-story building, and instead of a balcony, it had windows set up high, almost by the ceiling, and skylights up above. But despite these differences, the space felt the same; it was easy to recognize one after seeing the other. It felt eerily familiar, despite the lack of button mosaics and the absence of the giant fireplace.

There were portable tables set up in the open space of the hall. And for the first time in this timeline I saw people in medi-drones hovering about—the first physically damaged people I'd seen here. There was also more ethnic diversity at Morgana House, unlike back in Carolina, where everyone seemed to be a descendent of Catawba—the Native American tribe that inhabited the east coast when the Dutch arrived. Klaire's limited research had been very helpful in our understanding of this timeline.

A beautiful woman with long blond hair cascading down her back was dancing around the various tables, bring food and drinks to the ten or so families gathered in the great hall. My mom, I was sure of it.

"Hig!" Klaire called to me and rushed to my side. "Good morning, Charlie. Thank you for taking good care of my brother."

"You're welcome," he said. "I see you've met my sister."

I turned to see Ms. Marta waving us over to a table on the far side of the room, against the wall. My mom was serving her coffee. Ms. Marta caught my eyes—she knew.

"Ready, Hig?" Klaire asked. And I knew she was asking me about my readiness to meet my mother.

I couldn't answer, but I used the controls of my drone to navigate toward Ms. Marta. Klaire followed, her hand on my shoulder. Charlie left us to go assist someone else.

"And this is my godson, Hig." Ms. Marta introduced me to my mother as we reached the table. "Hig, this is Mevrouw Moira Labelle, Charlie's sister."

"Lovely to meet you, Hig." My mom extended her hand to shake mine. I barely managed to reciprocate.

"You must forgive Hig," Ms. Marta said. "We had a very difficult few days."

"But of course," my mom said. Same voice, same face, same smell even. "I'll leave you to your breakfast. Please, let me know if there is something I could do for you. This place might feel overwhelming at first, but we are all here to help. I promise." And she flashed each of us a smile. It wasn't as brilliant as Uncle Charlie's—it never was—but it was more than I'd ever expected to see in my lifetime again. I wanted so badly to... She walked away, and Klaire purposely blocked my view of her receding frame, tiny and delicate, just like Uncle Charlie's...like Nona's.

"Hig?" Klaire asked after she sat down at our small table and I finally maneuvered my drone into an appropriate position to have breakfast. "Are you all right?"

"Of course he is not," Ms. Marta said. "But he will be. Hig is a strong young man. He can handle this."

Could I? I had no idea. I wasn't handling it well at the moment.

"Your mom is lovely. I'm glad I've met her," Klaire whispered.

"Not really my mom," I finally managed. "But yes. Thank you. I guess we now know that neither Nona nor I exist in this timeline." I swallowed hard and saw Klaire and Ms. Marta do the same. "Charlie told me there was an accident that killed them...me and my dad almost two decades ago." And then, between waves of nausea, I told them everything else that Uncle Charlie managed to tell me.

"We don't know it was you who died," Ms. Marta said when I finally finished. "We just know a child died. Parallel timelines don't imply a one-to-one existence of the inhabitants within."

"Oh!" Klaire cried out and shoved her fist into her mouth to stop herself. Too late, many people turned to see what was wrong. Uncle Charlie rushed over to us.

"Is everything okay?" he asked and followed Klaire's eyes.

I had to turn my drone to see. On the other side of the room, a gentleman was floating in a contraption that suspended a young man in a semivertical position. The young man's facial features were twisted, wrong somehow. The older man helping him looked exhausted, almost gray.

"Oh," Charlie said after he realized we were all looking at the pair. "That's Roger Hill and his son Lucca. They've been here almost a decade. I've practically watched Lucca grow up."

"What happened to Mr. Hill's son?" asked Ms. Marta.

"He had brain cancer as a very young child. But while the treatments killed the cancer, they also devastated the boy's nervous system. It is a very unfortunate case. Nowadays, this simply doesn't happen. Or rarely, I should say. I haven't seen another case since Lucca. Roger have been taking care of his boy all this time, he refuses to give upon him. I admire the man."

"Yes," I said and remembered seeing Roger dive into some timeline from the Director of Destinies' stage. "He never gave up," I said, but I was talking about Roger from our history.

"If you folks are good," Charlie said, "I will go and help Roger and Lucca. Excuse me."

We watched him assist Roger in getting Lucca to sit up at their table. My mom brought over food—eggs, toast, and coffee for Roger and something that could be drunk through a straw for his son.

"As I've said," Ms. Marta said, "there are significant differences between timelines. I hope Roger found what he was looking for." So she too saw him fall into another timeline, chasing the dream of his son. Klaire just cried quietly. None of us could really eat right then.

Chapter Twenty-One:
Fitting In

Uncle Charlie came to us after breakfast, when most everyone had left the great hall.

"So how are you all feeling? I see you weren't very hungry," he said, glancing at our mostly full plates. I felt instantly guilty for wasting their food. Uncle Charlie looked tired—he did stay up late into the night with us and then obviously had to rise early to get the breakfast going here, and he probably had other duties too—and yet he smiled at each of us and made sure we felt welcomed. However timelines diverged, Uncle Charlie's nature was a constant. I loved him fiercely for that.

"I have to confess that we are still a bit out of sorts," Ms. Marta told him. "We had a few very difficult days," she repeated.

"I'm sorry," he said, and it was obvious that he was. "Please take all the time you need to recover, and when you feel up to it, I would like you to take a look at our chores scheduler. Here at Morgana House, we all chip in and work together to make this work."

I noticed he was holding a clipboard with a large stack of papers. This timeline didn't seem to have personal computing devices that were so ubiquitous in ours. I pointed to his clipboard. "Can we take a look? I think we…" I looked at Ms. Marta and the big dark bags under her eyes and amended, "I feel totally fine with helping."

He smiled at me. "Thank you, Hig. We don't usually require the patients to work, just their families." I felt my face fall—even Uncle Charlie didn't see me as a full human being here. "But I've always encouraged people to try," he added with a big smile. "Here, take a look at what appeals. And you too, ladies. I'm afraid helping out is not optional."

I read down the long list of chores, and Ms. Marta and Klaire leaned in to read along with me. There were kitchen duty, cleanup, laundry, gardening work, babysitting, carpentry and electrical, bookkeeping, help with medical exams—that job was starred with a notice that it required special training. The list was long, and there were many options, including teaching classes on various subjects. Curiously, that one didn't require additional expertise.

"I would like to help out with your garden," Ms. Marta said. I saw her eyes light up.

"Excellent!" Uncle Charlie practically beamed at her. "It's one of my favorite places here. We have a beautiful greenhouse up on top." He pointed to the ceiling. "We grow a lot of our own food there. It's not only saving us resources, but it's so much better than what we can get at the local markets. Wait until you try our salads. And our tomatoes are out of this world."

"Perfect," Ms. Marta said. "I've always liked working with plants. I have something of a knack for it. So put me down for that."

"We usually give folks a few days to adjust, so no pressure to start—"

"I would love to," Ms. Marta interrupted him. And I was

sure she would.

"I think I would like to help in the kitchen," Klaire volunteered. I was surprised, with her economics major; I was sure she would ask for a job in the office. But Klaire was full of surprises, always amazing ones. "But I have to be honest," she said with a shy smile, "I'm not a great cook. When I was younger, I helped my aunts in the kitchen before I left for school, but unfortunately, I haven't really learned much."

"I'm sure you'll pick it up in no time," Uncle Charlie reassured her. "Well—" He started to get up, but I stopped him.

"I know it's not on your list, but I would like to help Roger with Lucca, if that's okay?"

"You really don't have to, Hig."

"I want to," I insisted. "I think I could help...a little, and it would be good for me, too." I wanted...needed to feel useful, to feel fully human, to prove Uncle Charlie wrong about what he thought I could do.

"All right," Uncle Charlie agreed. He started to leave again, but Ms. Marta stopped him again.

"Charlie? You said that we didn't have to start helping right away." He nodded. "While I would love to go and take a look at your roof garden as soon as possible, I was hoping that Klaire would take Hig out to explore the neighborhood for bit around here. I think it would be good for him." I was about to protest, but she squeezed my fingers so hard that I almost yelled out. "Would that be all right?" Ms. Marta asked again.

"But of course!" Uncle Charlie said, that beatific smile flashing across his tired face. "Let's make sure your drone is fully charged first. And I'll give you a little map of our area. One of the kids from our program drew it. She is a true talent."

"Perfect. Thank you," Ms. Marta said, and finally Uncle Charlie was able to leave.

"Why?" I asked when I was sure no one was able to hear

us.

"I want you two to go and figure out if there is a Kismet meeting somewhere in the neighborhood," she said. "And good work, Klaire. The kitchen is a very communal place, and you will learn a lot by volunteering there. And I have similar hopes for their garden."

Klaire beamed back at her. God, I didn't even think of that. My women...my beautiful caretakers were so much smarter than me. I was one lucky guy.

✳✳✳

Uncle Charlie checked out my drone and in the process taught me some of the basic maintenance that it required. It was all those things I should have known but of course had never learned. He also gave us a color copy of a child's drawing of streets surrounding Morgana House. It was one of those illustration-like maps that had drawings of actual houses and even people walking the streets. By the amount of detail, it was obvious that the illustration started out as a much larger drawing and was scaled down to a practical-size paper by the copying process. So there was some tech here. A toyshop and a candy store were clearly marked, but so were a city civic center and a police station, and even a library. But while childish, the map seemed to actually be useful. There were at least ten blocks of streets indicated in either direction. Morgana House was the central and largest building depicted on this map, and the most detailed. It even had some trees on its roof, although we didn't see any when we first arrived. But then we arrived late at night—the evening train from Carolina to New Amsterdam took almost three hours and by then it was too dark to see much of anything. At the station, we got picked up by a specially sent drone, which delivered us directly to the front door of Morgana House. We didn't get to see a great deal on the way, other than the buildings were generally shorter in this timeline. Nothing was built above ten stories or so, and there was less electrical illumination. New Amsterdam was a much sleepier city than the bustling metropolis we came from.

As we got ready to go, Klaire helped me float back to the zipper door.

"Hey! Where are you going?" Uncle Charlie called after us.

"Out?"

"We only use the front door for new arrivals," Uncle Charlie said. "Please use the side door like everyone else." He pointed to a corridor behind him.

When we out of the earshot, Klaire said, "It's obvious that we couldn't have known not to use the front door."

"I agree, Uncle Charlie's reaction was a bit strange," I said. "But there are many strange things here. I'm sure we are just as strange to him."

"You shouldn't call him Uncle," Klaire said. "That sounds very strange coming from you." I agreed, but it was going to be a difficult habit to break. "So," she said, "where do you want to go?"

"Let's walk about the city and just look around. I feel a bit lost about...everything."

She agreed, and we stepped outside into the strange metropolis of a strange timeline where we were most definitely strangers in the strange land.

Everything was different. Even the smell was different. Since there were no internal combustion engines and no cars, that tell-tell odor of exhaust that was always there in our timeline was simply missing here. Instead, there were strange aromas of plants and cooking smells and perhaps a distant hint of disinfectant, just like the one at Morgana House. But the most striking thing was the total lack of vehicular traffic on the street—the entire pavement between buildings was devoted to pedestrians and plants. Drone traffic—and there was some of that, although it was mostly larger, bus-like drones—was assigned third and fourth story corridors above the street surface, way above the tallest treetops. Each elevation of drone traffic was dedicated to a particular direction. It seemed very efficient, except I didn't see how people changed directions or made stops until Klaire pointed out "bus stops" and traffic flow exchangers at certain street corners. They were hard to see because of all of the trees—down the center of all the streets we could observe was a green median, full of trees, shrubs, and some kind of grass. It was winter, and most trees had lost their leaves—one of the reasons we were able to spot the drone stops up above our heads—but shrubs looked rather green, and so did the strange grass.

The streets were all curved; nothing was straight in New Amsterdam. From the map Uncle Charlie...Charlie gave us, it was plain that the whole city was planned as a chain of concentric circles with parks at their centers, like bullseyes. It was truly lovely, even as we could only see a small portion of each street, for even the "radial spoke" streets that connected the great circular ones were curving.

"It feels like they used one of those pattern-maker spinner toys to do their city planning," Klaire said.

"A spirograph?" I asked. I used to play with one as a kid.

"Yes, one of those. I like it. I feel like with every step there is a surprise, something new comes in view."

"It makes it hard to orient oneself," I said. I wanted fewer surprises. I felt we had our share, more than our share in the last few days. My senses were overwhelmed by newness. I couldn't process more.

"Look, over there," Klaire said excitedly. "That must be the toy shop from our map." She pointed to the map and then to the building. She was obviously right.

The first two floors of the structure were painted red and decorated with children's books illustrations—even in a different timeline, one could tell drawings meant for children, even if the characters were not familiar to me. There was a large sign with letters made out of animals: *Missy's Kuklas.* The name sounded vaguely familiar, but I couldn't place it. The next two stories above the toyshop were offices, maybe? They seemed more officious somehow. The toyshop building was one of those with a drone stop off the third and fourth floors. There was a big round elevator that took people up and down the side of the building to access the public transportation from street level. Above that, there were several more stories of living apartments. At least that was my best guess— the windows all had different styles of coverings, some with colorful prints, some with window blinds, some lit, some not. They just didn't look like offices...at least not like offices from our timeline.

"They had to build all of these buildings to match the curve lines of the street," Klaire said. "This is wonderful engineering."

Looking at Klaire's face made me want to love this city too, but it wasn't home. Everything felt different, alien. Perhaps it was because I was trailing Klaire in my medically necessary drone, or the diapers I had to wear, or the fear I felt for what could have happened to my little sister. If Nona fell into another timeline, she was all alone there. At least I had Klaire and Ms. Marta. So while I couldn't share Klaire's joy of discovery, I tried not to ruin it for her. I floated carefully along, trying to avoid hitting plants and buildings. The few pedestrians we encountered were kind enough to get out of my way. I saw pity in their stares. I was the only person in a medical drone, the only crippopotamus out on the town. My mood was very dark indeed.

We kept walking, following the great circle of the street on which Morgana House was situated. If we never made any turns, we should theoretically get right back to it. Theoretically, because our hand-drawn map wasn't big enough to show the full circle. We needed to get a better map.

"Why don't we visit the civic center?" I suggested. It was indicated on our map, but we would have to traverse a few side streets to get there. "I bet they have tourist information and maps there."

"Sure, Hig. We can do that." Klaire didn't sound enthusiastic.

"We can finish the full circle and then go, if you like," I compromised. I didn't really care. I just wanted to find what we needed so we could escape this timeline.

"I saw something up ahead that I wanted to check out," she said. "Could we do that first? It looked interesting—a round structure like the ones back in Carolina. And it was taller than the others."

"Sure." I was very willing to do most anything to make Klaire happy. Floating a few extra blocks was no big deal, really. It wasn't like I had to push the wheels of my wheelchair myself. This drone did all the work. I just had to make sure not to fall off or knock down too many people in my way.

"And we should check out one of the central parks, too," she said. "We will be able to tell a lot about the culture from the kinds of recreating people do around here." That made sense, so we kept walking.

So far, we had seen nothing above twelve stories, and construction above seven was unusual. Most buildings were a combination of ground-level shops and apartment buildings with a few office buildings in between. All were curved to match the street, but some had secondary curves, like ripples at the bottom of a pond, to accommodate the delicate balconies on the sides. Each balcony was dripping with plants. The whole city, as far as we could see, was very green.

The drone stops all looked like four-story glass tubes, sometimes attached to adjacent building and sometimes free standing. The architectural style of New Amsterdam was nothing like the small town we arrived at first, with its combination of strange old-fashioned Dutch construction and round glass and concrete structures. There was more uniformity here, even if all the buildings sported wild color schemes and whimsical facades. My mom would have liked it here, I thought and then realized I could ask her directly if she did.

I pulled out my water bottle and took a big swig to control the nausea caused by thinking of my mother in two timelines. Klaire didn't notice. She seemed to be adjusting to the timeline transition far better than I. I hadn't seen her make that sick face in a while. It just figured I would be lousy at overcoming the SHITs, too.

I floated behind Klaire, numb to the wild differences between our old timeline and this one. I found it difficult to focus and pay attention. I realized that my back should have been hurting—or would have if I was back at home with the same injury—but the drone seat was too comfortable, too accommodating, arresting minor and even major aches and pains. I hated that.

Suddenly, Klaire stumbled backward into my lap. If I were paying attention to my surroundings, I would have stopped when she did. But I didn't, and my drone bumper cut her off at the knees, making her fall back on top of me. She yelped, and I gasped. The drone was able to hold up both of us.

"Sorry," we said at the same time. I should have gotten a thrill from holding the girl that I was crazy about on my lap, but I couldn't feel my legs; I barely felt anything below my waist. All I could think about was whether Klaire could feel the diaper underneath my sweat pants. I couldn't wait for her to get off.

"Sorry," she said again. "I should have been paying attention." It was my fault that she fell, but I was too flustered to stop her from apologizing. "It's just...just..." She finally managed to get back on her feet. We both looked around to see if people were horrified by what just happened. But there were few people out, and no one seemed to care...or they were too polite to notice. "I'm sorry, Hig," Klaire said again. "It's just that I thought I saw your mother up ahead."

"What?"

"Your mother. Moira Labelle? Well, I guess she is not your mother in this timeline." Her face turned a bit green and she swallowed hard but was able to continue almost instantly. I, in the meantime, had to grab hold of the armrests of my drone to keep from losing it. "You okay?" she asked. I couldn't answer, but I did nod slightly. "Sorry. It was just so unexpected." She looked in the direction she presumably saw my mother. I looked too. There was no one there. "I think she turned at the next corner, over there. Do you think we should follow her? See where she is going?"

"Why?" That was as much as I could muster at that moment.

"Well, I'm not really sure. Just a feeling, I guess. The way she was walking, furtively, like she was afraid people were following her. But even if I'm wrong and she was just out on an errand, shouldn't we try to make contact? I mean we are trying to learn things, right?"

I was starting to feel better, but my thinking was still sluggish.

"Hig?"

"Yes, of course. And I'm sorry I ran into you. It was totally my fault."

"Sure thing. It will probably take time to learn how to drive that thing," she said with an easy smile, completely misunderstanding what I was feeling. Just as well.

I demonstrably fiddled with the controls of my drone, which had shut itself off during the accident—a safety feature I was unaware of—and got it back up in the air and ready to go. Klaire turned to follow my mother. There was purposefulness to her walk now; she was no longer a gaping tourist.

We turned the corner into one of those side alleys that curved away from the grand circular avenues of the city. These side streets were narrower, or at least the one we were on was. There was no public drone traffic up above, and we saw no pedestrians in the limited arced view we had of the street up ahead. Since the buildings were closer together, the median planters grew only shrubs and grasses, no grand trees. But because of the closeness, some building had bridges between them on multiple levels with plants cascading down like living curtains. It was an interesting design, certainly very pretty. Even I could admit that.

"She isn't here," Klaire said, trying to look beyond the curve. "It's just been a few moments since she turned, so she must have gone inside one of these buildings." That made sense.

We slowly made our way up the street. There was a slight echoey sound to Klaire's footsteps. My drone, of course, hardly made a sound. I felt a giant drop hit my face and jumped. Klaire saw and grinned, pointing to the hanging plants above my head. I wiped my face with my sleeve and moved from under the steady drip of water.

"This place is so different from—" She gagged, I gave her a water bottle, and she drank, quickly overcoming her sickness. "I guess it's stupid to compare," she finally said. "How are you doing, Hig?"

"Perhaps not as good as you," I said honestly. "But I'm trying."

"Yeah, mind control is difficult to master."

She walked on, peering into each doorway on either side of the street. If she spread her arms wide, she could have almost touched the buildings on both sides. She stopped suddenly, and I almost ran her down again.

"Look." She pointed to a small carving of a galaxy just above an old wooden door. If she hadn't been looking so carefully, we would have been certain to miss it. "Should we go inside?"

I fingered the little pin I got from the social worker in the Carolina hospital. "Here." I pulled it out and gave it to Klaire. "Pin it on. Perhaps it will help with admission."

She took it and turned it over and over in her fingers, catching a few rays of sun that reached into the depth of this canyon-like street. The pin sparkled with deep blues and magentas and amber golds of the glass cloisonné design. "It's very pretty. Where did you get it?"

"A woman back in Carolina gave it to me. I think it was like a 'sorry you were robbed of your robe' or something."

"Hmm. This whole Kismet thing feels like a cult," she said, pinning the colorful pin to her shirt, under the jacket. I saw the cleverness right away—she could flash the pin or hide it in a hurry. "Everyone seems so ambivalent about the whole thing," she continued. "It's like they are tolerant, or pretend to be, of the believers and yet embarrassed about it at the same time. Charlie, in particular, the way he made us hide our robes."

"The police officers down south were strange about it, too. And the woman who gave me the pin made it into a big secret. I agree with you, it's all very strange."

I moved my drone over to the door, and it swung open automatically. Klaire gave a little cry of surprise.

"Do you think your drone will fit through the door?" she asked. It was narrow, certainly smaller than any of the doors I had to go through so far.

"We can try." I pushed ahead. The side edges of my drone touched the doorframe, and I was just about to back out when my drone did something very cool. It sort of collapsed on itself like some clever origami structure, neatly making itself narrow enough to fit through the door while still keeping afloat. I had a feeling that I wouldn't be able to move far this way, but I didn't have to. Beyond the entrance, there was a large hall lit by thousands of little lights...like stars in the galaxy. I floated inside, and Klaire followed. We were in what looked like the Church of Kismet.

Chapter Twenty-Two: Church of Kismet

The door closed with a soft thud as soon as we were inside. Klaire immediately turned and walked back. The door opened for her again, allowing her to leave.

"Well, that's good to know," she said. "And hey. Look at the wall, Hig." I turned around and saw dozens of galaxy robes hanging off the pegs on the wall next to the exit. "Do you think it's for people to wear?" Klaire asked. "You know, like a basket of spare yarmulkes in a synagogue for men who come without or one of those whore dresses they give out in churches for women with open-shoulder dresses?" *Whore dresses?* I'd never heard of either of those and so didn't really have an opinion. "I think we should put them on," Klaire said and took two. "Look."

I followed her gaze and saw a few people by the starlit stage in front. They all wore the same robes. So I guessed it made sense. Klaire put a robe over my shoulders; it looked ridiculous draped over the drone, and I had to worry that it would get caught in the motor. She, on the other hand, looked great. She always did.

"The quality is not as good as ours," she said. "Just cheap material without lining." That was true. But the robes Klaire and Ms. Marta got back at the Dream Land Music Festival were obviously exceptional; even the Carolina cops remarked on it. She walked around the back of my drone and pulled on neckline of the robe she just placed on my shoulders. "Huh. It says on the label it's made by Siming Enterprises."

"Just like your robes," I said. It was always strange to run into these direct parallels between timelines.

"Come on, let's learn things." And she walked on toward the Kismet followers. I hung back.

"Hello!" Klaire called to the robed group from halfway across the hall. "Is it okay for us to just come in? We are new in town."

Everyone turned in unison, and I could clearly see that one of the people in robes was my mother. She had that ethereal quality about her...and her long blond hair was easily visible, cascading down the front from under the sides of her hood. Klaire approached them and stopped a few feet away. "Hello," she said again, more tentative this time. I got ready to zoom over there and knock all of those people down like bowling pins with my drone if they gave her trouble...everyone but my mother. But a woman stepped up to Klaire and gave her a hug, and my mother turned to me and waved me over. So I slowly floated to join them. I didn't know what or how I was feeling about all of this. I just had to remember not to say "Mom" accidentally.

"Klaire, isn't it?" the woman that just hugged Klaire said. "Moira was just telling us about your family. You had an unfortunate encounter at the Kismet gathering down south?"

"Yes," Klaire stumbled out. "Our stuff was stolen. Hig's drone," she motioned to me over her shoulder, "and a few other things. IDs and such. It was scary."

"Of course it was," the woman said. "I'm Daila Megan." The name and her voice sounded familiar for some reason.

"Pleasure to meet you, Mevrouw Megan," Klaire said, and everyone laughed. It was a fake laugh to acknowledge a faux pas. "I don't understand," Klaire said. "Did I say something wrong?"

"Daila is a designation of my office, my child. I'm surprised you haven't heard of it, but perhaps you use other honorifics where you come from?"

Klaire looked from face to face, totally lost. I pushed myself forward, coming to her rescue. I might not be able to tackle bad guys for her, but I could certainly provide a distraction during an awkward moment, giving her time to think of something credible to say.

"Daila Moira?" I said, taking a chance. "You work at Morgana House too, right?"

She gave me a warm smile and nodded. I noticed that she was no longer furtive in her movements and expressions. My mom looked like she belonged among these people.

"I figured you two would make it here eventually," she said. "Did Charlie tell you where to go?"

"No," Klaire said. "I think he is uneasy with our Kismet beliefs. He told us to put away our own robes. We borrowed yours. I hope that's okay?"

"Of course it is, my child. That's what they are there for," Daila Megan said in a very patronizing voice. "And you are welcome to bring yours here, of course, if keeping them at Morgana House is such a problem." She glanced pointedly at my mother, and Mom withered under her gaze. I really disliked that woman. She seemed to be a bully. "We'll take good care of them here for you," Daila Megan continued. "Daila Moira told us that one of your robes was stolen. The prejudices against us and Kismet run at an all-time high. Unfortunately, we all have to be especially careful nowadays."

Other hooded Dailas nodded in agreement, and Klaire

and I did so as well. Mirroring was always a great way to gain trust. We were taught that in our marketing class back in college...back in another life...back in another... I coughed to hide my discomfort at thinking the "wrong" thoughts. Klaire instantly passed me our water bottle. I drank deeply to push down the sickness.

"You take good care of your brother," my mother said. "It's lovely to see."

"He is really my god-brother," Klaire said. "But we are very close."

"Charlie told me about Hig's unfortunate accident. What a wicked twist of fate not to get access to medical care when he needed it most," my mother...Daila Moira continued. "Do you know why he wasn't given the treatments?"

Klaire shook her head. I noticed that no one was really talking to me. They were all talking about me, in front of me, like I was some sort of village idiot. I had a broken spine, not a damaged brain. It was not okay, but I was so stunned that I didn't know how to stop it. It had been a long time since I was so pointedly ignored in social gatherings. I was obviously out of practice. I was grinding my teeth in anger...and shame.

"...too young," Klaire was saying. I missed what she said before, I was too upset. "I don't really remember it at all. Hig? Do you remember?"

I just shook my head. I didn't have a good answer. And it pained me that my inability to come up with one just reinforced what these Dailas thought about me.

"Well of course not," Daila Megan said, giving my arm a condescending pat. I had to restrain myself from pushing her away. "But you came to the right place."

"Really?" Klaire asked.

"Sure, my child. We work hard to guide fate into a better future."

It made no sense—fate by definition was what was destined to be. How could these women, for they were all women, believe that they could "guide" fate to better outcomes? It was crazy. No wonder Uncle Charlie didn't want to have anything to do with these Kismet crazies.

"And how do you do that?" Klaire asked innocently. She was focused on what we had to do, obviously. I was just fuming...stupidly.

"Well, I assume your family went down to the Carolina event to try to find an alternative fate for your *god*-brother," said Daila Megan, emphasizing *god* in the god-brother. When Klaire didn't respond, she continued. "There are many gatherings that are not true followers of Kismet."

"There are?" Klaire said. She actually batted her eyelashes. Her acting could win awards.

"People spend a lot of their credits to change their lives. There are always some who are willing to take advantage of the unfortunate," Daila Megan said. "You would be surprised how many people come to us with similar stories. Your family is not unique. And we work hard to help change happen."

"Thank you," Klaire said. "So what can you do for us? For Hig?"

"Well, now that Daila Moira told us your story, and we have had a chance to see for ourselves the extent of your *problems...*" She nodded over to me when she said the word, like being in a wheelchair...medical drone...and not being able to walk was the end of the world. These people were sick. But I held my tongue and didn't say anything. "Now that we know how bad your fate is," she repeated, "we can start the process of asking for a change. It will take time, of course."

"Of course," Klaire said.

"But there is another big conference in a few months—"

"In Iceland," I cut in. They all turned on me like I did

something unspeakable. "Yes, I know about Iceland," I said, enjoying their discomfort. "In fact, we were planning on attending." There, I hoped they choked on their precious events.

"Well, good," Daila Megan said after a few heartbeats, a fake smile plastered all over her face that never reached her eyes. "We'll work on that, shall we?"

"Thank you, Daila Megan," Klaire said. "Daila Moira. Everyone. Thank you." She bowed her head slightly to each robed woman in front of us. I pointedly refused to do so.

"Don't forget to hang up the robes on your way out," Daila Megan said. It was a dismissal and an accusation that we would steal their precious robes.

I grabbed my controls and made a wide turn, almost running over these Dailas. They jumped out of my way, and it made me happy. It was a petty thing, I knew, but it still made me happy.

"Bunch of old crones," Klaire murmured when we stepped outside again and the door closed. I loved her for that.

Chapter Twenty-Three: Same But Different

Klaire went to help in the kitchen. Ms. Marta was, presumably, working in the greenhouse up on the roof. I went to look for Roger and his son. I was directed to a room on the second floor. When I asked about the stairs to get there, Charlie laughed and pointed at my drone.

"Just zoom on up, Hig."

Just zoom on up...I hovered over to the center of the great room and used my elevation controls to slowly rise to the level of the second-floor balcony. I hated to have to use my drone, but this gave me a real thrill. I should have done something like that out in the city, when Klaire and I were wandering about. "I don't know what's around that corner, Hig," she could have said. I could have pulled her onto my lap, and we would have zoomed on high above the buildings and seen the whole city. And Klaire would have laughed and laughed... It was a good fantasy.

I saw Roger right away—the door to their room was open. Roger was sitting in the chair and reading something to Lucca, who was reclining in a complicated drone contraption. His personal mobility equipment needs were greater than mine. Lucca had to be able to "stand" and sit and move, but Roger was the one with the controls. Lucca's drone was remote-control operated.

Roger saw me though the open door and waved. I waved back and slowly flew toward the railing on the wraparound balcony that provided access to all the rooms on the second level of Morgana House.

Once I was safely outside their room, I called softly, "Do you mind if I come in? Charlie said it would be okay for me to volunteer to help you guys. Is it? Okay, that is?" I felt awkward. By volunteering like I did, I was implying that Roger couldn't handle his own son by himself, right? "If you would rather..." I started to say and backed off at the same time. Roger jumped up and grabbed the edge on my drone before I tumbled backward over the balcony railing. So much for providing support...

"Hig, isn't it?" Roger said after I was no longer teetering, ready to fall head-first onto the stone floor below. "Charlie mentioned you wanted to work with Lucca. I'm thrilled to have you. And I'm sure Lucca will be too. Shall we go inside?"

Roger in this timeline was thinner and more drawn than his counterpart in mine. His hair was grayer, and the face sported many more deep lines. But he grinned at me, and I saw that some of those lines were created by frequent smiles. I had imagined Roger as deeply unhappy, but my first impression might have been wrong.

"Thank you for helping me and letting me assist with your son," I said. This man literally just saved my life. My heart was still beating too fast.

"You know how many people volunteered to help Lucca in all the time we've spent in Morgana House?" he asked. I just shook my head; I had no idea. "Three. Charlie and his sister, Moira, and now you. I'm thrilled to have you with us. Lucca needs to interact with more people. Human contact is so important. Please sit down." He offered me the chair he just sat in, the only chair in the room, and then smacked his forehead with his hand and laughed, pointing to my drone. "See? I'm so not used to visitors. Please find a place where you are comfortable, Hig. Can I call you Hig?"

"Yes, please." I floated over to where Lucca was reclining. He was following our interaction with his eyes...sort of. "Lucca, I'm Hig," I said and smiled. The boy's expression changed a bit; it could have been an attempt at a smile.

"There we go!" Roger said enthusiastically. "I was just reading to Lucca. *Fairy Tales from the Big City.* Ever heard of it, Hig?"

I shook my head and looked at Lucca. He was older than me, not really a boy. But he was small, and his bones were easily visible underneath a thin coat of yellowed skin. His long fingers were twisting and untwisting, almost like spider legs, but not obviously under his own control. I tried to catch Lucca's eyes—they were big and gray and dim—but they never focused on me or on anything for long. I had to stop trying, for it was making me uncomfortable. Instead I studied the rest of his features. Lucca had a long, straight nose, almost bird-like, and a thin, long face. I saw some of Roger in him, but it was all distorted; it was like all the individual bits were there and had a familial resemblance, but they were put together wrong. There was a slight smear of drool on the corner of his thin lips. His teeth seemed big, oversized for his mouth, and they moved, continuously grinding. His hair was dark, and there was a lot of it, lovingly brushed from a strong widow's peak into a braid going down his back. Behind one of his ears, a scar was just visible underneath the hair. Our Roger's Lucca died of glioblastoma when he was a little boy. I wondered if it was the cancer in this timeline.

"Well, this book is Lucca's favorite." Roger kept on talking.

"We've been reading it together for years."

"I can read it to him," I volunteered. "This way it will be a new experience for both of us." I looked at Lucca but couldn't read him. Roger, on the other hand, was obviously thrilled. Perhaps I couldn't do much for his son, but I could make Roger's day a bit brighter. That seemed worth it.

I took the book from Roger's hand and flipped to the start of a new story: "The Frogs in the Walls." I read with feeling and tried to assign different voices to different characters. When I occasionally looked up, Roger smiled at me. Lucca was a total enigma.

I read for a few hours, through a few stories, until dinner was called. Frankly, I don't remember most of what I read; I kept thinking about Lucca's life. What was it like to hang there day after day, drooling, unable to control one's body, unable to think? I didn't know about the last part, of course. I just couldn't imagine what was going through Lucca's head... if anything. Could he even pass a mirror test? It terrified me.

"Thank you for your help this afternoon," Roger said when I left them. He had to get Lucca ready for dinner.

✳✳✳

We met back at dinner. Our table was far enough away from everyone else's that we had some privacy—we could talk openly about our day, together and apart. Klaire quickly filled Ms. Marta in on our encounter with the church of Kismet and all those robed Dailas, including my mother. We decided that Ms. Marta would approach Moira and pump her for more information. They had struck up a friendship back during Ms. Marta's transition into our timeline, so perhaps there was some emotional connection left over. And anyway, I couldn't do it. I felt like I would simply fall apart if left alone with my mother. That settled, we moved on to our chores.

"The rooftop garden is amazing," Ms. Marta was saying, her eyes shining. She almost looked young in her obvious enthusiasm. "They grow all of their own greens and vegetables." The food at Morgana House was mostly vegetarian, although very well spiced. If there was animal protein, besides eggs, I hadn't noticed it. Not that I was complaining. They fed us and took care of us and asked for very little in return...so far. "They even have chickens, for eggs only, of course," Ms. Marta added.

"Chickens, really?" That got Klaire's attention. I had to laugh, and she punched me. "What? I happen to like chickens. They are very friendly birds with unique personalities."

"I remember," I said. "But you know, when Klaire and I walked around the neighborhood, we didn't pass a single produce market or store, not a one. Strange, right?"

"In the kitchen, I saw packaged food in addition to the baskets from the rooftop garden," Klaire said. "So they must have some markets."

"Food can be apportioned and delivered according to some rules that we are simply not familiar with." Ms. Marta shrugged. "Don't judge everything by the measures you are used to. Things are different here, but that doesn't mean they are bad or that they don't work well for these people."

"True," Klaire said. "We haven't seen much poverty out in the open."

"And we are here, completely taken care of," Ms. Marta pointed out. "We had nothing and nothing to offer. And yet all of our needs are being met so far."

"Yes, so far," Klaire echoed. "It's strange, right?" We all agreed, feeling the same unease, even expressing it with the same words. "So my job in the kitchen was really to help these two women, these moms," Klaire continued, "to make enough food for dinner for everyone who lives here. It was busy. We didn't talk much beyond 'pass the carrots.' So I don't think I've learned much. But the women were very friendly. They were nice to me and took the time to explain how to do things the way they wanted them done. It wasn't confrontational, just not much time for gossip. Sorry I didn't manage to learn much."

"Hmm. I was first shown the garden by this young girl, about your age, I guess, " Ms. Marta said. "She has a younger brother living here. The boy was born without arms. They were both very nice. When the girl realized that I understood something about plants, she took me to see Charlie. He assigned me to teach a gardening class."

"Did you?" I asked.

"Tomorrow, maybe. There wasn't enough time today. How did your volunteer time go?"

"I almost died getting to the second floor," I said, making sure to sound like I was kidding. "Roger and I bonded over him saving my life, and then I read a book for two hours. That's all."

"I see," Ms. Marta said. "How did you find Lucca?"

I considered my answer for a bit. "I don't understand," I finally said. "I wouldn't want to be alive if I were like that. It seems cruel."

"Was he in pain? Badly treated?"

"Oh, no. Roger is like an angel, a self-sacrificing angel. He does everything for his son. And Lucca is not obviously in any discomfort. But I just don't know if anyone would even know if he was. I don't think Lucca would know. He seemed so empty. It was truly unsettling."

"Can Lucca speak?" Klaire asked. "Can he communicate at all?"

"I don't think so. I was reading, and it felt like it didn't even matter. Roger was enjoying it, I hope. But Lucca? I don't think he cared one way or another."

"How do you know?"

"How could I tell?" I really couldn't.

"Back home, we had computers that let people like that communicate, even those who could control just one muscle in their face," Klaire said and gagged loudly. People turned to see what was wrong. She waved weakly and pretended to cough, like there was something stuck in her throat. Ms. Marta got up and demonstrably patted her on the back. "I was just trying to say that Lucca might need something to help him communicate," Klaire managed to finish.

"They don't have computers here," I said and instantly regretted it.

"There are many low-tech ways of communicating," Ms. Marta said after we were done being sick. "I've heard of Ouija boards being used by people to spell things out. There are also card systems with images of objects and verbs that help those who can't read express themselves. I saw great apes use those quite effectively, too. Perhaps you can bring it up with Roger."

"Good idea," I said. But I didn't think so. Lucca felt less than human to me...less than an ape. Apes had emotions; Lucca felt vacant. I didn't understand Roger. And I prayed that I could end my life if something like that ever happened to me. I shuddered thinking back to how I almost smashed, headfirst, on this cold stone floor. What if I lived? I didn't want to live if I couldn't be me.

"I would feel horrible if something happened to you," Klaire said quietly, as if reading my thoughts. "I wouldn't give up on you. I understand how Roger can't give up on his son. You should talk to him next time, ask him what happened to Lucca."

"By the way, Roger keeps looking this way," Ms. Marta said. "And every time I catch him at it, he pretends he is just staring into space. But I wonder..."

"Yes?"

"Talk with him, Hig. Find out his story. I have a feeling it might be important."

***

A loud pounding woke me up in the middle of the night. I heard lots of commotion just outside of my door, but I couldn't manage to get out of bed without help. My condition seemed to be getting worse. I felt less and less in my lower body, and I didn't seem to have as much strength or energy overall. It was freaking me out. I lay in bed and listened as people ran around and talked excitedly. I couldn't catch the actual words, but it didn't sound bad. Not like a fire or some major emergency.

After a time, things quieted down again, and someone knocked softly on my door.

"Hig? Are you asleep?" It was Klaire.

"No. What's happening out there?"

She stepped inside and closed the door without turning on my lights. "They had a delivery," she whispered.

"What kind of delivery?"

"Twins. Someone left two little kids just outside the zipper door. They pounded the handle just like we did and ran, leaving the babies."

"Just like that?"

"Yeah, just like."

"Huh. What will happen to them now?"

"Somehow, opening that door notified the authorities of people asking for Morgana House sanctuary. I don't really get that, but there will be visits from city hall, Charlie said." That explained Charlie's instance that we use the side door. "But in the meantime, Mama said that she would take the night shift caring for the babies. She said she wasn't sleeping anyway. And then tomorrow we will all get a chance to meet the new members of the Morgana family."

"So they take unwanted babies, too?" I asked. "Is there something wrong with them? Do they have a way of caring for special needs kids here?"

Klaire shrugged. "I didn't really see anything obviously wrong. Two arms, two legs, twenty digits each, I think. They are very cute. I'd say they are about eight months old maybe? They have some teeth already. That's all I know."

"Huh."

"Well, that and that Mama was over the moon with the babies. The way she was holding and cooing over them..."

We looked into each other's eyes. Even in the dark, I could see that Klaire was worried. I felt a knot in my stomach too—Ms. Marta slid into our timeline to care for Nona and me. She wanted to have children to raise. And here were two perfect babies in need of someone to love them. *Coincidence?*

"Yeah," Klaire finally said. "Seems like a very crazy serendipity to me too. Well, I'll see you in the morning, Hig. Get some sleep." She leaned in, gave me a very chaste kiss on my forehead, and without another word furtively slipped out of the door.

I lay there in the dark and listened to the sounds of Morgana House. I spent the rest of the night thinking, but all my deep thoughts came down to this: I had to get out of this timeline before it was too late, before I was trapped here forever as a cripple with an adoring sister to care for me.

Chapter Twenty-Four: Crippopotamus Again

No one came for me in the morning. I tried to lift myself up with the help of my drone, but I just couldn't get the sling around myself. I crashed to the floor and couldn't get up. It was horrible. Even the thought of calling for help...what if Klaire came? I couldn't stand that, so I lay there halfway under my bed, with a full diaper, and wished myself dead.

When the knock came, I didn't bother to answer. Ms. Marta would let herself in if she was worried about me...she clearly wasn't. Uncle Charlie should have come a long time ago, but he obviously forgot all about me. And no one else was allowed in.

The knocking persisted, and my fear grew. I considered maneuvering my drone to block the door and keep everyone out. But before I could do anything, my door cracked just a smidgen.

"Hig? This is Roger and Lucca. Can we come in?"

"No!"

"You were supposed to come and work with us after breakfast, but you never came. We waited and waited."

"Sorry."

"Well, we are worried you. I asked, and you weren't at

breakfast. Can we come in, please?"

I didn't know what to do. But of all the people in Morgana House, Roger was the least objectionable. At some point Klaire might start to worry and come looking for me. She couldn't find me like this. I'd rather die.

"Could you perhaps call Charlie or Mevrouw Marta for me?" I asked.

"I wish I could," Roger said. "They had to take the babies to city hall for some paperwork early this morning."

So that's why they didn't come. It made sense. But I was still stuck here on the floor, unable to get up, even to change myself. "When do you think they will be back?" I asked, trying to hide the fear in my voice.

"I don't know, Hig. It's city hall—it could be fast, or it could take all day. That's why Charlie took your godmother. He needed help with the babies while he dealt with the government bureaucracy."

"I see." I was screwed. I again considered barricading myself in with the drone until Charlie and Ms. Marta came back. If I didn't eat or drink for a day, it would be fine. I was sure I would be able to get my drone to eventually obey. "I'm good, Roger. Thank you for coming by."

But he didn't give up. "Hig? It's okay to ask for help, you know."

"I'm good."

"You are on the floor." Roger's whole head poked through, and he saw me sprawled there.

"Just resting."

"Well, perhaps you can read to us in here. Lucca and I don't mind."

"Roger, I—"

"Hig. Please let me help you. It will be our little secret. I promise."

I was so embarrassed, I was practically crying. Couldn't people just leave me alone? A sob ripped out of my chest... *traitor.* But once I started crying, I just couldn't stop. It was all horrible. I was horrible. This timeline was horrible. I had no control over anything, including myself.

I felt Roger gently lifting me back onto my bed. Lucca was in the room too; he just stared into space as his dad changed me and put on clean clothing. He got me situated in my drone. And once I was sitting in clean clothing with hair and teeth washed and brushed, I felt more human. Somehow, Roger managed to help without taking away my dignity.

"Thank you," I said.

"It was my pleasure to help," he said with a big smile. "Why don't we go up to the roof garden? Lucca loves it there, and there is a place to make tea. I managed to smuggle some cookies from the kitchen," he added with a mischievous grin.

I couldn't even say thank you. I just nodded.

We spent the rest of the day up on the roof garden, reading Lucca stories and drinking tea and eating cookies and cakes. Roger carried out a whole basketful of sweets from the kitchen.

By dinnertime, I didn't even feel like I wanted to die.

✳✳✳

The next few days flew by. I'd spent all my time helping Roger and his son. I did as Klaire suggested; I cut out some images from old magazines and made communication cards for Lucca. The boy hadn't caught on right away, but we were both hopeful, and neither Roger nor I really knew what we were doing. So it was all early experimentation. I was actually excited.

Roger, in turn, helped me get out of bed in the mornings,

which was becoming more and more difficult with each passing day. Both Charlie and Ms. Marta offered to help, and Ms. Marta apologized profusely for abandoning me that way, but she did so while holding both twins up on her hips. All three, Ms. Marta and the babies, seemed so happy with each other. I couldn't pull her away from them. And Charlie looked exhausted. I don't know what happened during that city hall meeting, but he had to return there again and again. Something was obviously wrong, but there was no one to ask. Even Klaire looked exhausted. She had picked up extra chores from Ms. Marta and Charlie, working in the kitchen and doing some administrative duties on top of that to help out. Everyone at Morgana House shuffled around their chores to make things work. The place was humming.

When I had time to think about it, I freaked out that we could all just so easily fall into this crazy routine and get stuck in this timeline. And perhaps Ms. Marta would be happy here, raising her little twins. *But Klaire?* I assumed she wanted to go back. She had family, or at least her aunts, the only family I was aware of. She had career plans, and I didn't think being an assistant cook and a clerk were those. And I had to leave. Had to. Sometime by the fourth day in this timeline, I developed tremors in my arms in addition to losing most sensation in my legs. My body was deteriorating fast. I was running out of time.

"Hig?" Uncle Charlie's voice practically made me jump out of my drone...well, theoretically, practically, I couldn't do that even if I wanted to. He did startle me, though. "I would like you to meet Hugo Ulf. He works as a medical consultant for Morgana House."

I looked up and saw Dr. Ulf. *The* Dr. Ulf. *The same one.* My jaw dropped open, and I couldn't utter a word. Dr. Ulf's face became full of concern, and he leaned over me and placed his hand on my cheek and jaw in a freakishly familiar gesture.

"How are you doing, Hig?" he asked. "Can you feel my hand?" He placed his other hand on my knee. I definitely didn't feel that one.

"Yes," I lied. I hoped there was no drool on my face. "Nice to met you, Dr. Ulf."

He smiled, and I got the impression of a wolf's growl overlaying his expression. I vaguely remembered how nice this man was to me and my mother when I was a kid and then how he changed when he learned that I got better, chasing me to get some data for his paper, as if all I ever was to him was a test subject. This felt like yet another iteration of that Dr. Ulf. I noticed how deferential Uncle Charlie was with him, standing in a submissive pose, trying to please or appease. Roger too seemed nervous; he kept looking between us, trying to figure out what to do or not to do. What kind of power did Dr. Ulf have over me in this timeline?

I gagged. And everyone took a step back from me.

"Do you need a basket?" Uncle Charlie was the first to win his battle with fear and revert to his never-ceasing empathy.

"I'm okay," I said quickly. "Just too many cookies." I smiled weakly but noted that Roger looked worried and moved to block the cookies he had brought up for my afternoon tea from the kitchen. He'd been doing it every day since he learned of my sweet tooth. Funny, I never had one before.

"And here's Lucca." Dr. Ulf moved his gaze to Roger's son. "I see there hasn't been much progress."

"We are actually trying something new," Roger jumped in. "Hig here came up with an idea of making cards that represent different objects. We are hoping it will be a way for Lucca to communicate with us." Dr. Ulf stared blankly at him, and Roger's voice sort of petered out in the end, and he turned and stared at his feet, unable to meet Dr. Ulf's eyes.

"Why don't we go find Mevrouw Marta and the babies," Uncle Charlie said. "They are probably in the play area. We are all working hard to make them feel at home."

Dr. Ulf stood there and observed Lucca drool quietly for a few minutes and then turned and did the same to me. I didn't think I drooled, or at least not as much. Then he nodded to Uncle Charlie and turned to go. "Oh," he paused after a second, "why don't you come with us, Roger. You can tell me how this new card system works. Perhaps we can use it with other patients."

"It was actually Hig's idea—"

"Roger?"

"Yes, of course," Roger said. I noticed that his voice shook a little. "I'm sure Hig can watch over Lucca for a few minutes."

"Don't worry, Roger. I got this," I told him and watched the three of them leave the rooftop garden.

As soon as they were gone and the door closed, Klaire poked out from behind a bush of over-thriving tomatoes—Ms. Marta's influence, I was sure.

"Klaire?" I cried out. She put her fingers to her mouth and shushed me.

"What was that all about?" she asked in a hushed voice.

"I don't know," I said honestly. "But Roger and Uncle Charlie—"

"Hig!"

"And Charlie," I corrected myself, "both seem to be afraid of him. Do you know who he is? In this timeline, I mean." I swallowed hard, but Klaire seemed to be okay.

"Mama said that he works for the city," she said. I'd noticed that Klaire started calling Ms. Marta *Mama* even when it was just us. "He is here to inspect Morgana House to see that it meets the regulatory requirements."

"What requirements?"

"No idea. But it's been crazy. I had to file a stack of papers this big." She spread her arms out wide. "Listing everyone who lives here. How many patients they have versus how many volunteers, family, and staff. What are all of the different disabilities that our patients have. Crazy stuff. I didn't know the half it, and I got to meet virtually everyone here in the last few days."

"Huh."

"These are all nice people, Hig. I don't understand why the city is freaking out and giving Charlie such a hard time. But I don't really get how this whole operation is being supported. Does the city pay? Is this a not-for-profit shelter set up by Morgana family? If I weren't so busy, I'd go and check the city records. But... It's been crazy, Hig. Not at all like down in Carolina. Strange. And I'm sorry I didn't have much time to spend with you. So how are *you* doing?"

Everything Klaire said was very informative and valuable intel, but the way she said it... We had to get of here. It almost felt like Klaire was forgetting who she was...forgetting how we felt for each other.

"Hig?" She tried to get my attention when I didn't respond.

"Sorry, I was just thinking."

"Yeah, I'm trying to process all of this too," she said. "What could the city possibly want from us?"

"That's not what I've been thinking about." I looked into Klaire's face, and for a moment she stared blankly at me, and then her eyes lit up.

"Oh!" she said. "Funny, I keep forgetting."

"Yeah. I think this is what happens when the transition starts to become permanent."

"I have dreams of my life on the farm and my aunts, but none of it feels real." She shook her head; she looked bewildered. "Like that was all some strange dream or a story I've read. Like it wasn't real. *This* feels real, Hig."

"Klaire?" I took her hands in mine. She felt the slight tremor and gasped. "I can't stay here. I'm getting worse and worse with each day, each hour. I feel like if we don't leave soon, my life will... I just can't, Klaire. I can't stay."

She nodded and sniffed, a tear rolling down her cheek. "I will miss the people here. They've been more than nice to me; they feel like family. And I think for the fist time in my life I feel useful. Like I matter. What I do matters here."

"You always mattered, Klaire. Always." It was as if this timeline was trying to rip Klaire away from me. I felt horrifying dread watching her debate whether she wanted to stay or go.

"You know? The Beatles broke up in this history," she said.

"Really? When?"

"Right after they recoded the *Black Album*."

"I always liked the White one better," I said.

She chuckled and wiped away more tears. "I don't really want live in a timeline where the Beatles broke up," she said with a sad smile.

"Neither do I."

"When should we leave? Or I should say *how?* Do we go back to that Kismet house or something?"

"We should talk with my mom...Moira. Perhaps there is a meeting or a booth somewhere not too far from here. I don't think we can wait a few months for Iceland. It's just too far into the future. I'm scared that we won't last that long." I wouldn't, but I didn't say so out loud. Klaire could feel my body shaking. She knew.

"Yesterday morning, I found this under the door jamb," Klaire said and pulled out a piece of paper, a pamphlet with galaxies scrawled all over it as if by a child's hand. "I think Moira might have slipped it in through the door."

"You got it yesterday and didn't—"

"There was no time, Hig. I'm sorry. It says there is a large regional meeting of Kismet followers in Newfoundland a week from now."

"That's far."

"And it's the middle of winter. And we have no means of getting there. And only a week to find a way."

"We have to try," I said. "Did you talk with Ms. Marta?"

"About that." Klaire looked very uncomfortable. I squeezed her hands again—it was okay to tell me. I could take it. "I think she wants to stay here, Hig. Those babies... She is like a different woman. She loves them something fierce. I don't think she could leave them behind even for us...even for you."

I nodded, and it was my turn to cry. It felt like I was losing my mother all over again.

"I still can't stay, Klaire. I have to go. Even if I have to go alone."

She rushed into my arms, hugging me and sobbing into my shoulder. "I'm sorry, Hig. I'm sorry I almost forgot who I was, who we are. I won't forget again. I promise. We will be together. We will find our timeline. We will find Nona and bring her home. I promise."

And an evil thought passed through my mind—what if Nona didn't want to go back home either? What if she found a timeline where she truly belonged? Could I leave her? Could I force her to go home with me against her will? I felt sick.

Chapter Twenty-Five: Fellow Strangers

Klaire had to get back to work, so Lucca and I spent the rest of the afternoon alone together. I flashed cards, repeated words, pointed at things. I had no idea if I was getting through to him. I felt so bad for Roger. What was it like to take care of someone like that twenty-four-seven? What did it do to one's soul? At least I got to retreat to my room every night. I got a break. I didn't think Roger even wanted one. He was horrified when Dr. Ulf ordered him to leave his boy with me. What was it that Roger felt for his son? Was it love? Could you love someone when there was no chance for returned affection? After all these hours together, without Roger, I didn't even think Lucca noticed his dad wasn't there. Dogs at least showed devotion, but Lucca? I was so confused. But I worked with the cards nonetheless. I owed it to Roger to try.

"Tomato," I said as slowly and as distinctly as I could. I pointed to a photo of a red tomato we cut out from a magazine ad for home gardeners and then even showed Lucca a ripe tomato I'd picked from the bush Klaire hid behind earlier. Tomatoes in particular were doing very well under Ms. Marta's ministrations. Word, photo, actual fruit, repeat. I went though this sequence dozens of times and still had no

 Mirror Shards

idea if the boy even heard me. And Lucca wasn't even a boy... not that it mattered.

"There are my boys!" I heard Roger before I saw him. "Working hard, I see," he said and came over and gave Lucca a big hug. And then he just turned around and gave one to me, too. He was such a good man. I'd miss him.

"We've been focusing on words for various plants in the garden," I reported. "I figured we show the card and then the real thing. We let him smell it and touch it. He can even take a bite of a tomato, for example. Just hit every sense he's got. It might work?" I didn't believe, but I wanted Roger to be happy.

"Sounds wonderful. Thank you, Hig. And I hope I managed to explain your idea for communication cards to Mr. Ulf. He didn't seem very enthusiastic, unfortunately. Well, we'll just have to prove him wrong, right, Lucca?"

"So Mr. Ulf is not a medical doctor?" I asked. I almost added "in this timeline" but managed to stop myself.

Roger cocked his head and stared at me for a very long time. I was beginning to feel uncomfortable when he said, "Was Hugo Ulf a doctor where you came from?"

The world spun out of control. I felt sick. Bile rose all the way up into my throat. I felt dizzy; everything was spinning. I felt a water bottle in my hands and drank. I drank the whole thing, trying to get rid of the foul taste.

"Feel better?" Roger asked. I nodded. "It gets better with time."

"What? What gets better?" I asked, but I knew, of course. Roger was not from this timeline either.

"I suspected," he said. "Almost from the very first day I saw you three eating at the far corner table. There was an off-ness about you. And then I watched you all get sick. I recognized it. But you didn't say anything, so I didn't want to intrude."

"And you too?" I finally managed to ask.

"My son died in childbirth. I searched the world over trying to find a way to change that. Then I discovered Kismet, and here I am."

"But what happened to Lucca's parents in this timeline?" For some reason I could say the word now. Perhaps it was because Roger was like me, a stranger in a strange land. But he was a stranger who chose to stay; I had to find a way to leave.

"Lucca was abandoned as a child. I stopped searching when I found him."

"So you looked for Lucca?"

"Four timelines. Four different histories. In three, he died as a baby. In this one, he lived. It was a miracle. I found my son." Roger was crying softly. "I recognized him right away. And he me. I can't imagine being anywhere else."

I thought back on Roger from my timeline. He too was searching. That was probably why he was hanging out with Cherie. He saw her as a nexus for timeline crossing. And he grabbed on. Did he find his Lucca in the timeline he jumped into? I hoped he did.

"Did we know each other in your other timeline?" Roger asked. "Was there a Lucca?"

I nodded. "I met you a couple of months ago. Maybe a bit less. You were a friend of my uncle...Uncle Charlie." Roger's eyes widened, but he didn't interrupt. "My uncle was a nurse, and he took care of Lucca as a child."

"Did...did my son live?"

"No. I'm sorry. I don't know many details, but I know he died when he was around four or five years old. The other Roger loved him very much."

"What happened to him...me? If you don't mind me asking."

"We—my sister, Klaire, Ms. Marta, my uncle, Roger,

another friend named Vic, and I—we went to a music festival where one of the acts was a Kismet event." I didn't know how to explain Cherie, and it wasn't really relevant, I didn't think. "Somehow my sister was drawn to something we called the Looking Glass of Fate, but we don't believe it's actually a mirror. We think it's a device of some sort," I clarified. "It's a long and complicated story. We encountered this mirror-device when I was just a boy and my sister was a baby at the time. But somehow we got connected to it. My sister...I don't really know what happened to her. She said she felt a strong pull, like a rope stretching from her belly button to the device. She ran away from home to find it. We had been looking for her at the music festival. That's where I saw our Roger fall into an alternate timeline. Klaire, Ms. Marta, and I fell into this one."

"I heard of people like your sister," he said. "They are called catalysts, people who can help make rips in reality, gaps that allow people to move between timelines."

"Perhaps." I didn't want that to be true and wasn't prepared to write off Nona as any kind of supernatural catalyst. "But we...I can't stay in this timeline, Roger. I'm crippled here."

"I see."

"Can you help me get back? Please, Roger. I feel more and more disabled with each passing hour. I am scared of getting trapped in this timeline, in this drone, in this body."

"I'll see what I can do," he said.

Suddenly, we noticed a gentle humming. It was one of the Beatles' songs, "Here Comes the Sun." It was Lucca. Roger's face was beaming with pride. My mouth fell open.

***

Ms. Marta didn't meet us at dinner. Klaire and I ate with Roger and his son. I was able to quickly fill her in on our conversation. She was as shocked as I was, and we practically ate in silence after that, trying to adjust to all of the implications.

Charlie came to see us over dessert—a sweet tomato pie.

"Looks like the paperwork came through," he said, looking totally exhausted. "Mr. Ulf recommended that the babies should be granted a two-year stay, after which their developmental progress will be reassessed. He gave us two years..."

"I don't understand," I said. "What is wrong with them? And what does it mean to have two years? Two years to do what?"

"Sorry, I didn't realize that institutions like ours worked differently down south," Charlie said. "Basically, by law, we can't have more caretakers than patients in this facility. That would go against the Morgana House charter. We've already had extras—me and my sister weren't directly responsible for another person."

"But you two do so much around here," Klaire protested. "How could they demand more?"

Charlie smiled at her, and for the first time I saw him as a middle-aged man as opposed to beautiful, ageless youth. The strain of the previous week must have been more that I'd understood. But then I was really out of the loop, wasn't I? I was just a patient without much responsibility. It hurt to realize that.

"Thank you, Klaire," he said. "And thank you for all of the work you did. It really made a difference." Klaire smiled at him, pleased to be recognized. "When you three came, I figured that Mevrouw Marta would be seen as a dependent, not a family volunteer just due to her advanced age. But the city didn't see it that way. And when the twins arrived... Well, we managed to argue that three-year-olds should be able to walk and talk—"

"Wait! Three-year-olds? I thought—"

"Children without some kind of disability can't stay here, Hig. Even if they are abandoned and have no way to survive on their own yet," Charlie explained.

"But that's crazy," Klaire said. "It makes no sense. Does the city want to wait until the kids are harmed beyond recovery before offering help?"

Charlie shrugged. "That's our system. The twins' parents were responsible."

"But they abandoned them!"

"It doesn't make any difference. By arguing that they are older and thus developmentally challenged, we were able to secure permission for a two-year stay. And that also changed the calculus for Klaire and Mevrouw Marta. You see, while you could stay, Hig, only one them could have stayed with you here. And even that was a hard-won battle because Moira and I didn't have dependents. Mr. Ulf judged my sister healed a few years back, and so..."

"What? What is wrong with my..." I almost said my mother. "Moira?" I managed to change the first syllable in time.

"My sister lost her family in a tragic accident," Charlie said. "She has never been the same since...regardless of Mr. Ulf's pronouncements regarding her health. Moira is a deeply disturbed woman. And unfortunately I've recently learned that she has been a frequent visitor to the Church of Kismet." He shook his head, pain evident on his face.

I felt guilt spread through my gut like fire. We arrived wearing those stupid galaxy capes. Perhaps it was a trigger. I could have been the source of my mother's pain, even in this timeline.

"It's not your fault," Roger said quietly, as if reading my mind. "Moira was indulging in chasing Fates far longer than your stay at Morgana House."

"But we must have caused her to act on it," Klaire said. "I'm so sorry, Charlie. Your sister is a wonderful woman. I love working with her." I had no idea Klaire actually got to know my mother. It was another blow—I hardly said two words to her in all the time I was here.

"It will all work out," Charlie said. "And Roger is correct. It's not your fault, if for the simple reason you knew nothing about it. But with Mevrouw Marta adapting the babies and officially becoming their guardian, we are closer to solving some of our problems. Well, I just wanted to stop by and say thank you for letting your mother help in this way. It is very generous of you two to share her like that. It means the babies have a chance now. And that's a wonderful gift."

He stood up and gave Klaire and me a hug and left. All I could think was that we'd lost Ms. Marta for sure now. She wasn't leaving Morgana House. I just hoped Klaire was still interested in going with me.

"—for the next two years," Klaire was mattering. "And if they are particularly precocious, the city will just judge them developmentally normal and rip them out of the only home these kids have ever known. This is just wrong."

"It's how it works here," Roger said. "It's not an evil system. People who really need help get it. They have all of their needs taken care of. All of them. There is more empathy here than in lots of places I've visited."

He was right, of course. But it still felt wrong, and the look on Klaire's face made me worry. She could easily decide to take this up as her life's cause, dedicate herself to changing this society. And then where would I be?

"And whatever happens, Mevrouw Marta will be their guardian. The city can't take that away now," Roger added, fanning my fears.

***

It was very late, and I was still waiting for Charlie to come and help me get ready for bed. Despite his exhaustion, he had been coming every night. Roger in the mornings, Uncle Charlie at night—a cycle of living hell. But Charlie had been arriving later and later each day, it seemed, just as I needed his aid more and more. I promised myself that I would never complain, never ask for extra help, that I would always wait until assistance was freely given and then thank profusely all who gave it. The problem was an avalanche of humiliation my body was throwing my way. If Klaire and I left this timeline, just the two of us, could we manage? How would I?

The door creaked opened, and I almost sighed with relief. I was very tired of sitting in this drone. My muscles were spasming; my tremors wouldn't cease. It was torture to wait. I looked up, but it was Klaire at my door.

"Can I come in?" she asked. She always asked permission now. I guessed she felt my discomfort and wanted to allow me what shreds of dignity were left.

"What's up?" I said as casually as I could.

"I wanted to show you something. Do you think you can come with me for a few minutes?" She looked excited to share something with me, and I couldn't say no to that.

Klaire led me to the round glass elevator that serviced the three floors and the roof garden of Morgana House. There was also a spiral staircase on the outside of the elevator shaft that most people took to save time. I usually took the lift, though—after my near disaster of trying to fly my drone up to the second-floor balcony, I stuck with the conventional ways of getting around. We went up all the way to the roof, but instead of turning into the greenhouse, Klaire led me to the outside terrace. Surprisingly, I'd never actually gone there before. All my time was occupied with Roger and Lucca and my own personal maintenance now.

The view from the top was awe-inspiring. Morgana House was one of the shortest buildings in New Amsterdam, but the rooftop was far above the tree line and even above the drone traffic corridors. We'd noticed before that there was far less electrical illumination in this timeline than in ours, so the stars were clearly visible above our heads. The air was crisp and cold; it felt like it would snow. A few windows were still lit up in the neighboring buildings, even as it was getting close to midnight. People went to sleep early around here, and I peered into the windows to see what was making them stay up so late. This was a voyeur's paradise, but it couldn't have been why Klaire took me here.

"Hig, look there." She pointed to the round glass tower sticking out above all the rest of the rooftops. It was also one of the few buildings that were fully lit up. "Remember when we walked and I wanted to check it out, but we never got a chance?"

"Did you go afterward?" I asked, feeling a slight flutter of jealousy.

"Yes. It's not too far from the city hall." The way she said it seemed like an apology, and I felt instant guilt—an emotion I was getting very familiar with. "Hig, it's a dirigible anchor port."

"A what?"

"A dirigible? You know, one of those giant airships that float in the sky?"

"Like a blimp?"

"I guess. I'm not sure what the difference is, but it's not important. Remember how we never saw any contrails here?"

"I remember."

"Well, that's because they use lighter-than-air crafts to move cargo and people long distances, in addition to trains."

I looked, and suddenly, in the distance, high above the city, I noticed a giant oblong thing with lights flashing along its perimeter and on top and bottom, floating soundlessly across the night sky. There was grace and dignity in its movement as it neared the glass tower.

"I learned the landing schedule and wanted to bring you up to see this," Klaire said, her voice was full awe. "It's gorgeous, isn't it?"

"Yeah."

"And we can take it to fly to Newfoundland."

I wanted to kiss her right there and then. She wasn't going to abandon me. We were getting out of here. I felt tears burst out of my eyes. Klaire leaned in and hugged me. I pulled her close, all the way into my lap. My drone could take it. We sat together and watched as the massive airship anchored itself to the tower. Majestic.

Chapter Twenty-Six: Choices

R oger and Lucca came to help me in the morning.

"Moira is going to visit the Fates," he whispered in my ear.

"When?"

"Now!"

We rushed through my morning routine. I tried to help as much as I could, but I no longer could even trust my arms to do what I wanted. How much time did I have left before escaping this hell would be a physical impossibility?

"Hig. Relax," Roger said again. "You are making this difficult. Just let go. Let me do it."

"I don't know how."

"I know it's hard. Here, allow me to pull your arm through... Good, there we are. Are you comfortable?"

"Sure." I wasn't, but did it matter?

Outside my room, people were running around...a lot more than the ordinary bustle and hassle of the Morgana House residents getting ready for the day. I was very familiar with the normal soundscape of the mornings around here; I slept right next to the kitchen. Things were obviously different today. "Is there something going on today?" I asked. But Roger just shook his head.

"So," he spoke loudly as he opened my door and guided

Lucca's and my drones out of the room, "we are going to go for a walk outside today. I think the extra stimulation will be good for Lucca. Would you like to come along, Hig?"

I looked around to see if anyone was listening. There were people in the hallway, rushing around, but no one was paying any attention to us. Not obviously.

"Can Klaire come?" I asked quietly.

"I think she is helping Moira today," Roger said in full voice with an exaggerated wink. He would have made the worst undercover agent. The way he talked and moved and what he said just screamed that he was up to no good. I would have laughed, but I wasn't finding anything funny. "Come on, Lucca, let's go see the trees!" Roger said in full voice.

And Lucca surprised me again by humming "Walking in the Virgin Forest" from the Beatles' *Black Album*. Roger just nodded and whistled along, I was stunned. That was two days in a row the boy did something unexpected. Perhaps instead of the flashcards, we should have played songs for him. But did it change what Lucca understood? Was he even capable of understanding? Did Lucca know that Roger was planning to take him outside, for example? He *did* choose "Walking in the Virgin Forest." I shook my head. I couldn't focus on that.

As we passed the kitchen, I filled my water bottle and grabbed a piece of rhubarb strudel that someone baked for breakfast earlier that morning. I had been smelling the aromas from my room for many hours and was happy that there was some still left. Roger and Lucca had eaten before coming for me—Lucca woke up very early each morning. Roger called him his own personal rooster.

We got outside, through the side door, of course. The morning was sunny and cold. There were a number of people bustling to go wherever people of this timeline went each day. After all this time, I had no idea how anything really worked in New Amsterdam. I never even figured out how many states this United States had. I hoped I would never need that knowledge; I hoped to be gone soon.

Roger guided his son's drone down the street, while I floated along behind them. People stepped aside to give us room. They stared. Aside for people living in Morgana House, everyone here seemed perfectly fit, not even a cane in sight. I hadn't even seen people in glasses. Their medical care must have been far above ours in the ability to manage people's health. If I only cared enough to learn, I could have brought back some useful information to our timeline. I might have been able to save lives. I gulped loudly, and Roger turned and looked at me knowingly—I was sure my green pallor was a dead giveaway of my internal dialog.

I floated over next him. I wanted to ask what he had learned while moving between multiple timelines. Was there a flow of useful information? Could there be? But before I could ask, he spoke.

"This was the only place I found Lucca alive," he said in a low voice, hardly moving his lips. I had to strain to hear him. "I had dreams of taking him with me to other histories that might heal him."

"You did?"

"Of course. But I'm not a gambler, Hig. All I wanted was to share my life with my son for as long as I could. I have him—"

"But—"

"I had a choice of life with Lucca or without. I found it wasn't really a choice. I love my son, Hig. I didn't give up on him. I won't."

"I see." I didn't think "giving up" somehow prohibited Roger from trying to find a timeline where Lucca was whole. I found one myself...for me. Wouldn't there be one for Lucca?

"There is a concept that Dailas of the church of Kismet talk about during their sermons—the axis of desire."

"Axis of desire." I could almost intuitively grasp the meaning.

"We don't randomly move through possibilities, Hig. Some timelines are more probable than others. Some are more desirable."

"What does that mean? Practically, I mean?"

"Desire makes even unlikely transitions more possible."

"Like my desire to not be a crippopotamus?"

"Or mine to find a timeline where a life with my son was possible," he said. "I spoke with Rose...with Mevrouw Marta before...before..." He glanced at me. I wasn't used to thinking of Ms. Marta as Rose, but I knew what Roger meant—before Ms. Marta started to forget the life where I was her "gran chico." "Somehow your family's and Rose's needs wove together to form something much stronger than a normal bond between possible timelines," Roger continued. "Because despite of how much I wished for Lucca, I've spent years...many years looking for him. I didn't find him until he was almost an adult. I've missed my son's childhood, Hig. It ripped my heart out that I wasn't there for my boy. Life was so hard for him, and I wasn't able to be there to help. It still hurts even to think about it. But I'm here now. My son will never be alone or afraid again. Whatever fate has in store for us, we will face it together."

I never considered it like that. I always looked at Roger as the person who could have made a choice to walk away. But he found Lucca and chose to give his life to make his son's better. He didn't continue looking for a better Lucca; he stayed to help the one who needed him the most.

***

We turned into a familiar narrow alleyway, and I quickly spotted the small spiral decal above the door of the Church of Kismet—the only indication from the outside that this ordinary-looking building was something more special. Now that I knew what to look for, it was glaringly obvious.

Roger opened the door and held it for me to float through. Then I helped him get Lucca inside. There were no visitor robes hanging on the pegs by the door. The space was cavernous and empty.

"What do we do now?" I asked.

"We wait. I believe Moira..." He gave me a questioning look but didn't ask the obvious question. "Well, Moira left Morgana House before sunrise," he said. "Lucca and I were up by then, of course. So we wished her well."

"Does she know about you?" I asked.

"She suspects, but we never talked about it openly."

"Do you know what happened to Moira's family?" I asked; "in this timeline" was implied.

"Charlie told me about it in very broad strokes. From what I was able to gather, Moira's husband and daughter were killed in some kind of freak accident."

"Daughter?" That didn't make much sense. I was the eldest. "What about..." I didn't really know how to ask about what happened to me in this history. Could there ever be two of me in one timeline? Was that even permitted? Were there some cosmic laws that governed such things? Or was it all just random?

"As far as I know, Hig, Moira only had the one child. And it was girl."

"Huh."

"I've thought about it a lot. Did whatever research was

possible," he said after a few minutes of silence. Being inside the church set us both in a contemplative mood somehow. "Obviously," he continued, "there is not much information available about alternative histories. There are some fictional stories, movies, and such. Mostly fiction, not a lot facts or first-person accounts that are not written as fantastical stories. Some places had the equivalent of the Church of Kismet as an explicit religion, some didn't. But in my time, I've never came across another Roger. At most, I've met people like you who had interacted with 'me' in their own timelines. Jumpers like us tend to gravitate toward each other. I figured that if I stayed in Morgana House long enough, others would show up eventually. Not that it was the only reason to stay there, of course. Morgana House has been good for me and Lucca. Mostly..."

That was probably the most explicit discussion about multiple timelines I'd ever had. And surprisingly, I survived it without puking, although my head was pounding something awful. But from experience, I knew it would pass as soon as I stopped thinking about all of this. I wondered if Roger's timeline collision sickness was not as bad as mine, or was he simply better at hiding it? But even if he was in as much discomfort as I was, I wasn't ready for him to stop yet. I wanted...needed to know more, and I didn't think I'd get another opportunity as good as this to learn from someone as experienced as Roger.

"So there couldn't have been another me in this timeline because I came here, is that right?" I asked.

"I don't know, Hig. I think whatever laws govern the transition between timelines don't allow for multiples. But I don't think that precludes you having been born here and then dying prior to your arrival. Does that make sense?"

"Yeah."

"I wish there was someone to ask. But aside for the Dailas here, I never found anyone who specifically studied this subject. I've spoken with Daila Megan, Moira's friend, but we never got anywhere."

"What about the catalysts you've mentioned?"

"Like your sister? I assume those people know more, at least on some intuitive level, but I didn't find a way of having a meaningful conversation with any Mistress of the Mirror. Might be different for you, given that you are family."

"So a Mistress of the Mirror is a catalyst?" I felt sick, cold in my spine, thinking that Nona might become like that old blind woman at the county fair. That couldn't have been her fate, could it?

"Hig, what I'm telling you are just my guesses. They are based on my observations, my experience, but they are no more than a hunch about how things really work. I could be completely wrong about all of this."

"I understand. Thank you for sharing this with me. It means more than you know."

He nodded. And as my headache started to recede, I noticed that Lucca was humming another song. I didn't recognize it, but the style seemed very familiar. Perhaps it was a song that was never written in my timeline. I wondered if music was another thing of value that could somehow pass between timelines. There could be a history where John Lennon wasn't shot and wrote a hundred more songs. What a treasure trove that would be...

***

I didn't know how long we waited in the gloom of the church hall. Lucca hummed several more songs, some I recognized, some new to me. Roger closed his eyes and slept for a bit, leaning against the wall, holding Lucca's hand. It was peaceful somehow...like the calm before a storm.

When the front door opened, it was like a sonic boom. I bounced in my drone seat. Ironically, I was actually happy I was still able to do that. I looked back and saw Klaire and my mom walk through the front door. Mom was wearing an orange jacket, *the* orange jacket, the one covered with California puppies—I recognized it right away. Uncle Charlie gave it to her...to my mother the day we went to the county fair and encountered the Mistress of the Mirror for the first time. My heart skipped a bit; that was my mom, over there, just a few feet from me. I'd spent days avoiding her, and there she was, so painfully close.

Klaire furtively stuck her head out of the front door and looked up and down the street before carefully, practically soundlessly, closing it. It was almost like she and Mom were sneaking in, the way they both kept looking back over their shoulders to check that no one saw them, no one followed. What was that about?

"Moira! Klaire!" Roger called to them. "We are over here." He waved, even as we were the only ones in the whole cavernous hall, and we weren't hiding. Klaire rushed to our side. Mom approached more cautiously, studying me from a distance. I wondered...

"Roger, Hig! Good to see you, Lucca. Have you guys been waiting long?" Klaire was talking at a breakneck speed. "We got stuck in a city hall meeting again. I don't know why they need more and more information on Mama and me. We gave them everything we had." Which I knew was absolutely nothing. "But they said they just needed to make sure."

"Make sure of what?" Roger asked.

Klaire shrugged. "Beats me if I know. Moira testified as Mama's character witness this morning."

"Huh. I thought Charlie said it was a done deal? I mean about adopting the babies," I said.

"It's just the bureaucracy of it all, especially in cases of special needs kids," Roger tried to reassure. "It took a long time for me and Lucca, too."

I hadn't considered it, but obviously Roger would have had to adopt Lucca in this timeline. He wasn't always his father here. My mother...Moira walked up to me slowly and put her hand on my face...just like my mom used to do when I was just a child—a cross between a gentle caress and a medical exam. I shivered.

"So it's true," she said.

"What?"

"You are the son I should have had." The intensity in her eyes was like fire; it was the brightest thing in this giant cavernous room. I couldn't look away if I wanted, but I didn't know how to answer. I felt panicky. I glanced at Roger, but he just stared at my mother, obviously in shock, too. So he wasn't the one to tell her. Was it Klaire? I glanced at her, but she shook her head. So Ms. Marta. There was no one else. My mom testified for her, and in return for the favor she told her who we were. It almost felt like a betrayal somehow.

"Moira?" Klaire stepped up and put her hand the woman's shoulder, but Mom didn't move. She held my gaze, capturing my whole attention. Was she really my mom? In this timeline she didn't even give birth to me.

"Before I had my daughter," she said, staring into my eyes, "I was pregnant with another child." I caught my breath—there was a me in this timeline...a potential of me that didn't work out, obviously. "That child..." Mom's breath caught, but she pushed on. "That fetus had severe birth defects. We were told we couldn't keep it." Klaire gasped. "They didn't tell us the sex of the child, but I knew it was a boy. I felt it. Almost seven years later, I had a daughter." That was the exact difference in age between me and Nona. "I lost her as well," she said, tears rolling down her eyes. "She was only fifteen months old." I did a quick calculation—I would have been about eight then, around the time we first encountered the Mistress of the Mirror. Major life events seemed to track closely in dates between the timelines, even if the substance of what happened changed. "Mevrouw Marta said that your Nona is a Catalyst of Fate." I glanced at Roger; he looked guilty—from me to Roger to Ms. Marta to Mom was the flow of information that got us here.

"We don't know if that is what Nona has become. We are just guessing," I said.

My mother nodded. "But you are going to try to find her." It wasn't a question. "I want to come with you. I want to see my daughter once again." I noticed that she didn't say anything about wanting me...but then she never had me here, did she?

"What about Charlie?" I asked.

"If I leave, it might make things easier on him, actually," she said. "He feels like I'm his responsibility. He dedicated his life to taking care of me. If I was gone, he would be free to follow his own path in life."

I listened to her arguments, but I didn't believe them for a minute. Uncle Charlie would be devastated to lose his sister. He was always driven by his love of our family...even when he was Cherie, I believed. Losing his only sister, his only close family, would devastate the man. I loved Uncle Charlie. I loved my mom. But somehow, I think I understood my uncle better. I found myself empathizing with him over this woman. After all those years of feeling guilty for the miraculous life I'd gotten and then searching for my mother despite the possibility of losing everything, I wasn't sure how I felt about the person in front of me. Roger chose to be with his son, even when it was hard; my mother chose the opposite. I felt sick. I loved my mother, right? But this Moira wasn't her, was she? My mother chose death over taking care of me. Who said that death was easy, but living was hard? It must have been Ms. Marta. This woman in front of me was searching for a replacement daughter. But my Nona didn't know this woman. Nona and I had Ms. Marta as our mother. She was the woman who raised us, who took care of us when we were sick, when it was difficult, when no one else would.

It took only a moment to process all of that, only a moment to gain insight into love. I pressed the controls of my drone and pulled away from Moira. Klaire looked at me, and I just shook my head. I had a loving mother, a caring sister, a wonderful girl that I had high hopes of spending my entire life with. I had a body that was whole and very able. In other words, I had a future, and yet I chose to chase an old guilt trip. I needed to get my life back. And yet the life I was pursuing now, that life was gone for good, lost in the maze of timeline shifting. *So what now?*

"The airship is leaving for Newfoundland in a few hours," Moira said. It was amazing how something in my mind had clicked, and this woman was just Moira now. A stranger. "I plan to be on it," she continued. "According to Daila Megan, they are expecting the Mirror of Fate at this event. I've never seen one. But from what Roger told me, the mirror is a metaphor for seeing the possibilities. And it needs a Catalyst to make it work. Did I get this right, Roger?"

Klaire and I both looked at Roger; this all was news to us. He looked uncomfortable, moving from foot to foot, fidgeting with Lucca's drone. Even in the darkness of the hall, he looked a bit green to me.

"There really isn't a mirror. There is no such thing," he

finally said. "It's just an illusion. What we perceive as a mirror is actually a portal of sorts."

"But I saw it," I said; if not the mirror, then the device that seemed like a mirror. "I saw my own reflection in the mirror." But thinking back on it, the old woman was never seen moving the mirror or device about, and we never found an actual thing at her booth. Could it just have been an illusion this whole time?

"I saw it a few times, too," Roger said. "But I finally realized it wasn't a physical object. The Mistress of the Mirror, what I now call the Catalyst, is somehow able to conjure up an illusion of a mirror. She interviews and selects only those people she believes are capable of seeing between alternative timelines. The mirror itself might be just a hypnotic suggestion that triggers a rapture between histories. Or perhaps it's small device of some sort." He looked at me and shrugged. "I never figured that part out. Once I found Lucca, I stopped looking."

"Back at the festival, I saw multiple mirrors forming onstage," Klaire said. "Not just one. Roger...our Roger fell into one. We fell through another. We tried to follow Nona, but somehow we didn't end up in the same timeline."

"Do you remember seeing your own reflection in the rift?" Roger asked.

"Yes," she said.

"No," I said at the same time. All I remembered was falling and then waking up in the empty field.

"Well, it might be different for everyone." Roger shrugged again.

"But the Catalyst would be there," Moira said insistently. "I would be able to meet Nona."

"Maybe," Roger said.

"Well, that's good enough for me," she said. "I'm leaving.

I'm not passing on my chance to see my daughter again." She was almost militant in her demeanor. She was telling us that nothing was going to stop her—we wouldn't—even as Nona was probably not there. Even though Nona wasn't really her daughter, Moira was going to find her and...and what?

"We are coming, too," Klaire said. She opened her giant bag that she always carried with her whenever she went out and pulled out two galaxy robes—hers and Ms. Marta's. She put one on and draped another across my shoulders. "I'm sure they will allow the brother and close friend of the Catalyst to join the party." She smiled, but there was no mirth in her face. She was all hard edges, ready for battle.

Chapter Twenty-Seven: Escape

We walked into the winter midday sun together. Klaire moved next to me, and we held hands, our galaxy capes streaming behind us. Moira walked right behind us. I couldn't bear to see her. She broke something inside me...or set it right. I just needed time to process how I felt about her. Roger and Lucca capped our procession. People who saw us backed away in shock and dashed into doorways or turned into alternate streets. I wished I knew the emotional drive behind such extreme reactions. Was it our capes? Did people of this timeline view the Church of Kismet as some deranged sect? Or was it seeing two disabled men out on the street? What was it that freaked them out the most? My exposure to the society of this timeline was minimal, and yet I felt a strong current of intolerance. There were a lot of prejudices in my home history, but it seemed to be a different set than the one prevalent in this timeline. Or was it all the same, just with a slightly different emphasis? People in all timeframes might feel a natural disgust for crippopotamuses, the way we all normally experience an innate revulsion to blood.

I looked over at Klaire. She was scanning the street, looking at buildings, people, trees. She seemed intent on taking it all in, drinking in the differences. She was getting ready to leave, I realized. This timeline rubbed itself off on us...a bit. We changed by virtue of spending time here. But as we moved down the street, I felt like I was strutting...as much as that was possible floating in my medi-drone. Let them stare, let them judge me. As long as they couldn't hold me prisoner there, I could look down on them. I could be judgmental, too. I was a rebel...

The airship port building was not too far from the Church of Kismet. It was easy to see, even from the ground—it stood so much higher than all the other buildings of New Amsterdam. And now with a giant dirigible anchored to its top, it resembled a huge, shiny mushroom dominating the city's skies. If I ever doubted that we were somewhere else, the giant silver balloon with lights running along its perimeter was more than enough proof.

We stepped onto a broad avenue with several layers of drone traffic running above our heads. The port building was straight ahead. Moira sped up and overtook us. She rushed ahead, as if drawn to it by some unseen force, as if she couldn't help herself. I noticed that there was a strange hum all around us. Like I was seeing double, triple, multiple images overlapping themselves, making the world fuzzy. Klaire slowed. She must have felt something, too.

"Follow me," Roger said and turned into a side alleyway.

"But Moira?" Klaire said.

"Let her go," he said and led us down a small, circular street. With fewer drones and people, the world solidified again.

"What was that?" I asked.

"What did you feel?" he asked.

"It was like the world was bifurcating. And then splitting again and again," Klaire said—she saw what I saw. That was comforting.

"Splitting? Are you sure?" Roger asked. Neither of us was

sure. It was too confusing. My visual field became a puzzle of superimposed images. Some had people walking right next to us, while others showed trees as tall as giant sequoias overshadowing the buildings on either side of us. Roger nodded when neither of us answered. "I guess you are really not staying," he said sadly.

"I can't." I repeated my mantra.

"Leaving is never a guarantee," Roger said. "But I didn't know if you had already overstayed. Apparently not."

"What's happening, Roger?" Klaire asked. Her fingers squeezed mine so hard that it felt like the only real sensation I was experiencing.

"You are starting to drift between the timelines."

"But we didn't get up to that airship? We didn't meet up with Nona?"

"The Mirror of Fate and its Catalyst minder are just the more formal ways of shifting between histories," Roger said. "Some people skip over without outside help."

"Really?"

"I have a theory that it has something to do with your parallels in another timeline getting ready to slip between histories. They shift and somehow sweep others with them."

"Was that how you moved?"

"No," Roger said as he continued to guide us.

I could no longer navigate on my own; reality was too fragile. I held on to Klaire for dear life, pulling her closer and closer to me. I didn't notice when she slipped into my lap, riding the drone with me, clinging tightly as the world around tried to shimmer out of existence. She was whimpering gently. I held her close. I could feel the beat of her heart. It almost matched mine.

"Come on, kids. Mevrouw Marta is waiting for us." Roger urged us on.

Ms. Marta? I couldn't leave without saying goodbye. I rushed ahead, wind pushing against my face, wrapping Klaire's long, dark strands around my nose and ears and eyes. I felt the world warping around me. There were whole beats of my heart when Roger and Lucca were not even with us anymore. But I had to say goodbye. I had to.

"Gran chico," she called, and her voice sounded muffled, as if coming out of the mist. But with her next to me, the world stabilized once more.

"Mama," I called to her. Klaire and I reached for the woman who was my mother for thirteen years at the same time. She almost fell out onto the pavement; I managed to catch her at the last minute. I was not going to live in the world where Klaire was not part of my life.

Ms. Marta...*Mama* was standing in the middle of a small, circular park full of flowering trees. It was winter, but the trees had flowers...and no leaves. The wind blew the small white-pink petals down, and they floated to the ground like snow, piling in shallow drifts. I noticed that Mama looked younger. She appeared slimmer than the woman I knew; her hair fell loose around her shoulders, some white but mostly dark and wavy, like Klaire's. She was same and different at the same time. There was a doublewide stroller drone with two babies floating next to her. The infants were sleeping soundly inside. I could see the identical puffs of dark hair sticking out from the blankets. Mama had one of her hands placed protectively over them, and the other was reaching for me. She was wearing a galaxy cape, just like Klaire and I.

"You made it," she said.

"I almost left without saying goodbye," I said, tears streaming down my eyes. "I'm sorry, Mama."

"There is no goodbye, gran chico," she said.

"What do you mean?" Klaire asked. She wrapped one of

her arms around my neck, making sure to stay with me on the drone.

"The trees don't sing to me here," she said as if that explained everything. "I want my children to grow up listening to forest music."

"Are you saying you are going, too?" I asked. It was like being thunderstruck multiple times in a matter of minutes. First Moira, then the breaking of the world, and now Mama was coming with us.

"This world is not kind to differences," she said. "We'll go someplace where we will all be safe. Someplace where Nonaken can come, too. You didn't give up on your sister, did you, Hig?"

"No!" *Yes.* I was too focused on my own needs to see beyond my medi-drone and adult dippers. "We will find her, Mama."

"If Daila Moira is right, Nonaken is right here," she said, nodding toward the shimmering dirigible looming over our heads, anchored just a few blocks away. "I was able to secure the papers for the airship from the city hall. Apparently, they don't much care for strange old women and abandoned babies; we are just extra mouths to feed. I asked to be allowed to go to Newfoundland, and they were more than happy to hurry my paperwork. They even gave me this cape. The police officers in Carolina recovered it." That made no sense—there was never a third cape to recover. It was all just a story. But the world was shifting, and we were shifting with it.

"And Moira?" Klaire asked.

"They are happy to get rid of her too, as far as I can tell."

"It will break Uncle Charlie's heart," I said. "How could she do that?"

"We all follow our own axis of desire, Hig. Moira always wanted to leave." Yes, I saw that now. "I always wanted to stay and take care of my family." She smiled at me and then looked lovingly at the sleeping babies. "And now I have even more chicos to love."

"What about us?" Klaire asked. "Will they let us go?"

"Charlie advocated for you to stay at Morgana House," she said.

"No!" The scream was practically ripped out of my chest. "I can't stay. Please, I can't. Mama, I need to go."

"I know. You and Klaire, if she wants to leave, will have to take a different way up to the airship. Once we get going, I will find a way of getting you onboard."

"But..."

"Be brave, my gran chico." She smiled and pointed up to the top of the airship port building.

Klaire looked up, and I felt her other arm twine around my body. We were already floating about a meter off the ground—three feet or so. What was another ninety meters? I thought back on our lives in our sixty-seventh floor apartment. Ninety meters wasn't even half as high. I'd been preparing for this almost my whole life, looking down at the traffic and people below, watching whole lives go by. Thirty stories was nothing.

"We can do it, Mama," I said. And she smiled.

Roger came over and gave Mama a hug goodbye and then he kissed the sleeping twins. The babies didn't even stir. Mama always had a way with kids...and trees. Roger then came for us.

"So this is goodbye," I said. "Thank you for everything, Roger. I will miss you. And Lucca." As I mentioned his name, the boy started to sing "Hello, Goodbye." Klaire laughed and sang along: "You say goodbye, and I say hello."

"It's not goodbye forever, Hig. When Lucca won't need me anymore, I will find you."

What? And then it dawned on me—Lucca's life expectancy was no more than a few years more, even here, even in this timeline that had the medicine that allowed him to live while all the other histories let him down. I looked up and Roger smiled at me, seeing the realization in my face.

"I desire to find you," he said. It sounded like a promise.

"I desire to be found," I answered.

"I desire for all of us to be together again," Klaire said.

"I desire to live in a world where my loved ones are free," said Mama. "See you soon, my gran chicos." And with that she turned to go. She had an airship to catch.

We did too. I didn't want to linger. I felt the world start to spin again, twisting, drifting, getting less solid. I didn't want to get lost on the way to the top of the tower.

"See you on the other side," Roger called to us as we lifted up in the air, above the trees, above the average-sized building of New Amsterdam, way above the drone traffic.

"Don't look down," I told Klaire. "Just focus on the airship. And hold on!"

✳✳✳

We drifted up. Klaire pressed her face into my chest. I looked. I saw Roger wave to us; I saw Mama hurrying to the glass tower and getting on one of those transparent elevators on the outside of its wall. I never got to ride one of those. Never would. As I watched, I felt the world twist. One moment the giant blimp was overhead, the next it was just blue skies with a huge moon instead of the airship. The air vibrated. It wasn't like wind, even as I felt us being buffeted from side to side by air currents.

"Hig," Klaire said into my sweatshirt. I clutched her even tighter.

"Just don't look."

"I see trees."

I didn't, so I didn't answer. I just tried to aim our drone toward where I thought the ship was or ought to have been. We were high. Very high. The air tasted of smoke and ash. Were Klaire's trees on fire?

"Just a little bit higher," I told her. "We're almost there."

New Amsterdam was no longer below us. I couldn't bring it back, even as an afterimage. But I thought the airship was still above us. I felt it, even as I couldn't really see it, like a blind bat felt the top of the cave ceiling. It was like a great pressure from above.

"Mama and Nona will wait for us," I reassured Klaire, or perhaps myself. My head was pounding. I was scared.

"We should have stayed together," Klaire said into my chest. And I agreed.

We moved up and up. Klaire's body changed the center of gravity for our drone, and we were listing slightly backward. It felt like we were sitting in an extreme reclining chair. When the dirigible burst directly in front, like a mountainside revealing itself out of the dense fog, it was practically on top of us. I tried to slow us down, but the sheer momentum was moving us forward. I had to use my arm to keep Klaire from being smashed—I was nestled safe deep inside the medi-drone suspension, but she was lying on top of me, totally exposed. I pushed against the taut, smooth sliver skin of the airship while trying to stop the drone from drifting higher. But we got pressed into it anyway, crushing my arm. I did manage to protect Klaire's head, but she felt limp in my arms anyway. I had no way and no opportunity to check on her at that moment.

The airship shuddered and started to move, relieving some of the pressure of impact and twisting the drone even more back on itself. I could feel that a few more degrees and we would just slide out of it altogether, plunging thirty stories below onto the pavement. Into trees? We were sliding toward the back of the airship, facing away from the direction of its flight. Our capes were fluttering behind us like broken bat wings. We must have been visible to any ground crew looking up. Would they stop the ship to save us? I had no idea and no trust in the basic humanity of this timeline. What was it that Mama said about their priorities? "Who needed abandoned babies and old women? Who needed another crippopotamus to feed?" No, these people wouldn't help us.

I tried to feel for something to grab, something to hold on to, but it was just a smooth, slick surface, sliding past us. But there had to be seams, right? There were those lights that Klaire and I saw from the roof deck of Morgana House. I'd never got to see the dirigible up close, but from a distance, it looked like a fat football with six giant rotary motors above, a cabin for passengers suspended between blades, and four tails at back for stabilization. It was as if they took the design of one of their drone busses and scaled it to insane proportions. We must have come smashing into the dirigible's cabin somewhere near the bottom edge, where it started to curve up. We got lucky—we could have ridden straight up into one of those engines, and then we would have been toast. As it was, we were sliding past it as the ship was gaining speed. We might have survived the collision, but if we couldn't attach ourselves to the ship somehow, we were done. Maybe we could get the drone down safely. Maybe. But I couldn't see any lights below. I had a sense that the only thing that was anchoring us to this timeline was the dirigible itself. *We separate, and we could get tossed into another time stream, away from Nona, away from Mama and the twins.*

It was a trick to fly the drone, hold on to Klaire's limp

body, and try to find something, anything, to hook ourselves to. I tried to see around the silver bulge. There had to be something—a seam, a light, a wing, anything. My fingers felt ice cold. The air was chill and wet. It was a crisp winter morning when we left Morgana House. Now, it felt more like dusk. The air still had a vague smell of distant smoke, but now I could also sense water. New Amsterdam was in the same location as New York—a small finger of land sticking out into the Atlantic Ocean, or was it Hudson Bay? Either way, the smell of ocean wasn't a surprise, although I didn't think we'd made so much progress already as to be over water. If we were, our landing would be...I didn't want to dwell on that. There was nothing I could do about where we were going to crush land; all I could do was try not to separate from this airship.

My fingers slid and slid farther back along the surface... but slower? And slower still. And then, with a jerk, we were pulled slightly forward again; it felt like a rubber band snap. I yelped as my fingers were bent and crushed the wrong way... again. I clutched Klaire for dear life...hers and mine.

What happened? Why did we stop sliding back? After catching my breath and making sure that my fingers were still working, bruised but not broken, I tried to figure out what was holding us in position. The six motors of my medi-drone were still working, although they were making strange clicking noises that I'd never heard before. It was perfectly conceivable that we were running out of power—the drone was fully charged this morning, but it was working double its normal capacity by supporting Klaire's and my weight...and flying way above what it was designed for. I carefully turned one way and then another. From the corner of my eye, I saw my cape snagged on a big valve on the side of the airship. Below the valve were the metal rungs of a ladder. It took me a second, but then I realized that this must have been the intake valve for the lighter-than-air gas that was floating this giant contraption. A corner of my galaxy cape got twisted around the valve and anchored us in place; and my medi-drone's engines were working hard to break that connection, making pathetic noises trying to do so. Hot sweat erupted from every pore as I turned my forward engines off, leaving only the vertical lift operating. The clicking noises stopped.

"Klaire?" I gently prodded her dead weight on top of me. We needed to get to that valve and secure our connection to the airship. "Klaire?" I called again. But she didn't respond. I suppressed the fear trying to surge through me. Now was not the time to panic. I had to make us safe and then figure out how to help her.

The cape was tied around my neck, but Klaire's body somehow kept the pull from strangling me. I had to preserve that; I couldn't help Klaire if I was dead. So she had to stay exactly as she was. The valve was about four feet behind my head. I felt the silver side of the airship again with my nearly numb hand. It felt more solid somehow. I turned a little, trying to examine the fortuitous knot. The wind must have wrapped the end of my cape around one of the valve's protrusions, but it wasn't secure—it held because my drone was putting tension on it. If I moved and added slack to the cape, it would unwind and release. *Not good.*

Whatever I was going to do, I needed two hands to do it. I took the edges of Klaire's cape and pulled them behind me and back around again, tying the ends tightly around myself and Klaire, securing her body to mine. This was easier said than done. It took what felt like an eternity, all the while worrying about my cape slipping its anchor. But having secured Klaire to me, however imperfectly, I could now pull us along the length of my cape using both arms.

It was a painful affair. And when we reached the valve,

my drone's engines kept me from getting close enough to secure us to it—my arms were simply not long enough to reach
the valve from my position deep in the drone seat. To halve
the distance, I needed to collapse my drone the way it did
when I passed through the doors of the Church of Kismet.
But since I had never read the manual, I had no idea what col-
lapsing two engines to narrow the profile of the drone would
do our ability to stay afloat. It couldn't be good, I decided.
But what choice did I have? I pressed the controls, overrid-
ing a series of alarms; the drone collapsed, and we dropped,
dangling by my cape.

I felt the ties around my neck start to slide up against my
throat. Tighter and tighter. I took a deep breath, my last, and
tried to restart my engines, but there was no longer enough
power. My drone tried. It whinnied and clicked and desperately moaned. Then my cape ripped, and we plummeted
down.

Chapter Twenty-Eight: Crash

I woke with the sun on my face. I was lying in the grass, my cape fluttering in the breeze. I rolled over and got to my knees. I was in a cultivated field that was left fallow for the winter. There were patches of snow here and there. There was no drone, no Klaire. My stomached lurched, and I vomited. I had that dizzy, strange feeling of timeline shifting. The SHITs, as Klaire called it.

After my stomach emptied, I felt a bit better and got to my feet. From a higher vantage point, I saw another galaxy cape about fifty yards away from me. I ran, tripping over the uneven ground. When I got to within a few feet of it, I was gripped by terror. I didn't want to find a body underneath. I backed away.

"Klaire?" I called to the cape quietly. "Klaire? Please don't be dead. Please don't be dead."

The cape flapped a little, but I couldn't tell if it was wind or... I steeled myself and took the three steps to close the distance. I gently pulled on the edge of the cape. Nothing. I ripped the whole thing up in the air. There was nothing underneath. I turned around, looking in the distance in every direction. There were trees to my right and a cliff dropping off to the ocean on the other side.

"Klaire!" I screamed and screamed her name until I was

hoarse.

Finally, I clutched her cape to my chest and walked toward the cliff. I was terrified of what I might find there. But having emptied myself with screaming, I felt numb enough to look.

The cliff was about a third of a mile from me, but it took no time to get there. I walked sure and easy. At some point I even realized that I was walking, but the terror of losing the woman I loved...everyone I loved, made the realization flat, unreal. I needed to look below the cliff, so I made myself walk there.

I couldn't see it until I got to the edge, but then the full horror revealed itself. There was a terrible accident. A crash. A plane? A boat? A dirigible? Strange parts were twisted in and out of the waves. Scattered metal washed up on the shore, jagged edges sticking out of sand and water for more than a mile up and down the beach. There were people, too. Some were lying face down in the water. I'd never seen dead people before. I wasn't allowed to see Mom when she passed away. And seeing the inanimate, soulless objects lying about, I was glad of it. I wanted to remember Mom as a person, not a thing. But it wasn't only the dead down below. There were injured, and other survivors were assisting them. I needed to get down there to help.

But I couldn't stabilize the image of the crash in front of me. The plane was upside-down, with one wing buried in the sand bluff I was standing on and a broken wheel below it. There were four inflatable orange rafts. One was okay. Two were deflated and scrunched into the sand. And one was floating in the distance, bobbing up and down on the cold surf. The plane crash wasn't the only disaster I was seeing. There was a small cruise ship that obviously ran aground and somehow managed to split in half, just down the middle, left to right, like a broken fortune cookie. Instead of the inflatable rafts, there were three lifeboats—one was lying upside down in the sand near the water's edge, one still floating in the distance, and one listing sideways on the beach, having been dragged on land. There might have been another boat—I saw debris off in the distance that could have been a lifeboat at one time. And finally, I also saw the remains of our dirigible—a deflated silver coating was partly submerged right off shore, its structural supports sticking out like the ribs of some long dead goliath. I could see the remains of some of its engines, parts strewn in every direction as if a large explosion had ripped the airship apart. There was luggage everywhere too. I could see clothing, food, and even books floating in the waves.

Each time I picked out a person, dead or alive, one or another image of the disaster solidified...until I switched my gaze to someone else. It was completely disorienting. But I understood that I must have been looking at catastrophes in at least three different timelines. I could climb down and start helping the first person who needed it. It was the right thing to do. But it felt like a choice—once I started to help in one timeline, the others would fade, slip away. I shook my head. I knew what my choice had to be. I sought out someone from the dirigible explosion—that's where Klaire, Mama, Nona, and the twins were. I needed to pick a timeline where we could all be together again. I scanned the beach and tried to systematically focus on each individual. Some made the details of the plane crash sharper; others brought the cruise ship disaster into focus. I made myself push those away, regardless of the guilt I was feeling for not rendering aid. Finally, I found a man sitting in the sand; he was rocking back and forth, clearly in shock. And as I focused on him, everything and everyone but the dirigible and its survivors dissolved into the background. But as soon as I turned away to look for a path down the bluff, the views of different timelines crowded my vision once again, pushing each other for my attention.

There was a lot of debris everywhere, and it was hard to know which belonged to which disaster. I stood up and tried to find an easy to identify natural features that would allow me to find the man from the right timeline quickly. But the beach below was mostly sand and weeds, so I couldn't pick out anything useful. Finally, I noticed that my mark was holding some emergency equipment—a bright red and yellow striped noodly thing. It looked like a floatation device. And once I trained my eye on it, I could spot the noodle right away. That was my tell. Unfortunately, I also felt my body twisting and losing power when I focused on the airship disaster timeline too long—I was a cripple in that one. But that just didn't matter. As long as I had enough time to get to Klaire and the rest first, I felt...I believed I would be able to switch out of that history, sweeping all of my loved ones with me.

Now I just needed to get down. Unfortunately, the bluff was at least fifty feet high and sheer all the way to the sand below. I couldn't jump that; I'd break my neck. I had to find a way to climb down safely. There was no way to get down just below me, so I decided to search parallel to the beach until I found something. I ran about a hundred yards one way— nothing. Then another—all was just a sheer drop, not even grass to grab on to. Every few moments, I stopped and picked out my mark—the guy with noodle—stabilizing my view for a few moments. But the second I let go, my vision became a jumble of overlapping imagery. I had to be careful, or I could easily have fallen off the cliff—the shorelines of the different timelines matched, but they were not one-to-one identical. Once I nearly slipped, and after that I made sure to run a bit farther away from the edge. I was no use to my family if I killed myself accidentally. But as much as I searched, there was no easy way down, no way down at all.

"Damn." I cursed under my breath. I looked out on the ocean; there were people trying to get to shore. I watched as one went down, came up, but then went down and didn't reemerge. I felt tears of frustration and grief suffocating me. I didn't even know if Klaire or Mama or Nona or the kids made it out alive. I had to get down. I...

I saw a person swimming, holding on to the red plastic carry-on. And as I did, the embedded wing of the plane materialized just below me. I could jump down to it and then slide to the fuselage and climb down to the beach from there. It would put me into a wrong timeline, but what other choice did I have? I kept the swimmer and the red suitcase in my peripheral vision and jumped. I hit hard and rolled uncontrollably down the wing. The cape actually saved me it became my improvised sled. I hit the body of the plane hard and came to a stop, my eyes closed. I knew—I didn't know how, but I knew—that if I opened my eyes and didn't find a person from this timeline right away, I would just fall right through to the beach below. It was still a good fifteen feet down and I would probably be okay, unless I hit a piece of jagged debris stuck in the sand. The plane felt hot to the touch—there must have been fire somewhere inside the passenger cabin. But I didn't see open flames when I looked before, so it couldn't have been very bad. I used the second cape to protect my hands and carefully felt my way toward the edge of the wing, scooting on my butt.

I didn't notice right away, but as I turned around and lay on my stomach and pulled my body over the edge of the wing, I heard the sounds of helicopters. Rescue. Finally, there was real help for these people. And since I could still feel the metal of the wing, I assumed that the rescue I was hearing had to be from the plane wreck's timeline. I didn't know what would happen when I was spotted, so I made myself hurry. I dropped the second cape down below and got so that I was hanging off the wing by just my fingers. I counted to three and let go. I opened my eyes as soon as I was in the air. The wing and the plane disappeared almost instantly, yet I managed to glimpse a part of the airplane wheel directly below me...for just a fraction of a moment. Then it was sand. I hit and rolled. Nothing was broken, and I couldn't hear the helicopters clearly anymore.

I stood up and turned to look for the other cape—that cape was from the right timeline, right? It was confusing to keep track of how this worked. Were there identical capes in other timelines? We got these at the music fair...

The galaxy cape was lying in sand just next to my feet, not even ripped. I picked it up and tried to keep my eyes directly below me, on my feet. My visual field was a jumble of information, but now I was in harm's way—there were objects and people that overlapped in space and time. I didn't want to accidentally walk though or into something or someone. Up on the bluff, that wasn't a problem—it was just me and coastal grass and remnants of some agricultural field. This was going to be tricky. I needed to find the man and his noodle, but I no longer knew where he was in relation to where I was now. That was stupid. I should have tried to get relative positions of my mark to the plane. *Oh well.*

I decided to keep my eyes closed and then just to peek judiciously, retaining only a pinhole view of the world. Once in a while, as I looked, the noise of helicopters became deafening, and I was buffeted by strong winds. I stumbled away from where the plane wreck was and tried to walk along the beach, close to the tide line. There were so many injured, one of them must have been from our timeline. As careful as I was, I tripped and fell, and a child cried next to me. I opened my eyes. There were people face down all along the beach, some wearing life vests, some not. The child next to me was a little girl in a purple sweater with a big red heart in the middle; she was pinned underneath a lifeboat that must have carried her to the beach, to safety. I remembered that boat—it was the upside down one, partly buried in the sand. The tide was coming in fast, and the little girl wasn't going to make it if I didn't get her out from under the boat.

"It will be okay now," I said and pushed the spare robe under her head of soggy red curls to keep her mouth and nose above the water. "We'll get you out."

The little girl looked at me with huge brown eyes and nodded a little. She was about five or perhaps a bit older. I stopped being good at guessing the ages of kids once I stopped being one. She was brave, braver than I was. The boat was lying across her thighs; it made me sick just looking at it—it would be a miracle if this girl ever walked again. I stood up and got my fingers under the side of the boat.

"Tell me if it hurts," I said. She nodded, and I tried to shift the weight off her legs. I don't know why I thought I could move this behemoth off the child. The lifeboat was at least thirty feet long and could have easily carried fifty people or more. It must have hit something just off shore to flip like this. I vaguely wondered what happened to the rest of the survivors in the boat. But I put that thought out of my head and heaved. I gave it all I had, and the thing didn't so much as budge. I stood up, smiled at the girl, and leaned over to look what was anchoring the boat. It was immediately obvious—half the boat was buried in the sand already, and more sand was deposited with each wave.

I went down on my knees, smiled at the kid encouragingly again, and started digging around her legs. She was a wisp of a thing, I could just pull her out if...I felt the dead fingers clutching at the tiny bones of her legs almost imme-diately. I stifled a scream. The girl coughed as a large wave washed completely over her face.

I scrunched more material under her, adding my own cape and getting her to an almost sitting position. It bought me a few minutes. I stuck my arms under the sand again and felt for the fingers. Whoever was holding her—her parents, I guessed—died trying to keep her from falling out of the boat. Now their fingers were frozen around their daughter's tiny bones, dragging her under the waves with them. I started pulling up one finger at a time, practically breaking them off. But the water was coming in faster than I could release the child from her parents' dead grasp. I screamed as I pried the dead fingers off her. Someone heard me, and soon there were two more people, survivors of the shipwreck, trying to lift the boat off the girl.

"You lift, I pull," a woman in a torn white uniform told me. So I stopped what I was doing and started to work with the other guy to shift enough of the boat up for the woman to pull the girl out. I couldn't tell the woman that she needed to extract more than just a girl. I couldn't let the kid know about her dead parents. She was smiling me like I was some kind of hero. So I didn't look at her, just strained and pulled. And I knew it was hopeless, and so did the two people with me. The woman screamed for help—there were other people on the beach. Perhaps with a dozen more...

I let go of the boat and looked up. I saw a couple, just a few yards from me. They were cradling a child in a purple jacket and pink tights, who was obviously dead. Their little girl had red hair, all limp and wet. I looked at our girl and her red hair and her pink tights. It was the same in two different timelines. In one she died, in the other she was about to die. But in one, her parents lived. She smiled at me, and I knew what I had to do. I pushed the woman out of my way and held the girl to my chest, wrapping her in endless galaxy cape material.

"I'm going to take you to your parents," I whispered into her ear. I could feel her tiny heartbeat against me. She was going to die if I couldn't move her over. I held her tight and refocused on the grieving couple. Suddenly, the weight of the boat went away—there was no lifeboat in this timeline. The girl and I tumbled backward. She screamed. I looked back; the parents in this timeline were now only holding a child's purple jacket. I was holding their daughter.

"Mom!" she screamed. The man and a woman looked at us, coming out of the waves. It looked for all the world like I just pulled their daughter out of the ocean.

"Lucy!" The woman stumbled up and then ran to us. The man, the girl's father, looked blankly at me and then at the purple jacket in his fist, and then he too screamed for his daughter. They reached me at the same time. I passed Lucy over to them.

Was it wrong? Would they ever know there was a switch? I didn't know—but one child needed her parents, and these people needed their daughter. I was sure that the child they were just clutching in their arms a second ago was now being covered up by the tide, stuck under the lifeboat, buried by the waves with her family.

I stumbled away from them. The woman was holding her child and crying. The man still seemed stunned. The girl looked up at me and smiled. Perhaps she knew. Helicopters were landing on the beach. Rescuers were rushing over with blankets and medical support.

I looked around frantically. All I saw was the upside-down plane. Someone draped a blanket over me and was trying to guide me toward the medical team. I was still clutching the galaxy robes to my chest. I desperately tried to bring back the multiplicity of timelines that were practically incapacitating me moments ago, but now everything was crisp and clear.

I allowed them to walk me along the beach, swaying like a drunken man. Just as we were getting close to the makeshift triage camp, I stumbled and fell face first into the sand. Someone instantly got their arms around me, but as I came up, I pulled up a large purse out of the sand. Klaire's.

❊❊❊

They ushered me into a tent, covered me with a space-age blanket, took my blood pressure, gave me water. I was in a daze. I kept trying to push this reality out. I wanted...needed to get back to the crash site of the dirigible. My family needed me. Someone tried to pull Klaire's purse and the galaxy capes out of hands, but I held on for dear life. That was all I had... all I had.

Some nice man kept asking me for my name. He was talking to me as one spoke to a runaway dog—his voice calm, soothing, almost carrying a melody. I was rocking back and forth and muttering something, I was trying to concentrate, but they assumed I was in shock. I vaguely saw the parents of the little red-haired girl talking with someone who was obviously in charge—she had the most officious-looking uniform. They kept looking at me as the woman took notes.

I didn't know how much time had passed, but at some point I was too tired to try switching the timelines. It was getting dark. More rescue copters landed somewhere up on the bluff, and they were lifting survivors up in gurney to the top and, presumably, evacuating them out of there. Then it was my turn to go. I kept shaking my head, hoping they would just leave me here on the beach. But even I wasn't so stupid as to believe they would. They thought I was injured, and they were going to take me to a hospital whether I wanted to go or not. That was the rescue script, and they were following it to a "t."

"Son." The woman in charge came over once again to talk with me. I looked up and cried at how crisp her image was. I didn't even feel the SHITs anymore. She sat next to me on the beach and put her arm around me. "Do you remember your name?"

I looked at her, confused. I knew my name, but I wasn't sure if I should use "Hig" or "Fred Keen." Which one was the right name for this history?

"I assume you were one of the team members?" she asked, trying to catch my eyes. "You were flying to a soccer match, remember?"

"I was?" I might have been in this timeline.

"It's okay not to remember," she told me gently. "Sometimes it takes a few days, weeks even, for the memories to come back." I nodded like I understood. "You saved that little girl. You remember that?"

I looked to where Lucy's family was sitting before. They were gone now. "Lucy," I said.

"That's right." She seemed very pleased with me for re-membering the girl's name. "You are a hero." When I didn't respond, she gently tried to take Klaire's purse from me. I didn't want to let go...*never let go.*

"It's my girlfriend's," I said.

"Please?" she asked. "I was just hoping to find some ID. We want to tell your folks that you are okay. Please?" And I let go. The purse and the robes tumbled wet to the sand. The woman looked at the robes and glanced at someone. There were hands in blue latex gloves that were picking up and depositing the robes into a plastic bag. "Thank you," she said, meaning the robes, I guess. "Can I look?" She pointed to Klaire's purse. I nodded. She opened it carefully. It was full of sand and seaweed. I noticed that she too was wearing latex gloves. She rummaged inside the purse and pulled out a broken nail file, a sad scrunchy, a water bottle, a pocketknife. But our wallets and phones—hers, mine, and Ms. Marta's—were gone.

"Do you remember your girlfriend's name, son?" She kept calling me "son." I guess there was no better name...yet.

"Klaire," I told her, and my throat constricted and I made a sound like a strangled animal.

The woman's eyes went wide, and her face was all empathy. She looked up at someone but apparently didn't get what she was looking for. "We have the complete passenger roster," she said. "Can I read a few names to you? Perhaps you will recognize someone. It would really help."

I looked around the beach. Most survivors were already lifted up. Soon, it would be my turn. There was no point in even trying any more. I had a few happy months with Klaire and Mama and Nona, and now those days were gone.

"I'm Fred Keen, but everyone calls me Hig," I said.

The woman took a deep breath and smiled. "Captain of the team? Your dads would be so happy to hear you are okay."

Dads? But then I was being strapped into a gurney and lifted up the cliff. An IV line miraculously appeared in my arm, and I felt warm and fuzzy. Then, there was only beige.

Chapter Twenty-Nine: New Life, Again

I woke up in a hospital. *God, I hate those places.* It was white and sterile and smelled of cleaning fluids and death. I was pretty sure I was back in my original timeline...well, my second history—I could walk here.

I lay for a long time with my eyes closed. There was no reason to face reality sooner than necessary. No point to anything, really. They must have been giving me drugs to make me emotionally numb. I wondered how many people died in that plane crush? If my college team was on it, were the people who died the same as my friends? Not that it wasn't a tragedy either way; it was just how I would have to feel about it. This tragedy could be even more personal.

There were careful footsteps—someone was in my room.

"I think he's awake." That was Nona! *Thank god.*

"Nona?" I opened my eyes and tried to reach for her. My sister grabbed my hands, pressed them to her lips, kissed them, and covered them in tears. She was crying so hard, she was hiccupping now. "Nona, I'm okay. I promise," I kept saying over and over again. I was trying to find differences between my Nona and this one. Were they same? Did it matter?

"I was so scared, Hig," she whispered. "I thought everyone

was going to be dead. I saw so many dead people on the news clips."

"It's okay. I'm here, I'm okay." I wanted to ask her about Ms. Marta—did she and the twins make it? Did she hear anything about Klaire? But just then more people walked into my hospital room. I looked over my sister's long golden locks and saw two men dressed in impeccable matching suits—a light and a dark gray, like mirror images of each other. "Dad?"

"Oh, Hig!" Uncle Charlie, the man in light gray, rushed to me and threw his arms around Nona and me both. "You have no idea... They wouldn't tell us anything until just now. They couldn't ID you or something. Oh, Hig, we feared the worst. The worst." And he was crying just like Nona. I looked up and saw my dad standing over us. He was crying too, just a tear rolling down one of his cheeks, but he stood back to give Nona, Uncle Charlie, and me space to wallow in our feelings.

"Dad?" I said again.

"I'm sorry, Hig," he said. "She didn't make it." Nona let out a huge sob, and I felt the wetness of her face through my shoulder...like always...like home.

Uncle Charlie squeezed both of us, holding us tight. "I'm so sorry. I'm so sorry," he kept repeating, his voice gentle as a summer rain.

I didn't know how long we lay and hugged each other. Long enough for my mind to go numb. Finally, I looked at Dad and said, "I want to go home. I don't want to stay here another second." He nodded and left the room.

Uncle Charlie stood up next. He went to the bathroom to get a towel for my sister's face. He gently lifted her off me and wiped her tears with a cold, wet towel. I felt the stray drops on my arm. She was still hiccupping, and he gave her a glass of water from my side table. She drank like a little girl, sloppy and drippy.

"It will be okay. We'll get through it," he told her. "She didn't suffer, I was told." That seemed like a convenient lie given what I saw on that beach. But he shook his head at me, and I let it go. Nona didn't need to know the full horror of it all.

Dad came back almost immediately. He was holding bag full of clothes—for me, presumably—and Klaire's purse. "The social worker game me this," he said about the purse. "They said that it belonged to your girlfriend? Klaire?"

"You have a girlfriend?" Uncle Charlie smiled at me. And then his expression changed to horror. "Oh, Hig. I'm sorry. We didn't know. No one told us."

"But then..." I was confused. I looked from Uncle Charlie to Dad and back. "Who died?"

"Mom?" Nona said in a tiny voice.

✳✳✳

Dad drove us home...to the button factory. That's where the four of us lived, apparently. It looked just like I remembered it when Uncle Charlie was Cherie, except there were two stories now. Not three like in Morgana House or one like Cherie's apartment. The walls were covered with button mosaics of flowers and marine life, but nothing as exotic as in Cherie's place—just California puppies and giant red octopuses and some bright tropical fishes. I recognized them right away; they were not unfamiliar to me. There were photos everywhere—Uncle Charlie and Dad and my sister and I at Disney World, at Grand Canyon, on the beach, on a boat, hiking in the woods. The four of us happy together, exploring the world, making and sharing memories. There was even one of Uncle Charlie in a white summer dress walking on the beach holding Nona's hand, wearing matching sun hats, both smiling, enjoying the sun. There were some photos of Mom, too, but few and only with my sister and me; Dad and Uncle Charlie were not in those. There was one photo of Dad and Uncle Charlie getting married in the field of orange poppies at sunset, the sky a matching golden hue. Nona was just a tittering toddler flower girl. I was about eight there, dressed in a white suit and holding a pillow with wedding rings, grinning from ear to ear. All major life events seemed to coincide in many different histories...just like the plane-boat-dirigible disasters. I was starting to believe that it was not a coincidence but instead some kind of alternative histories law—knots in the timelines that bound histories together at important inflections.

I went around the main room of the button factory, exploring what my life had been like in this timeline. I looked happy. We looked happy. A happy family. I glanced at Dad and Uncle Charlie. They were busy making dinner in the kitchen. They kept watching me from across the room when they thought I wasn't looking. They both had worried expressions on their faces.

"The doctor said you might have trouble remembering things for a while," Nona said in a tone one used with a sick person. She wouldn't let go of me. She clutched my arm like her life depended on it. "But he said it will get better with time. Do you want me to tell you things about the photos, Hig? Perhaps it will help?"

I nodded. We were making the rounds of our life together, and Nona was providing a continuous commentary, little anecdotes about each of the photos that caught my attention. Some sounded familiar, some not at all. It was fortunate that they all thought I had amnesia. Brain damage made things easier; I could screw up with impunity.

I looked for photos of Ms. Marta. There were so many

back at our apartment on sixty-seventh floor. But there were none here. It seemed that Ms. Marta never came to raise us in this timeline. In this history, Dad married Uncle Charlie after divorcing our mom. And Uncle Charlie stayed a man who occasionally wore a dress—just as he wanted. He had it all in this timeline. I was happy for him...for them.

We had dinner almost in total silence—my family was watching me, judging the amount of damage or head trauma or whatever with every forkful of pasta. I finally had to excuse myself. I did have an insane headache and told them as much. But mostly I just needed to be alone to process what just happened...to grieve.

"They didn't think you had a concussion," Uncle Charlie said. Nona kept calling him Daddy Charlie, so I tried to make a switch to Charlie—"Daddy Charlie" was not something I could do. Not yet. I even tried to drop "Uncle" and just use "Charlie" in my head; I was getting better at that anyway after Morgana House. "But a bad headache could be a symptom..." Charlie didn't finish, just exchanged yet another meaningful look with my dad. "Yes, why don't we have you go to bed. The doctor did say to let you have plenty of rest in the next few days. And of course, no school." I totally forgot that was even a thing. Did I go to the same school in this timeline? "They lost the entire team...almost. So—"

"What?" I cried out. "The entire team? All but me?"

Charlie looked at my dad in panic, and he answered instead. "Hig." So I was still Hig here, even with my parents... my dads. "Hig, we don't have all the information yet. Until the authorities notify the families, we won't know. And there is an investigation going on." He looked at Charlie, and Charlie dropped his head. "There was a bomb on the plane."

"What?" I had no idea. "Is that why we crashed?" Did the bomb happen in all three timelines I saw? I sensed a rush of adrenaline; my skin was hot and sweaty. I felt dizzy.

"There were some Kismet terrorists onboard, apparently." Dad looked at me like I should say something now, but I just looked back blankly. I had no idea what he was talking about. "Those robes—"

"The galaxy ones?" I asked stupidly. And suddenly it made sense—the way they took them from me like evidence and all those questions they were asking. They thought I was... "Dad, Charlie, you don't think that I..."

"No, of course not, Hig." Charlie reached out and took my hands and looked at me, full of love. "Of course not. But the authorities will come back to ask questions. Do you know where those came from?"

"I..." I tried to think what to say. "I was holding a girl. The red-haired girl named Lucy. She was in the water. And I used the robes to...I don't remember. Sorry."

"That's okay, son," Dad said. The way he said it made me trust him somehow. "We told the authorities that you had nothing to do with those crazy people. But you will have to talk with them again. A lot of people died, Hig. They need to figure out what and who and why. You understand, right? Anything you can remember could be important."

"Yes." I would have to come up with something plausible.

"And this girl? Klaire?" Charlie said.

"Have you heard anything?" I was terrified to ask. I didn't really want to know the answer if...if...

"There was no one by that name on your flight, Hig. No one. Are you sure that was her name?"

"I...I... I have a really bad headache. Can I go to my room?" I asked and realized and had no idea where my room was.

"I'll take you," said Charlie. And he drew me into a warm hug, the one that always made my fears disappear. Oh, how I wished it worked that way now.

He took me up a spiral staircase behind the open kitchen. It was sort of in the same place that the stairs were in Morgana House. Nona followed behind, like a little mouse. Poor kid. Charlie led me into a corner bedroom at the end of a long hall. It had two big windows on the adjoining walls, looking out on the cross streets. There was a big bed in the other corner. The walls were covered with posters of soccer stars of this timeline. I didn't recognize any of them. There was a bookcase with several photos in frames, just like back in our apartment. But there were no crutches or a wheelchair anywhere in sight. I was never sick or crippled in this timeline, at least not obviously so.

I sat on the bed, a bit dazed. It was dark outside already, but there were lots of streetlights and electric signs visible. This was a bustling metropolis. Nothing like New Amsterdam. Everything was different.

"Do you want my help?" Charlie asked.

I shook my head. "I will be fine. I just need some sleep," I said and even managed a smile.

Charlie turned to guide my sister out of the room, but she squirmed away and sat on the bed next to me. He smiled. It was the same beatific smile. Made me ache inside.

"Don't keep him up too long, Nonaken," he said and left us alone in the room. My room.

✳✳✳

"I knew you weren't dead," she said. "I knew it. I told them so."

Nona was clutching at my arm again, but her other arm was wrapped around her waist. I recognized the gesture and felt another jolt of adrenaline hit.

"Nona? Does your stomach hurt?" I tried to sound

neutral, but I heard the panic in my voice. She did too. Her eyes got huge—two giant, shinning topaz gems in the dark on my room. She nodded. "Feels like a rope?" I whispered; just air passing my lips bypassing my vocal cords completely. She nodded again; and I took her hand in mine and held tight. "When did it start?" I asked.

"I'm not really sure," she said. "But it definitely was there when you got on that flight. Daddy thought it was indigestion. We left the airport early because of me. Remember?"

I ignored that little prod for information and instead asked, "But it's not indigestion, is it?"

"I don't think so." She pushed her face into my shoulder, just like when she was a toddler. "I don't think so because it's not the first time it's happened." She talked into my sweat-shirt, mumbling, scared. I could feel the words she was say-ing against my skin.

"And the time before, when was it?"

"When we went to the fair," she said. I shuddered, and I knew she felt it. "Will it be okay?"

"I don't know," I said honestly. "But I need you to tell me what happened at the fair."

"You were there."

"Yes, but I don't remember what happened." After a mo-ment of silence, I added, "Please, Nona. Please. It's important."

"A little over a month ago, you went to the fair with a bunch of your friends, remember?" I shook my head, and she continued. "Well, you didn't take me."

"I'm sorry."

"So the next day I insisted, and it was a Saturday, so you took me."

"Was it just the two of us?" I asked. I was barely able to breathe.

"Just us," she said. "We watched some chicken beauty

pageant and then went to a crafts booth. You were going to buy me and Daddy hats. You know how he loves hats? While we were there—"

"Yes?"

"We ran into Mom."

"She was there too?"

"She goes all the time," Nona said, and I heard soreness in her voice. "She never takes me."

"I see. So what happened then?"

"There was a stupid one mirror fun house." I stopped breathing altogether. "It had one of those stupid Kismet spirals all over it, the ones that Mom likes so much. Dad says that's why she goes all the time. She is a Kismet junky. But I didn't really know what that meant. I mean, I've looked it up a few times, but it is all stupid stuff about changing one's fate and crap. Daddy always talks about it like it's something only crazy people do. Dad doesn't even talk about it. But there it was. Galaxies and stars and swirls. And there was this woman with white eyes, and she knew your name, Hig. She knew you like she could see you. Only she was blind, so she couldn't. But she called you Hig, and Mom got scared and told us to go home. So we did. And that night I felt sick. I didn't know what it was. I was scared. I told Daddy Charlie. I mean, as a nurse he would know, right? He thought I just had my period. But I knew it was about that blind woman. But I couldn't tell him we went to the fair and saw Mom. He never let me go before. Dads think that all Kismet people are terrorists or something. And now they blew up your plane. And I felt it. I felt it, Hig. It was like a rope tied from my insides to that plane. And for a time when we knew the plane went down, I didn't feel it. And I thought you were dead. And I was terrified and couldn't tell. I thought I lost you." She was crying again. The whole thing just spilled out of her. And I held her and rocked her like I did when she was just a baby and Mom was dying...except that wasn't in this timeline. It was in another life. *Damn.*

She fell asleep on my bed, and I tucked the blankets all around her. It was soothing hearing her little snores. I loved that sound. But I couldn't sleep. I stood up and walked about "my room," looking at "my things." It all felt alien...and not. I stopped by the bookcase and looked at the photo of me, Nona, and Mom. Mom was wearing the orange poppy jacket Uncle Charlie...Daddy Charlie gave her the day we went to the fair that first time...in my first timeline. And here it was here. We went to the fair here, too. I remembered a similar photo in my bedroom, also on the bookshelf—Mom holding Baby Nona and me on my crutches. Uncle Charlie took that photo before we left the house that morning. He left his camera behind when he fled, and Mom had it developed, printed, and framed a few months after. She was real sick by then. And Uncle Charlie was missing...and so was Dad.

"I remember that day," Charlie said. I jumped; I hadn't heard him come in. "Sorry to startle you, Hig."

"I'm okay," I managed.

"I see Nonaken is sleeping in your bed again."

"Again?"

"Ever since you two went to that stupid fair a couple of months ago. Or was it is just a few short weeks back?" He shook his beautiful head. Uncle Charlie was such a beautiful man.

"What happened at the fair?" I asked. I wanted his perspective.

"You ran into your mom, and it got ugly. Nonaken got sick for a whole week. She always had a weak stomach."

"Do you remember when you took this photo?" I asked. I really wanted to know about that fair, the one thirteen years ago.

He looked at the photo with me, and his face had a sad smile. "I felt like I won the life lottery that day," he finally said. "I still feel guilt over breaking up my sister's marriage. But you had to know just how miserable she and Fred were. Staying together was killing both of them. And when I came—"

"You were like sunshine on a stormy day," I said. "Every time you came, you made it better. I never wanted you to leave. I always begged you to stay. And I felt guilt for years..."

He turned me around and pulled me into a hug. He was taller than Cherie...my Charlie. My head nestled into his shoulder like it belonged, the way Nona's head felt on mine. And I knew that he felt guilt, too. He loved us, and Dad, and his sister. And in this timeline, Uncle Charlie found a way to allow himself and Dad to be happy, even as Mom was never going to be.

"Did we go into the Kismet Booth at the county fair all those years ago?" I asked, even as I knew the answer. I felt him tense up and then nod.

"It was a silly thing to do," he said. "But back then, it was not like it is now. It was just a silly thing, not criminal. I thought it would cheer everyone up. There was a big fight that morning. Fred didn't want to go with us at all. But Moira thought that you would like it. She said we all needed a fun day out."

"What happened at the Kismet Booth?" I pushed.

"Nothing really. We looked into the mirror. We left. Fred stormed out. We—Sissy, you and Nonaken, and I—stayed a bit longer. But it was a sour experience after that, so we went home soon after, too."

"And then?"

"The short version is that Moira had a nervous breakdown and ran away. I moved in to help. About a year later, Fred and I were married. You were the ring bearer, which I'm sure you remember well." I didn't say anything. "Sissy spent a year in a mental hospital and has been in and out ever since. This Kismet cult totally messes people up. It's a blight. They are evil, Hig. You know that, right? The way they take the vulnerable and mess with their heads? And now her addiction cost Moira her life...and lives of so many others. It's such a tragedy. No wonder your mind decided to make you forget. It is so painful to remember." He hugged me tightly again. "You know that you can tell me anything, Hig, right? You know that? That I'm here for you, no matter what? I love you no matter what, okay?"

"Okay."

I said something about being tired again and the need to just be alone for a while. He kissed me on the forehead and left. I sat on the chair and stared out of the window until the sky started to turn gray, signaling the coming of a new day.

Chapter Thirty: Learning Curve

We received the invitation to the memorial services for my team the next day. I woke up late...well, in the afternoon. Nona crept out of my bedroom without me even knowing it. I was completely exhausted. When I finally got downstairs, the invitation was left on the kitchen counter, propped on a fruit basket for me to find along with a note from Dad—he and Charlie had to go and deal with the authorities. He was vague about it, but I'd bet it had something to do with me being questioned again. The thing was that I really didn't know anything, at least not anything useful to the police of this timeline. And I too needed information, and I had no ideas on how to get it. I didn't find a single computer in the house, but I saw Dad use something like a cell phone. How did people in this timeline get information? I needed to find out fast. I felt like I was walking on thin ice, and my amnesia would only save me for so long before even Dad and Charlie would get suspicious. And then there was Nona...

She was reading a book when I came down. Apparently she was off the hook for school, too. A city-wide week of mourning had been declared. All schools were closed.

"Daddy left you some eggs and bacon in the oven, but I'm

sure they are ice-cold by now," she informed me.

I checked the oven, and sure enough there was a nice plate of Charlie's eggs in there. All of a sudden, I was ravenously hungry. It didn't matter if the breakfast was cold; I wolfed it up. Nona joined me in the kitchen and watched me eat.

When I was done, she took my plate. "I can make more?" she offered. But I shook my head. What was left of my hunger was just in my head. My stomach was full; my brain just didn't know it yet.

"Can we talk some more?" I asked. "It helps me to remember."

She sat next to me at the kitchen table and asked, "What do you want to know?" The way she looked at me, it was like she knew it wasn't my memory that we were trying to jog.

"Do you remember Ms. Marta?" I asked. I figured she was a safe topic—if Nona didn't remember, I could say it was a name of an old babysitter when she was just a baby.

But she remembered. "She used to take care of us when I was little," she said. "I don't really remember her well. But she was nice, I'm sure. Daddy would never hire a mean person to take care of us."

"Do you know what happened to her?"

"I assume she went on to take care of other babies, right?" She shrugged, like it was an obvious thing. "Why, Hig? Why are you asking about Ms. Marta?"

"You don't know if she was on that plane too?"

Nona's eyes got huge again. "Ms. Marta? Oh god! I don't know. I don't think so. Daddy would have said something. Why? Did you see her on the plane? Oh, Hig. That would be just—"

"No, I didn't see her." That was the truth. "I just remembered her and wanted to understand why."

"Oh, okay." She nodded, visibly trying to calm down. "You really scared me, Hig. I don't want to know that more people I know are dead. I just can't take it."

"I'm sorry, Nona. I didn't mean to upset you. I—"

"It's fine. I get it, Hig. Keep asking." And she looked at me like she could read my soul.

I inhaled and continued, "What about a man by the name of Roger Hill? Does that name mean anything to you?"

"Uncle Roger?"

"Uncle?"

"Daddy and Uncle Roger work together. They run a house for very sick kids. He comes over all the time. Here." She rushed out and brought a photograph of Roger and all of us sitting at a dinner table, celebrating something. "Does he look familiar?"

"Yes," I said. It was Roger all right. So there was a Roger here, too. "And what about Klaire? Did I ever talk about a girl from school named Klaire?" I felt my nails digging into my flesh as I tried to be casual.

"You mean your girlfriend?"

"You know her?" I was hyperventilating again.

"No. But that was the name you told Dads. The purse? You said it was Klaire's. Right?"

"Yes. But do you know her?"

"Sorry, Hig. I've never heard you mention her." She looked at me with pity.

I tried to collect myself. This didn't mean that Klaire wasn't in this timeline, just that in this history we weren't dating. So even if I did find a Klaire, she wouldn't be *my* Klaire. And so it wouldn't do. I didn't realize right away, but that was the moment I made my decision to go. I couldn't stay. I would never be happy here in this timeline. Nana, Dad, and Uncle Charlie would all be okay without me. They all seemed happy, well adjusted. They didn't need me. They would mourn, but they didn't need me. I needed Klaire. I also needed to find out more about her. Like I had no idea which farm she grew up on, I never met the aunts who looked after her; I hardly knew anything of her background other than she raised chickens as a kid. But to find her again, I might need to know all that.

"How do we search for things?" I asked. I knew I sounded dumb, but I had to know.

"You mean like a library?"

"Well, do we have computers?" There I said it, and my head didn't explode or anything. Good sign...

"There are computers where Dads work," Nona said. Her eyes held mine like a vise. She knew there was something very wrong with me. "Dad uses it to evaluate stocks and some financial things. Daddy Charlie has a database that has all the stuff about the children he works with. A database is like a computer library or something."

The way she explained it made it clear that personal computers were not a thing in this timeline. Whatever I was going to do to try to get back into the timeline with my Klaire would be much more difficult without easy access to information. You'd think that computers and the Internet would have been invented in all timelines, but obviously not.

"I see," I said as Nona patiently waited for me to figure things out. "Can I ask a few more weird questions?"

"Sure. But you can probably look up Klaire's address at your school's record office or simply use the address book in the library. You do know where Klaire's family lives, right?" I must have made a grimace because she said, "You don't, do you?"

"We just didn't get around to asking about that," I said and felt some strange combination of guilt and shame.

"I know about the families of all my friends," Nona said.

"Huh."

"I just find it strange. Didn't you care?"

"I did. And I know a lot about Klaire. I know she grew up on a farm with her two aunts."

"But you never bothered to ask where the farm was? I bet you don't even know her aunts' names." That was also true and very painful.

"Look, Nona. I know a lot about Klaire, okay?"

She shrugged. "If you say so."

I inhaled and tried to put that aside. I loved Klaire. I was pretty sure she felt very strongly about me. All the while, Nona was watching me, and her gaze was making me squirm. "Look, I know how it was...is between Klaire and me. Now, please. I want to know...to remember a few other things. For example, how did Charlie and Roger meet?"

Nona nodded, noticing my slip-ups, but answered right away. "Uncle Roger's son died. Daddy was the one who took care of him in the end. They have been friends ever since. But this was way before I was born, Hig. I don't really know any details, sorry."

"That's fine. That's good." So this too was similar. Roger from Morgana House did say that in most histories, his son died very young. So this made sense. And this Roger didn't go looking for a way of getting his son back. He started a company to help other sick children. That was his way of filling the void. Kismet was toxic in this timeline, so it made sense that this Roger didn't go chasing fate across histories...like I was planning on doing.

"Don't leave me, Hig," Nona suddenly pleaded and grabbed on to me. "Please, Hig. Don't go."

I wrapped my arms around her. She was crying again. In a few moments, my shoulder would be wet. "Do you still feel it?" I asked gently. She nodded into my shoulder, and I felt the wet grounded in. "Which direction?" Her arm shot out and pointed toward one of the walls. I didn't know which way that was; I'd bet it was pointing exactly at the disaster beach. "Would you tell me if it stopped or changed directions?"

"Yes." I could hardly hear her; her voice was so quiet.

"Thank you, Nonaken."

***

I noticed an unmarked police car parked outside our home...well, I assumed it was police. I first spotted it by accident, looking out of my bedroom window. I caught the woman inside looking at me. She quickly pretended that it was just an accidental brush of gazes, but she was still there three hours later and then again the next morning. I was being watched. Someone believed that I was connected with Kismet gang—not wrong—and the bomb—dead wrong.

At home, our family dynamics were crazy, too. Dad and Charlie spent a lot of time at home—Nona said it was very unusual; they both worked a lot. My sister was my source of all things normal...and not. Our dads would often come over to me and pat me on the back or ruffle my hair or just smile in my direction. It was as if they couldn't get enough of me. This was not normal behavior. And yet we never talked, really talked. Klaire never came up again; I didn't even know what happened to her wet purse. Dad had it at the hospital, and then it vanished. Nona too was exceedingly clingy, never letting me out of her sight for long. It was like they were all waiting for something, for me to make a wrong move. It felt practically claustrophobic.

At the same time, we were all getting ready for the memorial services to be held on the grounds of my school. I was asked to say a few words about my dead team. I refused but somehow wasn't really off the hook. The whole city seemed to be planning on turning out. There were many discussions about it on the news on the radio—they had radios, but no TV here, just movies with daily changing news clips. Everyone was talking about the bomb, and the Kismet terrorists, and all those people who died. It was the worst terrorist act on record. People just didn't kill to improve their fates. It was crazy. Out of one hundred passengers and seven crew members, sixty-seven died. Yes, the same number as the floors in my old apartment, but coincidences like those no longer fazed me.

I was hailed as a hero who saved the little girl. Dad said that the city was planning on awarding me a medal...after the memorial service, after the full investigation into the bombing was closed. It was like someone somewhere was worried that I might also be a bad guy, and if so, it might not do to give me honors, even if I saved a kid. All this attention, negative and positive, put insane constraints on my movements. Basically, I just didn't leave the button factory. Frankly, I didn't really have anywhere to go...in this timeline.

Yet I wanted to go back to the scene of the disaster, to that beach. But it was five days now. What would be left? If there were survivors, they wouldn't have stayed there. The only thing that gave me hope was Nona's stomach—she still felt that strange connection to the mirror, and it still pointed north, she thought. I didn't know how long that connection was going to hold, but in a previous timeline, it lasted days. So I didn't have a ton of time. If I wanted to find that rip between timelines, I needed to go as soon as possible. With everyone watching me, that was going to be difficult. The memorial service was really my only opportunity to slip away unnoticed, however unlikely. So I planned.

I found an old backpack in the back of my closet and

started to fill it with useful things—matches, change of clothing, a pocketknife. It was amazing just how parallel the parallel timelines really were. It seemed that a foldable knife, matches, and backpacks were a universal constant. Money must have been too, but I hadn't solved that puzzle here yet.

"Nona?" She was back in my room, watching me go systematically through everything I owned. I knew she suspected me, but I was trying to make it more difficult for her by looking at everything.

"Yeah?" She looked up from her portable tablet. That was another strange thing about this timeline—they had computers, but they were used very differently from how I grew up using them. Mostly, there were these giant things—I imagined them giant, but they might not have been for all I knew—that powered organizations like Charlie's and Roger's charity for sick kids and my dad's financial firm. But there were no home computers, just these portable tablets that people used to text each other and to read books and newspapers. The tablets only showed text, no images at all. If one wanted colorful photographs or videos, one had to buy paper magazines or go out to the movies. It really changed how society behaved. Sure, people texted each other all the time. Nona was in constant communication with dozens of her girlfriends, but things remained private and contained in a smallish circle of friends and family. There were no Facebooks or Twitters or Instagrams, no way to publicly shame and humiliate or spread misinformation and gossip on a national scale. It that way, this timeline was actually far superior to ours. It also limited my exposure to strangers. Sure, people knew my name and had seen some photographs—mostly the official photo from our school team—but I didn't think I would be easily recognized by everyone. I was a celebrity, and yet I had a modicum of privacy. This gave me hope.

"Yeah?" she asked again. "Stop thinking so hard all the time, Hig. It's not normal even for you."

"Normal?" I asked.

"You did tell me to tell you—"

"Yeah, sorry, Nonaken." I noticed that I was the only one who called Nona Nona here. Everyone referred to my sister as Nonaken. I had to get used to that again.

"Nona is fine," she said as if reading my thoughts. "So what do you want to know now?"

"Money. I want to know how money works. How do we pay for things?" I asked and felt intensely stupid. How did one not know how money worked?

My sister gave me one of those "really?" looks, but went on to explain patiently. "It's like what Dad works with. You put your hand on a recognizer, like so." She demonstrated holding her hand out and cupping something like a ball, fingers down, knuckles up. I mimicked her, feeling very dumb. She laughed. "You've done this thousands of times, Hig. Dad set you up with your own account when you were thirteen."

"But I don't remember," I said and saw pain flash across Nona's face. "Sorry," I added. I hated causing everyone around me pain. "I'm trying to remember, Nonaken. And you are really helping. Please go on."

"Okay," she said. Her face was serious now, worried. "The recognition device reads your hand print and gives you access to your accounts. You can pay for anything this way. All stores and train stops have them. It's easy."

"So it's all biometrics?"

"Bio-what?" she asked. And I felt a wave of sickness. I was getting used to those and hid the effects well now, I hoped.

"So there is no paper money or coins?" I asked.

"Not for many decades. Daddy Charlie showed me some coins he got from his father when he was young."

"I see." This was going to be a problem. We never did do a DNA test of Cherie, so we never figured out if the same individuals from different timelines shared biological traits. What was the chance that their Hig had the same—or close enough—fingerprints to mine? I couldn't walk to that beach from here. I had to take some form of transportation. And I had pay for it. I needed money. "Nonaken, I know this sounds stupid, but do you mind going out with me and showing? I don't mind you knowing how I'm screwed up, but I would rather seem smarter to strangers. Okay?"

"Sure." She jumped off my bed and went downstairs. "Coming?" she called from below. I ran to follow.

*****

This New York City was different from the metropolis where I grew up and from New Amsterdam, although on a first glance it was closer to my city. There were no cars, but there was plenty of traffic on the streets, directly on the streets. Most were trams, but some were these cool taxi things that also traveled on rails. Nona said there was also an underground rail system that connected everything and moved faster than street traffic. We, of course, didn't have any form of underground where I grew up. There was just too much construction built up on the streets. How would they have dug up all those foundations? But Nona said that here they started the underground railway before the tall buildings were built—that's foresight!

We walked on the wide pedestrian lanes of the streets between buildings. It felt like we were walking in canyons. Everything was rising so high up above our heads that we could hardly see the sky. There were no trees, but most buildings had some sort of living walls. Nona said that it was necessary to keep pollution down. Apparently a lot of city kids got asthma here, so the city put up the living walls as one of the solutions to the epidemic.

Nona was giving me the grand tutorial on *this* timeline and *this* New York in particular. I worried at which point it would be too much. I already knew that my sister suspected me. She might not be clear about what it was, but she was keeping a close eye on me, making mental notes.

"Don't tell our dads, please," I finally said. "They would just freak out."

She nodded noncommittally. "I overheard Daddy talking with Dad about you," she said.

"And?"

"Daddy thinks we should take you back for additional medical tests after the memorial."

"I see. Thanks for letting me know. Can you keep me undated? I don't want more people messing with me, okay?"

She nodded again, and we kept walking. Evidently, the neighborhood we lived in was completely residential—not many places to buy things. And the button factory was the only two-story building I'd seen thus far. Nona said something about it being a historical landmark, and I didn't press further. Most buildings around us were built in what Uncle Charlie of my childhood would have called Grand Art Deco style of architecture. They looked a bit like a cross between a medieval cathedral and a Lego construction set—cool shapes and angular decorations, almost toy-like. The living walls were attached to most and mostly at odd angles. It wasn't unattractive, just strange to *my* eyes.

We walked along a number one tramline. There were stops every few blocks. Nona offered to take me on a ride, but I was worried about sitting still among people long enough for them to recognize me—my photo was in all the papers and newsreels. I wanted to stay anonymous as much as was possible, and thus we walked. I thought my sister understood.

We walked out of the apartment building labyrinth and into a Disneyesque sugary insanity of a shopping mall neighborhood. It hit me so hard, I stumbled back.

"What—" I didn't have the words to describe what I was seeing. Things were spinning and flashing and shinning and pushing themselves on us. There were hordes of young people strolling around, gawking at an insane collection of incomprehensible wares—schools were closed for a city-wide period of mourning. And then there were very deliberate shoppers, adults maneuvering expertly through the crowds of kids to get the items they came here for.

"You never liked shopping." Nona smirked. "Just like Dad, you've always got Daddy to get you all the things you've ever needed."

"But how can one find anything?" I was looking around and felt almost a physical need to step back into the cool canyons behind us.

"Come on." She pulled us into the madness, and in a few short steps I was completely disoriented. It wasn't like I'd never shopped before. I went to Abba's corner store all the time to get things that we were out of. But Ms. Marta did most of the major shopping. And I guess Dad used to order things online—we got packages of things we needed delivered to the door of our apartment. When I couldn't walk, I didn't go shopping at all. And when I could, I never got into the practice. I preferred to watch the city from above. Being in this mosh-pit in the flesh seemed...not dangerous, exactly, but certainly anxiety-inducing. Nona was as happy as a fish in the water; this was clearly her native environment.

We took a glass elevator on the side of the building about two dozen stories high. I couldn't tell because the floors weren't marked with numbers, just with destinations. It made sense—what could a number really tell me other than height? The floor we got off at was a movie theater. They were playing six movies, none of which I recognized.

"Come on," Nona said again. "It's dark in there, and it will give you a better sense of the world." She was right, and that was terrifying.

At the door to one of the screening rooms, there was a line of people waiting to "pay." We stood, and I got to observe how each person did it. I saw people grab this giant doorknob-looking thing, and a small screen next to it showed the name of the movie and the price per ticket. A person could select how many tickets they were buying.

"Don't worry," Nona said. "If it doesn't work, I'll pay for it." I squeezed her hand—we had been holding hands since entering this crazy neighborhood. I was grateful for her help.

When it was our turn, I placed my hand of the spherical knob and squeezed, like I'd seen others do. Nothing happened. Cold sweat exploded down my back. I adjusted my fingers and tried again. A light flashed on the console just next to my fingers: Error. *Please consult with a customer representative at the sales booth. Sorry for any inconvenience.* I jerked my hand back, but the error message remained. People in line behind us were looking at me now. I guessed this didn't happen much in this world. Did it brand me as some kind of criminal?

"Is that Fred Keen?" someone spoke behind me. "Hey, man. You're a hero!"

Then other people started to point at me. I moved back and away from the ticket pay station, wishing myself to disappear. Nona grabbed my arm and pulled. We rushed into the crowd, and it parted like water. People were pointing at us, shouting out my name. It was overwhelming. In the confusion, I felt another set of strong arms tug on me and push me into a side door. The noise cut away, and I turned and saw Dad.

"This way," he barked at us and led through another set of doors and into a white service corridor. The doors shut, and the noise cut away. We were the only ones there. "Now," he turned on me, "it's time you told me who you really are and what you've done with my son."

Chapter Thirty-One: Family

I looked from Nona to Dad and back. My sister's face was contorted with guilt, but there was defiance in her too. She was about to say something, but Dad stopped her.

"Let him talk, Nona," he said. She let go of me and stepped behind our dad. I felt totally betrayed.

"I'm Hig," I said, meeting my dad's eyes in defiance. "I was born Fred Keen Jr. I'm the son of Fred Keen and Moira Keen—you and Mom. I have a sister almost eight years younger than me. Her name is Nona Keen." I glanced at my sister, and she flinched as if I hit her. "I was born in a small suburb of metropolitan New York City, next to the county fair grounds. Charles Labelle is my uncle." Dad listened without so much as blinking. So I went on. What did I have to lose at that point? "Thirteen years ago, the five of us—Uncle Charlie, Mom, Baby Nona, you, and I—went to a county fair. There, at a crafts booth pavilion, we walked into a Looking Glass of Fate exhibit run by a blind woman." Dad inhaled deeply but didn't interrupt. "We all took turns looking into her mirror. The Mistress of the Mirror said that Nonaken was too young to pass the mirror test, so she was carried into the booth by Mom." I paused, trying to discern some reaction from Dad. He was like stone. My sister was hiding behind his back, her eyes dilated, full of horror.

"Go on," Dad ordered.

I shrugged and continued. "I stood up from my wheel-chair and used my crutches to get to the mirror in the back of the booth."

"What did you see?" The way he asked, I knew that Dad looked into that mirror, too. I wasn't telling an unfamiliar story.

"I saw me, just as I am today. Healthy, no crutches."

"Anything else?"

"After about a year, Mom was dead." Nona made a hysterical gasp. "I no longer needed even crutches," I continued. "You," I looked directly into Dad's eyes, "were a successful businessman, and we moved to a high-rise apartment in the heart of the metropolis. And Uncle Charlie went missing."

"Uncle Charlie?" Nona's voice sounded scared, uncertain. "Daddy?"

"Uncle Charlie and Dad were never married. Thirteen years later, Uncle Charlie came back into our lives as Cherie Hydrargyros. She was dating you. I'm not sure if you knew who she really was, though."

"I see," Dad said. "Were you on that plane? Before the crush?"

I shook my head, and Nona made another gasp. "I was on a dirigible with my girlfriend Klaire and Ms. Marta and the twins."

"Ms. Marta?" Dad asked. I nodded. "Are they...are they all dead?"

"I don't know. I don't know." And I felt tears running down my face again. It was actually good to tell someone the truth. The burden of not knowing, of not knowing even what to do... "I woke up on the bluff. My medi-drone—that's like a wheelchair that floats—was gone. I had two galaxy robes on me, and not much else. Klaire and I were together, but when

I woke up, she was gone. I screamed and ran—I could run again—but couldn't find her up there. So I went to the edge of the cliff and saw...and saw..."

Dad put his arms on my shoulders. He was no longer glaring at me. He was almost gentle. "Hig? What did you see down on that beach?"

"I saw a plane crash, a cruise ship run aground and broken in half, and the remains of our dirigible floating in water. There might have been more, but I'm not sure. I did see at least three disasters clearly. And there were dead and dying people everywhere, from every disaster. I had to get down to help. But there was no way down." I was sobbing, and Dad pulled me into a hug. He was taller than me, and I practically collapsed into his broad chest, crying like a little kid. I felt Nonaken reach out and stroke my back. These strangers loved me. I was not alone. And slowly, between sobs, I told them the rest, including how I swapped the little girl from one timeline into this one. "I'm no hero at all, Dad," I said. "I'm even not sure I'm your son."

"Hig." Dad put his hands on the sides of my head and looked directly into my face, just inches away. "You are still my son. And you are as much a hero as everyone thinks you are. You reunited that child with her parents. Her *living* parents. She will grow up being loved by her mom and dad. That's a miracle."

"But—"

"There are no buts, Hig. You did good. Now we need to find Ms. Marta and your girl. Klaire? Do you know where she lives?" I shook my head. I had never bothered to learn. "No matter," Dad reassured me, "we will find out. Charlie and I have many ways of finding people." And it was like a huge burden was lifted off my shoulders. These people, perhaps they were not strangers. "Let's go home, okay, Hig?" Dad said.

***

Dad led us out of the shopping neighborhood via a series of white hallways and service elevators. I was totally lost almost instantly, but I trusted Dad to get me home safely.

Charlie was waiting for us. He looked drawn, frightened even. Nona rushed into his arms as soon as we walked in. Charlie held her in his arms and my dad with his eyes.

"He is Hig," Dad reassured him. And I saw some of the tension drain away from Charlie's face. "But he is not *our* Hig." He led us into the living room, and we all sat down. Dad held my hand, and it felt like an anchor of security in world that had lost all semblance of stability. I didn't want to let go. Strange. All those years I had barely tolerated Dad, and here I was needing him. If nothing else, this was proof that I was living a very different history now.

"What does it mean?" Nonaken asked. She was holding on to Charlie like he was her island of peace amid the storm. Back in my first timeline, I probably would have chosen Uncle Charlie for emotional support, too. That Dad was not available that way to me. To anyone, probably.

"Do you still feel that knot in your stomach?" Dad asked my sister gently. She nodded. So she told him everything, even that. I couldn't really blame her. "Is it still pointing north? Does it still have a direction?" he asked.

Nonaken concentrated, and her eyes rolled as if she was looking deep inside herself. "I don't know," she finally said. "When the accident happened, the direction was clear. I could have walked there with my eyes closed. But now? It's all fuzzy. I still feel the sick feeling, but I can't tell where it ends, only where it begins." She rubbed her middle; Charlie pulled her even closer, loving the pain away.

"I don't know how Kismet got hold of you—"

"Stop it, Fred." Charlie cut Dad off. "Those people are evil. We don't have anything to do with them. Ever." His eyes were begging for Dad to stop.

But Dad didn't. He held my hand and continued, "Thirteen years ago, I took Nona and Hig to the county fair. Moira didn't want to go. She had another anxiety attack, or at least she said she did. It didn't matter; I wanted to take you kids someplace fun, with sunshine and happy people. We saw the chicken competitions."

I smiled; that seemed to be a constant, too. But then I saw Charlie and remembered—his story of what happened then was different. There was a shuffling of timelines for this Charlie, and this Dad, and this Nona. It wasn't just I who was different, an outsider. We might all have been.

"After the chickens, we went inside to grab some food and buy something fun to take home to Moira." Dad continued his version of the county fair family excursion. "She texted me by then and said that she was sorry for not coming. I told her to meet us at the crafts pavilion. Nona was asleep in her pram. And Hig and I wandered about, looking at all the cool things on sale. There was one guy that made swords and knives, and he showed Hig how he tooled leather sheaths for them."

"Vic," I said, and they all looked at me. "The guy who makes knives and such, his name is Victor."

"Could be," Dad said finally. "I don't really remember. Nona woke up, and I took her over to the apple-faced kuklas booth. I think the woman's name was Missy or Messy." He looked at me.

"Missy," I said. He nodded.

"Missy. I got one of those dolls for Nona. The Kismet Booth was just across from Missy's. It was not a big deal back then. Now, it's a bunch of crazy radicals. Back then, it was just something silly and fun one did, like reading a horoscope in a Sunday paper. Harmless fun. In any case, your mom came just then and found us there. She insisted that we do this one thing together."

"You went into the Looking Glass of Fate booth," I whispered. "It's like all of the timelines were somehow tied into a knot around that one event, that one stupid mirror."

"At the time, I thought it was just harmless fun," Dad said, a bit defensively. "And it was. I went in and carried Nona in my arms. She was just a baby and it didn't matter, the blind woman said. Then Moira went and came out screaming. It was a scene. I rushed all of us out of there. Moira wouldn't calm down, so an ambulance took her away. She was committed into a psychiatric ward. Charlie came out from California to help us. Our marriage was over even before then, but after her breakdown, I just couldn't...couldn't... Well, Charlie and I were married about a year later." He looked at me. "So our past was different from what happened to you." I saw Charlie nodding. His past was different, too. But it was his story to sort out with Dad.

"What did you see in that mirror?" I asked.

Dad took a long time to answer, but he finally looked at Charlie. "I saw him. And that's when I knew." I saw Charlie was crying too now. Nona crawled into his lap and was trying to hide herself in his embrace. Poor kid.

"Did your Hig look into that mirror?" It was a strange thing to ask. It pushed me away from them, but I had to know.

Dad turned to me and pulled me into a hug. "It doesn't matter, son. It doesn't matter."

Somehow we all ended up in one huge group embrace. I let the moment last as long as Dad and Charlie and Nona would allow it. I wanted desperately to belong in this timeline.

Chapter Thirty-Two: Sliding

We went to the memorial service the next day. Dad forbade the city from forcing me to make a speech. It was good; I had no idea about what happened back there on that beach. I didn't know any of my soccer team members, not really, not in this timeline. Still, going to the service felt like going to my own execution. My legs felt leaden and my head ached. I wanted to stay in this timeline; I wanted to be with Klaire; I wanted to make sure Ms. Marta and the babies were all right. How did one reconcile so many desires? Was there one history, one fate that had it all? Everything on one axis of desire... Could I find it? I couldn't even make this reality shift. I wasn't even sure I wanted to. How did one choose between the love of a family and the love for a girl? *A lifetime of love versus weeks?* I didn't think love was measured by time, like ingredients in a cake.

The service was held in a building that in my timeline would have been a cathedral. Here, it was a giant library. I could see millions of books stacked away on the upper levels, along multiple stories of balconies. Down below was a great hall, with all of the library tables removed. There was enough space to let a thousand people or so sit there comfortably. It felt like I was inside the church of literature. I was an English Lit major, and yet I didn't know any of the books up above—they were written here and thus had no reason to be the same as the ones I grew up with and studied. For someone who skipped between timelines so much, that sure was a poor choice of majors.

The library couldn't accommodate everyone, but the park grounds outside—the university oasis inside the heart of the city—were converted into an extension of the memorial service with video projectors, speakers, and heat lamps—it was the middle of winter, even in this timeline. But everyone who was directly affected by the tragedy was ushered inside, of course.

Some of the injured ended up in Charlie and Roger's care. Their families and those who lost loved ones in the bombing all sat up in front. Our family sat together in the front row, not the optimal position for someone who wanted to slip out unnoticed. Our dads sat on either side of us, Nona and I sandwiched and protected between them. Nona held my hand and leaned against Charlie's shoulder. Dad held my other hand. He held it like he was never going to let go. After our conversation in the living room, Dad practically didn't leave my sight. He was worried I wasn't going to stay. I didn't know either, and yet it was going to be harder and harder to leave the longer I stayed. I felt like this timeline was putting roots in me very fast. In any case, I left my backpack at home—I couldn't really be inconspicuous about wearing a beat-up and overstuffed bag on top of my suit.

Roger sat just behind us. He, like Charlie and Dad, was dressed in a dark three-piece suit with a silver silk tie. His hair was nearly gray, worn stylishly long, all the way below his shoulders, tied in a ponytail by a silk band that matched his tie. I didn't know why Roger's appearance struck me so, but I couldn't take my eyes off of him when I first saw him. There was just something about him, something that reminded me of my Roger...my first Roger. The Roger from Morgana House was nearly bald and didn't bother much about his appearance. His whole focus was his son. This Roger cared what other people thought about him. But that was not all. There was a look he gave me when he first approached us to say hello. There was something predatory about it. But his demeanor changed in a flash, and moments later I wasn't even sure what I saw, but it left a sour taste. Perhaps it was because Roger had agreed to speak at the memorial service when Charlie declined. Charlie was asked to give a speech because he suffered the loss of a sibling and almost lost a child in the plane crash. But he refused, and Roger was a close family friend, even as he was at one remove from the tragedy, perhaps making it a bit easier for him to talk in public. Dad refused the request to speak as well.

The lights dimmed, and on a giant projection screen at the front end of the hall we were shown images of the plane crash...after all of the bodies had been removed from the scene. Some important person spoke of the importance of carrying on even in the face of the unspeakable tragedy.

Then it was Roger's turn. He spoke of the toll this *misfortune*—his choice of words—had on the community. He said all the right things, and yet I felt the unease persist. When he was done, a youth chorus from my university, supposedly, arranged themselves in a semicircle behind him and started to sing. They sang a sad melody *a cappella*, without words. The lights dimmed and the screen started to show a stately procession of victim portraits as Roger read out their names.

I heard people all around me crying. But I was all cried out...and I didn't know these people. Somehow, even those young men from my soccer team who seemed to have corresponding selves in my timeline were completely unrecognizable in the flat portraits on the screen. People are more than what they look like; they are a collection of all the experiences they have shared with their loved ones and friends. That inner light that shone through those eyes was foreign to me, and I was glad—my friends, my soccer team might be just fine, living their best lives in some other alternate timeline where there were no Kismet terrorists trying to force fate into giving them something extra by paying a blood price.

I zoned out for a time, but something brought me back. *A low sound? A slight movement in my peripheral vision?* Later, I would try to remember what it was that caused me to sit up, adrenaline pumping into me like a fire hose. And as soon as Dad felt me go rigid, he was on high alert, too.

"Jane Doe is the last victim we want to remember today." Roger's voice reverberated through the great hall. I looked up on the screen...

"What is it?" Dad leaned in to ask, but it was no longer necessary. Everyone in the hall gasped.

"This young woman still remains unidentified," Roger said. Above him there was the dead face of Klaire. "But perhaps someday, we might find answers to this mystery." He was looking directly at me as he said it.

I stood up, and my chair fell backward with a loud bang. The hall became dead silent. Roger stared at me, and there was a strange smile on his face. Everyone was staring at me. Dad and Nona were holding on to my arms for dear life. I think without them, I would have collapsed. Klaire was dead... in this timeline. And Roger had known it. He was looking at me, and I at him. He knew all along.

There was a moment of total silence as people all around us tried to process what just happened. And then the world literary exploded. There were people up above on the balconies, running, throwing what seemed like loud firecrackers into the audience below. Books were flying down from above.

There was foul-smelling smoke. People were screaming. Everyone seemed to jump up and move in a random direction, completely disoriented.

Dad grabbed my sister and me. Charlie was holding Nona on the other side, stooping low, his arm over her head, trying to protect her. Everyone was trying to get back to the entrance; Dad pulled us toward the front, behind the podium and the screen with Klaire's dead face. There was no time to argue. The four of us ran, hunching low. Behind the movie projection screen were speakers and other equipment. It looked eerily familiar—like the setup behind the Kismet stage of the Dream Land Music Festival.

"Come with me!" Roger screamed. "This is a Kismet attack," he said, and Nona whimpered. "We have to try to get out of here."

"Are people hurt?" Charlie asked. "I can help—" He tried to turn around, but both Dad and Roger stopped him.

"It's not safe, Charlie," Roger said. "And we have to get the kids out of here." He looked and Nona and then me, and there was something in his eyes that I didn't like. But Charlie and Dad were instantly agreeing with him. "There is back door that way." Roger motioned somewhere behind us with his head. "I know the way." And he grabbed my sister's hand and ran. We couldn't do anything else but follow.

He took us behind all of the equipment and into a small office just off to the side of the main library hall. The door was hidden behind a swinging bookcase. It was a strange thing to know, unless you worked for the library, and Roger most certainly didn't. I saw that Dad and Charlie were both surprised, too. Roger pushed us in and slid the bookcase back.

"We can wait it out in here," he said and turned to put himself between us and the door. I looked around the room; the secret door was the only exit.

"Roger, what have you heard? What's happening out there?" Dad asked. He was still holding my hand. Charlie stood behind him, hugging Nona. We were all looking at Roger. And I didn't know what everyone else saw, but I saw a mask slide back across Roger's face. It was for just the briefest of split moments that I noticed something very ugly and hungry on his face...something that reminded me of my Roger, the one that jumped away from us into an alternative timeline, all those weeks ago at the music festival. That expression of intense need flickered and then was gone, replaced by a concerned Roger, a scared Roger, a determined Roger, a Roger who was a friend and was here to help our family. And it was all a lie. I was sure of it.

"Roger?" Charlie asked. And I heard a note of doubt in his voice.

"The Kismet terrorist group learned that your whole family was here, and I believe they were going to grab Hig," Roger said, rubbing his forehead. It was a good technique to conceal micro-expressions, the ones that would have betrayed him as lying. "Just as I was getting ready to finish my speech," he said, "I saw these people way up on the balcony, over my head. They were wearing the capes like the ones Hig was found with." I wondered how he knew about that. As far as I knew, it wasn't common knowledge. I didn't think Dad or Charlie said anything; I wasn't even sure they really knew about those. The robes were collected back on the beach. I'd never seen them again or even heard them mentioned. "These people were not even sneaking in," Roger continued. "They were just marching down the balconies. And then the explosions started to happen. I looked for you guys, but you were gone. So rushed to find you."

"How do you know they were after Hig?" Dad asked. His tone wasn't confrontational; he was just asking. But I felt his fingers squeeze tight around my hand. I squeezed back. I wanted him to know that I was suspicious, too.

"I've heard people talking about how Hig is some kind of fate catalyst."

"A what?" Dad asked.

"A fate catalyst? I'm not really sure what that means, but I gather they think he is very important."

"Like how?"

"They believe Hig can create rifts in reality and allow people to slide between alternate timelines, to choose their fates. That's why I believe they are after him. They don't really believe Hig is from this reality."

"And what do you believe, Roger?" Charlie asked.

"It's all nonsense, of course. But those people are crazy, right?" He looked from Dad to Charlie and back. He was trying to convince them or seed doubt about me. "Hig suffered a brain injury. It's not magic; it's amnesia. Right, Hig?"

Dad squeezed my fingers again, and I didn't answer Roger. What could I say?

Outside, we heard another explosion, and every book in our little room shook and snowed dust down on our heads. Nona sneezed just as Charlie used his body to shield her.

"Well, we can't stay here," Dad said. "They will find us. We are like sitting ducks."

"I have a plan," Roger said. I felt cold inside. "We split up. Fred, you take Nona and run toward the back entrance. From what I've seen, the front of the building has completely collapsed. Charlie and I will run with Hig. We have a better chance if we split up."

"I won't go without Daddy!" Nona cried out. But of course not—Roger must have known that Nona wouldn't separate from Charlie.

"Well, if we ran as a group, we are easy pickings. We have

to split up. So perhaps it's best that you go with your dads, and Hig and I run the other way. We are both very athletic. We'll give you time to spirit away Nona and get the authorities on the scene. It's the only way," he added.

Suddenly, Nona collapsed to the floor, clutching her middle. Dad and Charlie were immediately at her side. But I knew. I felt it too...I saw it. The world started to bifurcate again. One moment I was in the secret library room, the next I was back in the metropolis of my youth, in the middle of my college campus uptown, at the commons. There were students all about, wearing their caps and gowns. It was the winter graduation ceremony, I realized. I looked around and saw people I recognized. I saw recognition in their eyes. This was definitely back in my original...second timeline. Something was going on there, too. People were screaming, running. There was a building on fire. The administration building.

I was moving my head back and forth, looking at two different time streams. And then I felt hands holding me tightly by my upper arms.

"What do you see, Hig? What do you see?" It was Roger. The intensity was twisting his features into something grotesque.

Another explosion rained books on us. Roger stumbled, and we both fell next to Nona. She was moaning in pain. Charlie had a bloody gash on his forehead. He looked confused, disoriented. I looked at him and saw all of us on the graduation lawn—Nona, Charlie, Roger, and me...but no Dad. Of course—Dad was still in that timeline. We all left, but he was still there. No duplicates! I pushed that reality away from me, and we were back on the floor of the secret library room.

"What was that?" Roger yelled at me. "What was that? Is Lucca there? You know, don't you? You can switch fate. I knew it. Moira was right."

"Moira?" Charlie asked, his face covered in bright red blood. Face wounds bled a lot, I remembered Uncle Charlie telling me after one of my nasty falls as a kid. He told me not to be scared. I was crying, and Uncle Charlie told me that everything was fine, and I believed him. "Moira knew about the bomb?" Charlie asked.

"Of course she knew," Roger said. "She planned the whole thing. A big enough event repeats itself across many histories, creating echoes and tremors up and down the timelines. Once we knew who Hig really was, we needed to get him to do his thing, to start the rifting. Moira was supposed to have jumped. I don't know what she did to screw it up. Hig was her son. Once they were together..."

Dad sat up and punched Roger hard across the face. "You knew? You orchestrated all of this? You killed all those people? You used my family?"

"Roger, how could you?" Charlie asked. "My sister was a sick woman."

Roger wiped the blood from his lips. "She wasn't wrong, though, was she? This Hig isn't *your* Hig. You know it. He is just some doppelgänger that slid across the timelines. He couldn't even use the pay system here, did you know that, Charlie? This Hig doesn't even have the same handprints as your boy. So stop pretending. Stop pretending like you didn't know, like you weren't going to use him yourselves to improve your fates. With him, you can go anywhere you like, anywhere in the universe. Even where my son still lives," he added quietly.

"Roger?" I finally forced myself to speak. "Lucca doesn't live. Well, he does in very few timelines—"

"See!" Roger looked at us triumphantly. With blood across his face and his eyes blazing, he looked deranged.

"I knew of only one place, only one, where Lucca lived to

adulthood. His father searched history after history to find the one where he survived."

"I'm his father. Me!"

"That Roger, a very gentle man who helped me very much, is taking care of his special needs son at Morgana House, which exists where the button factory used to be, where my family lives here. I assume Morgana House is something like the house for special needs kids you and Charlie run. Things repeat over and over in strange permutations—same people, same places, same circumstances...just slightly altered in various timelines. But that *adult* Lucca won't survive much longer. He lived a happy life...the part of his life after Roger found him. You won't find a timeline where you get to be with your baby son. Histories march forward, even if you jump between them. You can't jump into the past, Roger. You can't get your son back. I'm sorry."

I watched as Roger wailed and pulled his hair. We all scooted away from him, but there wasn't anyplace to go. Charlie looked at his partner in complete shock. Dad's face was like stone. He held my sister with one hand and me with the other. He wasn't going to let anything happen to us. He looked determined. As determined as Charlie seemed undone.

"Roger." I reached out to him. "Lucca is a grown man now," I said again. "Switching timelines won't change his age. And the one place where he lives, he is loved. He is happy. Another Roger is doing a good job taking care of him. Your son is not alone. You have to let go."

But by that point Roger was obviously beyond reason. I could see all those years of pain, of mourning his son. He never got over it. Every Roger I knew never got over that loss, but one found a way of coping that didn't cause additional pain. And suddenly, I realized that it was the Roger from my other timeline who stole away my sister. He found a way of getting me to chase Nona all the way to some major Kismet event. He convinced Cherie and Ms. Marta and Klaire and me to go to South Carolina. He told us it was Nona who was the catalyst, when all the time he knew it was me. He got me where he wanted me, and I made the rift. I didn't mean to, but somehow, with so many infinitely intersecting lives, I opened a possibility to switch fate. And as I was feeling the rift open up again, all I wanted was to get Klaire and Mama and the twins here, into this timeline. That's all I needed to be happy, I believed.

I closed my eyes and searched. I felt thousands, millions of timelines twisting in front of me. One of those had a Klaire that survived the dirigible accident. In one of those Ms. Marta and twins were alive. But how did I find which one it was? *The* one. I probed and combed through the many variations of history. I saw great tall glass buildings and trees taller than any skyscraper I'd ever seen. There were timelines filled with fire and those that felt impossibly beautiful. Dirigibles, rockets, gliders, suspended trains, good old buses. There were people riding on horses and other places that were full of bikes and trikes and hover-boards. All I was getting was glimpses and micro impressions before the timelines slipped away. I cried out—there was no way to find Klaire by randomly rummaging through timelines.

I felt Roger trying to hold on to me as I kept sliding away from him from one timeline into the next. But Dad gripped my hand the whole time, never letting go. Where I moved, he moved with me. And with him, I felt Charlie and Nona move along, too, the whole family staying together. After that first time of separating from Dad and finding myself, ever so briefly, back in my home timeline, my family stuck together. I felt it—they would go wherever I went, and that in itself limited my options. But my family didn't want me to be alone—that was their axis of desire. And moment by moment, the frantic pace of timeline change slowed down. The walls of the hidden library room solidified again, and we were all back in the timeline where Dad and Charlie married, where Nona and I were happy, where Mom and Klaire and Ms. Marta and the twins died at the hands of a crazy Kismet cult.

"Don't do that, Hig," Nonaken said and slid into my arms. "Don't go. I need you."

"I'm sorry," I managed. I didn't have strength left for anything else.

As I relaxed, I noticed that Roger was gone. He was simply no longer in the room with us. I looked around, confused. Our dads did, too. Only Nona didn't seem concerned.

"He slid away into one of those other lives," she explained. "Perhaps he found a fate that will make him happy."

"Shh," Dad said. "Do you hear that?" We listened; it was quiet. No rumbles of explosions, no screams, no pounding of feet just outside the secret door. "Hig?"

"Yes, Dad?"

"The visions...the rifts that you were spinning up, were they only in this room? Or did they bubble up out there too?"

I had no idea. "Maybe?" I said. "I've never really done this before."

"Is it over?" Charlie asked.

"I think so. I only see this one reality."

"Is it ours?" my sister asked. And I honestly had no idea, but there was no dust on this floor, no books scattered on the ground around us. Nona understood and clutched me even closer to her. "It is now," she whispered.

"I will go and look," Dad said and stood up. But we all jumped up after him, holding him, all of our hands and arms intertwined. "All right," he smiled. "We all go together." He pushed the bookcase door a little, and we all leaned out to look.

Outside was quiet. It was dusk already, so we must have been in that little room for hours. It didn't feel that way, but we had slid between so many possibilities. It could have taken a long time. We pushed the door all the way open and stepped outside, still gripping each other tightly, even as I knew there were no more rifts; I would have felt them. All the possibilities were closed now. And I had no idea how to open one, even if I tried. Roger theorized that traumatic events caused me to spin the doors between alternate histories, but that was just a hypothesis, and we surely weren't going to test it some more by blowing things up. I planned to live a very uneventful life from now on, if I could help it. I would mourn Klaire. I would mourn Mama. I would even mourn the twins, though I didn't really get to know them. But I couldn't put my family though this again.

There were no signs of explosions or debris or shredded books or dust or injured people. It was just a calm winter evening inside a giant library hall. Even the great library tables were all set up in neat rows down the middle. But the great library was empty, closed; it must have been after hours.

"We should try to go home," Charlie said, and his voice sounded unnaturally high. I looked, and he seemed shorter to me. But now was not the time to mention it.

We walked toward the front door. On the way, I saw my backpack bulging with all the crap I had packed the night before leaning against one of the library tables. I picked it up. Nona looked but didn't say a word. It was obviously mine even as I left it back home...in the other timeline.

We were able to push the doors open—they were closed from the outside but not trying to keep anyone locked inside. The air was cool, chilly even. I pulled out a sweatshirt from my backpack—I remembered packing it, and it was there just like I expected it to be—and handed it over to Nona. She was wearing only a thin black dress for the memorial service, appropriately somber but not very warm. We were all dressed in suits. I also pulled out water bottles and some sandwiches and distributed them. I was starving and figured my family was too.

"You really were going to leave us," Nona said. "Don't you get it? We are your family! We take care of each other. And thanks." She took a sandwich and water, after adjusting the oversized sweatshirt and hood over her head.

"She is right, Hig. No more running away," Dad said. "Whatever happens now, we will figure it out together. Now, do you know where we are?" It was obvious we were not back where we started from this morning. I shook my head. I had no idea. "Okay. Let's see if our house is still here."

"And if it's ours," Charlie said. I could see that soon he'd be Cherie. I hoped he was good with it. Uncle Charlie was always such a beautiful woman.

Chapter Thirty-Three: Home

It was dark when we finally made it back to the house. The streets seemed to be pretty much the same, but the architecture was difficult to discern at night. We did find the button factory without any problems, though.

The front door sported the cool zipper door, just like Morgana House. Both Dad and Charlie were freaked out by the change. Nona was too tired to care. I stepped up and used the zipper slider to knock. What did we have to lose?

After a terrifying several moments of waiting in the cold, the door opened. Ms. Marta smiled at us from inside.

"Well, come in," she said. "We've been expecting you."

With the light spilling from the doorway, I saw that the whole building was covered in button mosaics of galaxy swirls. A woman in a Kismet robe stepped from behind Ms. Marta. Her eyes were blank white, and her face was Klaire's.

###

Acknowledgments

My friends and family have been full of encouragement and support, often reading a paragraph hot off the press, asking what happens next, and pushing me to go on. Their support means everything to me.

My husband Christopher helped with editing the story and grammar on this book. He is also the amazing genius that makes the ebook version as good as it is. Occasionally, we also co-write stories. Together, we run Pipsqueak Productions: *pipsqueak.com*. I also write a blog on design at *interfaces.com*. I'm on Twitter at *@OlgaWerby*.

It took over a year to get this story out into the world. Allister Thompson was my editor and motivational support; my partner in writing, Christopher, was the there for the whole drama of pandemic writing. In addition to fixing seemingly endless errors, these men sharpened my work, making me look good. I am the better writer because of them. Allister can be found at *AllisterThomson.com*. You can't have Christopher. All errors between the covers and on them are entirely my own.

If you liked this story, please consider recommending it to others. Reviews on Amazon and Goodreads are very much appreciated. Word-of-mouth endorsements and reader reviews are the holy grail for indie authors. Without these, our stories just gather e-dust.

Most of all, thank you for reading. Your imagination makes my stories come alive!

Notes on Illustrations

Too few adult books include illustrations now. When I was growing up, I loved illustrations in the books I read. I particularly loved the edition of *Captain Blood* by Rafael Sabatini that contained etchings; and the Sherlock Holmes stories were greatly improved by Sidney Paget's illustrations.

The illustrations for *Harvest*—a short snippet of this story to follow—are my original pen and ink drawings augumented by NASA photogrphay and images that are in the public domain (fractals). My goto place to find a lot of ideas and components for my illustrations is Pixabay.com. The artists that share their work there are amazing! I owe a debt of inspirations and creativity to their imaginations and skills.

Other Books

If you enjoyed this book, I hope you'll consider reading some of our other stories. Most are available on Amazon.

Harvest (the first few chapters included)
    Fresh Seed—a prequel novella to *Harvest*

The God of Small Affairs

Good Girl

Becoming Animals

"The Chronicles of the DaDA Immortals" series:
    Lizard Girl & Ghost

"Many Worlds, One Life" series:
    Suddenly, Paris (book 1)
    Coding Peter (book 2)

"The Ornis Experiment" series:
    Pigeon (book 1)
    Birdie (book 2 is coming soon)

The FATOFF Conspiracy

Twin Time

I occasionally send out newsletters with free promotions for my own and other indie authors' books. If you sign up, you can download our first book, *Suddenly Paris*, as a gift. Just visit Interfaces.com. Thank you!

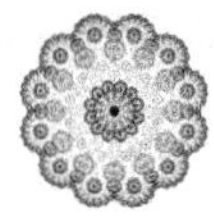

Notes on Names

I believe that character names should have special meanings and allow for a bit of surprise, an unexpected joy of secret discovery. Not only do names hide secret meanings, but their origins—cultures, languages, geographic locations, historical time periods add a bit of spice to the stories for those willing to look things up.

Every one of my stories is filled with little Easter Eggs... Enjoy!

HARVEST
Olga Werby

ProLog

"The exton controls are not responding!" Marc shouted into his exoskeleton spacesuit helmet.

His exoskeleton was the heavy-duty dirt-and-boulder-mover type. *Move a ton with exton.* Right now, Marc was really just an intelligent bulldozer with life support. But the suit had disconnected from his D-tats, the personal computing device tattoos embedded in his lower arms and jaw, and his directional controls were busted. Now his exoskeleton acted with a mind of its own, moving him away from the construction site and out into the open Martian landscape. He needed to get back to the Malfy—an affectionate acronym for Martians Live Free, a city-sized habitat being built for the next wave of planetary immigrants.

"Marc?" his SB responded from the inside Malfy's operational center. "What's on the fritz this time?" Every contractor working outside was in constant communication with a personally assigned *safety buddy.* "I can't seem to toss the controls over to my side." In an emergency, Marc's SB could take over the controls of his exton and bring him in, even if he was unconscious.

"I've got nothing!" Marc was more irritated than scared. This was his second equipment failure in as many months, and their group of union builders had reported three more to the management since the start of the project about two hundred days ago. It was always the same MO: at the end of a shift, the movement controls failed to respond to their operators' commands, taking the builders out into the desert; and yet, after the rescue when the equipment was checked out, the engineers found nothing wrong with the extons. The first time it happened to Marc, he was even accused of faking the failure to get extra time off for hazardous conditions. As if construction work on Mars wasn't dangerous in and of itself. Fortunately, Marc's supervisor made everyone carry extra oxygen and a spare battery pack after the first few incidents. Just in case. Inconvenient for sure, but it was better than being stuck out of breath without a heater among the Martian dunes in minus 125 degrees Celsius.

"Send someone out to get me," Marc said. "It's an official request."

"Are you sure, Marc? You know if they don't find anything again—"

"I'm telling you, I've got nothing. Everything is dead on my side."

"Yeah, mine too," Marc's SB agreed. "I'll get Greg out there. But he won't be happy. He just got his exton off and you'll be cutting into his three days off period."

"Tell him that I'd go if it was him out here. And tell him to hurry up about it." The earliest he could expect Greg to arrive would be at least an hour, probably more—it took time get these darn things on.

Marc felt funky. His D-tats itched like crazy, probably from all of the energy pushed through them to try to reconnect with his exton. And now his comm was down, too. As soon as he'd gotten over the rim of the crater, he'd lost touch with his SB.

It was lonely out here in the Martian landscape with no one to talk to and all the human structures obscured from view. Marc could only look ahead—his suit didn't allow him to turn his head—and before him stretched miles and miles of nothing but rust sand and red rocks underneath a yellow

sky. Someday this would be paradise, but Marc didn't expect to live that long. Still, it was decent pay, and the benefits were great. And, most importantly, all the construction workers were to be awarded a family subdivision inside the new MLF. Marc looked forward to moving his wife and a new kid he'd never seen out here from Luna Colony. Kids should run around on the surface of a real planet, his mother always said. In a few years, Marc would make his mother's dream a reality right here, on this dusty red rock. And when he did, he would be able to tell his kids that he built this place with his own hands. He would point to a boulder and say, "See that rock? Your daddy placed that rock." It was a satisfying thought…if only the equipment worked right.

He tried to will his suit to obey. Heat erupted around his jaw and down his neck. It took him by surprise—not an emotion he was used to. The off-world building crews went through years of training, and part of that training involved controlling one's thoughts. Spend too much attention on extraneous thoughts and emotions—like surprise and worry—and space got you. Cognition was a limited resource.

This fact about human nature was drilled into Marc, not just during training but from an early age. All Luna Colony children learned to focus and control their attention. Those who couldn't didn't make it to adulthood. It was different there now, in those modern Luna Live Free habitats—Elfys. But when Marc was young…

"Ahhh!" The scream seemed to rip itself out of Marc's throat without his conscious control. Pain twisted his arms inside his suit. He felt himself hyperventilating. Something was seriously wrong with *him*, not just with his exton. The horror of that realization hit him hard as the exoskeleton kept marching him inexorably farther from the base. He smelled cooked meat. It took all his willpower not to think where the

smell was coming from. The life support systems should have noted his elevated heart rate and responded.

Since his D-tats weren't working, Marc tried to blink commands directly into the suit. He drilled down several menus and selected a painkiller injection. He needed to get himself under control. Rescue was still at least thirty minutes away.

Sweat trickled into his eyes. It was difficult to see now. He felt cold and yet heat burned his arms, neck, and jaw. His teeth felt out of alignment. There was a constant buzzing in his left ear, different in tone and structure from the one in his right. But at least it was something he could focus on. He poured himself into the strange, asymmetric tinnitus. Bzzz, bzzz, swish, bzzz, bzzz, swish...

"I found him unresponsive."

Greg sat in front of a board of inquiry. Marc's death was the first among the Martian chapter of the Off-World Builders Union this year. Given that Mars was deemed a relatively low-risk environment, the death had attracted extra scrutiny from both the union leaders and the insurance representatives for the Martians Live Free project.

"Are you saying Builder Mark Kelly's communications were out? Or was he unconscious when you found him?"

"At first it wasn't clear, sir," Greg testified. "The exoskeleton continued to walk into the desert and wouldn't stop until I caught up with it and patched into it directly."

"So the comm was completely out?"

"Yes, sir. I wasn't able to control the exton from a distance, and Marc lost his communication a while before that." Greg wiped the sweat from his forehead. He hated answering stupid questions. Everyone already knew what had happened. Marc's D-tats had fried from some bad connection to his equipment. *Shit happens. Get over it. Move on.*

The interrogation went on for another hour, but at some point, even the insurance representative recognized that Greg had nothing more to add to the report he'd filed with the union. The conclusion was that this was a freak accident caused by improperly implanted personal computing device tattoos a decade earlier. The Luna Colony medical board was granted jurisdiction over the case.

Chapter One

"Sentient life's colonization of the Earth is fractal. Even within a single ecosystem, there are many species that possess intelligence and self-awareness. But only one species becomes dominant."

Professor Volhard took a theatrical pause here. Everyone in the audience knew where she was going with this, but it never hurt to add drama to a presentation.

"Obviously I am talking about humans. We are not the only intelligent, self-aware species on our planet—but we got lucky. We were blessed with favorable initial conditions, and our dominance was almost guaranteed. Lack of luck tends to permanently retard progress. Dinosaurs' loss is our win."

There were a few chuckles from the audience, but no big laughs. Varsaad Volhard sighed inwardly and moved on. She never knew how the lay audience would react, but this was all part of doing the book-selling lecture circuit.

Vars was tall and skinny with short, unruly, dark red hair and glasses to match. She looked a bit like a stick insect in her black pants and black sweater. For the tour, she was trying to dress more interestingly than normal—per instructions from her publisher—and so had added the bright orange scarf that her publisher sent in the mail. The instructions that came with the scarf told her to wear matching orange shoes, but

Vars didn't own any orange shoes, so matching black was as good as it got.

She hadn't failed to notice that the cover of her book—*Luck & Lock on Life & Love: The Human History of Conquest of Resources on Earth, Luna, and Beyond*—had the same color orange titles as the scarf. Her agent or someone in the office was obviously trying. Vars made a mental note to figure out who that was and thank them.

Vars talked for a while without paying attention to what she said—that was a gift that came with giving the same talk for the hundredth time. Fortunately, she was almost at the end of her book tour. Two more lectures and she would be done. She could go back to teaching and research—get her life back. This nomadic lifestyle wasn't for her. But before she got out of there tonight, Vars still had one more surprise argument for these people: a defense of space exploration.

She looked into the dark void in front of her. The stage

lights made the hundred people in the theater disappear from view—a plus for a shy researcher. And she was a true believer in the "what you can't see can't hurt you" principle. Not only had she opted out of vision-correction treatments, she regularly taught without her glasses, leaving all but the front row of her classroom a Monet-like blur. The trick worked well to relieve her agoraphobic anxiety.

"So, what are the prerequisites of space travel?" she asked.

There were a few shout-outs from up in the gallery—the cheap seats usually occupied by students. "Civilization." "Faster-than-light travel." "Aliens." They were on the right track, even if their sources were limited to science fiction movies. But Vars was an evolutionary socio-historian, and that meant she was trained to look both into the future *and* the past. She liked to think that her ideas about possible human future scenarios were well informed by historical precedents and intelligent extrapolations of cultural trends—meaning she wasn't just talking science fiction here.

"Let's start with something simple," she said. "Time." Time was never simple, but people always assumed it was. Everyone had experience with time, so everyone felt like they were experts on the subject. "Humans have a relatively long lifespan for a mammal. And we have the longest childhood of all animals." Well, that was true now. Neanderthal kids had enjoyed a longer childhood, but Vars didn't want to complicate things further. "Not only are we able to learn a lot before we plunge into adulthood," Vars continued, "we also have the time to use that knowledge. I'm sure we would all like to live even longer, but nature has ensured that we live long *enough* to transfer wisdom from one generation to the next, so our species can build on that, expanding our collective grasp of how the universe works. Each generation stands on the shoulders of all those that came before. Without a sufficiently long lifespan to learn and apply that collective mastery, space travel would just not be possible."

Vars tried to peer into the audience to check that they were still with her.

"So why not elephants or whales, you might ask. Both species live a long time and spend a significant proportion of that life as children." Vars didn't wait for answers. "Unfortunately, neither were lucky enough to evolve hands. Even the elephant's prehensile trunk can't compare with the nimbleness of human fingers. And whales have the additional disadvantage of living in an underwater environment. These are significant handicaps to developing space travel. So again, humans got lucky. We evolved to live on land, and we have the right appendages to be able to tinker with objects in our environment. To bend it to our will."

"Language!" someone screamed out of the dark.

Vars smiled. Language came up over and over again at each of her lectures. "Yes, language," she said into the darkened auditorium. "It's been said that language is the ultimate tool of mankind. Its greatest invention." There were sounds of agreement from the audience. "But are we the only species on Earth to possess language? Sure, human languages are incredibly sophisticated and versatile, far more so than those of any other species we have encountered to date. But until a few decades ago, we didn't even believe that there *were* nonhuman languages here on our planet. Now, of course, we know better. Dolphins, elephants, and even some birds have been observed using rudimentary languages unique to their species."

Vars stopped to listen to the audience. There were murmurings of assent, but also a few mutterings of rejection. The idea of animals inventing languages was very new still, but it was no longer controversial among her colleagues. Of course, politics was always way behind science. If humans were to widely acknowledge that dolphins communicated via language, then we might also have to recognize them as having some legal form of "personhood"—and that just wasn't tenable in the current political climate.

The dissent told Vars what proportion of the audience held human-centric views. It was about forty percent or so, judging by the noise. That was about average for this part of the country. In places like Berkeley, California, only one or two people in the audience dared to express such backward opinions loudly enough to be heard on stage. Most dissenters kept quiet, she knew. People were herd mammals, after all, and needed to be surrounded by others with similar views. That was how social echo chambers worked in the age of mass e-media.

"Language," she said, "particularly written language, is essential to passing information from one generation and one community to the next. Written language saved us from having to invent things over and over again—"

"Oral traditions!" someone yelled.

"Oral traditions are fantastic for capturing and communicating culture," Vars replied. "But they are lousy for transmitting technical information. There is no oral tradition of calculus." There was a murmuring of agreement. *Good.* "And before someone brings up apprenticeship, let me just say that I'm a believer in learning while being embedded in a community of practice. We see such educational approaches in species other than our own. Chimps routinely teach their offspring how to fish for termites with specially made twigs. Birds teach their chicks how to hunt and which foods are good and where they can be located. Cerrado, a species of monkey from South America, use giant hammer rocks to break tough palm nuts over carefully selected anvil boulders.

It takes years for the youngsters to learn how to select just the right hammers and anvils and to perfect the technique for bashing open the nuts. So yes, apprenticeship works—but it has its limits. We are the only species on Earth to develop *other* intentional ways of passing on knowledge. Without written information, we wouldn't be in the process of colonizing Mars, or mining the asteroids, or having permanent bases on the moon."

Vars gave the audience a few seconds to absorb this. She wasn't done having fun with them yet. "But before written and oral language traditions, before the apprenticeship form of passing knowledge from generation to generation, there was another way. Nature's way. Evolution's way."

She stopped, giving her listeners a moment or two to guess the answer. Some nights, the audience got it almost immediately; other nights, there wasn't a clue in the house. Tonight, there was only silence.

"Evolution couldn't wait for humans to invent language. Survival depended on passing some information down the chain of generations." *Well? Still nothing?* "I'm talking about instincts, of course. Our drive to mate, to reproduce, to protect our children. Our will to survive against all odds. We've all experienced, or will experience, these instinctual needs. It's in our DNA, so to speak. But that's not the only hard-coded knowledge that we pass along to our offspring.

"I will focus on humans here, because that's what I wrote my book about. Which reminds me: I will be signing copies in the lobby right after the end of the lecture. I'm required to say this by my publisher." There were a few chuckles. *Good.* Vars hated dull groups. It was hard to speak without feedback. "Agoraphobia and claustrophobia, fear of dark places and of heights, ophidiophobia and arachnophobia, instinctual disgust of bodily fluids—blood, urine, pus, feces—all of these are innate for us humans. We are born to avoid tight places and grand expanses. We naturally avoid snakes and spiders even if we've never seen or heard of them before. But we have also learned to overcome these fears. We had to if we were going to go into space. Our spaceships are extremely cramped, and they float in vast expanses of space. Astronauts are forced to recycle their bodily fluids and to no longer be afraid of extreme heights and absolute darkness. Although I may never overcome my fear of snakes and spiders..." She shivered dramatically and earned a few more laughs. "And perhaps, one day, we will meet other explorers out there. And we might have more innate fears to shed."

Vars talked for another quarter hour about the importance of different sensory apparatuses and the need for access to easily extracted raw resources, but it was getting late, and she could feel that the energy had drained from her audience. She was tired, too. She needed to catch a redeye tonight and try to squeeze in a few more hours of sleep before another lecture tomorrow.

Before she was even aware of it, there was hearty applause, and then it was time for smiling, handshaking, and book signing. She'd come to learn that the only people who still bought paper books were the ones who attended these book tour lectures. She was grateful to all of them, and yet she couldn't wait to get out of there.

"Dr. Volhard?" The voice was a nice soft baritone. "May I have a moment of your time after you've finished autographing?"

Vars raised her head, a fake smile plastered on her face,

and tried to identify the speaker. There were still half a dozen people waiting, each clutching a copy of her book. But none of those was the speaker. So she went back to signing, and soon enough, like magic, it was done. She rubbed her wrist, which had started to cramp up, and slid the contents of the table—brochures, pens, and leftover business cards—into her bag. She would deal with sorting it all out later.

"Coffee?" the baritone asked again. "I know you take it with sugar and milk. But I wasn't sure of the proportions."

Vars looked up again. A tall, slightly graying man in rimless glasses with a slight yellow tint was standing in front of her, holding a recyclable coffee cup. He was dressed in jeans, a dress shirt with no tie, and a wool jacket—easy elegance, her literary agent would call it. She tried to do something similar for these lectures—approachable, smart, and interesting were her original goals. But at this point in the lecture tour, all she could hope for was clean, awake, and present. Dressing in all black helped.

"I beg your pardon," she said. "Do you have a book for me

to sign?"

"That would have been lovely," the man said, "but I bought an e-version of your book."

"I can sign your data pad," Vars offered. She still didn't take the coffee from his extended hand. And she wasn't planning to.

"What a lovely idea." He smiled. "Do you mind if we talk a bit? I know you're tired—"

"And I have a plane to catch." Vars spoke more harshly than she'd meant to; the man did buy her book, after all.

She tried to go around him, but he wouldn't budge. She looked past him for a security guard at the door. Shouldn't someone be getting everyone out of here? Perhaps escorting her to a taxi? She was getting annoyed and a bit alarmed.

"My name is Ian Rust," the man said.

"Dr. Vars Volhard."

"Of course." He smiled again.

"I really do have to go, Mr. Rust," Vars insisted. She tried to push past the man, her suitcase ready to roll behind her.

"The thing is, Dr. Volhard, we really need your expertise as soon as possible," Rust said.

"Sir, I'm an evolutionary socio-historian. My direct expertise is rarely required on an *emergency* basis. Contact my university office, and I'm sure I would be able to fit you in during one of my ample office hours after I get back."

"Ah, but there are exceptions," he said. "We've read everything that you've published—"

"Everything?"

"Everything. And you have a unique set of expertise that my team at Earth Planetary Space Agency urgently requires." He pulled out his EPSA credentials. "Our car is waiting outside, Dr. Volhard. Won't you please follow me? Do you mind if I call you Vars?"

"Sure," Vars said automatically.

"Then please call me Ian." He handed the coffee to her.

EPSA was the umbrella agency that had taken over for NASA, ESA (European Space Agency), ASA (Australian Space Agency), and JAXA (Japan Aerospace Exploration Agency). So it wasn't entirely "planetary"—China and Russia still ran their own space exploration programs—but it *was* the largest and best-funded agency, and it was the one that was actively pushing the Mars colonization program and comprehensive exploration of the solar system.

Vars had always dreamed of working for EPSA, even as a girl. But somehow, somewhere along the way, her academic career had veered into anthropology, and then evolution, and then...well, here she was. The evo devo diva of anthropology.

And now she was riding down the dark, empty streets in the back seat of a black driverless car, with Dr. Ian Rust, head of the exobiology research team at EPSA, sitting by her side.

Chapter Two

Vars slept on the plane...or tried to. She was too confused, too keyed up to really sleep. That coffee might have been a mistake. Ian said that he couldn't tell her anything until they arrived at his EPSA office in Seattle, which was conveniently her own hometown where she lived with her dad. The man just smiled a lot and talked about how much he had enjoyed reading Vars's new book.

There was a strange edge to their interaction. If Vars hadn't believed Ian's credentials, she would have bailed on him a long time ago. Even so, she felt like she was being kidnapped. And, in a way, she was. She'd had to cancel the last two lectures of her book tour and apologize to her agent over and over again. Ian had promised that EPSA would send an official excuse letter, but Vars still felt like she let her agent and publisher down.

They landed at a general aviation airport, and another black car whisked them to EPSA's headquarters, just outside of Seattle's city limits. She was taken to a conference room on the top floor of the EPSA science building, which Ian called the "tree house." She immediately understood why—it was surrounded on all sides by a balcony planted with a row of trees and some shrubbery. It was quite nice, but Vars couldn't enjoy it; she was simultaneously exhausted and adrenalized.

It was just a matter of time before she crashed.

She must have looked it, too, because someone handed her a very big, very steamy cup of coffee. She sipped it gratefully, completely oblivious to how she came to be holding it. It was still very early in the morning, way before Vars even liked to get up, much less attend a meeting.

About a dozen EPSA people joined her and Ian around the conference table. Vars noticed that several paper copies of her book were laid out; some even looked read, with cracked spines and dog-eared pages.

"So," she said to Ian. "Is *now* a good time and place for you to tell me what this is all about?"

"Now is perfect," Ian said with a big smile. "We are very grateful to have you with us today, Dr. Volhard. This is my exobiology team." He pointed one by one to the people on one side of the table. "Dr. Alice Bear. Dr. Greg Tungsten. Dr. Bob Shapiro. Dr. Saydi Obara. Dr. Evelyn Shar. And Dr. Izzy Rubka."

Vars had heard of some of these people by reputation, of course, but never met any of them personally. EPSA people were a reclusive bunch, tending to mix with their own to the exclusion of others, even with the same research interests. It was one of the reasons Vars always wanted to join the organization—to get access to the best and the brightest minds and a chance to discuss the origins of life over coffee... But the introductions were happening so fast, there was no chance that she would remember how any of these names linked up with faces. Vars doubted she would even recognize these people walking down the street.

But Ian just continued. "And this group," he gestured to two men and a woman, "is on loan from JPL—Jet Propulsion Lab in Pasadena. Trish Cars, Dr. Ron Silverman, and Dr. Benjamin Kouta." Vars gave up on remembering who was

who. "And these two," Ian said, nodding to a pair of identical twins sitting next to him, "are Ibe and Ebi Zimov, our computer science wunderkinds from EISS, European Institute of Space Science."

Ian pronounced their names as *eye-bee* and *ee-bee*; it was the only introduction Vars was likely to remember fully, as the siblings were the most interesting looking pair in the room. They seemed young—Vars guessed not older than twenty—and she was honestly uncertain whether they were male or female or one of each. They were dressed the same— sweatshirts with the EISS logo embroidered on the left, black jeans, black canvas shoes—and both had their hair dyed jet black, shaved on the sides and long on top, falling over their eyes. Vars could see impressive sets of D-tats on the exposed parts of their necks and jaws and peeking out of the twins' sleeves. Other people around the room presumably had

D-tats too, but nothing so obviously ostentatious as these two.

"And before you ask," Ian said, "yes, they are related to Dr. Sergey Aphanasievich Zimov."

That name sounded vaguely familiar, but Vars had no idea who Dr. Zimov was.

She also noted that the other two people present—two men in military uniforms—were not introduced.

"It's a pleasure to meet you all," she said. "Please call me Vars." She smiled at everyone, then turned to Ian. "But once again... Please, I'd very much like to know why I'm here."

"I was just getting to that."

She noticed that he looked tired, too. He hadn't slept much on the plane either. Then again, pretty much everyone in the room looked haggard. Deep circles under the eyes were the norm, not the exception.

Before Ian could continue, one of the women from the exobiology team spoke up. "In your book, Dr. Volhard, you mentioned an example of how robots developed by collectivist cultures would be less likely to kill. Would you mind elaborating on that?"

Vars didn't know what she expected—but it wasn't this. "You flew me out here before dawn to talk about *killer robots*?"

The discussion of robots in her book was just an illustrative example, and a frivolous one at that. It was just a funny way of explaining the differences in value systems between collectivist and individualist cultures. She'd almost cut it from the final draft, but David Gatewood, her editor, had insisted she keep it in.

"Of course not," Ian said. "Robots are just a small part of it. But if you don't mind answering Alice's question..." He gave Vars a pleading look.

"You're serious?" Vars still couldn't believe it. She'd

worked four years on the book, and what had caught EPSA's interest was a stupid joke. *I guess David was right,* she thought. *People, even smart people, grab on to the most flamboyant metaphors.*

"Should I explain the differences between collectivist and individualist societies first?" Vars asked. She looked around the room; she didn't want to assume what these people knew, but at the same time, talking down to the top minds of the Earth Planetary Space Agency was completely unacceptable.

"If you don't mind," Ian said. He composed himself as if awaiting a lecture. In fact, every face in the room had that look of composed concentration that Vars was used to seeing in her grad students.

"Okay." There was nothing to do but move forward. She launched into her introductory lecture on socio-evolution. "While there are many ways of classifying the various human cultures that arose in the last fifty thousand years or so, one division that can be made is focused on the perception of the role of an individual within the group. In collectivist cultures, the group needs are judged *above* the needs of an individual; in the individualist cultures, it's the opposite, naturally."

"Naturally," echoed an older, tiny, dark-skinned woman with bottle-thick glasses and tightly cropped hair, the one who asked the original question. *Alice something.* Vars wasn't familiar with the woman's work. And she hadn't encountered too many people, other than herself...and well, Ian, who wore glasses. In his case, Vars was almost certain it was all about self-image. She wouldn't have been surprised if they were simple tinted glass. But Alice's glasses were thick corrective lenses and far from attractive. Most everyone had their vision corrected in this day and age. So either Alice had a strange affectation or an aversion to treatment. Or perhaps she had a defect that couldn't easily be fixed, which was rare.

"Logic clearly dictates that the needs of the many out-weigh the needs of the few," said one of the youngish-looking men from the JPL team. Vars knew enough popular culture to know he was quoting a character from an old space-exploration series. *Star Trek?*

This is too basic, she thought, and she raised her discourse up a notch. "Let's just jump right into the robot anecdote. Robots designed by collectivist cultures would be less likely to kill. They would have a stronger focus on the *theory of mind,* understanding and taking perspectives of others—"

"Can you backtrack a bit?" Ian asked.

"Sure." Vars thought she now understood the Goldilocks zone she was to lecture to. "Consider guilt. Guilt is one of the strongest human psyche compulsions. We use guilt and embarrassment as tools for social compliance all the time. Guilt is motivational, so to speak. Our social media landscape is full of guilt traps. We finger people who don't pay taxes or contribute in a positive way to our society. We name people who don't recycle or who drop trash on the road or who still use personal transportation vehicles. We social-shame not only the anti-social behavior but even the way people dress and look."

A man in the back spoke up. "We are all familiar with cyber bullying, Dr. Volhard. EPSA is a large, multicultural organization, and we're all required to take classes and work-shops in antisocial behavior and sensitivity training."

"I do too, as a university professor and researcher," Vars assured them. "But my point is that social shaming works."

"On robots?"

"I'm getting there," Vars said with a smile. "People from collectivist and individualist societies experience guilt differently. A person from a collectivist culture feels guilt as 'What will people think of me?' While someone from an individualist culture perceives it as 'How will I live with myself?' See the difference?"

"So outcomes vary?" Ian asked.

"Precisely! Consider a criminal," Vars said. "A person who commits a crime in an individualist culture can't escape guilt, for the feelings of guilt are experienced internally, whether anyone is aware of the crime or not."

"Are you implying that in collectivist cultures, a criminal won't experience guilt the same way?" Alice asked.

"That's precisely it, Alice." Vars made herself say the name of the woman to reinforce it in her memory—a simple mnemonic trick. "It's easier to commit a crime if you're convinced that no one will learn of it and you live in a world where it's only the opinion of your group that matters."

"So a murderer won't lose sleep over his deed if he was raised in a collectivist culture?"

"I'm saying that the guilt is assessed differently," Vars said. "And it's always about the extremes of the spectrum: the extreme form of collectivism, the extreme form of individualism. Of course, we live in a world that is both a little collectivist and a little individualist. I'm giving you the very antipodes to make my point clearer."

"Of course, Dr. Volhard," said Ian. "So the robots?"

"Yes, the robots. I'm getting to that, but first one more point." Vars took a big gulp of coffee. It was cold and bitter now, but she needed the caffeine.

She must have made a face, for Ian was instantly on his feet, getting her a refill in a fresh cup. She waited for him to sit back down.

"Thank you, Ian," she said, taking a sip. "Much better."

"My pleasure."

"And this is a perfect example of my next point: the theory of mind. Ian saw my expression when I took a sip from my cold cup and guessed that I was dissatisfied with my coffee."

"It was obvious," Ian said.

"To *you*."

"I think it was obvious to everyone in the room," he said with a smile.

A few people chuckled.

"That bad? Well, good. Then everyone here has a good theory of mind. You were all able to interpret my feelings, thoughts, and experiences even though you had no direct access to my taste buds. The theory of mind is necessary for higher-order thinking skills. It's necessary for communication, for understanding multiple points of view. Not all animals on Earth have this ability, and even human children take several years to master this skill. Before the age of about four, kids are unable to switch perspectives and understand what motivates others. And even after that age, the theory of mind continues to develop into and throughout adulthood."

"The development of empathy," Alice said.

"That too. Empathy requires that we try to put ourselves in another's situation to understand how they might feel. This is different from sympathy, obviously, which doesn't require such cognitive acrobatics. So a child of five would flinch and hold their hand after observing someone get hit on the hand. It's almost like the pain of another is their pain."

"Are you saying that there's a difference in the development of the theory of mind between collectivist and individualist cultures?" Ian asked. He'd clearly read her book and was now helping his team to quickly get up to speed on the subject.

"Yes. In a collectivist culture, the theory of mind is paramount. The focus of collectivists is on others, so the success of the culture is dependent on nuanced social interactions that require complex cognitive activity and deep understanding of the feelings and motivations of others. In individualist so-cieties, the focus is on the self, so the theory of mind is of less central importance."

"Thus robots designed by collectivist cultures would be less likely to kill," Ian said.

There were murmurs among the people around the table. Apparently not everyone was buying the conclusion about the robots.

"Didn't you just say that in a collectivist society it is easier to commit a crime?" Alice asked.

"Not easier, but with less guilt—and, even then, only so long as the crime isn't discovered by others in your group. In a collectivist society, as long as the crime remains hidden from the group, there are no ill consequences to the individual. But note that committing a murder requires a deep understand-ing of what others know, how they will react to the crime, and how they will feel about the perpetrator. One would need a deep understanding of the entire web of social interactions." Vars paused. "Again, I'm talking about extremes. But it stands to reason that robots created by collectivist societies would be designed with a focus on the theory of mind, with the abil-ity to analyze problems from multiple perspectives. And such social cognitive flexibility puts more restraints on antisocial behavior than guilt alone."

"So the robots we design are more violent?" Alice asked.

The "we" came up a lot in Vars's classes. Everyone as-sumed that Western cultures were the most individualistic.

"Only if we design them so," Vars said. "But most of this is discussed in my book, and you clearly all have access to my work..." She trailed off meaningfully. All of this *was* in her book. It didn't make sense to her to be dragged urgently across the country for this predawn meeting. What did EPSA really want from her?

"Ibe," said Ian. "Could you run the short version of our presentation for Dr. Volhard, please?" He turned to Vars. "It's really the best introduction to our problem, and we can fill you in on details after."

The way he said "problem" made Vars uncomfortable.

Ibe and Ebi both got up and set up the presentation. One of them pulled up the oversized sleeve of his black sweatshirt and exposed an ostentatious set of D-tats on his right arm. That twin was a lefty, Vars noted, and a body-computing junky. She'd bet there was another, equally extravagant set of D-tats on the other arm.

She glanced around the room and noted a few other PCD tattoos peeking from people's clothing. Vars heard that EPSA was heavily invested in cyberhumatics—the science of human implant technology and its connectivity with global

networks and robotic extensions—so it wasn't surprising that D-tats were the norm among this group. But Vars had no implants, and it made her feel even more of an outsider.

Dark shades descended over the wraparound windows, cutting off the rays of the morning sun. The lights turned off, and the room was swallowed in a soft purple gloom. Vars yawned into the darkness—it would be so easy just to fall asleep in here, even with an almost full cup of coffee in hand. She heard others yawn as well. Yawning, she knew, was contagious among primates and other empathetic animals.

A 3D projection of the solar system lit up in the center of the conference table. The planets slowly rotated in their orbits. It was a very nice model, but of course it would be—this was EPSA.

"This is our solar system," Ebi said. Her voice pegged her as a girl.

Ibe spoke next. "This is Saturn. And this is Mimas." Based on the timbre of his voice, Vars judged him male. *So not identical twins.*

Using a combination of hand gestures and rapid tapping on his D-tats, Ibe zoomed in on Mimas, Saturn's closest moon. One side of the small whitish moon had a giant crater with a dimple in the center. "Mimas is primarily made of water-ice. As you can see, it's heavily cratered. The big one is named Herschel and is nearly a third of the moon's diameter."

"That's almost eighty miles wide and over six miles deep," Ebi added. "That pimple thing in the center is a mountain that's almost four miles high."

"That must have been some impact," said Vars. Based on the initial questioning, this was not how she'd thought the rest of the morning would go.

"It liquefied the little moon," Ibe said.

Most of the Saturn moons were well explored, and EPSA

was actively working on establishing permanent science stations on some of them. But as far as Vars knew, none of the moons of either Jupiter or Saturn harbored anything more complex than simple bacterial life. Impressive, certainly, but old news now. And not something that an evolutionary socio-historian could help with. Vars's specialty was the development of self-aware cultures.

"A year ago, we detected a signal coming from Mimas," Ian said.

Ibe zoomed in on the giant crater and focused the image on the mountain. The rotation stopped, and the holographic image froze on a close-up. Vars could clearly see something protruding from the ice—a small, dark structure near the base of the central mountain.

Vars inhaled. She was no longer sleepy; all tiredness had been wiped clean. "What's that? One of ours?"

"No," said Ebi and Ibe in unison.

"And that's the main problem of the day," Ian said.

"You mean you don't know?" Vars asked. "It's been what? Twelve—"

"We have been able to divert one of our probes, and it arrived on site a few weeks ago," said of the men from the JPL team. *Ben?*

"So this picture..." Vars said.

"Yes, it's from that probe," said Ben. "We have detailed close-ups."

Ibe zoomed in even further, until the structure occupied most of the conference table.

"Wow," Vars whispered.

Chapter Three

The meeting lasted until late morning, until Vars just couldn't go on. Too tired, too much information, too much. Ian, seeing that Vars could no longer absorb anything new or contribute in any coherent way, insisted on taking her to an on-campus guest suite.

"My dad and I live just thirty minutes away," Vars protested, but Ian wouldn't hear of it. He and one of those guys in uniform—neither of whom had said a word the whole time—led her through the labyrinthine hallways. And without ever setting foot outside, Vars arrived at a small bedroom with a view of redwoods.

"I'll pick you up in a few hours and take you to lunch, okay?" said Ian. He smiled broadly and closed the door.

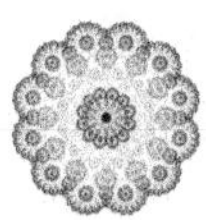

Vars's suitcase had made it to the EPSA guest room ahead of her and was waiting next to the bed, as was her backpack, which held her tablet and a few copies of her book. Even her raincoat was hanging on a hook by the door.

She took off her shoes and the fashionable orange scarf and thought about everything she'd heard. She still wasn't sure why EPSA wanted to talk with her, although she was thrilled to be included. This was the biggest thing ever. She was thankful for the alone time to process the information a bit. She needed to get a handle on what they were telling her. It was all so…so…incredible!

She pulled up her computing tablet and set it up on a desk by the window. Like her dad, Vars abhorred the PCD tattoos and had never even considered having one implanted. Well, nothing more than an ID microchip, which was required by law anyway. And the personal tablet, too, was an old-fashioned affectation. In her whole life, there had never been a circumstance or a place that didn't provide all of her computing or communication needs at any time she wanted it. Equipment was ubiquitous; in fact, for those who opted to get the new D-tats, it was never farther than their skin. But Vars's dad always used his own computing equipment, and she just picked up the habit.

She needed to get in touch with her dad. Even when work took them to different sides of the world, they talked every night, if only to exchange a few words. But last night, Vars had never gotten around to it, and she knew he would be worried about her. It was just the two of them—Vars's mother had died when Vars was just an infant, and they had no other family left, unless you counted some distant cousins on the other side of the world, in Norway or something. Her dad communicated with them only once or twice a year, and even then only out of a sense of obligation rather than familial closeness.

She considered *versing* with him but, at this time of day, her dad would be out in the field collecting samples. He did research on the effects of microplastics in the environment and tended to spend his mornings dredging through coastal tidal plains. It made more sense just to send him a note. She would tell him about her insane trip to EPSA later tonight when she got home. The idea of spending a night as a guest of EPSA seemed totally ridiculous—she lived just a short ride away.

She recorded a brief *vers*: *Dad, I'm back home in Seattle. Got invited to EPSA! Don't worry. All is good—talk tonight. Love you.*

She hit send. And nothing happened.

She tried again. Nothing. The blinking light on her tablet indicated no connection.

That made no sense. There was no longer a place on the Earth or the moon where communication devices didn't work. Even as far out as Mars, people complained when the services were down. Everyone was fully connected to the planetary network everywhere at all times. How else could anyone function?

Vars tried multiple times. She even restarted her PCD tablet—something she had never done before. But still nothing. Perhaps it was the room? *All those redwoods outside?*

She took the tablet out into the corridor. The man in uniform was standing just outside her door. He smiled. Vars smiled back, but her stomach did a double flip. She told herself that she hadn't been kidnapped, but clearly this man was guarding her in some way. *Holding me prisoner?*

"I'm not getting any connection in my room." She felt the need to explain and immediately got angry with herself. They couldn't keep her here against her will...could they?

"Dr. Volhard." Vars was sure the man was just about to salute her before relaxing his arm again. That was reflexive—years of training taking over. "Dr. Rust asked me to stay with you and help you navigate the facility when you were ready to resume work. Would you like me to escort you back to the tree house conference room?"

"No. I didn't get a chance to rest yet," Vars said uncertainly.

"Is there something I can get you? Coffee?"

"My connection doesn't seem to be working," Vars said again. She lifted her portable PCD to the man's face as evidence.

"Oh. Yes. Dr. Rust mentioned that the connection might not work here."

"Well, I need to get in touch with my father. Is there someplace I can go to do that?" Vars asked. "I didn't see any equipment back in the room." As soon as she said it, Vars realized it was true. There had been no public terminals there, which too was very unusual.

"I was only told to take you to the conference room if you were ready before Dr. Rust picked you up for lunch," the man said.

"I just need to send a message to my dad to tell him I'm okay," Vars tried again. "It's short. See?" She played the brief recording to the man and immediately hated herself for acting like a child who needed permission to talk to her own father.

"I'm sorry, Dr. Volhard. All I can do is take you back."

"Well, I don't like being out of reach like this," Vars snapped. Again she felt like a kid, whining about not getting what she wanted. Not that she had ever been that kind of kid.

Embarrassed, she stepped back into her room and closed the door. Perhaps she was just tired and misinterpreted what was going on.

She climbed into bed and placed her PCD tablet on the pillow. She watched the connection indicator show an error. She blinked. Blinked again.

The next time she opened her eyes was when a knock sounded on her door, four hours later.

"I should have introduced you earlier. This is Major Terry Liut," said Ian.

Vars smiled thinly at the man sitting across the table from her in the small EPSA cafeteria. She recognized the officer as the other uniformed man in the back of room during the morning conference. "Nice to meet you, Major Liut," she said.

Ian smiled. "Terry—we are very informal here—explained to me that you tried to contact your father?"

Tried and repeatedly failed. Even here, in the cafeteria, Vars had no connection on her tablet, and she had yet to see a single public terminal anywhere in the building. Perhaps that was because of EPSA's military component—the agency was a mixture of civilian workforce and the air force of its active member nations. Or perhaps all EPSA employees were required to get a PCD tattoo, so no terminals would be needed.

"Yes," she said. "I just want to let my dad know that I'm all right."

"And we're working on that," Major Liut said. "But you see, we ran into a little problem. We don't have Dr. Matteo Volhard's DNA profile."

Every human had their genetic code registered with authorities the moment they were born—or even sooner in cases of prophylactic genetic testing to identify possible medical problems. After the Keres Triplets asteroid fragments hit the Earth in 2057, wiping out half the human population and ninety percent of all other life on the planet, genetic testing had become a must. Even over a hundred years later, it was the only way to maintain a healthy gene pool.

"I assume it's just some error," Vars said. The Human

Genome Heritage Project was regularly underfunded. Glitches were bound to happen.

"That's what we assumed at first. But it doesn't seem to be a glitch," the major said.

"So...what are you trying to say?" Vars asked. She was getting irritated.

"We ran your DNA sample this morning while you rested, to check it against your officially registered sample—"

"You did *what?*" Anger simply erupted out of her.

Ian raised his hands in a soothing gesture. "Vars, I know you feel like this is a big violation, but—"

"Violation?" Vars felt herself trembling with rage. *First kidnapping, then cutting off all my communication with the outside world and keeping me prisoner, and now this?* "So that's what the coffee was all about!" A dark realization hit her. "No wonder you kept giving me fresh cups. And, like a sucker, I just assumed you were being considerate and nice. All the while you were *stealing* my DNA from me."

"Vars—" Ian began.

"I think we should stick to formal address, Dr. Rust."

"If I may," Major Liut interjected. "Ian was very much against gathering your DNA sample without your explicit permission—"

"But he did it anyway," Vars spat. She needed to get out of here. As she scanned the room for exits, she saw that several other military personnel were stationed around the cafeteria, and all of them were now staring at her.

"He didn't have a choice," the major continued. "When your work was identified as necessary for this project, we had to look into your background. Your father's lack of genetic credentials was flagged."

"I assure you that was in error," Vars said.

"And *I* can assure you that EPSA doesn't make mistakes,"

said Liut. "At least not in this area. By law, we have to track all of our people's genetic material. We are charged with creating a genetically diverse population for off-Earth colonization. We take genetic diversity seriously."

"And I think you might have made a mistake this time," Vars said quietly.

"The only way a citizen of Earth, or of any off-world colony, would not be part of the Human Genome Heritage Project database is if he or she was born in one of the human seed vaults," the major said. "Are you aware of any information that might lead you to believe that your father might be a former Seed?"

Vars felt her head spin. There were several human seed vaults on Earth, one on the moon, and one planned on Mars. There was talk about establishing yet another one in the outer reaches of the solar system. The establishment of the Vaults was one of the governmental responses to the cataclysm that followed the Keres Triplets asteroid strike. As the nations of Earth recovered, they worked together to build the Vaults partly in order to ensure the genetic diversity of humanity. Individuals were selected by a secret set of criteria and spirited away into underground catacombs that were supposed to be impervious to all disasters. That was almost three-quarters of a century ago. And, in each year since, a genetic lottery had been held to deposit a few more babies into the Vaults.

The Seeds, as the humans who grew up in those communities were called, developed an almost monastic lifestyle. All were required to donate sperm and eggs to the outside world. The resulting embryos were highly prized by those interested in embryonic adoption. Seeds who reached the age of maturity at about thirty years old or so—Vars wasn't too familiar with their secretive ways—were allowed to make a choice to leave their society and join the general population or to stay and spend their entire lives below ground. Vars had heard horror stories of Seed children and adults being exploited for their unique genetics. She found the whole system detestable.

Now these men in front of her were hinting that her father was a Seed. That just couldn't be.

"My dad would have told me," she said. But even as she spoke, doubt wormed its way into her heart. No close family except for the "distant cousins" who lived in Norway, which just happened to be the location of one of the Vaults. *And Dad's extreme aversion to public communication terminals and D-tats...*

The major and Ian sat quietly, waiting. Furious as she was, Vars still appreciated the space to think. Would EPSA have a reason to lie to her? *They are the good guys, right?*

"I need to talk to my dad," she said finally.

"I figured as much," said Ian. "We've sent a representative to talk with him."

The major added, "And we would also like to run a blood test on you."

"You didn't get all you needed from my coffee cup?"

"We just want to be sure," Ian said. "I...we want you on our team, Dr. Volhard. You have a tremendous contribution to make to our understanding of how to even approach what we're dealing with. This genetic thing," he glanced over at the major, "will be straightened out, one way or another. If you could just overlook this very...this awkward start to our relationship, I'm sure you will find working at EPSA very rewarding."

"Are you offering me a job?" Vars asked.

"If we can straighten out this genetic mystery," said Major Liut.

Ian glanced sharply at the man and said, "Yes."

"I see," Vars said. A job at EPSA was what she had always

wanted. *It's just…*

"And I would like you to start immediately," Ian added. "My department will smooth everything out with your university—"

Everything was happening too fast. Vars felt confused and conflicted. "I still have a few classes left to teach this semester," she said and realized that she was agreeing to the offer.

"That won't be a problem," Ian assured her. "We need you, Dr. Volhard."

"Where do I go to take the blood test?" Vars asked. She noted that as soon as she said it, not only did she feel better, but Ian seemed to relax. Even Major Liut's face was drained of some of its tension. *They really do want me.*

"If you'll follow me, please, Dr. Volhard," said Ian.

"We can go back to Vars."

"Perfect! Thank you, Vars."

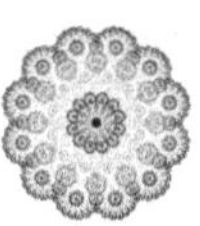

The test didn't take long, or at least the top-level pass at the results didn't. The more detailed analysis would take a day or so. Vars felt herself holding her breath as they stood around the display in the medlab. It read:

The paternal haplogroup is E-M5021—a relatively common haplogroup, associated with Ashkenazi Jewish ancestry.

The maternal haplogroup is U5a1—a very old mitochondrial haplogroup that was part of the initial human expansion into Europe after the retreat of the ice sheets, 30,000 years ago.

*Top-level analysis of potentially
problematic variants:*

- *increased risk for age-related
macular degeneration*

- *hereditary hemochromatosis variant detected*

- *lactose intolerance*

- *less likely to be a deep sleeper*

- *wet earwax variant*

- *variant for a high number of freckles*

- *dark red hair variant*

- *light skin pigmentation*

- *likely to taste a wide range of bitter compounds*

- *likely to consume more caffeine*

It continued on, but Vars stopped there. She'd never paid much attention to genetic testing—she always figured if there was something truly problematic, her dad and her pediatrician would have fixed it or kept track of it. At a minimum, she would have known about it. She did note that the list of traits didn't explain her slight epicanthic eyefold—but then who really cared?

"Your results are excellent," Ian said.

"And they match your genetic ID profile," added Major Liut.

"In fact," Ian said, "there's nothing there that would preclude you from going on an outer planetary mission—"

"Wait, what?" Vars was taken aback by the suggestion. Sure, she had always been interested in participating in some space program mission, *theoretically*. But to hear it said so casually...

"We've already obtained your health records, and you are in fine physical shape for your age," Ian continued.

"You obtained my health records?" Vars felt violated all over again. How could her personal doctor hand over medical records without her explicit permission? There were laws against that.

"Your agreement to employment at EPSA—we have the recording of your assent for legal purposes—gave us permission to initiate a full background check on you and your father," the major said. "Medical records were obviously part of that."

Had she actually agreed to take this job? Vars wasn't sure she had, at least not without ambiguity. She never actually came out and said she would take the job offer...she didn't think. Then again, she knew she wouldn't turn down a chance to be part of Ian's team—and potentially go *into space* to investigate the strange alien artifact. Yes, of course she was taking the job. She just hated how all of this was being handled.

"And my father?" Vars wasn't sure what she had agreed to with regard to her dad.

"Once we explained the situation to him," said Major Liut, "Dr. Volhard volunteered to take the genetic test."

"When did you even have a chance to talk to him? No, hang on. You're saying he *volunteered*?" Her dad was a very private man; that would had been very unlike him to agree to genetic testing.

"Once we told him we realized who he was..." Ian said.

Who he was? "Do you mean to say that my father admitted to being an ex-Seed?"

Neither man answered the question. "We have his preliminary test here," the major said. "Would you like to see his results?"

Vars could only nod. This was all happening too fast.

The major typed a few commands on the D-tats embedded into his left arm, and the medlab display lit up with genetic information for Dr. Matteo Volhard.

The paternal haplogroup is E-M5021—a relatively common haplogroup, associated with Ashkenazi Jewish ancestry.

The maternal haplogroup is U5a1—a very old mitochondrial haplogroup that was part of the initial human expansion into Europe after the retreat of the ice sheets, 30,000 years ago.

Top-level analysis of potentially problematic variants:

- *increased risk for age-related macular degeneration*

- *hereditary hemochromatosis variant detected*

- *lactose intolerance*

- *less likely to be a deep sleeper*

- *wet earwax variant*

- *variant for a high number of freckles*

- *dark red hair variant*

- *light skin pigmentation*

- *likely to taste a wide range of bitter compounds*

- *likely to consume more caffeine*

"Something is wrong," Vars said. "This is identical to mine."

"At the top level, yes," the major said. "We will, of course, do a complete analysis of both of your DNA profiles. In the meantime, would you like to see how similar your genetic profiles really are?"

"Major, are you saying...?" Ian didn't finish. He looked as surprised as Vars felt.

"Dr. Varsaad Volhard and Dr. Matteo Volhard share over 80% of their genetic traits, according to preliminary DNA profiles," the major read out from his report. He looked Vars in the eyes. "Dr. Matteo Volhard is both Varsaad's father and sibling."

Vars felt her head spin. Her vision tunneled as she lost all of her peripheral sight to darkness. Someone kept repeating her name, but that was all she was able to process.

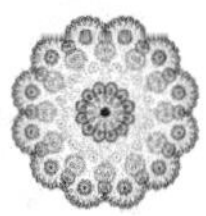

"Vars? Vars?" A woman's voice. "It will be okay. Here, drink this."

Vars felt cold water trickle past her lips. She took a real sip and swallowed. It felt good going down her throat. The cold spread into her chest.

She slowly opened her eyes. She was lying down on a hospital bed, still in the same medlab where she'd learned of the genetic results. The thick-spectacled woman from Ian's team, the exo-biologist, stood beside her. There was no one else in the room.

"Alice?" she said.

"I got here as quickly as I could." Alice had a look of real concern etched on her gentle face. Why had she come here? Why did she care how Vars felt?

"I'm okay," Vars said. "I'm just tired. No sleep. The stress of the book tour. The artifact you found. And now all this."

She waved her hands feebly in the air. She wasn't sure how much Alice knew. "Did Ian tell you he offered me a job at EPSA?"

"Yes. And that you've accepted."

Vars sat up, picked up the glass of ice water, and finished it. Dehydration was never a plus. "Do you know how complicated my genetic relation is to my father?"

Alice flicked her eyes up to the ceiling in a gesture that Vars somehow understood. *She's telling me that they're*

recording us. Vars double-blinked to indicate that she'd received the warning.

"I know about you and Matteo," Alice said in answer to Vars's question. News certainly got around fast at EPSA.

"So…do we need to call someone in order to leave the medlab?" Vars asked. They clearly couldn't talk about anything here—not privately, anyway. And she wanted to learn more about the Mimas artifact. She wanted to know why Ian thought she could help. And she wanted to know why Alice seemed so invested in her well-being. She needed to know if she could work here.

Thank you for reading! The full book is available on Amazon and other places books are sold.